Also by Sharon Clark:

Tears Don't Become Me
Into the Mist
A Majestic Affair

THE CHAOS SERIES
Chaos Beneath the Moonbeams
The Magic Found In Chaos

THE SPEAKEASY SERIES
Speak Easy, Speak Love

Speak Easy, Speak Danger

Sharon G. Clark

Yellow Rose Books
by Regal Crest

ISBN 978-1-61929-434-9

First Printing 2020

9 8 7 6 5 4 3 2 1

Original cover design by AcornGraphics

Published by:

Regal Crest Enterprises

Find us on the World Wide Web at
http://www.regalcrest.biz

Published in the United States of America

Acknowledgments

Thank you, my fabulous editors, Patty Schramm and Mary Hettel; and, thank you Regal Crest for allowing the opportunities provided to me and my imagination, which can't stick to a single genre. And, thank you, to Ann McMan for always providing wonderful covers for my books.

Dedication

To my amazing son, Jeremy, and wife Cassy for giving me two
beautiful granddaughters,
Keira Nicole and Alexia Haylee-Jean.

Prologue

October 1922

"THAT'S ENOUGH. YOU may desist."

One overenthusiastic fellow managed a last booted kick to Nicholas's lower back. A good thing he already lay on the floor or Nicholas would surely have fallen when the two men abruptly released him and stepped back. Their brutal assault was thorough. Nicholas doubted any spot on his body had escaped the pounding, but he'd reached the point where pain throbbed in piercing steadiness that made isolating the worst of the aches impossible. Nicholas felt rather than saw Blanche's approach and heard the rustle of paper. He forced an eye to open by a bare slit, focused on the daintily clad, too large, foot of his former lover Blanche Bowman. At least he assumed the beating marked their breakup.

"This should cover it." Her voice sounded coolly detached as if they hadn't shared an intimate relationship. "Remember, no one is to hear of this because it didn't happen."

"What about him, miss?" asked a deep voice. "Want us to chuck him somewhere?"

"Thank you for your concern, but Nicholas and I have a few more things to discuss before he leaves." The overloud slam of the door marked the zealous departure of the hired thugs. Nicholas tried to focus on the slippered foot, which hadn't moved away. Blanche had yet to utter a word.

Well, if they were to have a chat before he left tonight, Nicholas refused to do so curled up and laying in his blood on the floor. The slow movement to obtain a seated position brought stabs of pain, some sharp, some dull. Silent but for the wheeze of his breathing, Nicholas finally regained his feet, focused with the only eye not completely swollen shut, on the blonde woman before him. Nicholas resorted to the defensive mechanism that stayed him through many rough or uncomfortable times. "So, I guess our courtship is over?"

An expression of rage and disgust flushed her face before Blanche said, "It should never have been. If I hadn't wanted this matter to remain private, I'd have told those goons the truth. I can't believe I let you—" She stopped with the grinding clamp of her teeth.

Nicholas winced as he pulled a handkerchief from a pocket and carefully wiped the blood that dripped from his mangled face. It would be days before he'd be able to see and breathe properly. "Let me what, Blanche? Never let me provide orgasms leaving you crying out my name in pleasure. Make you whimper and moan when I caressed you?" Her horrified expression told Nicholas she remembered how she'd reacted during their lovemaking. He took an unsteady step forward. "I love you, Blanche. Please, don't let this little matter erase the fact."

"Little matter?" she said. Her mouth moved in the silent imitation of a beached fish gasping for air.

"We love each other, which is why I told you the truth. No secrets between us, as relationships should be conducted." Nicholas took a hesitant step toward her. "Did you not profess your love for me? I would do anything to make you happy, to prove I am worthy of your returned love."

Blanche burst into hysterical laughter. "You think I meant it?" She snickered. "You were merely a means to piss off Daddy."

"But—" Nicholas's heart broke, the pain more excruciating than the beating.

Blanche continued her tirade. "I settled on you because you're easy to look at and chivalrous to a fault. Unlike other available suitors, you didn't paw at me with awkward, rough hands."

Nicholas stared at her in confusion. Had there been signs he'd missed, signs she hadn't returned his affection? Blanche's responses toward him had always felt genuine. "Then why let me bed you?"

The question seemed to sober Blanche. She stepped away to the sideboard, which held numerous crystal decanters of various colored liquids. Blanche selected the brandy, splashed a generous amount in a glass intended for liquor that required ice or soda water. She downed the entire contents before she turned around to glare at him. Her once beautiful blue eyes cold, calculated, and resembled shards of ice. "I was curious."

"Curious?"

"Yes. I wondered if your overly polite manners followed into the bedroom. Which is why I only did it in the dark."

Nicholas's emotional pain built into a rage that effectively overshadowed the physical pain. He hadn't realized Blanche was a slow learner as it took more than once for satisfying curiosity. "And what did you learn?" he asked.

Unaware of the shift in Nicholas's emotions, Blanche rolled her eyes, her tone laced with boredom. "You were tolerable and easy enough to manipulate with a few sappy words of praise."

Nicholas stopped mere inches from Blanche, smiled as best he could through swollen, split, and bloody lips. He stared into her eyes, close enough to note when Blanche realized she lost control of the situation, the fear replaced sarcasm. "You used me as a game piece to piss off your father." He took a barely discernible step forward. "You professed to have feelings for me, which you never meant." Closer. "You knew I loved you, would do anything for you. Hell, honey, I can even forgive and forget this beating. Just tell me you love me. Tell me all that's come before is due to your shock from hearing my confession of the truth. Tell me—"

"That you disgust me, and I can never live with your secret?" She snickered again. "That your touch didn't inspire a pity fucking? I should get those men back here to teach you a proper lesson."

Nicholas's rage, like a fire, hit the level where heat burned cold. Before consciously aware of doing so, Nicholas had a hand around Blanche's throat, his grip tightened, tightened more. "Trust me on this, Blanche. Your thugs can't teach me anything new. There's nothing their Neanderthal minds can come up with that hasn't already been done to me, physically or emotionally, by my own father." He squeezed. "You had my heart and my soul. I would have moved heaven and earth to please you." His grip continued to tighten as he brought his face so close to hers that he could see her panic reflected in the ice-blue depths.

Face flushed, nails clawing at the already damaged flesh of his hand, she gasped, "I...can't...breathe."

"Why should you be allowed to?" Nicholas barely registered when her body slackened, wedged between him and the sideboard, the only thing holding her up. He placed gentle kisses on her face. Tears burned the torn flesh of his face before Nicholas realized they were his own. "Why, Blanche? Why did you have to be like everyone else who professed, or supposed to by blood, love me? Why did you crush the love I presented you beneath your beautiful heeled foot?" Blanche didn't respond.

A moment ticked by before Nicholas realized she had yet to respond. Nicholas guided her unconscious form to the floor and slowly released her. He took a step back. Pain and panic consumed him, worried Blanche might never respond again—to anyone. Without another glance, Nicholas used every ounce of stealth his tortured body could expend and snuck out through the back of the house.

Chapter One

Pueblo, Colorado, April 1924

FIONA CAVANAUGH BOLTED upright with a cry lodged in her throat, her nightclothes plastered to her skin from the sweat drenching her. With trembling hands Fiona swiped damp locks from her forehead and gently shifted the covers off to the side, careful not to disturb Margaret, soundly sleeping beside her.

She dressed quietly, then made her way downstairs. In the kitchen, she put the percolator on the stove and sat at the kitchen table. Her body felt the exhaustion from the nightmare—memories—returned to haunt her sleep the last couple of months, usually accompanied by pounding headaches. She wouldn't be able to keep the ailments from Margaret for much longer. What Fiona couldn't let her wife know was the new and frightening addition to the headaches.

Fiona was going blind. The first time it happened, Fiona brushed it off as a fluke occurrence due to working too hard in the workshop. Serious harm could have come to her if Jo hadn't worked alongside her, she knew. Her greatest fear, though, was how she could protect and support her family if she couldn't run her business. Someone was breaking into homes in the city, the female owners killed if at home, presumably so the thief could maintain anonymity.

When the percolator finished its job, Fiona retrieved a china cup from the cupboard and poured herself a cup of coffee. She walked to the sink, gazed out the window at the first hints of dawn, and took a couple of restorative sips.

She'd fought so hard to leave Boston and its gangsters and those wanting to be gangsters. She'd uprooted Margaret, Brigid, and Sunny and kept them all in one piece. Now they safely lived a new life in Pueblo, Colorado.

She smiled at the old name, Sunny, given to her by Fiona when she tried to earn the young girl's trust. Sunny had grown into a beautiful woman and now went by her middle name, Josephine—shortened to Jo.

Fiona knew she couldn't lose her livelihood. These women were her family through the bond of shared support and love. So much love. Her duty was to protect and provide for them. To give back all the strength their love gave Fiona, which buoyed her above her self-doubts. She feared, as had happened with Jimmy Bennett, she'd fail to stop danger from harming them.

She shivered at the memory. Fiona filled the sink with hot water and soap flakes, prepared to wash up the dessert dishes from last night. It had been Friday night, the night all four provided updates from the week and made plans for the next. It was a habit formed when they first moved from Boston to assure each had what they needed, shared the positives and the negatives for the emotional support to move forward or find closure, and their version of girl time.

Fiona ignored the pounding ache in her head as it increased, as she shoved her hands into the soapy water. She knew what was coming. She washed her cup, placed it on the drying board, and returned her hands into the water for the next dish. Then, eyes fully opened, darkness descended.

JOSEPHINE CAVANAUGH WAS excited about the day's activities to come. She would introduce Tessa Langford, the town's new seamstress — a woman who resided in Jo's heart from the first moment they met — to her family. Her feelings for Tessa proved love at first sight could truly exist. A simple thought of Tessa invoked an uncontrolled smile to Jo's mouth. The euphoria she rode quickly dashed when she stepped into the kitchen and saw her sister, Fiona, bent over the sink.

"What's wrong?" Jo asked as she rushed to Fiona's side. Fiona wasn't her sister by blood, the dark brown hair, caramel-colored eyes, and skin tanned from hours in the sun differed from her own curly-blonde hair and light-blue eyes. Fiona's wife, Margaret, had the appropriate papers prepared for Jo when they lived in Boston. Fiona saved Jo, born Thelma Josephine Winton, from a fate worse than death, at least to Jo. Her parents sold her for drug money to an aspiring gangster, Margaret's brother, for his whorehouse. That was a little over four years ago, at the age of fourteen.

A single tear trailed down Fiona's cheek. "It's happening again." The words so soft, Jo barely heard them.

"You're eyesight?" She placed a hand on Fiona's back. "How long has it been?"

Fiona gave a shaky sigh. "I don't know exactly, but long enough for the dishwater to grow cold."

Jo looked down, saw Fiona's hands submerged in the water,

and pulled them into her own. She released one hand long enough to grab the dishtowel from the counter and gently dry Fiona's water-wrinkled hands. "Guess it's been a while. I should have been in here to help sooner. I'm sorry, Fiona."

"Hey, stop it." Her voice still soft, but the tone reflected Fiona's sternness. She raised a hand and awkwardly fumbled toward Jo's cheek. The chilled, pruned skin of Fiona's fingers also lessened the severity of the demand.

"Your fingers feel weird."

"Guess I could have pulled them from the water sooner."

"Well, you didn't pull them out at all," Jo said. She smiled broadly so Fiona would feel the expression on her face. Fiona looked so weary. This strange illness took a toll physically, emotionally, and wearing her to a frazzle. "You realize this could be marking the time where I start the journey of saving you after all the care you've given me."

Fiona gave a derisive sniff. "You make it sound like you've been a burden, and I've done so much for you. Not close. You've had your normal teenage angst, but I wouldn't have missed a moment of having you in my life. You know that, right?"

Jo pulled her into a hug. "The feeling is entirely mutual." She leaned back, tucked a lock of Fiona's dark brown hair behind an ear, and asked, "Are the headaches getting worse, too?"

With a nod, then wince, Fiona said, "Yes."

"Fiona."

"Yeah, I know. I can't keep this from Margaret much longer. It's just—"

Movement and the sound of heeled steps from the doorway stopped Fiona as Margaret entered the kitchen. "Can't keep what from me much longer?" Margaret gave Fiona a quick kiss on her lips, "Morning, honey." She turned to grab a coffee cup from the drying board and went to the stove where the percolator sat.

Jo steered Fiona toward the table, guided her into a chair, and placed a hand on Fiona's shoulder. The partial truth would keep the wrath of Margaret at bay—for now. "Fiona's worried about ruining the outing with her migraine."

Margaret sat at the table beside Fiona, placed a hand on her thigh. "Fiona, this can't be good, having them as frequently as they've been." Margaret looked away from Fiona and focused on her cup. "Your nightmares have returned and become worse recently, too."

"I'm sorry," Fiona said. Then her face paled. "Have I hurt you?"

"Oh, honey, no. Even if you had, I know it's not intentional."

Fiona bit her bottom lip, and Jo could tell she was upset with the thought of harming Margaret in any way, no matter how minor or unintended. "That means I have or come close already."

"What it means is we need to consider doing something about getting you better. Maybe Jo can rearrange her plans, ask Tessa to come here." Much as Jo wanted them to meet the new seamstress, Jo wanted Fiona's ideas and help with some work Tessa had hired Jo to complete for her shop. The job would be the first carpentry project Jo would take, which didn't specifically come through the *Cavanaugh Sister's Crafts* business. No matter the significance, Jo knew Fiona shouldn't push herself, so she tended to agree with Margaret.

"It can't be healthy for you to have so many headaches," Margaret said.

If Margaret only knew, Jo thought. Fiona reached up and squeezed the hand Jo rested on her shoulder, silent indication her sight returned to her. "Quit worrying. I just needed a minute to get myself collected. I'll get breakfast going, and then we can get ourselves to town."

Fiona started to rise, but Jo increased the pressure on her shoulder. "I'll do breakfast," she said.

"Oh, no, you will not, brat," Brigid said as she entered the kitchen. "I'd like to be well and calm when Nicholas and the Walters' come by to pick me up."

With feigned indignation, Jo asked, "What are you implying, Cousin?"

Brigid was twelve years older than Jo, which didn't stop them from acting like siblings closer in age. She was also four years older than Fiona and Margaret. Age wasn't an important factor when deferring to Fiona, even for the Friday family meetings.

"I'm not implying anything, squirt, but stating a known fact. Besides, when you get done the cooking—" Brigid raised a hand to forestall Jo's intended objection, "I know, it's not intentional, but the food is nearly unrecognizable. Cooking is not a task for everyone." Brigid smiled and tapped a hand on Jo's cheek. "You handle the building tools, and I'll handle the kitchen tools."

"Then, I respectfully defer to your superior skill." Jo gave a formal bow. "The stomachs of all present, thank you."

"But it's my turn and not fair for you on the one day you aren't scheduled," Fiona said. Jo could see the anguish overcome the pain on her face.

"I wouldn't offer if I objected, Fiona. Not even to save us the indignity of food poisoning."

"Ha, ha," Jo said. "I'm calling Eddie Cantor to tell him he's lost one of his radio comedians and should come to get you." Brigid began breakfast as Jo sat down across the table from Fiona.

To the room in general, Jo said, "I appreciate you going into town to meet Tessa." She nodded to Fiona. "And for letting me take this project before we've finished Jane Parker's hope chest."

Fiona shrugged. "We're close enough to the finished point on that, so it won't be a hardship to complete on my own. Besides, when the school year is over, I want to take a week or so off from the shop to spend with Margaret." Jo wondered if Fiona would use the time to tell Margaret about the spurts of blindness that accompanied her more severe migraines.

As Brigid cooked, Margaret asked, "So, Jo, is this strictly a working friendship, or more?"

"Yeah," Fiona said, "your words say this is only a job, but your voice and expression change so much when you say 'Tessa' that I wonder if she means more to you."

Margaret gave an exaggerated batting of her eyelashes, a hand to her chest, and whispered, "Tessa, Tessa."

Jo felt her cheeks heat with her embarrassment. She could only wish there would be more for them, but Jo hardly knew Tessa, even if their few interactions suggested Tessa encouraged opportunities to share more time.

Chapter Two

THEY CLOSED THE house up, all four women standing on the porch soaking up the good weather when Brigid noticed Nicholas pull up in his 1922 Renault KZ, with the soft-top pulled up in place even though the day was beautiful. Ethel would not want her hair mussed.

"Guess we're ready to go," Brigid said. "My ride has arrived."

"Yes, and your date is rather exuberant, too." Margaret smiled and gave her a wink. Poking the upper portion of his torso through the opened back window and enthusiastically waving, hung little five-year-old Richard Walters.

"You should charge Ethel for all the times she pawns the kid off on you," Jo said into Brigid's ear. She waved back, pushed her shoulder into Jo's in a silent reprimand. "What? Anyone watching would think him your son."

"You know I enjoy doing it." Brigid walked ahead of the others down the sidewalk. She did enjoy time with Richard, even though she too, worried about the depth of their relationship's bond. Brigid hoped Richard, being young, wouldn't notice how often his mother pawned his nursing off onto someone else — usually her. With her advanced years, she was almost thirty, and no prospect of a serious suitor, Brigid wanted to enjoy the child before her dotage settled in, or he grew too big for her attention.

Nicholas popped out of the driver's door and rushed to the back passenger door. "Scoot over, little man. Miss Brigid doesn't need you climbing on her like a monkey."

"I'm not a monkey," Richard said indignantly.

Nicholas slapped his palms to his cheeks and gave a moue of surprise. "You're not? What are you then?"

"A little boy." Richard sighed as if the answer obvious.

"Oh," Nicholas said. "Then, again, I say scoot over, and let us see if you can be a proper gentleman."

Richard glared and sat correctly, patted the space next to him while he tossed a glare toward Nicholas. "Come on, Miss Brigid, we goin' bye-bye for the ride."

"Thank you, Richard." Brigid glanced behind her at her family. "We'll meet you downtown." As she slipped onto the seat, Brigid heard Jo tell Nicholas, "Shop's on Union Street, by the depot. It's called *Seamlessly Stylish*."

Nicholas nodded and slid behind the steering wheel. "Everybody ready?" After everyone voiced their response, Nicholas pulled onto the street.

IT COULDN'T BE a more beautiful Saturday morning, and the majority of town seemed to be out and enjoying the day. The day made more exciting with her family meeting Tessa Langford, the woman who unknowingly held Jo's heart. They managed to find a parking spot and got out in front of Tessa's dress shop. Although the closed sign hung in the window, the door was ajar in anticipation of their arrival. From close by came the sounds of raucous male laughter. When Jo turned sideways to glance down the sidewalk, she noticed three of the boys who had graduated with her. They were roughhousing, pushed each other, slapped each other on the backs, and their bad jokes carried on the wind. Some of the families out for a stroll purposely stopped and crossed to the other side of the street.

Jo tried to usher Margaret and Fiona into the shop before Thomas Gendry and his boys, Donald and Walter, got to them. Unfortunately, they caught sight of Jo and picked up their pace. "Hey, Cavanaugh, what's the hurry?"

"Yeah, don't want to chat with men?" Thomas sneered. Men was not a word Jo used to associate with the trio. Thomas was average in height and weight, with blond hair and blue eyes. He came from money, which was the only aspect to make him stand out and gave his excuse to break people who didn't kowtow to his whims.

"Just move along, boys," Jo said.

Tessa tried to close the door behind her, but the three boys weren't going to make their departure easy.

Thomas shouldered his way inside, seemingly determined to focus his harassment on Fiona. "Hey, I heard you're some tough guy, wearing trousers and hanging with gangsters. Is it true? Are you hard-boiled?" Fiona ignored the taunt and placed herself between Thomas and Margaret. Thomas glanced around the store's interior. "Maybe while you're in here, you can finally get you and Jo a dress. It's degrading or should be, girls traipsing around town like men. Bad enough, isn't it, that you're doing men's work?"

"Leave her alone, Thomas," Jo said.

He smirked. "What's either of you going to do about it?" He

poked Fiona with a finger in her chest, stabbed the digit in heavy jabs. Walter and Donald flanked Jo.

"Leave this shop. We aren't open for business." Tessa made her way beside Margaret, a pretty, auburn haired woman with dark green eyes, who stopped Tessa's approach with an upraised hand.

"We don't want any trouble," Fiona said, her tone low. "I'm sorry you take exception to my attire, but I can't see how it's any of your business. My family and I wish you to leave us in peace."

"Nah, can't do that," Thomas said. "Need to point out wrongs." Thomas lunged toward Fiona, only managed to trip, whether purposeful or not wasn't readily discernable and landed solidly against Fiona. Both crashed to the wood floor. Jo's human bookends grabbed onto her arms, prevented her from going to assist her sister. She panicked when Fiona's forehead smacked into one of the crates on the floor. "Need me to teach you the differences between men and women? Do you need to be fucked?"

Blood oozed from her wound, but what Jo feared most was the glassy-eyed expression on Fiona's face as she let out a terrified whimper, "No, Jimmy."

Thomas's expression was confused. "Who?"

Before she could think better of it or think it all, Jo slammed a heel into Donald's shin, yanked herself out of Donald's grip, and practically dragged Walter until he released her. Then, Jo grabbed Thomas roughly by the collar, pulled him to his feet, and tossed him out the still-open door. He landed hard, his friends rushed to his side and laughed jovially — until seeing the furious look on Thomas's face.

Thomas brushed himself off, and the heavy reek of alcohol breath assaulted Jo. They'd been drinking harder than she'd originally suspected. Thomas glared at her and asked, "What the hell was that, bitch?"

"Get on your way before I call —"

"Jo," Brigid yelled from across the street. She stood beside Ethel with Richard cradled in her arms.

Nicholas dodged cars in his haste to cross to her. "Jo?"

"What's going on, Jo?" Jo turned to the voice to see her friend and new police officer, Randall Braddock, a tall, gangly boy of nineteen. During the last couple of years of high school, Randall's interest in Jo had increased, until Jo had to tell him they couldn't be more than friends. Randall suggested they could get to know each other as friends, see if the relationship went beyond.

Jo didn't have the heart to burst his disillusionment. So far, friendship worked. "These boys," Jo said distastefully, "have accosted my sister."

"She okay?" Randall asked, real concern in his expression.

"Not sure, but she's bleeding, which has Margaret unsettled." Jo couldn't explain the possible flashback Fiona may have suffered.

Thomas stood to his full height even though he swayed. "The clumsy bitch did it to herself."

"Yeah, just having a little fun," Donald said, fat lips pursed. He tried to cross his arms over his chest, but his fleshy rolls didn't make the action easy.

"Not ladylike, sprawled on the floor," Walter agreed. He was a visual duplicate of Thomas, though from the other side of the tracks, which precluded him having two bits to rub together, carried on the mental match of Thomas's bullying with a more violent lean.

"Only you appreciate your idea of fun." Randall glanced at the store before he turned back to the three boys. "I'm going to see if Miss Cavanaugh intends to press charges. Maybe the storekeeper intends to." He glanced at Nicholas. "Keep an eye on them. They'll probably turn tail and run, but don't let them back in the shop." Nicholas gave a silent nod.

"My father ain't gonna stand for this," Thomas said.

"Don't care if he does, Thomas. I'll do the paperwork either way. Plus, I know where you live." Randall went inside the store, and Jo followed. "Too bad he's right. Daddy'll make sure this goes away."

Margaret sat on the floor, Fiona was in her arms while she applied a handkerchief to the wound on Fiona's head. Tessa held a glass of water out to Margaret.

Jo knelt in front of Fiona and placed a hand on her shoulder. "Fiona? Are you all right?"

Margaret answered for her. "She's fine, considering, and doesn't want trouble. She won't press charges," Margaret said, her gaze on Randall. "Won't do any good with his kind."

Randall stepped closer to them. "Are you sure? They're drunk, and they've done this bullying before. They shouldn't get away with it."

Fiona shut her eyes. "I'd rather not make more of this than necessary." She stood, Margaret on one side and Jo on the other helped her until certain her balance okay before they released her. "Just let it go, Officer Braddock."

Jo didn't like how pale Fiona had become. She also worried about the effect her head injury would have on her eyesight issue. But from the glazing in Fiona's eyes, and the worried look on Margaret's face, Jo knew the blow wasn't what had Fiona out of kilter.

Randall moved to the door with Tessa, and Jo followed. As Tessa held the handle on the doorknob, Randall turned to the room. "Let me know if you change your mind. Hooligans may come from money, but don't mean they should get away with stuff."

"Thanks for being here when we needed you, Randall," Jo said. She needed him to leave, preferably with Thomas and crew so she could tend her family, and before personal aspects were wrenched from the dark and pulled into the light.

Randall extended a hand to Tessa. His sea-green eyes gazed at her from a heavily freckled face. "Randall Braddock. I work at the station with your brother, obviously." He blushed. "Wish our first meeting were different."

Tessa nodded. "I wish it had happened that way, too, and I thank you for assisting."

Randall glanced down at Jo, who returned his gaze steadily. "I'll send these boys on their way. I hope to see you again soon, Jo."

Thanking Randall, Jo nodded to Tessa to close the door. They returned to where Fiona and Margaret stood, Fiona visibly shaken. Margaret glanced at Tessa and asked, "Is there a private room I could take her to make sure she's okay?"

"I've locked the door, so we shouldn't be interrupted," Tessa said. She pointed toward the back of the room. "There's a set of stairs to my apartment. Take her up, and we'll let her rest while we have tea and get to know each other." Just as they started toward the back of the room, there came a pounding at the front door. Jo and Tessa turned to see a worried Brigid and Nicholas, Ethel and Richard beside them. Brigid appeared frantic. Tessa glanced at Jo, as if in silent question on their suitability to enter. Jo nodded.

Once they were inside, Brigid immediately rushed to Fiona's side. "We saw some of what happened from across the street. She okay?"

Margaret shrugged. "It's just disconcerting for her. With her recent nightmares, it brought back — "

Jo, worried about the same thing. She didn't want the matter blurted before Tessa and Ethel, which could effectively destroy any hope of friendship, let alone more. Jo said, "Let's take this upstairs." She turned to Nicholas. "Thank you for your assistance. Would it be too much to ask for you to take Ethel and Richard home? We'll give a raincheck on the outing." With a nod, Nicholas picked up Richard and escorted Ethel from the shop. Once again, door locked, and then inside Tessa's little apartment upstairs, Margaret sat with Fiona on the small couch.

Chapter Three

MARGARET HELD FIONA'S hand like a lifeline and Tessa wondered what underlying demons the crude drama downstairs managed to release. She suspected, from Fiona's reaction and the conversation with Brigid and Jo, trauma in Fiona's past caused the dull eyes and pale complexion. Tessa suspected a close mirroring of Fiona's reaction just from the disgusting words Thomas spewed. She set the percolator to boil and took out a coffee set specifically used for visitors. Tessa glanced over her shoulder toward Margaret. "I don't believe this is the introduction Jo had in mind, but I'm glad you've stayed."

Margaret said, "Glad the invitation is still open. Sorry for the display, and our current—"

"Think nothing of it. Let me get some ice on your forehead," Tessa said as she started for the icebox.

With a trembling voice, Fiona said, "No, that's not necessary. Don't put yourself through any trouble. I've been enough already."

Jo, from her position beside the door, straightened and said, "Thank you, Tessa, for letting us invade your apartment. Of course, this isn't how we intended to introduce my family to you." She pointed to each one as she spoke. "The one with the cracked skull is my sister Fiona. Beside her is Margaret, our sister-in-law." Tessa looked at each woman in turn as Jo made the introductions. But from what she'd noticed downstairs and what she saw here right now, Tessa wondered at the true relationship between Margaret and Fiona. Although it outwardly seemed sisterly, they appeared closer, made her "my" rather than "our" sister-in-law. Tessa wondered if Jo would take offense if she questioned aloud but then decided the conversation was for much later in their relationship. If their friendship progressed, she internally reminded herself. Jo pointed to the only other woman in the room, Brigid. "She's our cousin."

Tessa smiled. "I'm happy to meet all of you."

Jo shrugged, flashed a beautiful smile at Tessa before her face flushed. Jo shoved her hands in her pocket and said, "Guess we could talk about the work you need to be done."

Little over an hour later, Tessa prepared to usher them down the stairs to leave the shop but heard the pounding of heavy footfalls on the stairs. Tessa recognized the tread as belonging to her brother, Warren. She winced and knew the scene would not go well. The women flinched in unison as Warren slammed through the door. He wore his usual scowl, and the glance he gave Margaret, Jo, and Fiona bordered beyond disrespectful. His glance, however, seemed a little more inviting and friendlier toward Brigid. As he glared at Tessa, he said, "I heard about an altercation. What the hell happened, Tessa?"

"Just some drunk boys getting out of hand."

Warren nodded absently. "Yes, I'm sure they're celebrating graduation."

"Doesn't give them an excuse to be ruffians." Jo snickered.

Warren's scowl deepened. He glared at Jo from head to toe with a smirk on his lips. Tessa knew he was about to become more insulting than his visual perusal. "Maybe they mistook you two as ruffians. Probably didn't recognize you are ladies." He sneered on the last word.

Brigid stood in front of Warren. "And would you? Would you recognize a lady?"

"Of course," he sniffed.

"Wasn't certain, as you apparently can't act like a gentleman," Brigid said. She slammed her fists on her hips. "Disrespecting my family proves you aren't one."

Warren furrowed a brow in concentration, and Tessa knew he was working through how best to approach Brigid on this subject. With an eyebrow quirked, he put on what Warren considered his devilish smile and flashed it at Brigid. "Maybe I can rectify your poor opinion of me by taking you out to dinner."

Brigid guffawed. "You insult my family and then ask me on a date?" She shook her head. "No, I don't think you're the type of man I could find interesting." Brigid turned to the others. "Are you ready to go?" Then to Tessa, she said, "Thank you for your kindness and your invitation. Sorry we can't stay longer. We hope you'll come to visit us at our home." Tessa smiled when she emphasized the last words. Brigid shouldered Warren out of their way, assisted Margaret with helping Fiona navigate the stairs. The cut to Fiona's forehead stopped bleeding, but the cloudiness hadn't left her eyes. She also appeared miffed at accepting assistance but not willing to put up a fight.

Tessa wanted to applaud Brigid for standing up to Warren, as very few women ever did. As Warren stared with mouth agape, Tessa went to Jo, who stood uncomfortably in the doorway to the stairwell. She lowered her voice so Warren couldn't hear. "I'm sorry things worked out the way they did, Jo. I don't know what your schedule is, but you're welcome to begin work anytime if you're still interested in the job. I'd apologize for my brother, but what you witnessed is how he is regularly."

Jo glanced at Warren before she looked Tessa in her eyes. "I, too, wish the day finished better. I'll be back first thing in the morning." Jo gave her a bright smile and a quick wink before she turned and rushed after her family.

When Tessa heard the downstairs door close, she spun toward Warren. "What the hell was all that about? I finally get friends, not to mention assistance in getting the store put together for a price far lower than anticipated, and you have to be horrible toward them."

Warren gave a one-shoulder shrug. "They aren't the type of people you should be friends with, little sis. You're new and don't know the talk. I'm looking after your welfare." She doubted that the case. Warren didn't want her associations to rub off on him.

"Well, you can stop. The gossip doesn't matter. I like the Cavanaughs, who have been nice to me ever since I arrived." Tessa started toward the sink to clean up from the visit. She smiled, remembered how adamant Margaret and Brigid were about cleaning up. She'd put her foot down about their washing of dishes, and now she was glad for her decision. It gave her a chance to turn her back and avoid looking at Warren. She feared, if she did, she'd give him a proper dressing down, and might say something she'd regret later. Like admitting how much she wanted to get to know the adorable Jo Cavanaugh better.

Since the very moment Jo introduced herself, Tessa felt a connection she hadn't had with anyone else. "I know you promised to watch out for me, but I don't believe Mother and Father planned on you going so far as to choose my friends."

The sound of chair legs as they scraped on the hardwood floor made her cringe. Warren could be such a Neanderthal. The apartment wasn't his, but he'd insisted on having a key. In case of emergency, he'd professed. Tessa knew the real reason. Warren wanted to come and go as he pleased while helping himself to her cupboards and her privacy. "Not trying to pick your friends, just letting you know the people you should avoid."

"You spoke your piece, and I listened, but I won't avoid them. I've heard nothing but wonderful things about all of those women." She turned and gave him a pointed glare. "You seemed mighty interested in Brigid. Guess you won't be pursuing that particular skirt."

"Why not?"

"You openly insulted her cousins, Warren. Would insults put someone in your good graces if I'd been the recipient of the gossip?"

"Brigid just needs to get to know me." Warren furrowed his brow. "I didn't say anything that hasn't been tossed about town long before me."

Tessa shook her head. "Aren't you afraid to be seen with Brigid then? What about guilt by association?"

Warren gave a smug grin. "Dating me can only bolster her position, keep her above the taint."

Where did men get the lofty images of themselves? Warren wasn't a catch. He was husky and boringly plain, with dull brown eyes and even duller brown hair. Heck, he was the heavier male version of her. The internal reminder of their sameness caused her to reconsider Jo's kindness. Tessa wasn't the type to attract attention. Had she misread the subtle hints she thought Jo gave? Maybe Jo was interested only in friendship. Tessa could use a friend as well as the carpentry work on the dress shop.

No, there was something in the glances she and Jo shared, which caused Tessa's rapid pulse, and a twinge in her private lady-place. She shook her head to clear the self-doubts. "Sometimes, I'm happy you're my brother. But honestly, most the time, you're a complete ass."

"Yeah, I get that, little sis." He slammed a hand down on her table. "Since I'm here, how 'bout lunch? I found another dead woman this morning, and I've been busy investigating. Police work's got me hungry."

Tessa felt a shiver run through her with the news and the callous way he presented it. "That's three so far?"

"Nothing to cause you to fear. No one's gonna hurt the sergeant's sister." Warren sat back in the chair roughly. The wood groaned in protest. "Besides, you needn't worry, overmuch."

"Maybe not, but what happens when this person believes you'll never catch them, and killing me would be a fun incentive for you to try harder."

"Not gonna happen. You worry too much."

As she prepared a sandwich for him, Tessa wondered if Warren worried too little.

Chapter Four

ETHEL WAS UPSET, forced into postponing their outing. Nicholas and Richard looked forward to a day together and didn't care how they spent it, more into the bonding than the excursion itself. Not so with Ethel. In his attempt to make up for the canceled plans, Nicholas offered to treat Ethel and Richard to lunch at the Vail Hotel's restaurant, just up the road from Tessa's shop, on Grand and Union. They sat at an intimate table for two; a third chair pulled up to fit Richard between them. A white lace tablecloth covered the top with a small hurricane lamp in the center, and floral bone china and silver tableware properly arranged on top. The light meal was pleasant enough, with Nicholas entertaining Richard with tales of his life as a photographer.

"When I get bigger, can I be 'togaffer too?" Richard asked.

"Don't see why not," Nicholas said. He reached over and ruffled Richard's hair. "If there's one thing I've learned, it's if you try hard enough, want it bad enough, you can accomplish anything. I know college will be wondrous for you. You can have any career you want."

"Don't encourage the child, Nicholas," Ethel said. Her tone implied any vocation unattainable to her son. "There's no way Richard will see the inside of some fancy school. He'll have to make do just like his daddy."

Richard nodded solemnly. "If I could, I'd start with pictures of Mr. Teddy." Nicholas internally applauded Richard's small show to dream bigger than his mother and promptly avoid joining in her negativity.

If a five-year-old could move beyond his mother's negativity, so could he. "Mr. Teddy would make a fine model." Nicholas enjoyed his time with Richard, especially lately, but not so much with Ethel. Ethel was never a demonstrative woman, but recently she seemed to pull further away from the growth of a serious relationship. The situation became commonplace to Nicholas. The unfortunate part was that this was his first relationship, which involved the addition of a child. The very idea of losing the friendship between him and Richard was heartbreaking, and why he hadn't disengaged from Ethel already. It had long since been apparent Ethel was not one to look beyond anything, focused on her own needs and wants, and would never accept his past.

As a waiter came by to pick up their empty plates, Ethel rose from her chair. "I need to powder my nose." Then, she walked away.

"Why does Mommy need to have powder on her nose?" Richard asked, innocently.

Nicholas didn't see a reason not to be honest with the child. "That's a woman's way of saying she needs some private time," he leaned close to Richard's ear, "in the ladies' room."

"Why didn't she just say that?"

"That would be an indelicate conversation for a woman." Nicholas caught sight of the dessert trolley in the corner of the room. He waved a server in his direction and announced the desire to purchase a few delicacies. He turned toward Richard. "What do you say to some sweets? We'll get something light for your mother and us now, and a little something special for you later." Nicholas put in his request for half-dozen petit fours, cannoli, and two oatmeal cookies. Nicholas asked them to wrap the cookies in wax paper. With the desserts placed on the table, Nicholas promptly picked up the wrapped cookies. Since he gave Richard the teddy bear, Nicholas knew of the hidden pocket in the toy's back seam. "Hand over Mr. Teddy, my man." Richard complied, and Nicholas stuffed the two cookies into hiding. "Now you have a little something for later. But you can't tell your mother about it cause she might not like it."

Richard's smile fairly beamed at Nicholas. "I like you better than Mommy's other man."

The comment from a guileless source startled Nicholas. Not wanting Richard to think he had done something wrong, he attempted to be as nonchalant as possible in his next question. "Mommy has another suitor?"

Richard nodded as he bit into one of the petit fours Nicholas placed atop the small plate in front of him. "Ah-huh, that Sergeant, leastways that's what Mommy calls him, and he makes me play outside when he comes."

"Is he grumpy?" Nicholas asked, wrinkling his nose. "Probably only does boring stuff anyway."

"He's not grumpy, he's mean. He don't likes me." Nicholas didn't believe Warren Langford liked anyone, except maybe himself. Would also explain Ethel's behavior lately. Was Ethel weighing the merits of one man against another? Good thing he hadn't invested more than time in this alleged romance. Maybe he was learning his lesson.

Richard finished both small cakes and clasped his hands in his lap. Nicholas noticed Ethel's return approach to the table.

"Don't worry, Richard. We'll keep this between us men."

Richard's smile grew so wide with inclusion in the adult world, the obvious flakes of cake stuck to his teeth. "I like it when you and Brigid visit. You don't ignore me."

"We don't have to mention this talk to your mother, or the cookies," Nicholas said.

Richard took a sip of water and stared down at his plate as his mother sat. Nicholas suspected Richard enjoyed having a secret from his mother. What child wouldn't?

Ethel returned to her chair and stared at her plate. She picked up one of the small cakes, and said, "You needn't have ordered dessert," as she shoved the entire treat into her mouth.

"Anything I can do to make up the unexpected changes to your day, sweetheart, is of no consequence." Nicholas flashed her a sugar-sweet smile. "Can I get you anything else?"

Ethel shook her head. "No, nothing else. Wouldn't want to ruin my figure."

"As if anything could make you unattractive, my dear."

She flashed a false smile. "But, you are sweet to think about how the situation today has affected me."

Nicholas hoped his confusion wasn't written on his expression when he asked, "And how has the situation affected you?"

"Being dismissed by that child, Jo, the way we were. Didn't we have as much right to be there? It is rather disconcerting." Ethel gave him a strange look as if he suddenly grew another head on his shoulders. "We've known the Cavanaugh family far longer than the shopkeeper, which means we had just as much, if not more, of a right to be there during Fiona's time of need."

"Oh," Nicholas said. "Quite right." Narcissistic, much? Nicholas wasn't a stupid man. He knew the proper time to correct a woman, and when, specifically, correcting Ethel was appropriate. This moment was not that instance. Doing so in public would only bring on such histrionics as to embarrass the other patrons and Richard. And, to bring any discomfort to Richard was entirely out of the question, in Nicholas's book.

Finished with her cakes, and Nicholas his cannoli, Ethel wiped her hands clean on the cloth napkin beside her plate. "Shall we go? I'm distraught and think I need a lie-down." And then there was this. Lie-down? When had Ethel gone from the simple farm girl to attempts at posh? He'd been there before.

Haughty women were too much trouble. He needed to heed his lessons.

He assisted Richard from his chair and pulled out Ethel's. Nicholas tossed some extra bills on the table, having already charged the meal to his room, and escorted Richard and Ethel from the hotel. Maybe it was beyond the time he moved on.

Chapter Five

TESSA SAT IN the back room and finished the dress for Mrs. Sabre. She needed to stretch her legs, and if honest with herself, needed an excuse to interact with Jo. She went up the back stairs to her apartment to get coffee, and, after much internal deliberation, placed a few of the oatmeal cookies she'd baked last night on a small plate.

Downstairs again, she stood in the curtained doorway and looked out at the shop's front as she watched Jo sand one of the bookcase-style cabinets she built shelves for this morning. Tessa felt her heartbeat pick up. Jo wore a one-piece overall made of heavy black cotton denim, which Tessa knew to be a less common color in denim, though she didn't understand why the color hadn't more popularity. Black hid dirt much better. The front bib held many pockets with Jo's smaller tools and supplies. The overalls had additional large pockets on the back as well as side pockets and large fold-up cuffs.

The vest extended the denim full up the back with V cutout straps continuing over the shoulders. Jo had removed the blue cotton long sleeve work shirt earlier, apparently preferring to work in her T-shirt. The overall was baggy, but on Jo Cavanaugh, Tessa could only see it as a venue to make the woman sexier and inspiring. Jo's muscles strained against the T-shirt. Tessa was also captivated by the fluid motion with which Jo worked. The female form enamored Tessa, and Jo had a beautiful form. Not only was she long and lean, her face expressive and beautiful, but her physique continually drew Tessa's gaze and filled her fantasies. Tessa's attraction to women created much of Warren's chagrin. Finding beauty in the more boyish women kept Tessa happy and less depressed with her solitary love life.

The singular time Tessa allowed her attraction to flourish outside her normal venue cost her dearly in a broken heart and embarrassment. In Kansas City, when she went against her desires and fallen for a beautiful and feminine woman two years her senior. Her name was Catherine Dubois. Catherine stealthily pursued her, although Tessa suspected it because Tessa was unable to hide her interest, which she now blamed on her youthfulness. For all intent and purpose to Catherine, Tessa was just another notch on her busy bedpost. The situation precipitated

Tessa's move to Colorado when her parents, loving as they were, wiped their hands of Tessa when the tittering of rumors began — rumors Catherine probably initiated.

From what she could gauge, although she admittedly knew little on the subject, Tessa believed Jo's interest in her to be sincere. She should be extremely cautious, she knew, intent on avoiding prior mistakes, but the pull toward the adorable blonde was too strong, silenced any internal dialogue before it could roar inside her head. Tessa cleared her throat loudly and stepped into the room.

"Brought you something to drink," Tessa said, raised the plate, "and a light snack." When Jo looked up, Tessa's heart stopped in her chest. The look of appreciation beamed from Jo's beautiful, light blue eyes. Tessa's fate then sealed. She knew she would give herself body and soul to have Jo look upon her with the same gaze for the rest of her life.

"Thank you, Tessa," Jo said. She stood and wiped her hands on a handkerchief pulled from a back pocket of her overalls. The muscles in Jo's biceps seemed to pulse with the action, and Tessa inhaled a slow breath to keep herself from openly gawking. Jo stepped closer, took a cookie off the plate, and then took a hearty-sized bite. "Thank you. I was getting a bit famished." Jo glanced with astonishment at the cookie in her hand. "Gosh, Tessa, this is delicious." The heat of embarrassment at the compliment flushed Tessa's features. "You can bake for me anytime." Jo raised her head and stared at Tessa with a mischievous grin.

"If you cook as great as you bake, I'm up for playing guinea pig. To help you, of course." Her face flamed hotter, and she stepped back, when Jo advanced toward her, needed distance before she did something she might regret. Jo must have noticed because she stopped abruptly with a pained expression on her face. "Gosh, I've upset you. I'm sorry," Jo said.

Tessa shook her head adamantly. "I'm not upset, Jo, just surprised." Jo frowned in her confusion. "No one, not even Warren, compliments my time in the kitchen." Tessa shrugged. "I expect I'm adequate, but not great."

"Adequate?" Jo said as she stuffed the last bite in her mouth. "Better than. The cookie is fantastic. Don't tell Brigid, she's proud of her baking. Rightfully so, but not great like you."

Tessa decided to change the topic away from herself. She glanced around the room and nodded at the work she saw. "You know you do wonderful work yourself. Carpentry is a task I could never do."

Jo shrugged. "Nah, anyone could do it given the proper training."

"And did you have the proper training?" Tessa asked.

"I learned from the best. Fiona taught me all I know."

"And who did she learn from?"

Jo sat down on one of the crates and began a careful study of her boots. Just when Tessa thought she wouldn't answer the question, Jo raised her head and met her gaze. "Mostly, she learned on her own. Fiona is good at watching, studying, and then applying what she's seen." Jo glanced out the window. "She had to learn self-reliance, and she passes the importance of it on to the rest of us. We rely on her, for support and knowledge, to be independent ourselves. I don't know where we would be without her. Well, I do know, and I wouldn't change our now for anything."

"You sound worried when you speak of her. Is there something wrong with Fiona? Other than the incident with Thomas?"

Jo's bottom lip slightly trembled. From the furrowed brow, Tessa knew Jo needed to share with somebody, but had taken on a large dose of Fiona's self-reliance. Tessa wondered what happened in Jo's life to make her so distrustful of others. Of sharing feelings. She wished she could walk up to Jo and say, "trust me," but knew she must earn Jo's trust. Tessa didn't know if she could, or to what degree she may already have done so. It would be best if she just dropped her cards on the table and hoped Jo realized the honesty with which her comment was given. "I'd never betray your confidences, Jo. If you ever want to talk to someone, I'm here for you."

"Maybe you should be careful about what you offer." Jo stood from the crate.

Tessa felt the increase in her pulse when Jo took both her hands and walked her toward the counter littered with the larger pieces of Jo's tools and sawdust from her cuttings. Covered with an old skirt of Tessa's, too worn to wear, was a cash register ready to tally daily accounts when the shop officially opened. Jo shifted to sit on the floor, tugged Tessa down with her. Tessa held her knees to her chest. Jo stretched her legs out and crossed them at the ankle. They both leaned their backs against the counter.

Jo said, "Some of this story isn't mine to tell. I'll have to glaze over those parts. Let's stay simple and say things weren't so good in Boston, and tragedy came to our family. We weren't sure Fiona would survive the passage out here, by the time we left. Fiona worked so hard for all of us to make this move, away from danger. She could've come here on her own and avoided the worst of what happened, but that's not Fiona's way. Fiona took us on as her family. She wasn't leaving Boston without all of her family."

"But I thought—" A gentle finger to Tessa's lips halted her question. Tessa felt sparks alight in her body, a yearning strained for release.

The corner of Jo's lip quirked upward, and Tessa had the sudden urge to kiss her. "Don't pretend you haven't noticed the obvious differences between Fiona and me. I feel I can trust you with private stuff, so I'll give you a chance. Hope you don't disappoint."

"I couldn't do anything to hurt you, Jo. Or your family by extension." Tessa prayed Jo could hear the sincerity in her words. She trusted Jo more than her brother. Tessa hoped Jo recognized it.

"Okay." Jo quirked a smile. "Suffice it to say we're a stronger family than any blood could've created. And in our hearts, and thanks to the power of Margaret and her paperwork, Fiona will always be my legal sister."

Tessa shifted so she could glance into Jo's eyes. A blind man could have seen the love and adoration when she spoke of Fiona. How different her life would be, Tessa thought, if Warren had one iota of the same form of affection toward her, his biological sister.

"Do you think you will ever be able to tell me the whole story?" Tessa asked, prepared for Jo's antagonism at the requested personal invasion.

Instead, Jo placed a hand on her bent knee and said, "I would like that, to share my past with you and how Fiona's became entwined with mine." Jo gave her a serious look and then ran a forefinger across the line of her jaw, leaving Tessa's flesh heated with its trail. "I'm afraid if you hear the story, you'll think differently of me. I don't have a nice past."

Tessa could see emotions warred within Jo. Much as Tessa wanted to know of her past, she didn't want to be the one to cause Jo more pain. It was enough for now, but Tessa knew they wouldn't be able to sustain a healthy relationship without total disclosure. Tessa would also have to share her history with Catherine. What she asked was, "So Fiona healed well enough to travel?"

"Yes, but it was a trial. We were all battling our individual and shared demons," Jo gave her a strange look and lowered her voice, "our common deviances, except for Brigid, who's normal. And we were looking into an unknown future."

Ah-hah. Tessa did have the right of it about Fiona and Margaret and with Jo's possible interest in her. A bit of her tension released. "How long ago was this?"

"About four years, maybe a bit more."

"Well, you all seem to do well for yourselves. You're as normal as any family. But there's something still bothering you, isn't there?" Was Tessa pushing Jo too hard? Insinuating herself in her need to be part of Jo's life.

Jo took in a deep breath, held it for a moment, and then exhaled loudly. "When we left Boston, Fiona had just undergone serious surgery, been in a coma for over a week. But it seems despite the healing she accomplished, another matter was hidden. I don't know if the doctors missed something, or we're on borrowed time with Fiona's good health. We didn't know then," Jo's voice cracked. "But now —"

Tessa hadn't seen Jo's quick emotional reaction coming. Her arms flew around Tessa's shoulders and buried her face in Tessa's neck. Tessa felt the warm dampness of tears. Jo's silent sobs tore at her heart. "Jo, honey, it's all right, I've got you. If you don't want to talk anymore, we won't. I never intended to upset you like this."

After a few long — somehow not long enough — moments more, Jo moved away, pulled the ever-present handkerchief from her back pocket, and angrily wiped the remaining tears from her eyes. "Guess you think I'm a big baby, don't you? I wouldn't blame you if you did. I've spent a lot of time learning self-control, so I'm not sure why I'm so emotional with you."

Tessa felt the moment Jo tried to pull away. She latched an arm around Jo's waist and held her close. "I hope it's because you're comfortable enough to trust me and trust in me. Thank you for sharing something so personal. I'm sorry if I brought pain to you somehow."

"Nah, I've wanted to talk to somebody about how worried I am. Fiona's sitting on the ledge of anxious and probably obsessing about this, and Margaret isn't supposed to know until Fiona has thought it through in enough detail to tell Margaret what's wrong."

Tessa knew she shouldn't be so focused on the comfort she felt with Jo's warm body pressed into hers, vaguely aware her fingertips drew circles on Jo's hip. If it weren't for the depth of

Jo's emotions, Tessa would want to stay clasped like this forever. "Well, if you ever feel you can trust me with your secret, I'm glad and willing to listen." Tessa didn't know how long they sat together, neither getting anything accomplished.

A niggling in the back of her mind worried Warren could walk in on them anytime. Tessa didn't want this moment to end. And for an odd second, Tessa realized she never had one of these moments with Catherine Dubois. She wanted many more with Jo.

Barely able to hear, Jo whispered, "Fiona might be seriously sick."

"What makes you believe that?" Tessa asked.

"She's been getting a lot of migraines, and she's had moments where she can't see." Jo swallowed hard. "Heck, she probably wouldn't have told me, but there was an episode when we were working in the barn. That's our workshop." Jo's gaze became unfocused, stared at what may be a memory. "She was working with the electric saw, cutting up pieces of wood we'd measured for one of the projects, a hope chest we're building. I'm not sure what made me stop work and look up then. But when I saw the pain on her face, and then the fear as she just stood there, as if she wanted but not sure how to do something important. When I walked over to her, Fiona's hands were shaking. I wondered why she didn't turn off the power." Jo shook her head slightly. "I teased her. The look on her face when Fiona admitted she couldn't see, didn't know where the switch was without taking her hand off the machine."

Tessa softened her voice when she said, "The teasing may have helped take some of the tension from her, Jo. It's a good thing you were there for her."

Jo sniffed. "Kind of my point. What if I hadn't been? How long would Fiona have been forced to stand there, holding the saw, waiting for her sight to return long enough to turn the power off and safely put the saw down? What if that had been the time her vision didn't come back?"

"So, it does come back?" Tessa asked. Now, her first meeting with Fiona here at the shop, before and after the mishap with Thomas, became clearer. Jo believed Fiona had become more fragile, waited for the straw that would break her. Take the family pillar from them.

"So far. But the migraines are getting worse and more frequent. And, Fiona's episodes of blindness are lasting a little longer each time." Jo blinked, then focused on Tessa. "I'm sorry, Tessa. I shouldn't lose all this on you. It's just I want to do something for her, and I feel helpless. I don't know what to do."

Tessa released Jo's waist and used both hands to hold one of Jo's. "Seems to me you love Fiona very much. And Fiona fighting her helplessness, which I guess I understand is difficult for her, has created the same feelings for you."

"We'd do anything for her. She's given up so much for us. Shared so much with us to become a true family."

"But it's frustrating because Fiona doesn't realize this, right? She doesn't see this the sharing from the loving family she built, that she should rely on you. Maybe the hardship is Fiona sees herself as becoming a burden to you all?" Jo nodded to each question. "I wish I could give you sage advice, Jo. But Fiona needs to come to terms with this before she can accept any form of intervention."

Jo snorted. "Stubborn as she is, realizing it may come too late."

"I get the feeling you're her mirror image there." Tessa used the pad of her thumb to wipe a stray tear from Jo's face. She loved the feel of Jo's flesh, soft and warm, where the rest of her exuded strength. Tessa stood and then reached out her hands for Jo until they were face to face. "Fiona seems a strong and capable woman. You should give her a little more time. I have faith she'll do what's right before it's too late. I also have faith Fiona knows you're there for her, and she will come to you and Margaret when she's ready."

"Yeah, guess you're right." Jo gave her a small grin. "Worrying now isn't getting your carpentry work done, either. Sorry 'bout this."

"There's no hurry, Jo. I can do my original work without opening the shop for the new business."

"Maybe, but a major part of your income is in selling the pretty stuff in boxes in the storeroom." Jo leaned down and placed a soft kiss on Tessa's forehead. "Thank you for the tasty cookie and the talk."

"I'm always here for you, Jo." No sooner had the words escaped her lips, honest as they were, Tessa wondered if she'd said too much, gone too far in their new relationship.

Jo nodded and quirked the corner of her lips into a smile. She swiped another cookie from the plate. "An admission and invitation I won't forget either, honey. Thank you." Jo winked and stuffed half the treat into her mouth.

Tessa's heart hammered in her chest. Did Jo mean to call her honey? Had she meant the word as an honest endearment? Or only been a slip of the tongue, buddy to buddy? Oh, please, let it be more than a casual word.

"Tessa?" Jo gave her a thoughtful and nervous stare. "Would you be my girl?"

Surprised, Tessa stared for a moment. "I would like that very much, Jo." Jo grinned wide, nodded, and returned to work. Tessa smiled too, as she picked up the snack dishes and brought them upstairs to wash. I'm Jo Cavanaugh's girl. Happiness filled her entire body.

Chapter Six

MARGARET WATCHED AS Nicholas walked to Fiona and, after a short pause, sat on the bench beside her. The school year would end in little more than a month. Could whatever matter bothering Fiona wait that long? She didn't know what concerned Fiona but hoped Nicholas could somehow get Fiona to share — even if she weren't the one privy to the problem first. She frowned, tried to decipher what secret Fiona kept from her. Margaret loved Fiona with all her heart, and, although they'd been busy with their respective careers and lives, she didn't believe the chasm too lengthy to cross. Was she wrong? Should she be more worried?

Jo wrapped an arm around her waist and pulled her closer. "You okay?" Margaret nodded. "You aren't worried about Fiona and Nicholas having a tryst, are you?

"No, not at all," Margaret said, grateful for Jo's attempt to lighten her mood. "That's the farthest thought. I'm hoping whatever is upsetting Fiona, Nicholas can get to the bottom of it before Fiona cracks." She felt Jo stiffen beside her. Margaret turned, grasped Jo's hands, and gave a smile. "I suspect you know what the matter is but are sworn to secrecy."

"It's nothing to do with—"

"I don't believe it has anything to do with our relationship, Jo," she lied. "I wish she'd be less worried about upsetting me, and more focused on letting me shoulder some of the burdens, her burdens."

Jo sighed. "I believe she will soon. Fiona needs to work it out in her head first." She smiled and added, "Then it's family meeting time, and all will be clear."

Yes, a family meeting to work out the finer details of the situation, and each could move on in a consolidated mission. Any other time, anyone else, they would have had the meeting by now. The delay is what worried and, if she were honest with herself, panicked her, and gave credence to Margaret's fear this problem would be monumental. Would she be prepared for Fiona's revelation? She hoped so because this distance Fiona put between them broke her heart. Margaret missed her wife. How much longer before she got her loving Fiona back?

Enough of this, Margaret silently chided herself. It was near the end of another school year for her, another group of third graders ready to move on to the fourth grade. She started what became a tradition in her first year of teaching to applaud the students for finishing the grade level while ushering in the summer break. She'd offered finger sandwiches and snacks, which Brigid prepared and baked, respectively, with lemonade and iced tea for the first two years. The offering quickly morphed into a barbecue setting and had the parents bringing the snacks.

Also, this occasion provided a means to meet some of the adults in the community, while it opened avenues for Fiona and Jo to better integrate into their new home. The effort provided mixed results. Jo realized no one could know of her past unless she told them, so she blended in almost seamlessly.

Fiona had a harder time integrating. She was too conscious of her healing body and the facial scars she perceived to be hideous.

Margaret tried to explain they by no means disfigured, but Fiona was too self-conscious of them. It wasn't until she slipped away—much like now—into the barn, converted into a workshop when one of the parents (either concerned or curious) followed. Fiona's standard way to release stress was wood carving. When the parent peaked into the barn, he not only witnessed Fiona carve a pattern into the pie chest she'd built, but all the other woodwork she'd crafted. Up to that point, Fiona had sold a couple of pieces to local businesses on a commission basis. Since the man walked inside, much to Fiona's consternation, Fiona was hard-pressed to keep up with the demand for work. All because of the man's praises he shared with others.

Of course, the incident also prompted the verbal requirement for an invitation into her workshop—for safety sake, Fiona insisted. Now people drove down from as far as Denver to place an order for a piece of specialized woodwork. The incident helped bring Fiona out of her shell, gave her more self-assuredness. And yet here they were, Margaret worried as Fiona pulled away emotionally again.

Margaret must've telegraphed her concern in her body because Jo squeezed her waist and said, "She'll be okay. We'll all be okay."

She wondered if it were true. Margaret held a nagging premonition balled in the pit of her stomach that life would get worse before it improved. With the smile Margaret strained to wear, she said, "What about you, sweetie? Has your friend Tessa arrived?"

Jo scowled. "No, not yet. Her brother insisted he would bring her when I offered to pick her up. Don't know what he suspected would happen between us once all alone." Jo gave a derisive snort. "Guess not even your professional safety blanket as a schoolteacher can make that man like me."

Margaret leaned her head against Jo's shoulder. "Trust me, honey, it's his loss. You are more spectacular than even we suspected you'd turn out to be."

"You have to say that, I know where you sleep," Jo said, then chuckled.

Margaret tapped the hand still at her waist. "You and Fiona are so alike. Often it's kinda scary."

Richard skipped up to them, interrupting Jo. "A lady's looking for you, so I bringed her."

"Brought her," Margaret corrected automatically. As Jo dropped her arm, picked up Richard, and perched him on her hip, they turned to see Tessa and Brigid headed their way. Brigid flashed a mock scowl at Richard, who giggled in response. Tessa, whose expression mimicked absolute comportment initially, beamed in delight once her gaze landed on Jo. Oh my, Margaret thought excitedly. Jo's feelings weren't one-sided, after all.

"You were supposed to walk with us, you little scamp," Brigid said to a grinning Richard. Away from his condescending and grumpy mother, Richard was cheerful and precocious. They all enjoyed the time he spent with them, but Margaret knew that to be truer for Brigid. Even as the family disliked Ethel's abuse of Brigid's generosity of time, Brigid fairly beamed into life when with the little boy. Brigid stretched her arms toward Richard, who promptly switched from Jo's hip to hers. "As you can see, Jo, your guest has arrived, so I'll take this rascal off your hands — or hip as it were — and get him a plate before he fills up on cookies."

"But your cookies are the bestest," Richard said.

Brigid smiled, even as she feigned indignation. "Flattery won't get you another until you've had your lunch. Excuse us, please." Brigid spun on her heel and headed to the house. Richard beamed, with his arms possessively wrapped around Brigid's neck.

Margaret's attention returned to Jo and Tessa, who stared and smiled but hadn't budged toward or away from each other. Oh goodness, Margaret thought with the equivalent of a mental eye roll, I hope Fiona and I weren't like this when we courted. The observation brought a stab of pain to her heart. Of course not, they hadn't resembled them at all, their courtship mired in danger, death, and disguises. Well, Fiona's disguise anyway.

Fiona posed as a sixteen-year-old boy, using her dead brother's nickname, Finn. As Finn, Fiona had saved her from a group of bullies intending her harm. Her brother was so grateful that he hired Finn as his driver. Margaret hadn't known then about her brother's entrance into the profession of mobster since he used the family restaurant business as a front.

She shook her head, hoped to dispel the pain-filled memories. If Margaret hadn't been in that precarious situation, Fiona would never have accepted the job. What would her life be like if Fiona had never come into it? Would Fiona's father have succeeded in beating her to death? Despite the pain and hardships to them all, she couldn't imagine her life without Fiona and Jo.

No maudlin thoughts, she chided herself. Margaret sighed and said, "I'm so glad you could join us, Tessa."

With only a slight pause, Tessa broke eye contact with Jo and turned toward Margaret. "Thank you for inviting me, Mrs. Cavanaugh."

"It's Margaret." She gave a glance around the yard. "Was Warren able to join you?" she asked, as she hoped for a negative reply. Margaret couldn't put her finger on why, but she didn't like Warren, and it had little to do with his rudeness toward them.

Tessa nodded. "He's on the back porch chatting away with Mrs. Walters. Keeping her company in her beau's abandonment, he told me."

Margaret raised an eyebrow wondering if Nicholas cared about the encroachment and his supposed journey into dereliction of his date. She glanced at a smitten Jo. "Why don't you two get some barbecue and mingle." She thought about the last part and amended the directions. "Find a quiet corner for yourselves." At their tandem silent nod, Margaret said, "I'm going to check on Fiona." Margaret gave a gentle nudge to Jo's back. "Off with you two." She stared after them until they reached the long tables of food.

Comfortable Jo and Tessa would entertain themselves—albeit in silence apparently—Margaret turned back to the barn to see Nicholas follow Fiona inside as he pulled an object—his camera most likely—free from his ever-present satchel.

"He must have got her talking about her work," Margaret said quietly. Her heart lifted as she wondered, Is Nicholas the hope I need to get Fiona to open up about her trouble? If he did get her to talk, she would willingly kiss him full on the lips as a thank you. Margaret shuddered. No, she couldn't go quite that far, especially not with his mustache, little or no.

Chapter Seven

FIONA SAT ON the bench outside the double doors of the barn, one opened to allow the scent of cut wood to seep out to her. She didn't care for the number of people who showed up for this yearly event, hated so many people in one place. She did love the joy it brought to Margaret's face. The excitement thrummed through Margaret which made her body tremble. Not as if anyone else would know that without holding her; and, heaven help anyone who touched her. But Margaret understood her need for personal space and smaller crowds, preferably family only crowding. And understood Fiona's need to walk away.

She knew it was past time she told Margaret about what was happening with the headaches and the blindness, especially since the whole matter scared Fiona into being less communicative. Once Margaret became aware, she wouldn't let up until they had a medical diagnosis. The thing was, in her heart, Fiona suspected the medical conclusion would be worse than the symptoms offered at present. How do you prepare for bad news? More importantly, how do you prepare your loved ones to hear bad news?

From her peripheral, Fiona caught Nicholas Tirrell's approach. He stopped about two feet away and pointed to the empty area of her bench. "Mind if I sit for a moment?" Normally every fiber of her being would telegraph a negative reply, surprised when she automatically nodded instead.

"Margaret has done a wonderful job with the picnic. Brigid tells me it's now a yearly end of school event."

"Her way of saying goodbye," she said. "Margaret gets quite attached to the children."

"She's a good woman," Nicholas said.

"Yes, she's one-of-a-kind."

Nicholas unstrung the satchel he always carried from his neck and placed it between them, like a barrier. Which of them, she wondered, needed the barricade? "I noted all the women in your family are quite remarkable."

The comment elicited a chuckle from her. "Says the man with a bit of a crush on Brigid."

Nicholas also chuckled, rubbed a finger on one side of his thin mustache. "Quite observant of you. You probably think me a cad."

Fiona shook her head. "Only if you do something to hurt her." She glared at him sternly. "I wouldn't recommend that course of action."

"At the risk of incurring your wrath even a bit, I need to state Brigid will be the heartbreaker."

She would vehemently disagree if she didn't recognize the truth of it herself. Brigid had left her life, her family, all to follow Fiona to Colorado. Her help with Fiona's healing, with raising Jo. She maintained the homestead while Margaret and Fiona worked outside the home, and while Jo went to school, it was invaluable. But Fiona sometimes wondered if Brigid didn't believe she left one housekeeper job for another, even if more liberated. She never complained, but Brigid also hadn't done as much socializing as needed for a young single woman.

Fiona wondered if Brigid felt backed into a corner of responsibility. She felt a modicum of relief when Brigid befriended Ethel Walters at the grocers, where she plucked an excited Richard from climbing the shelf to reach something which caught his eye. Brigid and Ethel purported a friendship, but Fiona wondered, especially when Ethel went out at night and left Richard in Brigid's care.

Hence, Ethel's meeting Nicholas, which was also a conundrum, as their pairing seemed off too. Fiona hadn't missed the wistful glances Brigid gave Nicholas when she believed no one watched. The problem for Fiona was she believed Brigid was attracted to Nicholas more for the thrill than for any true chemistry. "You may be right."

Nicholas leaned back against the barn wall. A long moment of silence stretched between them before Nicholas spoke. "You may not know this, Fiona, but I've done a good deal of traveling in my nearly thirty years." He paused. Fiona wondered where this conversation was going and stiffened in anticipation. "I've seen a lot of tragedy and joy, marked some of my travels with my photography, and garnered a career."

She always assumed he came from money because of his clothing and the fact you could find him available nearly anytime, day or night. Leading Fiona to conclude work, for Nicholas, was a pleasure, not a necessity. Did he make a great deal of money with his photographs? The silent question was probably written all over her face because he gave a wide grin.

"Don't expect most people to know who I am since I use a pseudonym, and photographers are usually only celebrities to other photographers. Not popular like radio and silent screen stars."

"Can you tell me your other name?"

"My full name is Nicholas Allen Tirrell. My photos present under N. Allen. I earn a respectable income as a freelance photographer, but it did take a small inheritance from a relative to allow me the opportunity to eat regularly while building said career."

"I think I've seen a couple of your photos in the paper. They were of tragic events like the aftermath of hurricanes and such, weren't they?" Nicholas nodded. "You have quite the eye for catching the human condition in the wake of devastation."

Nicholas snorted. "And you have quite the way of naming me a ghoul who exploits people with my film. Trust me. I've heard the negativity before."

"No, I truly didn't mean it that way," she said. "I think a lot of people may see the photos in that way and the chance to sigh, 'glad it wasn't me' in the process. Your images, though, reflect the human condition in the wake of that very devastation. The pain of loss. Humanity, when people work together to pick themselves up and dust themselves off, so to speak. The moments when one's station in life isn't a consideration in the moment's destruction. No matter your station, we bleed, grieve, and die the same."

"Not everyone mirrors your views on the subject. No matter. I have thick skin, and don't let other people's insecurities become my own."

"How hard was that to achieve?" Fiona asked, knowing his resolve couldn't have happened overnight.

He lowered his voice conspiratorially. "Actually, about as easy as swallowing crushed glass."

Fiona's laugh was an unexpected outburst to her, even as it was genuine. "I bet. So, what brought you here to Pueblo?"

Nicholas shrugged. "The train. When I stopped at your depot, I got off and had a bit of a look-see. The people and sites were different enough from Denver to pique my interest." He locked his gaze on hers, and Fiona suspected he debated whether to voice whatever thought in his head. He rubbed a finger along the side of his mustache again, prompting Fiona to wonder if it were a conscious or unconscious habit. "Less of me, and back to my original point. As said earlier, I've witnessed any number of tragic experiences, Fiona, the impact both physically and emotionally from these events, and been the character in my own tragic drama."

Nicholas gave a heavy sigh. "Having said this, I'm going to voice an observation, and then I'll drop the matter. I hope you aren't too irritated with me and will give me a tour of your workshop."

Fiona eyed him cautiously. What could he possibly say to warrant an obvious forewarning? She gave a hesitant nod. Curiosity outweighed her caution. "Okay. If it's too upsetting, I can always lock myself in my room. Even if I have to navigate a hundred people first." The levity was more for her than him.

"Noted." Nicholas inhaled deeply. "I don't know your past and could be off base here, but I don't think so if the scar on your forehead is any indication. It doesn't look like a childhood injury. Brigid commented—nothing intentional, just in conversation without understanding implications, I'm sure—about your migraines. Having witnessed our boys returning from war, and hearing of your symptoms, I think you are doing Margaret an injustice by not letting her know about them."

"How do you know I haven't?" Fiona asked defensively, although what he'd asked her not to do.

"The pain in her eyes when you distance yourself." That was unexpected. Fiona hadn't realized her actions, motivated simply to help not harm Margaret, were obvious to others. Nicholas seemed intent on breaking the tension. He feigned adjusting his already precise tie. "Not that anyone other than a devastatingly handsome and charming photographer would notice such a thing."

Relaxing only slightly, Fiona got off the bench and moved to the open doorway of the workshop. "Come on. Get the tour before your ego swallows you completely from my view."

Chapter Eight

TODAY, THREE DAYS after the picnic, Ethel was supposed to pick up Brigid for a shopping day. Brigid became tired of the wait and wondered what happened to Ethel. She'd borrowed Fiona's truck, and currently barreled down the road to Ethel's country home in a near-blind panic. It wasn't like Ethel not to answer the phone. It wasn't like Ethel not to let Brigid know her whereabouts if she were going to be late. Some of the habits stemmed from Ethel's twinge of narcissism to be the most important person worthy of attention at any given moment. Despite Ethel's distractions, Brigid had a real fear something was amiss.

One disconcerting thought was Nicholas arrived for a visit, and Ethel was too preoccupied to remember her prior plans with Brigid. Ethel's self-absorption tended toward frustrating. Also, the visual image she'd initiated saddened her. Brigid had no claim on Nicholas, wasn't sure she wanted one. Brigid also knew Ethel was about to, if she hadn't already, break off her relationship with Nicholas.

If Brigid were honest with herself, she'd considered taking Warren up on his offer of a date. Something about Warren, more her type in the social realm, kept her from accepting. He wasn't attractive like Nicholas, and he certainly didn't share the same sweet characteristics of his sister Tessa. Maybe it was his rough, bad boy side. She was attracted to the good boys, like Ian Donnelly and Fionn Cavanaugh, and it had led nowhere in the end.

She mentally corrected herself. Brigid would probably be with Fionn right now if it hadn't been for the fire, which took him and his mother's life and left Fiona at the hands of her abusive and drunken father.

Leaving Brigid without a marriage license and ring.

Brigid slammed a foot on the clutch and brake pedals, slid to a stop on the gravel before the front porch, punched the shifter in gear before racing out of the truck. She called out for Ethel as she burst through the house's front door, not bothering to knock. The home appeared empty at first glance. Ethel's handbag lay on the side table by the front door. She called out again, still no response. She moved further into the home before she heard the muffled crying from Richard's room.

"Richard?" Brigid called softly. "It's Brigid, can you tell me where you are?" she asked, as she entered his room and glanced at the empty bed, toys neatly in their toy box, everything in its usual tidy spot. Ethel, after all, would have it no other way.

Brigid stood in the doorway, stared around the room before she identified the crying came from the closet. She rushed over, jerked the closet door open, and bent to meet Richard's gaze. "Richard," Brigid said softly, "it's me, honey. Are you okay?" She reached her hands out, and Richard catapulted into her embrace. "Where's your mother?"

Richard cried in earnest. "Mama's hurt in the barn."

Brigid furrowed her brow. Something was seriously wrong with Ethel if Richard wasn't sitting with her. Under normal circumstances, Richard would be the first to offer his mother assistance. A knot of fear clutched leaden in Brigid's gut. Giving Richard one final squeeze, Brigid placed him on his bed, and said, "Stay here until I check on your mommy. Okay?" She waited until he nodded. "I'll be right back, honey."

Despite what she might find, Brigid exited the house and hesitantly made her way toward the barn. Both the large barn doors were closed, the first indication of something wrong. Ethel made a habit of keeping those doors open so she could hear and watch Richard's activities from the kitchen window when he played inside. She tugged the door open just enough to squeeze her way through.

Richard was right. Ethel was in the barn, but far from simply hurt. Whereas Brigid expected Ethel to be lying wounded on the floor, possibly unconscious from a fall, she didn't expect to see Ethel hanging from a rope tied to the rafter. Ethel's dress was torn and bloodied, her face damaged by multiple blows and bloated from strangulation.

With a stifled cry, Brigid took a step back, her body contacting the door before she twisted around and ran back into the main house.

Using the phone installed in the kitchen, Brigid picked up the receiver and placed it to her ear. Ethel had a party line. Due to cost, she put in a rural line but hadn't been able to afford a single. As voices chirped away, Brigid grew perturbed. "Ladies, I need you to hang up. Operator, please connect me with the police. There's been a murder."

The women on the line tittered as if it were a joke, until Richard screamed, "Momma's dead, Momma's dead" behind her.

Once the operator assured her help was on the way, Brigid called the only other person who made her feel safe. Fiona agreed to come immediately, so Brigid returned her attention to Richard. She clutched him tightly to her body, they both cried at their loss.

FIONA TELEPHONED NICHOLAS. He was the only person with a schedule as flexible as her own. Nicholas also owned a vehicle. She needed transportation since Brigid took her truck. Nicholas, as luck would have it for her, had been in his hotel room.

Nicholas must have broken every speed limit to get to her house, screeching to stop where Fiona nervously waited. She slid in, and they were underway before the passenger door closed.

"She didn't say what was wrong?" Nicholas asked.

Fiona could tell Nicholas searched for the facts rather than making it a matter of disbelieving her. "All I know is Richard was near hysterical in the background, and Brigid was barely holding it together." She gave him a sideways glance. "You may need to prepare yourself that something serious has happened to Ethel."

"Not to be sarcastic, or cruelly melodramatic, but I certainly hope that's the case. I'd hate for this to be some form of punishment of hers toward Richard and Brigid." Nicholas gave a quick one-shoulder shrug. "Ethel told me two days ago, our relationship is over. She wasn't in a mood to pretend interest when all she wanted was a new daddy for Richard."

Fiona shook her head. "I'm sorry, Nicholas. The situation appeared so to Margaret and me, but we didn't feel comfortable questioning Brigid on the situation. Not that Ethel would have shared, or did share, this newest fact that we are aware of. Poor Richard. You were good for him."

Nicholas's grip on the steering wheel tightened. "You want to hear a sad truth?"

"If it makes you feel better to share."

"No, not better." Nicholas exhaled heavily. "Truth is I figured it out for myself. Ethel was always so distant yet had no trouble with me spending time with Richard, even if it meant I also spent time with her best friend, Brigid."

"So, you already decided she used you?" Fiona felt bad, but it brought a niggling question to mind. Could Nicholas have harmed Ethel in anger at rejection? She felt a moment of unease. No, Fiona had many faults, but judging character usually wasn't one them. Nicholas had secrets, but murder wasn't one. And, in her experience, usually, the man dumped the woman, not the other way around.

"Do you believe she purposely placed you with Brigid?"

"No, Ethel also used Brigid to take on responsibility for Richard when she didn't want to deal with motherhood. Ethel has always been interested in what makes Ethel happy. That's why we still had s—"

Fiona smiled at the sudden rush of red to Nicholas's face. His embarrassment at alluding to shared intimacy was refreshing. Most men seemed pleased to announce anything physical, which gave credence to male prowess. Nicholas was so different from the average male. Fiona took pride in their growing friendship, mostly because his reactions appeared genuine and honest. She gave a soft chuckle. "Okay, you don't have to spell it out for me. I get it."

The relief on Nicholas's face nearly made Fiona laugh aloud. Fiona was glad she hadn't laughed then when they closed in on Ethel's home and saw Sergeant Langford's vehicle and another police car in the yard. A teary-eyed Brigid held a near-catatonic Richard in her arms that confirmed the situation was more dire than anticipated.

Fiona and Nicholas exited the vehicle and made their way to Brigid's side.

Warren said, "Need you to go through what happened one more time."

Brigid gave a watery sniff, readjusted her grip on Richard, and sighed wearily. "I've already told you the sequence of events three times." She shook her head. "Are you even interested in doing your job? Do you plan to spend the rest of the night asking the same questions of me?"

Warren shrugged indifferently. "I need to make sure I got this all straight." Fiona and Nicholas stepped closer, and Warren glared. "And what's your reason for being here?"

Nicholas returned his glare, apparently able to step in where he needed to be, and Fiona wanted to congratulate him for standing his ground with Warren's bullying. "Friends of the family, as both Brigid and Richard, are obviously in distress and need support. We came to make sure they safely get home."

Warren didn't appear happy with Nicholas's assertion. "Weren't you and the deceased, Mrs. Walters, dating?"

Fiona sucked in a breath. "Ethel's dead?"

"I'd say hanging by a rope from a rafter would achieve that end," Warren said.

The coldness of the reply brought fresh tears to Brigid and Richard. Fiona prepared herself to reprimand Warren for his insensitivity, but Nicholas beat her to it. "Could you be any more of an ass, Sergeant?" With the tilt of his head, Nicholas indicated the women and the little boy. "Can we at least allow Brigid to take Richard inside? Better yet, can Fiona take them home? I think the matter is emotional enough without having to listen to your cold declarations about someone they love."

Warren gave a dismissive snort. "I know where you all live, so I'll find you when I need you to answer more questions."

When the sergeant turned and walked toward the barn, Fiona asked, "Do you believe this is associated with the other murders in town?"

Not turning around, Warren snarled, "How can it be? Ask Brigid. Nothing was taken. Suggests to me this was someone Ethel knew." He snorted. "Guess the killer might'a changed his methods."

Fiona wanted to place her fist firmly into Warren's nose. She suppressed the urge. Barely. Fiona wouldn't give the insolent Sergeant Langford any more reason to disrespect her family and friends.

Fiona walked to Nicholas, who stood beside her truck. "I should probably take them home." She stretched out a hand to him. "I thank you for driving me here on short notice. I need to stay with them."

"I understand. If you need anything, you know where to find me."

"I do, Nicholas, and I appreciate the offer," she said. "As soon as we find out any information, we'll let you know, not that I expect the sergeant to be forthcoming."

Brigid, Richard still held tightly, said out the window, "Why don't you come by for supper. Once I put Richard down to bed, we can discuss this matter."

"Aren't you afraid the topic will spoil your appetite?"

Fiona hid her surprise at Brigid's invitation, and responded, "It just may, but I think we need to collaborate on this, as we appear to be the only ones interested in a speedy resolution in catching the perpetrator." Fiona quickly glanced toward the barn before returning her attention to Nicholas. She smiled at him, realized he had done the same. "Guess we have the same expectations."

"That we are the only ones who haven't all the faith in the world in our esteemed Sergeant Langford?" Nicholas said.

"Yes," Fiona said as she climbed behind the wheel. "See, we are reading the same story." She didn't bother to hide a smile. "You know, Nicholas, I appreciate you more and more by the moment."

Nicholas closed the driver's door. "Then, I consider myself blessed, indeed."

"Supper is at seven. We look forward to your opinions." He gave Fiona a wink, and she shook her head. "Be on your way before I change my mind."

"And here I thought I'd sufficiently charmed you."

Fiona started the truck and put it in gear. "Watch your step, young man. I have tools at my disposal to swipe the grin and attitude completely from your face."

As she turned the truck around and headed down the long driveway, Fiona glanced in her rearview mirror. Nicholas watched their departure with arms crossed over his chest, a wide grin exposed his white teeth. Yes, she wasn't sure why, but something about Nicholas was beginning to heal her fear all men were of the same ilk — heinous.

Chapter Nine

DINNER TURNED OUT to be a somber affair. Fiona hadn't expected it to be otherwise when they'd invited Nicholas to join them. Fiona sat at the head of the table with Margaret and Jo on one side, and Brigid and Nicholas on the other with Richard's chair wedged between them. Brigid excused herself once she'd finished pushing her food around the plate with her fork, seldom using the utensil to bring it to her mouth. Fiona didn't blame her as they all had a difficult time eating while Richard would frequently break into tears over his plate. They each tried to get him to lie down, but he insisted on staying with them through the meal.

"Time for bed, Richard," Brigid said. She gave up her pretense of eating. She tenderly carried him from the room.

Hearing Brigid's footfalls above them, Margaret asked in a near whisper, "Do you think Ethel's murderer is the same killer as the other women?"

By voicing the question, Margaret probably suspected otherwise. Nicholas and Fiona glanced toward one another, both shaking their heads.

Fiona said, "No, honey. Although I could be wrong, I don't think so." She covered one of Margaret's hands with her own and squeezed.

"Hopefully, Warren is doing all he can to find the creep," Jo said. "Wish I had faith in him that that will be the case."

"Yes, as do I," Nicholas said. "Too bad, the initial impression of his personality belies the possibility."

"We have to do something," Margaret said. She cast a glance to the ceiling, then an apologetic look toward Nicholas, added in a quieter tone, "Ethel wasn't my favorite person, but I would see her murderer punished, for Richard's sake if not for justice alone. No one deserves death at another's hand."

Nicholas cleared his throat and glanced at Fiona. "Maybe you and I could do a little investigating on our own."

Fiona nodded. Nicholas was proving to be a wonderful friend and, so far, a positive addition to the family sessions. If Warren didn't solve the matter, they could give any information learned to someone else in the police department. Fiona wished, not for the first time in the last few years, she could bring her suspicions and suppositions to Ian Donnelly, her old sounding-board on many matters. But he was still in Boston and, if this were his case or his old beat, Ian would have moved heaven and earth to find the murderer.

"No, you most certainly will not," Margaret said. Vehemence laced her tone.

Fiona placed her hand on Margaret's thigh. "This won't be a repeat of Boston, honey. Nicholas and I will only see if we can learn something Warren will overlook, whether accidentally or intentionally. Trust me, please."

Margaret stared at her for a long moment. She bit her bottom lip and nodded. "I do trust you. But I certainly hope you two are careful. Not only is a killer out there, but Warren Langford doesn't strike me as a man to take kindly to interference from people he looks down on." Margaret shook her head, cast a pleading glance toward her. Fiona understood her wife feared a recurrence of previous situations ending less than pleasantly, worried for the outcome as Fiona aligned herself with another man in the position of trust.

"Warren doesn't strike me as someone who takes kindly to anything, no matter who is involved. However, he can't stop Fiona from showing me the sites for my photography work." He stared at Margaret for a long, intense moment. "I give you my promise, Margaret, no harm shall come to her when she's with me, or from me."

Fiona noted the slight drop in Margaret's shoulder's as a little of the tension released. Fiona wondered if Margaret felt the same sense of ease from trusting Nicholas. Jo, probably unconsciously, showed her relief with a quick squeeze to Margaret's hand.

Fiona felt some of her pressure dissolve. She now had a mission to take her mind from her problems, and an opportunity to assist with the resolution of Ethel's murder, as well as the other women. Despite the modicum of reprieve, Fiona knew she couldn't avoid her migraines and blackouts much longer. Or avoid telling Margaret.

BRIGID ENTERED THE lawyer's office, the door opened into the vestibule, from behind Nicholas who held Richard's hand clasped in his own. She considered leaving Richard at home, but the lawyer hadn't given direction one way or another on the best course of action on the matter, even though the matter concerned him and his future. Her surprise to learn Ethel had written a will, let alone included her in it, was a tremendous surprise, but not nearly as surprising being no one had come to take Richard away from her yet. Granted, only a day passed, which begged the questioning of such speed for the will reading, but some family response should have happened. She suspected that would occur today, which is why she and Richard hadn't parted company for more than necessary except for sleep and such since she learned of the will reading. And why she included Nicholas for the support of her what she expected to be a broken heart at Richard's loss.

A young man, barely out of his teens, sat behind a table converted to a desk. A single pen in a holder, a desk calendar, and a phone were the table's only adornments. The only other furnishings in the vestibule were four chairs with embroidered flowers, lined in a row in front of the office window, and a thin four-legged wooden stand with a potted philodendron on top, its vines snaking around the legs made of half-inch dowels.

To the left side of the room was a closed door.

Stepping to the table-desk, Brigid announced herself. "Hello, I'm Brigid Connor. I have an appointment with Mr. Meloni."

"Yes, of course," the young man said with a nod. Why 'of course'? Did she fill a preconceived expectation he had? Of course, because his boss had no other appointments scheduled for today? Or, of course, because there would be no others present for the Ethel Walters reading? Had Ethel no other family?

She spoke as if she did but had once referred to them as the biological past. Brigid assumed an argument might have separated Ethel from her family — due to the dislike of Richard's father — but that at least relatives existed. Nerves are making you distrustful, Brigid chided herself. "I'll let him know you are here," the young man said while standing. He moved to the door, knocked once, and returned to his seat. "If you'd like to take a seat, Mr. Meloni will be right with you."

She nodded and turned to find Richard settled into a chair, Nicholas stood protectively beside him with a grin lifting one side of his mustached lip. Brigid sat beside Richard, reached for one small hand, and clasped it on her own. She intended to exact as much physical comfort from the child as she could, a little boy she loved as her own. The thought of losing this remarkable child was breaking her heart.

Brigid barely settled into the chair when the door opened. A rotund, impeccably attired man, dressed to the nines like

Nicholas, stepped just past the threshold of the room. His coloring was painfully pale, his mousy brown hair was thin, the fingers on his hand resembled little hors d'oeuvre sausages she would serve at the dinner parties the Grahams used to host, back when she worked as the family's maid.

She shuddered at the correlation. That was so long ago. Back when Margaret's parents were alive, and the house filled with love and laughter. After their deaths, Eldon Graham had decided to try his hand at being the head of a gangster organization, and goodness was eclipsed with the darkness of fear.

"Ah, thank you for coming," Mr. Meloni said. He swung an arm behind him. "Please come to my office, Miss Connor. We should be able to conclude rather quickly." He disappeared back into his office, as Brigid rose, and gave a nervous glance toward Nicholas. At his nod, Brigid followed Mr. Meloni into his office.

Compared to the outer vestibule, the lawyer's office was heavily furnished. There were three filing cabinets, a large wooden desk and chair, scenic prints on every wall, a leather couch, and two leather chairs in front of the desk. Mr. Meloni indicated she take one of those chairs.

Meloni took his seat behind the desk, his chair groaned under his weight. "I'll make this meeting go as quickly as possible so you can get on with your day."

Brigid was puzzled. "Will no one else be joining us? Have you already settled Ethel's estate?"

"No, aren't any others coming. Most of the direction is simple paperwork, except your part in Mrs. Walter's will." He gave her a smile, which she assumed supposed to instill confidence or comfort in his presence.

Forty minutes later, with multiple questions asked and answered, Mr. Meloni escorted an emotionally numb Brigid to the vestibule. Her hands were shaking, and on seeing Richard, tears fell from her eyes as she rushed to him and dropped to her knees in front of his chair. She pulled him into a tight hug, noticed Nicholas give a glance toward the lawyer, and the lawyer nod in return. Brigid rose with Richard in her arms. With a mixture of joy and trepidation, Brigid grinned at Nicholas. "Shall we go home?"

Nicholas beamed a smile back. He crossed over to Mr. Meloni and shook his hand, shook the hand of the young assistant, and returned to her side. With the gentle hand to the small of her back, Nicholas said, "Lunch at the hotel?" Brigid nodded. "Thank you, gentlemen, and have a good day," Nicholas said with a slight tip of his hat.

In the hotel restaurant, his go-to spot he'd said, Nicholas treated them to a wonderful light lunch. They hadn't spoken about what happened in the lawyer's office. Brigid assumed Nicholas waited for her to broach the subject. Satiated, and Richard enthusiastically devouring a slice of chocolate cake, Brigid gave her attention to Nicholas, who asked, "Dare I ask what transpired?"

Brigid realized her hands still trembled. "It appears," she said with a glance toward Richard, "I am now the legal custodian of one dashing young boy by the name of Richard Walters." Richard's focused concentration on his dessert stopped as his gaze swung to her incredulously.

"Honest?" Richard asked.

Brigid nodded, "Yes, honest."

"That is wonderful news," Nicholas said. "Are you able to share the extent of what Mr. Meloni read in the will?"

"I don't see why not. I'm sure the whole town will know before long, now the will's been officially read." Brigid took a drink of her hot tea. "The most important part, of course, is my custody of Richard for now and always. The house is to be sold off, and the small funds she managed to save in her account will be transferred to an account Mr. Meloni set up for Richard." The entire situation was surreal and frightening for Brigid. She had sole custody of Richard, which was a great thing, but quite the responsibility. Not that she doubted raising him would be done with little trouble. After all, as Cavanaugh clan, their combined efforts did an exceptional job of raising Jo into a strong and determined woman. No doubt, they could all do the same with Richard. The difference now being Richard needed a male influence, and that wasn't present in their home.

Brigid dated, but the prospects lacked long-term potential. Most recently, the addition in Pueblo of Warren Langford and Nicholas held possibilities for a future, a family of her own. The problem was Warren intrigued her with his bad-boy attitude but was an ass. Nicholas was good for his attentiveness and handsomeness but with a job that could take him away at any time. Could she count on his return to them after an assignment? Possibly. Neither could ever have her heart. Not like Fionn Cavanaugh. Not like even —

"Are you all right?" Nicholas asked.

"What?" Brigid blinked rapidly to dispel the images of the past.

Richard would need a father eventually, but she had a mourning period for Richard to work with, where no one would think it untoward if Brigid didn't provide what would be considered a normal and stable home. Warren didn't strike her as able to provide that kind of home. Richard and Nicholas got along well together, and Nicholas was helpful throughout their recent association. She could do worse, although probably not better, as Nicholas possessed a brilliant career, was easy on the eyes, and would make a great father. Could she look at him as more? Brigid realized she would do whatever she needed to do to give Richard a good life.

"Yes, I'm fine. Trying to come to terms with today's changes and how it will affect the future for Richard and me."

"I'm here to help if you need me," Nicholas said.

Would he feel the same if he knew the turn her thoughts had taken? "I appreciate the offer, Nicholas. Thank you."

"You've had a stress-filled day. I should take you home." Nicholas rose, removed Richard from his seat, and extended a hand across the table toward her. She took it, and he tucked it under his arm as he grasped Richard's hand, and they left the restaurant. "I bet your cousins will be happy for you both."

From the backseat, Richard asked, "You think they'll be mad to have a boy around?"

"Heavens no," Brigid said, twisting to look at him over her shoulder. "You are already a part of our family, sweetie."

"And on the bright side," Nicholas said with a glance into the driver's side mirror. "They get a wonderful boy, and the boy-photographer gets a house full of beautiful women to take pictures of." Nicholas wriggled his eyebrows exaggeratedly. "Hubba, hubba."

Richard laughed. "Hubba, hubba."

Brigid playfully slapped Nicholas's shoulder. "Careful what you teach him. He's an impressionable boy."

Nicholas gave a feigned pout of chastisement and said, "Sorry." He ruined any authenticity in the apology when he winked at Richard sitting between them, which produced a round of giggles from the child.

The playful bantering continued the entire ride home. As Nicholas pulled up to the house, Brigid realized she could make the best of this moment. She didn't have feelings beyond friendship for Nicholas, but he could be useful as the head of the household to raise Richard. Nicholas would be the perfect father figure. Bonus, he had money and probably expected it would draw women's attention. She could use his help, so best start setting a to-snare-a-father-slash-husband plan in motion. Brigid halted Nicholas with a hand on his shoulder when he pushed open the driver-side door. He turned to her with a questioning expression. Before he could speak, Brigid kissed him full on the lips, quick but firm. "Thank you, Nicholas. Your support has meant the world to me."

Nicholas gave a surprised grin. "My pleasure, Brigid."

See, men were predictable, Brigid thought. She could do this. She needn't be alone to raise Richard.

Nicholas walked Richard into the house. Brigid leaned against the car and squeezed her eyes shut. What the hell was she doing? She missed her friend. Missed their agreement to disagree—on a great many topics—and the fun in coming to resolutions regardless. Even missed Ethel's self-centeredness.

Brigid previously considered what she would do for a child, much like Richard. That more obvious with what she was willing to do now, to Nicholas. Ethel managed to be a mom alone, but Ethel had the advantage of her marriage. Brigid wouldn't be truly alone with the Cavanaugh's.

She rubbed her forehead. It didn't wipe away her confusion or her disgust with herself. Brigid needed to concentrate on Richard. Needed to focus on mourning her lost friend.

Chapter Ten

NICHOLAS, EVER GALLANT, picked Fiona up from the house, and checked up on Brigid and Richard's state of well-being as he did so. After they left, they'd driven up and down the streets where the women had lived when murdered, focused on the surrounding layouts — access sites, hiding places, etc. — when they both seemed to come to the same silent conclusion that they would learn nothing today. Having garnered as much information as they could in their mobile investigation, Nicholas parked the car, and they consented to continue on foot.

As suspected, the specific homes of the murdered women were close to areas where a perpetrator could easily hide from view. Neither she nor Nicholas believed, though they hadn't ruled the possibility out, Ethel's killer was the same person. They'd been up and down the street where the last woman had been murdered and realized this area also within a short walk to the railroad tracks.

"The similarities are compulsive enough to believe the train tracks are the quickest means for our killer to escape. My money is on a hobo," Nicholas said. He was going through the motions of snapping pictures as they walked, hoping anyone who watched would believe them sightseeing.

Fiona roughly scrubbed at her forehead, she tensed as a throbbing began behind her eyes. Of all the times for a possible episode, out in the open and so far from home, from safety. "Despite the tracks, we still agree Ethel's murder is unrelated, don't we?"

"The train tracks are the only clue in common." Nicholas stopped and shifted, so his body blocked Fiona from the road. "Shit. Warren is across the street, about 200 yards east of my left shoulder. We aren't doing anything wrong, but a confrontation with Warren is not on my fun-things-to-do list."

Fiona squinted and casually looked in that direction. Warren was currently in a heated conversation with a disheveled man in tattered and filthy clothes. A vagabond or tramp? Could it be possible Sheriff Langford was conducting a real investigation?

"We should leave," Fiona said as the pain in her head increased. Having any interaction with Warren, especially without sight, wasn't her idea of fun either. As if the deities were against her, Fiona stumbled when the pain increased, and her gaze spotted toward grey darkness.

"Fiona, are you alright?" Nicholas asked. "Hold on to my arm and follow my lead."

A ball of panic grew heavy in her chest as she latched a hand on his arm, her fingers biting deep in desperation. "Nicho—"

"Don't worry. I know it's not easy for you, but trust me and try to relax." Nicholas placed his hand over hers. "Okay, here he comes. Just follow along with me." He nudged the camera into her hip. "Pretend you're focused on the camera." Fiona dropped her head slightly. "Of course, you're right. The angle of shot and light trajectory are all important, but not crucial. I've found—"

"What the hell are you two doing here?" Warrens' accusatory tone barked loud and sharp. Fiona flinched.

"Good afternoon to you, too, Sergeant. Didn't realize you'd restricted areas of the city to visitors. Or is it just restricted from us?"

"Answer me."

Nicholas shifted in front of her, his shadow crossed her face. Fiona suspected he'd moved to block her from Warren's view. "Now really, officer, isn't it obvious?"

"Don't call me that. It's Sergeant, not officer."

"Then don't be an ass. Beg your pardon, Miss Cavanaugh."

Fiona dutifully took her cue and squeezed his arm. "Understandable and forgiven."

"Thank you, my dear." He gently tapped the hand on his arm, then rested the palm over hers. "Miss Cavanaugh kindly offered to show me the city in all its aspects. In return, I share my craft so she can show young Richard. After all, it's up to us to keep his mind off his mother's brutal death. One which is still unsolved, I gather? Sergeant?"

"It's not like these matters are resolved overnight." Fiona could feel Warren's anger like it was a physical thing. There was something else in his defensive tone, something she couldn't quite grasp. "Guess I'm just a bit confused," Warren said. His tone changed to one more recognizable. Hateful. "Why would someone with your obvious money and snobbery hang around this thing anyway?" She couldn't see it, but Fiona could image his pudgy finger stabbed in her direction. "I can't even decide if it's a woman or man, traipsing around town in men's clothing."

Fiona was used to people like Warren and learned not to react openly. Well, for the most part. Reactions were what ignorant people of Warren's caliber thrived on, making them feel all superior to the person they insulted. Nicholas tensed, though, and Fiona could feel it. She just hoped he'd maintain his temper and not do anything rash. She was about to recommend they left when Nicholas gave a small chuckle. "Ah, and that is what truly sets us apart, officer. Not the money and upbringing. I see the heart of a person. You see the cut of a person and will never delve deep enough to reach the treasure."

"What?" Warren's tone indicated he hadn't a clue what Nicholas just imparted to him.

"Precisely. If there is nothing else, I'll take Miss Cavanaugh home to her family." With a nudge to her arm, they turned from Warren and walked away.

"I know what you were doing here," Warren yelled at their retreating backs. "I won't have it. Get in my way, and I'll make you pay."

Nicholas guided her with caution and asked softly, "Do you think anyone will back us if we complain about his threat?"

"Not on your life," she said. That's what troubled her. When it came to figures with more power, no one remembered or heard a thing.

"Was afraid you'd confirm my conclusion."

Fiona chuckled, then winced at the piercing pain. "Probably no consolation for you, but I believe either one of us could take him."

"Agreed but, be that as it may, men like him don't play fair."

"Yes, I'm aware of that fact. I also have the scars to prove it."

"We're at the car." She felt him shift to open the door. He gave her a hand inside before he gently closed the passenger door.

Fiona heard his door close. Then silence for a few moments. "Um..." Nicholas hesitated. She worried about what he might say next. Would he ask personal questions Fiona was not prepared to answer? Would she ever answer them if he did inquire? Fiona needn't have worried. When he spoke, his voice low and holding a tenderness she rarely associated with men, Nicholas said, "I don't put much stock in gossip, but admit I've heard enough. I know your comment on scars was not lightly made, either. Just let me say that anyone who can't see you as, not only a woman, but a beautiful one no matter what you wear, is blinder than your illness has you at this moment."

Fiona sensed his seriousness, and not given as flattery to win favor. She decided it was best to inject humor to lighten the mood. Nicholas had often used it as a go-to response to tension.

"Mr. Tirrell, are you flirting with me?"

Nicholas gave a warm chuckle as he put the car in gear and drove away. "No offense, Miss Fiona, but not on my life."

"Your life would be in jeopardy, huh?"

"Yes, ma'am. You have powerful protectors. They'd rise to your defense if they believed me playing fickle with you. Honestly, upsetting Miss Margaret is not smart, not at all. But the whole Cavanaugh clan?" He chuckled. "I value breathing and hope to continue doing so for a long time."

Despite the pain in her head, Fiona guffawed. "We're not that bad."

"You're right," he said, his tone turned serious. "Not bad at all. Surprisingly remarkable." He sighed heavily, his next words barely a whisper. "Once knew a girl who could have used the protection of the women of your clan."

A bit less quiet, Fiona said, "If she's anything like you, Nicholas, she would be most welcomed." She could feel the headache abate a little, and with it, her vision returned.

Another whispered reply. "More like me than you could imagine."

Fiona frowned at the sadness that swirled through the remark. Her vision was returning, going from nothing to cloudiness like a thick fog. Fiona again decided to resort to humor. "Impossible, Mr. Tirrell, as you are one of a kind, all dashing and debonair."

After only a slight hesitation, Nicholas shook his head and laughed. "Too true, Miss Cavanaugh. Too true, indeed."

Chapter Eleven

BRIGID WAS GLAD to finish the last of the packing after a full day of work to box and clean Ethel's home. Nicholas took the last box to the truck he'd borrowed from Fiona. She would be glad not to have a reason to ever return to Ethel's house. She offered to make supper for them before Nicholas presented a picnic lunch prepared by Margaret. She was thankful to have one less worry today. Of course, now she had a bigger worry than closing the house up. Now she had to explain her charade toward Nicholas.

She was leading him on. Not that Brigid didn't like him. Goodness knew Nicholas was handsome. She appreciated his masculine physicality, without being too bulky or awkward, his thick black hair and Greek nose. The thin dark mustache neat above his nearly too-red full lips, the piercing intensity of his grey eyes.

But, despite all his gorgeous attributes, she didn't care for him in the same way she perceived he cared for her. Her fault, of course, since even when it was clear to everyone else that Ethel washed her hands of Nicholas, Brigid implied her interest for him. Looking back, Brigid realized how inappropriate and unfair she had been. Deep down, and all things reconsidered, Nicholas was a wonderful man who didn't deserve her deceit, even for Richard's benefit. The spark expected with her feelings whenever they were together never occurred.

Today, she played with his feelings to her advantage. She gave him every indication she thought of Nicholas in more than a friendly way. Even going so far as to suggest, due to possible exhaustion from closing the house, of course, they spend the night in Ethel's home. Brigid needed to tell him the truth. She hoped it didn't backfire — or she could lose a good friend. Or worse. She played a dangerous game with spurning a man's advances. Would Nicholas be the type to take the original offer even if she rescinded? Was Nicholas prone to violence?

Brigid picked up the last of the dishes from the table.

"That should do it," Nicholas announced. She heard the distinctive click as the front door closed. She returned to the sink with her dishes.

"I'm about finished in here," she said.

Nicholas walked behind her and stood nearly flush against her back. His whisper feather-soft against her ear, his mustache tickling. "Shall I start a fire? I wouldn't want you to get a chill." He wrapped his arms gently around her waist. "Have I told you—"

"Nicholas." His name came out harsher than intended. Brigid felt him stiffen in anticipation of her next words.

He gave a self-deprecatory chuckle. "Am I to assume your increased interest was solely to use me for labor and protection tonight?"

Brigid inhaled deeply. "Yes." She dropped her head until her chin hit her chest. "If it's any consolation, I do care about you." She felt the warmth of Nicholas's body leave her as he stepped back. Brigid felt a pang of regret.

"I thought my days of playing the fool were behind me." He barked a short laugh. "I guess an attractive woman can still trap an intelligent grown man. I should know better."

"I didn't start out trying to use you, not wholly." She raised her head, stared into the darkness outside the kitchen window. "I'd given up hope of finding someone for myself. Or of knowing what it was to feel love, someone's adoration and attention. There you were with your caring ways toward me, tender and gentle hand with Richard, your burgeoning friendship with Fiona. I thought maybe, with all that, it could be enough, and that feelings would grow between us with time. And it nearly is enough," she said, unable to stop the escaped sob of her shame. "I want to be intimate—"

A human-shaped shadow darted past the window, and Brigid screamed.

Nicholas wedged himself between her and the sink. "Brigid?"

Trembling, Brigid said, "Someone was in the window. I don't know who."

Nicholas rushed to his satchel by the front door, pulled out a gun, dashed outside, slamming the door closed behind him. Brigid turned off the overhead kitchen light and hoped the evening illumination was enough to see by and decrease her chances of being a target. She strained into the depths of darkness, watched what she assumed to be Nicholas's shadow in the yard. Concern for him turned to more internal guilt as she prayed he not be harmed before she could explain herself.

WHEN THE LIGHTS in the kitchen went out, Nicholas blinked rapidly to adjust his sight to the sudden darkness. There was just enough moonlight to make out his car in front of the barn. The barn doors appeared to still be locked with the padlock and chain he'd attached himself when, as the first project of the day, the barn emptied of the few tools and Richard's miscellaneous toys. From off to his left, the rustle of dried leaves indicated someone trespassed. His internal reasoning allowed it could be a wild animal, though he doubted the possibility. He didn't want whoever was there to come back. Raising the pistol at an angle slightly higher than an average-sized man's head, Nicholas fired two rounds into the wooded darkness.

He waited, ears straining for any sound before he accepted whoever frightened Brigid was no longer there. Nicholas doubted whomever, for whatever the initial intent, would return tonight. He stuffed the pistol in his pocket, gave one last look around, before reentering the house.

Still standing in front of the sink, Brigid turned toward him, her face damp with tears. "Whoever was outside, they're most likely gone now." He locked the door and slid the bolt in place. Nicholas picked up his satchel, removed the pistol, and tucked it inside. "You'll be safe to sleep tonight. I'll be in Richard's room."

Brigid rushed toward him, stopped him with a tug on his shirt sleeve. "Please, Nicholas, let me explain."

"I understand, honestly, I do. You needed a patsy, and I filled the bill."

"It's not like that," Brigid said. "I didn't intentionally set out to hurt you."

"But, you did intend to play on my attraction?" Admittedly, his attraction to her had a lot to do with a ready-made family. Easier to assume the mantle of respectability, normalcy.

Brigid nodded as fresh tears fell down her face. She swiped them away with the back of her hand, gave a watery chuckle. "It wasn't supposed to end this way. I would've given myself to you. We could both have satisfied our needs and walked away."

"And what changed you from your course?" Confused, Nicholas needed clarification. Her words suggested she still wanted him intimately. But is that all she asked of him? One night? Was this the I-care-for-you-as-a-friend-but speech? Brigid had to know he cared for her, and in time, could learn to love her. After his previous experiences, Nicholas didn't give his heart too lightly. He inhaled deeply. There it was. Although her tactics were inappropriate, her purpose mirrored his own. With all that had gone on recently with Ethel, and after her death, they both needed companionship.

What was wrong with him? He didn't have an answer for himself.

Was he doomed to be attracted to women who didn't truly want him?

Brigid must believe she lost ground. "I care too much to use you, Nicholas. I thought, with you, I could know one night of masculine attention, where I could feel safe. We would both get a little enjoyment out of it, or so I hoped." Brigid took a step back, her gaze aimed at the floor. "Was I so wrong?"

"No, no, you weren't wrong." Nicholas cupped her cheek with his palm. "I would wish more from you but understand what you are asking." He leaned forward and pressed his lips to hers, gently at first, until she returned the pressure. Nicholas would have laughed if the situation wasn't so emotionally stressful. And now, realization filled him. If they had kissed before now, they both would have realized the feelings for a future relationship just weren't there. They would never mean more to one another than convenience. But the sensations weren't unpleasant enough that he couldn't give her this night of pleasure without expectation. "We do this my way?"

"What...what do you have in mind?" A flash of fear crossed her face before replaced with the resignation of giving him something to get her own needs met.

"Nothing as sinister as you may just have envisioned. Only, pull the curtains to keep all light from the bedroom, at least as much as possible. Wait on the bed, completely naked." Her brow furrowed in question. "This way, you can imagine me as your true dream lover." He controlled a snicker picturing who she might imagine. "Even if it's our onerous sergeant." He didn't imagine her blush before she spun away and headed toward the master bedroom. "I'll make sure the house is completely locked up before I join you," he said to her departing back.

Nicholas slung his satchel over his shoulder. He made his way to all the windows and the back door, checking they were secured. He blew out any lit candles and switched off any lights still on. With no other tasks left to perform, Nicholas stood before the bedroom door, reached into his bag, and retrieved the object to allow him to complete his intended objective of bringing pleasure to them both.

With a deep, bolstering inhalation of breath, Nicholas opened the bedroom door.

THE ROOM WAS darker than Brigid expected. Had it been wishful thinking when she put clean sheets on the bed? Yes, she originally planned for the evening to end this way. Her body craved human touch. The last and only time was Fionn. There were other opportunities, but Brigid was old-fashioned. She couldn't sleep with a man solely for sex. Brigid required more depth of feeling; and, she did have some feeling for Nicholas. Right this moment, she desperately needed a lover's touch.

She did as Nicholas asked, closed the curtains before she removed her clothes and slid beneath the sheets. Nervous, it felt like hours had gone by, though she suspected it only been a few minutes before she heard the doorknob disengage from the lock. "Nicholas?"

There was a soft chuckle. "Maybe silence is the best course if you're that unsure of who I am in an otherwise empty house. Especially, I guess, if you plan for me to fill in for a fantasy lover." Brigid couldn't have spoken even if she knew what to say. "Stand up, Brigid, take a single step toward the door," Nicholas whispered from the doorway, a hint of a smile in his tone. His voice was so soft, nearly inaudible. "Then turn around."

Brigid did as commanded, even as anxiety of the unknown thrummed through her. Brigid suddenly felt she could trust him implicitly. Then, any residual light disappeared as Nicholas secured a blindfold—she suspected it to be one of his neckties—in place. He drew her hair aside and pressed a warm kiss to the back of her neck. Goosebumps skittered down her arms. She inhaled deeply, catching the scent of him.

His fingers trailed down to her wrists before he grasped her arms so suddenly that Brigid gasped. His soft laugh pure seduction.

"What are you doing?" she asked, aware her voice rose with a mixture of excitement and panic. She provided feeble protests when Nicholas pinned her wrists behind her back, restraining her with one hand. He slid his fingers between her legs and teased her folds, and then his exploration ceased. Brigid felt him lean into her, and his thumb traced her bottom lip. Another shift and fingers tweaked one nipple. Brigid sighed her pleasure. With the blindfold on, the familiar fragrances she associated with Nicholas seemed more intense. Brigid nibbled her bottom lip as shards of pure pleasure shot straight to her center.

Suddenly, he swung her hands to her front and loosely bound them with another necktie. She nearly barked a laugh, wondering how many he carried with him in the satchel. One for different occasions? she wondered. Focus. Focus. Nicholas lifted Brigid, and she realized he was still fully dressed. He placed her on the bed and secured her hands to the headboard, stretched high above her head.

The bed dipped, and Nicholas's body moved to stretch out at her side, his lightly calloused palm touched and caressed her. His mouth brushed her jaw, her cheek, and then he kissed Brigid slow and sweetly. If his lips hadn't moved to her ear, she might not have heard his next words. "Rely on your senses. In the darkness, I can be anyone you wish. No names, no guilt. Only pleasure."

Then the exquisite torment of his light touches began in earnest.

A path of fire followed his fingertips. The careful, slow way he grazed, nibbled, traced, and tickled her with his breath, lips, and tongue roused Brigid's desire in unparalleled ways. A low throb beat in her center, her blood rushed through her. Nicholas leaned over Brigid's body, his hot breath skittered along her skin.

Hot and wet, Nicholas's mouth closed on Brigid's nipple, and it took everything to hold back the moan rising from her throat. Brigid was barely conscious of the tickling sensation from his mustache. Moving more briskly, with a bit more pressure in his touch, Nicholas freely ran his hand across Brigid's body. Her other breast was treated to a wonderful exploration while Nicholas's mouth remained on the first. Brigid's breath came harder, faster.

After alternating between her nipples numerous times, Nicholas slowly kissed his way down her body. He sucked, licked, and nipped with teeth in his wake. Brigid's body trembled, over-sensitized when he reached the top of her thigh and bit the sensitive skin joining her leg to her hip. Brigid jerked, the action sending a shot of energy through her, drenched her in her body's response to her excitement.

Soon, the hot breath moved directly over her mound, and Brigid's body tensed with anticipation. If her breasts responded so astonishingly to being touched, then her nether folds would surely explode from the attention of his mouth and tongue.

An eternity seemed to pass while his slow hot breaths rained down on her. But Nicholas wasn't finished teasing her. Nicholas sucked her clit into his mouth, the tip of his tongue flicked once, twice, and then teeth gently nipped. Oh, dear lord, had she ever been so excited, so wet, so wanton? Heaven or Hell, Brigid was ready to be transported.

Nicholas stopped and pulled away. The bed shifted, and his body moved between her legs. His manhood nudged her open, and she instinctively spread her legs wider to accommodate him. Brigid jerked as much as her bound hands allowed when the tip of his manhood ran through her folds, then in one quick motion, he pushed himself fully inside. The stretch in her intimate folds nearly had her crying out in a mixture of surprise and pleasure.

Nicholas gently rocked in and out of Brigid. Brigid found herself on the edge of giddiness by the need to feel and not speak, and the torturous rub of his clothes against her hypersensitive bare skin elicited a strange dynamic. Nicholas sped up. Brigid wondered how he managed not to make a sound other than the increased tempo of his breathing.

Despite her best efforts, small, short moans escaped Brigid. She felt Nicholas tense, repeatedly thrusting inside Brigid, and near his orgasm, if the tense, trembling in his body was any indication. They maintained their relative silent act, quivered and jerked with the struggle to contain the pleasure in their bodies for the last possible moment. The waves of her climax rolled through her and sent Brigid into blissfully dark heaven behind her blindfold, where all that mattered was the length of Nicholas penetrating her depths, his smooth fingers as he rubbed her clit.

Her orgasm was powerful and long. Her body trembled with the aftermath. Nicholas slowed the speed of his thrusts, sliding to a quivering stop before he collapsed on top of her. They stayed in that position for a long moment, Brigid mostly because she remained bound. With time, Nicholas shifted to her side, untied her hands, and pulled the covers over her. Without a word, he rolled her onto her side, pulled her into his chest, and wrapped an arm around her waist. In less than a minute, Brigid fell asleep.

Chapter Twelve

FIONA WAS RELIEVED to let Nicholas do the driving. She hoped to enjoy, for a little while, the beautiful and warm May morning. Not unusual for early in the month. They both were quiet for the ride to Ethel's house. She had a lot on her mind and assumed Nicholas did too. Brigid had acted strangely, flirty toward him, then stopped doing so, to the point of blushing when his gaze fell on her. It wasn't Brigid's normal behavior, which worried Fiona. Was Brigid playing a game? She suspected Nicholas had feelings for Brigid, but even those appeared to have altered to a tamer level. Both were adults and able to work this out, but Fiona worried one or both could get hurt in the process.

She didn't fault Brigid, as Nicholas was a handsome man and Warren, a prominent figure in society. Fiona couldn't understand why she thought them mismatched, just felt they weren't right for each other. She wasn't a connoisseur of relationships. Heck, after almost five years, Fiona still didn't understand what Margaret saw in her, or why she professed that love on many occasions. She just hoped someday Nicholas would find the same affections, the same love she shared with Margaret, and which Jo appeared to feel for Tessa.

Fiona enjoyed Nicholas's company for more than his caring and politeness. He was quickly moving up the appreciation ladder to a spot previously only held by her Boston friend, Ian Donnelly.

"Here we are," Nicholas said. Fiona realized they had arrived at Ethel's. "Brigid saw someone over by the barn. I came outside and fired a shot or two," he said, pointing off to the left. "In that direction."

She nodded. "That's in the direction of the train tracks, isn't it?"

He raised an eyebrow. "Yes. It would also be a good point of ingress and egress."

"Should we check out the house just to make sure there are no squatters?" Fiona asked, glancing at the front door. "At least to make sure whoever you saw last evening didn't return?"

"That's probably not necessary," Nicholas said. "There shouldn't be a need for Brigid or Richard to return. We packed everything yesterday. The lawyer's problem now. No need to poke the bear if we can avoid one in the first place."

"The lawyer is already working on selling the place. Brigid's taken anything of importance. Richard has settled into the house with us. You're right. I see no need for any of us to go back inside, either."

Nicholas gallantly offered his arm. "Then shall we?" he asked, indicating the trail beside the barn with his other hand.

"Are you truly offering to escort me?" Fiona asked as she stared at the still offered arm. "My dressing as a man, entirely comfortable, tends to put most men off. Although I can't attest to it doing much for the ladies either. Unlike them, you insist on treating me with respect."

"That's because most people aren't me," Nicholas said, with a quick swipe of his finger across his mustache. "And they're basing most responses on what other people would do rather than enjoy the time spent with an intelligent, often amusing, and entirely beautiful woman."

Fiona playfully slapped his arm away and started toward the trail. "Often amusing? I have a great sense of humor, though entirely misunderstood." Once Nicholas closed the distance and walked beside her, Fiona gave a feigned skeptical sniff. "And I'm not beautiful. Margaret prefers to call me handsome, even if I don't agree with the assessment."

"Ah, well, from a woman's point of view, I suppose handsome would be suitable for you. But, as a significantly educated man, I plan to go with beautiful. Which, whether you believe it or not, is a precise assessment."

Fiona chuckled. "Significantly educated?"

Nicholas raised an eyebrow. "Do you doubt my pedigree?"

"Oh, saints preserve us, boy-o," she said in imitation of her dead mother's lilting brogue. "Perish the thought. I'd never disparage a fine man, such as yourself."

Nicholas just gave her a harrumph.

As they continued down the trail, nothing seemed out of the ordinary. If someone had come this way from the railroad tracks, they probably didn't stick to it. Fiona said as much to Nicholas. She asked, "Should we leave the trail?"

"Not quite yet," Nicholas said. "Let's get to the tracks, have a look around. If that is where the intruder originated, then we'll find our evidence beginning there."

It wasn't too long a walk before they were in sight of the tracks. Once there, it was evident someone, possibly many someones, had camped there and may have only recently abandoned the site. Nestled between a scraggly bush but thick with greenery, and a tall, thick tree, someone had hung a five-by-five frayed square of oilcloth. When they moved closer, they saw a rusted tin plate, a bent spoon, and a tin cup. There were also square discarded pieces of newspaper and butcher paper complete with grease stains. Footsteps were many and in random directions. Above the tarp and nailed to a tree, was a broken slab of wood fence with writing on it. On closer inspection, Fiona recognized it wasn't writing at all, but crudely drawn pictures.

Nicholas moved closer to her. "It's a hobo code."

"For?"

"Well, for the hobos to send messages to others. Not all hobos are thieves. Some are just folks without a lot of money or means for travel. You'll always get those people with bad intentions, too. These signs alert them about the mood of the area. For instance," Nicholas pointed to one drawing that appeared to be a large X with the top closed and eyes on either side. "This one indicates this place is a safe camp." He pointed to what appeared to be a blocked U. "This means can camp here."

"Some appear to have been scratched out," Fiona noted.

"That could indicate whatever message was left is no longer valid.

Fiona studied the sign, noticing only two other messages were still visible. "And the last two?"

Nicholas stepped closer as he studied the drawings. After only a few seconds, he shook his head and said, "This message could be disturbing."

"What you mean?"

"The blocked T states food for work, which could indicate an interaction at Ethel's at some point. The stick figure with a dress and the triangles indicates 'kind woman-tell her pitiful story.'" He focused his attention on her, and Fiona nearly shivered with the look of distress in his eyes. "Ethel's killer may be a more unsavory hobo, more specifically called a tramp."

"We should probably take this information to Sergeant Langford. Whether or not a hobo or the like is responsible for her murder, we can't ignore the possibility the killer isn't a local. And from the number of footprints, I would say the activity is recent. The weather would've destroyed these tracks before now."

"I agree. We can only hope the esteemed sergeant accepts well-intentioned assistance." Nicholas glanced at the tracks in the area surrounding the camp.

"Do you see something?" she asked him.

"No, but that doesn't mean someone isn't out there." Nicholas nudged her shoulder with his own. "Let's go. I'd rather not incur the wrath of Margaret or Brigid should anything happen to you. I have mentioned my fear of this possible occurrence rather recently, I do believe." Fiona shook her head.

They retraced their steps back to the house. They almost reached Nicholas's car, when a sharp pain lanced through her skull, dropping Fiona to her knees. Nicholas fell to a knee beside her and clamped a hand to an upper arm in an offer of support. Fiona feared not being able to find a resolution to this illness and have time to tell Margaret before the worst happened.

"You all right?" he asked, his voice low.

She hissed a breath through her teeth. "Fine."

Nicholas cleared his throat. "This is stronger than the last one. Let me help you into the car."

Fiona roughly pulled away from him. "I'm entirely capable of taking care of myself." She managed to get to her feet on trembling legs. Even her hand shook as she reached for the door handle.

Nicholas gently nudged her aside and opened the door. In a voice barely above a whisper beside her ear, he said, "Of your ability, I've no doubt. I offer the assistance of a friend to a friend, not as strangers. Why are you so averse to my assistance this time?"

Fiona slid into the seat. Nicholas closed the door before racing to the driver's side and sliding behind the wheel. The pain in her head had Fiona taking deep breaths through her nose while gritting her teeth. The frequency of the attacks was increasing.

The severity of the pain grew stronger for most of them. The accompanying waves of nausea were building, and Fiona thought she might be ill. She started to get out of the vehicle, not only reluctant to vomit in front of Nicholas but to soil his vehicle. "I just—"

Again, in softly spoken tones as if aware of her pain, Nicholas said, "Continue taking deep breaths. Your stomach will settle. If it doesn't, I'll deal with any mess later."

In the silence, which seemed to last forever, Fiona realized he was correct. As the pain decreased, so did her nausea. Only to be replaced with guilt. Once sure this episode nearly passed, and her sight moving to the greyish blur, Fiona said, "I am sorry, Nicholas, for my rudeness. I hate feeling out of control, and you're correct, this episode was more severe than the last. In my heart, I know your intentions are as a friend, and I truly appreciate them. However, in my head, I have difficulty trusting goodwill from a man without an abhorrent recompense expected."

"And that dear lady is where you have miss-stepped. I'm not just any man." Nicholas gave a toothy grin, waggled his eyebrows exaggeratedly. "I am the incredible and distinguished Nicholas Allen Tirrell. Haven't you made the distinction recently yourself?"

"That you are, and that I have," Fiona said, the tension lessened with his playfulness. Nicholas drove them toward her home.

"TIRRELL?" NICHOLAS LOWERED the newspaper, folded it in fourths, and tossed it on the table when he recognized the voice of Warren Langford. He looked up. "What can I do for you, Sergeant?" He picked up his coffee cup, took a sip, silently replaced the cup to the saucer.

Warren yanked a chair away from the table and plopped down. "Hear you've been to the station, claimed to have a suspect in the Walters murder?"

"More a direction you could focus on." Nicholas didn't offer he'd originally given credit to Warren for the same conclusion when seeing him with the vagabond near the last murder scene.

"Where did you get your case solving skills and information anyway?" Warren smirked. Nicholas knew the question rhetorical. Warren didn't seem concerned with finding a killer, but with the possibility of someone showing him up.

He could play along—for now. "Miss Cavanaugh and I went out to the Walters place and had a look around after I'd caught someone sneaking around Ethel's place. We found a placard with hobo code and believed the matter warranted further investigation." Nicholas feigned plucking lint from his jacket sleeve. "I believe looking into the possibility is your job."

Warren's face flushed a dark red. Nicholas was surprised he'd be so easily volatile. "Look you...you..."

Quirking an eyebrow, Nicholas supplied, "Photographer?"

"Pansy," Warren said, nostrils flared.

Nicholas hid his grin, not surprised Warren resorted to name-calling. Just because Nicholas enjoyed the proper coordination of his suits, didn't suggest him effeminate in any way. There happened to be a lot of work in putting together colors, patterns, the proper vest, the number of pleats to the trousers, and shirt combinations. These decisions were needed before the accessories selected. For today, Nicholas had settled on double-breasted blue pinstripe with a white pointed collar shirt with French cuffs and tie, finishing with black wingtip boots.

Warren was a Neanderthal and would never recognize the height of fashion. All sense of amusement drained from Nicholas when Warren added, "And, shit, you're hanging around in public with that perverted person."

"You're quite disrespectful, Warren, and have little room to talk." Nicholas put as much ice in his tone as he could muster. "If you have questions, I suggest you get on with it. I refuse to entertain your intolerant bigotry."

"You sure are sensitive, aren't you?" Warren seemed done with baiting when Nicholas picked up the folded newspaper. "Hold on." Rolling his eyes purposefully in an expression of distaste, Nicholas settled back into his chair. "Explain to me this theory created with you and—" Warren paused. Nicholas suspected the sergeant considered the feasibility of further derogatory name-calling. "Okay, the photographer and carpenter theory."

Nicholas ran a forefinger across his mustache. He suspected this information would lead nowhere, but it was his civic duty to share what they'd found. He owed it to Ethel, and to all the other women killed recently. "Less than a quarter-mile from Ethel's is the railroad tracks. We found evidence of a recently used campsite. There's a placard with hobo code on it." Nicholas wouldn't offer the translation as it might rouse too many questions. Questions he'd rather not answer if avoidable. "When Brigid and I were closing the property, someone was sneaking about outside. When I attempted to confront them, they ran." He raised his hands in a supplicated gesture. "Could be something to look into, could be nothing. I know at least one of the first victims lived close to the tracks, too. Maybe this is the common denominator."

Warren stared at him for a long moment. What he said next had Nicholas gritting his teeth. "How do I know you didn't murder her, and this is your fancy way of misdirecting me?"

"Are you suggesting I'm a suspect, Sergeant?" He should've known Warren would resort to invective again. "What motive would I have to kill her?"

Warren gave a snarky grin. "Maybe she insulted your carpenter friend? Maybe for you to move on without the possibility of female dramatics? Maybe Ethel was tired of you, and you weren't ready to move on?" Warren shrugged casually as if proud of his deducing.

"I see," said Nicholas, standing up and retrieving his satchel from under the table. "So, that would make you a suspect too. Wonder to whom I should communicate this particular tidbit of information?"

A startled expression quickly replaced with a cold guarded one, when Warren barked a laugh. "Who gave you that ridiculous idea?"

"A few someones, to be honest." Nicholas would never reveal a source, not unlike a reporter, he wouldn't expose Richard, especially to this man. He didn't doubt Richard's honesty, either. "And I've no intention of revealing any more information."

Warren rose and took a menacing step closer to him. Nicholas stood his ground. "You should be careful who you cross, Nicky, my boy. Life could get difficult for you. Any skeletons to uncover if I did some digging?"

"Is that another threat, Sergeant?" Nicholas wouldn't rise to the bait, although the image of Blanche Bowman immediately presented in his mind.

"Take it has helpful advice."

As Warren glared and threatened, Nicholas noted the advance of Governor Alva B Adams. They met the year before at a fundraiser in Denver. This unexpected entrance could work in his favor. Nicholas ignored Warren, extended his hand toward the governor. "Governor Adams, so good to see you."

Alva gave a warm smile. "Why Mr. Tirrell, how good to see you again. Here for photos?"

"Well, actually, Governor, I'm taking a bit of a hiatus to spend time with friends. But I wouldn't ignore an opportunity for work if one presented itself."

"Good to hear. You've quite the eye for imagery." Alva turned slightly to acknowledge Warren. "This man, one of the friends you spoke of?"

"No, business with him. This is Sergeant Warren Langford. A close friend of mine was murdered. Warren is providing an update on the status of the investigation."

Alvin nodded solemnly. "Then my condolences on your loss, Nicholas. I'm certain Langford will do all he can to bring you peace."

"I'm sure he will, Governor."

"Well, it's been nice seeing you again but, if you'll excuse me, I have a meeting to attend. Good day gentlemen."

Once Alva was out of earshot, Warren said, "Don't think Adams can protect you from me. You need to be careful who you make your enemy."

"You should show caution too. Threats or any harm come to me, and especially after whispering my link to Ethel in the right ear, will raise some powerful eyebrows. Be prepared yourself."

Warren balled his hands but kept them by his sides. Nicholas suspected he wanted to slam those fists into Nicholas's face. Instead, Warren spun on his heel and stomped from the room.

Nicholas followed him in his departure, at a more moderate pace, and wondered if Ethel's death truly was linked to the deaths of the other women. He hadn't believed they were related but hadn't enough evidence to prove that one way or the other. He suspected Warren of killing Ethel when she got too clingy. Warren would have given her the social respect Ethel craved. More importantly, Warren was a bigger hothead than even Nicholas. Who knew what threat or action created the final push to murder? Now Nicholas would be troubled with the notion he had provided Warren a means of covering his tracks.

Chapter Thirteen

FIONA COULDN'T BELIEVE she and Nicholas thought this was a smart idea. It was just shy of three full days since Nicholas took their suspicions to the police station. She suspected this would turn out to be a waste of time, but couldn't, in all good conscience, not do something to stop a murderer. "We might not even have the right person."

"Then again, we might be right," Nicholas replied from beside her. Fiona stared at him in surprise. "Didn't think you spoke aloud, did you?"

"No, I guess I didn't." After seeing Warren talking to a possible suspect, she and Nicholas decided—harebrained as the idea was—to do some investigating on their own. Yes, it was possible for Warren to actually be conducting an investigation and questioning an alleged suspect. And, she had to admit after Nicholas explained his conversation with Warren, the perfect means to supply a scapegoat in Ethel's death. He was a police sergeant. However, the interaction between the two men nagged at her. As it had for Nicholas, which is why they sat in his car watching for things out of place. What had they learned? Everybody, innocent or not, did suspicious things. Fiona wondered if her own simple daily chores and responses to her surroundings could be considered suspect to curious eyes. How hard would it be for an innocent task to be construed as criminal activity? Possibly too easy.

Earlier in the morning, while the weather was still cool, she and Nicholas started their search by retracing the areas where the murders were committed, focusing on egress of the train's tracks.

Fiona couldn't believe how many people were about this time of day. Their drive found people going off and on shift for the Colorado Fuel & Iron Steel Mill, Pueblo's main manufacturing business, and some to other various jobs throughout the city. Kids playing in the streets before taking themselves to school. Women hung clothes, swept walks, and performed other daily chores in the home. Trucks made deliveries of various items from milk to diapers.

Also, among the activity, the less expected populace. Fiona hadn't anticipated children among the throngs hurriedly raiding various available cans for food or other necessities from behind bakeries and restaurants and shops. Children with haunted and determined expressions as so many from her own childhood, with a hint of resignation in their expressions. The amount of activity this early showed Pueblo wasn't too different from any other city of hard-working blue-collar workers. A person was expected to rise, work hard for a long day, go home to the family, and early to bed so the process could start over again the next day. The sight was both familiar and sad.

Then Fiona saw him. The same hobo who spoke with Warren days earlier. He currently walked down the street with two other men. Each wore tattered and dirty clothes of trousers, shirts, and worn footwear. The two new faces, to Fiona's recollection, showed signs of trying to clean up their appearance with washed faces and slicked-back hair. Fiona hoped the men found *Brilliantine* to use, and not some other fouler type of oil.

She and Nicholas were currently driving in the residential area close to where the last victim lived. "There," she said, pointing. Nicholas pulled to the curb. From the safety of their vehicle, she and Nicholas witnessed a disagreement with their hobo and the other two men, with arms waving, scowls, and gritted teeth.

"What do you think is going on?" Nicholas asked.

The argument seemed to be two against one, their man the odd one out. "Take it our guy is tipping their applecart." All three men began walking again, but barely a few feet ahead, at the corner, the two men veered right, heads shaking. The third man, their chosen suspect, continued straight ahead. As the morning progressed, activity increased. Maybe their own actions wouldn't be obvious amidst the growing influx of people. "What are the chances of following on foot and not being seen?" she asked.

Nicholas patted the satchel on the seat between them. "We could try the picture taking excuse again."

Fiona smirked. "Or catch Warren in the act of being an asshole."

"I don't think a picture of that would surprise, let alone interest, anyone," Nicholas said. They shared a quick laugh. "Let's go. We don't want him to get so far ahead that we lose him."

"What about the other two?" she asked. Fiona doubted the murders were perpetrated by more than one man, and gossip didn't support the evidence either.

"Expect that they're up to no good," Nicholas said. "Don't think it is of the nature we are looking for." Agreed, they exited the car and followed as discreetly as possible.

The tramp did a lot of walking and stopping, staying in the shadows when he did pause. Fiona noticed he stared into windows where curtains had been pulled open and provided a view of the inside. He'd watch for a little while, possibly studying, before he moved on. The adrenaline of anticipation made Fiona jittery. She didn't want this man to hurt another woman but wished he would do something to either prove or disprove their theory; he was the murderer. She was certain of it.

Fiona startled when Nicholas put a hand on her arm.

He pressed a finger to his lips in a shushing gesture and tugged her toward a large tree in the yard beside them. Nicholas pulled out his camera. As he fiddled with the device to prepare it as well as explain their presence should someone see them stalking about, Fiona chastised herself for not having paid more attention. Rather than be unprepared for whatever would happen next, Fiona owned up to her abstraction. In a whisper, she asked, "What did I miss?"

"He's been focused on the houses across the street too long. He may not be up to what we think he is, but he's definitely up to no good."

Fiona focused across the street. She noted two homes, in particular, stood out. It wasn't the homes themselves, but the activity presented. One home, closest to them, displayed an attractive young woman of about twenty, pacing back and forth in front of a parlor window, holding an infant in her arms as she fed the child a bottle. Her actions were keenly displayed by the lighting inside. She appeared to be alone, as no other movement occurred the entire time Fiona watched.

The second, three homes down, also well lit, showed another woman. This woman a couple years older and only slightly less comely as the first. As Fiona watched, a man in a business suit opened the front door, planted a quick kiss to her cheek, plopped a hat on his head, and walked to a car parked in front of the home. Once the man drove off, Fiona caught movement about twenty-five feet to the side.

Whatever this tramp planned, he seemed ready to put it into action. What were the chances, Fiona thought with a little trepidation, this tramp was the killer? Looked more positive now. And that they just happened upon him the day he planned to kill again? Obviously, he was up to something other than a stroll. If they could stop him or alert the police of a possible crime, they'd have done their civic duty. No matter.

The tramp shifted, gave a quick glance around, and crossed the street. His focus apparently not truly on his surroundings — probably on his intended task — he didn't seem to notice her standing beside the tree. With determined steps, the tramp walked down the street, slower than he had before his concentration on these two homes. Targets?

She heard the distinctive click of the camera's shutter, then Nicholas was next to her. "Shall we?" Fiona said. Nicholas followed.

At the end of the street, the tramp turned left, then left again into the alley behind the homes. Fiona hesitated. On the main sidewalk, their presence was less noticeable. They would be conspicuous in the alley. "Suggestions?" she asked.

"He can't miss seeing us if we follow him, but our proximity may prevent a dire outcome." He shoved the camera into his satchel.

"Better preemptive then —" They heard a startled cry. The decision was made for Fiona and Nicholas, apparently, and both of them bolted down the alley. Most of the yards didn't have fencing, so it was easy to see the ones without activity. Fiona expected the home with the recently absent husband would've been the intended target, surprised it turned out to be the home of the woman and infant.

As Nicholas pushed through the yard's gate, Fiona vaulted over the five-foot fence, using a discarded milk crate as the jump point. A basket of laundry had been tipped over, once-clean clothes ready for the line now scattered across the ground. Beside it, another basket sat. An infant rested inside, swaddled in blankets, and asleep. The tramp wrestled a young woman through the back door. He had one arm around her waist, a hand clamped over her mouth. He used his heel to push the inside door closed.

Nicholas had the screen door flung open with his right hand while his left hand reached for the tramp's collar, followed by the sound of rending material. Fiona had an instant to realize Nicholas only held a handful of dirty material and not the culprit. She dove through the opening and wrapped her arms around the tramp's legs bringing their three bodies crashing to the floor. Nicholas reached down and pulled the tramp from the pile.

From the corner of her eye, Fiona caught the tramp's booted foot shooting toward the woman before he'd made it to his feet. She covered the woman with her own body, taking the brunt of the blow. With a better hold of him this time, Nicholas tossed the tramp out the door.

Fiona remembered the baby in the basket. She raced outside, tackled the man again, and was rewarded with a kick to her stomach. The tramp stumbled, regained balance, and slammed through the gate and down the alley. At least I don't have to smell his vile stench anymore, Fiona thought, wrinkling her nose.

"Saved the day, lost the culprit," Nicholas said with an extended hand. Fiona let him lift her to her feet. The young woman rushed out of the house and dropped to her knees by the baby's basket. "Your little one is a sound sleeper, ma'am."

"Nora. Nora Spiegel," she said. Nora picked up the baby and clasped him to her chest. She turned tear-filled eyes toward Fiona and Nicholas. "How can I thank you? You saved me from—" Her voice cut off on a sob.

Fiona put one hand on Nora's shoulder, the other clutched at her tender stomach, trying to rub the discomfort away. "You and the baby are gonna be all right. You should take your baby inside. Call the police and report this. If you can specify, ask for Officer Braddock. He'll do right by you, I promise."

"Maybe you should call your husband," Nicholas suggested. "Or someone. Having a loved one's support will help calm you." He smiled. "Can always use the loved ones close by to feel safe. Especially at trying times."

As soon as the woman was securely established inside the home, the police called, and the car arrived outside, Fiona and Nicholas left. They took their time to walk back to the car, her more gingerly.

"You think we should have stayed?" Nicholas asked.

Fiona snorted. "Yeah, and have Warren show up? He's going to hear about this and our part soon enough."

When they got to the car, Nicholas opened the passenger door, then closed it when she was inside. Once he drove away, he said, "There's a place in Colorado Springs that will let me develop my film any time, day or night. I'll drive up after I drop you off. I snapped a picture of him before the incident, which should assist with the investigation. How about early in the morning, we take the picture to Jo's friend, the kid cop?"

"Randall," Fiona said.

"I know." He smirked. "Making sure you're still with me." Fiona shook her head. "How are you feeling by the way? A couple good kicks you took back there. Better you than me."

"How gallant of you to say so."

Nicholas gave a short nod. "Glad you understand. Bad

enough that I touched the wretched, filthy creature and will need another bath. Can't imagine if I'd become disheveled in the nasty process."

Fiona broke out into a full belly laugh, which quickly reminded her of a tender and abused stomach. "Ow, ow," she moaned exaggeratedly. "I'm in pain, and you're worried about being disheveled."

"Certainly. Knew you would understand," Nicholas said, then flashed her an exaggerated wink.

FIONA MADE HERSELF a cup of tea and sat at the kitchen table. She hadn't turned on any lights, preferring to sit in the relative dark, lit only by moonlight streaming through the open curtains. Her head hurt again. Nothing new or unexpected, even if she didn't know the cause. On top of the migraine, Fiona's stomach remained tender from the tramp's kicks.

One thing was clear. She never had to look for trouble. Trouble followed her like a second shadow. Fiona scoffed. Well, she did kind of put herself in a dangerous situation today. On the positive side, had she and Nicholas not followed the tramp, the young mother may have been, more than likely, another victim of a murderer. Fiona didn't want to think about what the poor woman would have suffered at the hands of that brute. Even if he weren't the killer, his intentions were less than honorable. She hoped, when they took his picture to the police, the man would quickly be apprehended. One problem on her long personal list would be solved.

Now? Fiona needed to figure a way out of her current dilemma. Clearly, the matter of her migraines and periodic blindness were not issues that were going to evaporate on their own. She didn't know what to do. Fiona had a family to care for, to protect, to support. The idea of being incapacitated, even for a little while, was inconceivable. She knew it wasn't a certainty, just a probability. It was enough to put her in a panic. Enough to consume her feelings of helplessness and dread.

Fiona finished her tea and brought the cup to the sink. Dammit. How much longer could she postpone the matter before she had no choice but to tell Margaret? She hated not having a plan. Not having specifics in tidy order before she could approach Margaret with the matter — which would affect them all.

She needed more time. More time to think about the subject and find a resolution. Margaret was her heart, her soul. Fiona couldn't crush either for her wife. Margaret had to be protected and cared for, and Fiona's job to accomplish that task. If she believed prayer could work, Fiona would be on her knees. However, that avenue never worked for her in the past. Never brought her mother and brother back. Never kept her father from beating her near to death on so many occasions. Never protected her from Jimmy Bennett. No, Fiona had no expectations prayer would work now, either.

The silence of the house and the privacy of her thoughts were broken by the soft snick of the back door lock being turned. Fiona twisted toward the sound, reached behind her, and into the drawer, pricked her finger before pulling a knife free, as a dark figure slipped into the room. The stench of unwashed body and dried sweat and food filled the kitchen. Fiona clenched the knife handle tighter, holding it beside her leg and out of sight. Geez, did he smell this strong earlier?

"I believe you're in the wrong house," she said quietly. Fiona didn't want to alert or frighten the women sleeping upstairs. "Leave now, before the situation gets uglier than you are."

He snorted, raised his arm, and wiped his nose with the back of his hand. The move, though disgusting, was deliberately made to make Fiona aware of the gun in his hand. "Funny, bitch. Have a good laugh before I kill you for spoiling my fun today." He grinned. In the faint illumination of moonlight, Fiona could tell he had few teeth. Those remaining were stained and rotted. He cocked his head to the side. "Then I'll enjoy time with the ladies of the house since you got in my way once." Smirking, he asked, "Should I kill you outright, or let you watch?"

Fiona clenched her teeth. Why did men have to be so loathsome? Why did everything boil down to the degradation and abuse of women? With extremely few exceptions, Fiona could see the world rid of men and not feel deprived or bothered by the loss. She took a step toward him. Fiona only had to be quick enough to bury the knife blade before he got a shot off. "Get out." Fiona propelled herself forward, knife raised in her fist, as he pointed the gun in her direction.

A shot rang out, deafening her, as a blaze of burning pain flared in her left arm.

A spray of warm, sticky blood landed across her face when she buried the knife blade in the upper left shoulder of the tramp.

A bright and blinding flash as the overhead light consumed the darkness.

Two voices rang out.

"Fiona!"

Two bodies slammed to the floor with muffled grunts.

Two sets of feet rushed into the room.

Fiona slowly managed to get to a knee before a fist slammed into her jaw as she was pushed onto her back.

"No, Jo, let him go," Margaret yelled out, kneeling beside Fiona as Fiona tried to get to a seated position. She glanced up in time to witness Jo halt on the threshold of the back door, clearly anguished. The tramp got away. "Fiona, honey, are you okay?"

Jo turned toward them as Brigid rushed into the kitchen. "I could have caught him, Margaret." Jo crossed her arms over her chest after she slammed the door closed and reengaged the lock. "Fat good that's gonna do." Jo dragged a chair over and shoved it under the doorknob.

"Oh, of course, because he didn't succeed in killing Fiona, so let's give him a second chance with you." Margaret's voice rose with every word. "And you, always the knight looking for a dragon to slay. Do you even care how your actions affect the rest of us?" Margaret's words hurt, but Fiona understood she was scared.

Fiona glanced at her and saw the panicked expression on Margaret's face as tears streamed down her cheeks. She reached up and wiped at them, as Brigid brought a dampened towel and pressed it to Fiona's arm. She'd managed to forget about the injury until that moment and responded with a hissing intake of breath.

Margaret glared at her. "Is there something we should know about our late-night visitor?"

"Did you and Nicholas learn something?" Jo asked, more eager than accusing. Fiona nodded. "You must be on to something if tonight's any indication."

"We need to get to you to a hospital," Margaret said. Her hands were shaking as they reached for her. "A doctor needs to tend to..." Margaret swallowed hard, new tears flowed. "I can't believe you've been shot again."

Fiona pulled Margaret into a tight hug. Margaret's sobs increased, and Fiona felt the tears dampen the material at her shoulder. "Hush, honey. We're okay. I'm okay." Fiona placed a kiss to Margaret's temple. "We don't need the hospital. There will be too many questions, too many people to get involved."

"You mean with Warren, don't you?" Jo asked from beside them.

"What does Warren have to do with this?" Brigid asked, a tad too defensively. Fiona wasn't certain how best to reply. She didn't need to worry.

Jo shrugged. "There's oodles of paperwork, a lot of wasted time answering questions with obvious answers. And truly, the only cop I trust entirely is Ian." She wrinkled her nose. "Well, Randall, too, but I don't want him to get so deep in our affairs he gets into trouble."

Margaret appeared to have regained her composure. She pushed Fiona back an arm's length. "Brigid, would you get some antiseptic and bandages, please? Sit down, Fiona, and take your shirt off."

Fiona gave a mischievous grin. "Should we do this in front of the kid?" She sat back down in the chair, felt a bit woozy, hoped it was due to stress, and not because the wound was worse than she wanted it to be.

Jo shoved her hands on her hips. "Hey, I'm not a kid anymore." Brigid returned with the items Margaret requested, placed them on the corner of the table, and then filled a bowl with hot tap water. Once that was brought to the table, Margaret began cleaning blood from the wound.

"So, fill us in. What's going on?" Jo said, impatiently.

"Nicholas and I followed a hunch. In the process, tonight's visitor attacked Mrs. Nora Spiegel." Fiona explained the events of the morning. "Nicholas got a picture of him and went to a friend in Colorado Springs to get the film developed. We planned to take the picture to the police station in the morning, so they know who they're looking for."

"Do you think he knew you took the picture?" Brigid asked.

Fiona shook her head. "No, I think he was ticked off I spoiled his intended assault and murder. If nothing else, we could describe him." She winced when Margaret hit a particularly sensitive spot. Fiona glanced at Margaret, who focused on tending to her injury. In a soft whisper, she asked, "What's the verdict, my love?"

Margaret gave a wry smile. "It's a flesh wound mostly. Should have stitches, but I'll do what I can. Going to be sore for a while."

"Why don't you two go back to bed," Fiona said. "Margaret and I will clean this up." Jo, after a sympathetic glance toward Fiona, and Brigid left the room. Margaret finished by tying off the bandage and took the blood-tinged bowl of water to the sink. Fiona moved to stand behind Margaret, wrapped her arms around Margaret's waist, and kissed just below her ear. "I'm sorry, love. I didn't anticipate that he'd come here. I love you and wouldn't consciously put you in harm's way."

"I know this isn't your fault, Fiona. Not really. It's just—" Margaret's shoulders began to shake. Fiona realized she'd begun to cry again. "I understand you're upset we followed this person, investigated on our own, but I could never forgive myself if I thought I'd been able to stop this tramp from harming that defenseless woman."

"You don't know he's the murderer," Margaret said, her voice shaking and watery from her crying.

"No, and neither Nicholas nor I intend to do more. We have a piece of evidence to supply the police. They will have it first thing in the morning. But I've done what I thought I could, what I thought right, to give Richard the peace of mind his mother's killer has been caught."

Margaret spun in Fiona's arms and squeezed hard. "I couldn't handle it if something happened to you again. I nearly lost you once, Fiona. Please be careful."

Fiona inhaled deeply, Margaret's flowery scent filling her nostrils, soothing her taut nerves. She cupped the back of Margaret's head, threading her fingers in the thick fullness of her dark auburn hair. "I'm here to stay, honey. I'm done with the investigating and will leave it to the proper authorities after tomorrow. Everything will be fine, I promise." Fiona winced inwardly. She couldn't keep that promise, not until she addressed her migraines, the blindness. But what else could she do? Margaret needed to feel safe, needed to be safe. Fiona would say and do whatever it took to make sure that happened.

Chapter Fourteen

JO STOOD AT the top of the ladder, working in the backroom of Tessa's shop. She replayed events of last night's intruder to their home when she heard Tessa come down the apartment stairs. She finished tightening the last screw holding the top of the cabinet in place. Jo wanted the space to be comfortable. The room in back would be the area where Tessa did most of her work and spent most of her daytime when not out front with customers. She'd hung a rod and attached a curtain to separate the front from the back, so Tessa had privacy but could hear the entrance of customers.

"Just about done," she said, leaning back and putting the screwdriver in one of the pockets of her coverall. She must have overcompensated her position because she lost balance and stumbled down the bottom three steps of the ladder. Before she could right herself, Jo felt sturdy arms wrap around her. Jo turned slowly in those arms.

"Are you all right?" Tessa asked, her voice barely above a whisper.

"More than all right," Jo said. She reached her arms around Tessa and pulled her closer into the embrace. Jo smiled. "This is nice. I should slip from ladders more often." Tessa smiled openly at her. Jo couldn't help herself. She stared at Tessa for longer than intended before she lowered her head and brushed her lips across Tessa's. Tessa's eyes sparkled as she drew closer, shifted when Jo's lips touched hers. Jo tugged her closer, and Tessa slowly relaxed in her arms. She lost track of time. Finally, Jo leaned back. "Gosh, that was—" The rush of exquisite pleasure coursed through her. She couldn't get enough of Tessa. The quiet woman was smart, funny, caring, and above all, the first thing Jo thought of in the morning and the last thought at night. Now, kissing her, Jo recognized a deeper need for her.

When Tessa spoke, her breath brushed across Jo's lips. "I give you permission to kiss me anytime, without the ladder's involvement."

Jo's heart beat increased. "You do, do you?" Jo caressed the smooth skin of Tessa's face along her jaw, then trailed a finger down to her neck, her shoulder, down her arm, resting the hand on a hip. She pulled Tessa tighter until they were flush against one another. Tessa's arms went up to Jo's neck, where they rested clasped behind Jo's head. "Then let me see where the permission might end. It's almost time to close for the day."

Jo opened a couple of the front buttons on Tessa's dress, sliding her hand inside and smiled when Tessa inhaled a sharp breath. Jo kissed Tessa long and deep, the returned kiss just as demanding. Jo wanted to do this all day whenever Tessa was in the same room with her. It seems she needn't have worried. When she tried to pull back, Tessa grasped and pulled harder, refusing to release Jo completely.

And this, Jo thought, was the divine moment when you realized the woman in your arms had burrowed into your heart. The singular one intended for you. Words escaped her.

Probably just as well neither had spoken. The curtain shifted, and Randall peered in after he cleared his throat. "Sorry for the interruption, ladies," he said, averting his gaze from their direction.

Jo shifted them, Tessa's back to Randall, as she closed the buttons she'd opened. "Something I can do for you, Braddock?" Clothing returned to normal, Tessa stepped away so quickly, shame reflected in her expression, Jo felt a pang of hurt. It wasn't like they were outside in a public place.

Attention directed at Jo, he said, "Well, this explains a few things for me. Someone may need to explain the situation to the sergeant."

"Oh my God," Tessa said. "Is he—" She tried to see behind him.

Randall shook his head. "Stormed out here so fast I thought I'd make sure everything was okay." His face flushed. "Seems all is better than well here. I'll leave you to it." With a precise about-face, Randall left the shop.

After Randall left, Jo returned her attention to Tessa, who, even with the distance Tessa put between them, Jo could tell was trembling. "Are you okay?"

Tessa gave a nervous laugh. "Says something for your kisses, doesn't it? I never heard the door or footsteps either time. I should have locked the door first." Jo moved toward Tessa, but Tessa hastily stepped back. Jo felt a keen ache. She couldn't have been more taken aback if Tessa had physically struck her. Jo picked up the jacket she'd tossed over a chair on her arrival, shuffled to the front door, her hand on the doorknob before Tessa spoke. "Jo, stop." Jo did. "My reaction is from confusion. Please come back here."

"Are you embarrassed by me? Or because Warren and Randall caught us kissing?" She tried but didn't believe she'd kept the distress from her tone.

"Oh, Jo," Tessa said. She hurried across the shop and stopped beside Jo, placing a hand on Jo's on the doorknob. "Startled to be caught kissing surely. That's because Warren will surely bring it up, and quite vocally, too. He knows how I am and who attracts me. He knows you are more than a friend to me. Knows but refuses to acknowledge this isn't a matter of me going through a phase to upset him or my parents."

Tessa moved closer, and Jo felt heat suffuse her upper arm where Tessa's breast pressed against it. "Embarrassed by you? Hardly. You're why I get up in the morning. You're why I look forward to the future of each new day. You're always in my thoughts. But, embarrassed? Never. If I didn't think we'd be stoned, or worse, I'd hold and kiss you in the middle of town. I'm so proud to have you. Proud that you're my girlfriend."

"Then why pull away from me? You understand the depth of my feelings for you, don't you?" Jo asked. Did Tessa not comprehend the full extent of Jo's affection for her? Would Warren's disapproval keep Tessa from moving further with a relationship? She should leave now, let Tessa come to terms with whatever caused her hesitation. "What should I do now? I want to keep you safe, not create more trouble for you." Jo didn't trust Warren not to respond with violence toward his sister.

"You mean we. You're not alone in this, honey." Tessa clasped a hand in Jo's. "First, you come to dinner tomorrow night, with Warren and me. Let him see for himself how wonderful you are, how important you are to me." Tessa locked the front door, turned the window sign to the "closed" side, and tugged their joined hands. "I'd like to go to my apartment and spend more time kissing."

Jo smiled as they walked through the shop to the stairs. "Do you think we need to practice?"

Tessa snickered. "Heck no. I was thinking more along the lines of refining the methods. Find a way to last all day without needing to take breaths in between."

"That's quite the undertaking."

"Think you're up for it?" Tessa asked, raising an eyebrow.

"I may have been labeled as being an overachiever from time to time. One thing you should also know about me is that I do love a challenge."

"And I do love kissing you. Wouldn't want to be the cause of you failing a challenge."

Jo laughed. They'd reached Tessa's apartment. Jo shifted, which allowed her and Tessa to gaze at one another. "When you look at me, Tessa, I get all warm inside. One thing I know for certain, I can and want to do everything for you, with you."

"I've never been this important to someone before," Tessa said, tears building in her eyes.

When a lone tear fell, Jo carefully wiped it away with the pad of her thumb. She gently tugged Tessa to the couch. "Careful, sweetheart. Tears could drown us before we've accomplished our pursuit of the day-long kiss."

Tessa pulled Jo into a tight hug, and her tears flowed freely. Jo suspected their kissing-fest had turned into simple bonding time. What the heck, hugging was wonderful too.

JO HEARD HER name called from the front of the barn's workshop. She stopped planing the cabinet door and looked up to see Randall standing outside. She waved him in, but he didn't budge. Jo knew he was upset with finding her and Tessa in an embrace, but she wouldn't deny her affection for Tessa. She'd told Randall many times they'd never be more than friends. If his feelings were hurt, too bad, as he should have heeded her warning. Jo didn't have time to coddle bruised feelings from some unfounded expectations he may have about them.

She just hoped he didn't tell the wrong people. People who could make life more difficult for them. People who could harm them as Fiona was hurt. "No time for games. Randall, I've things to finish."

He must have sensed where her thoughts had taken her. "No, Jo. It's about Ethel Walters, her murder."

She squeezed her eyes shut and exhaled. Was this how it would be? Were her and her family automatic suspects because they didn't conform to normal expectations, so they must be criminals? Well, so be it, she certainly wasn't going to make it easier for him. Jo put down the plane, dusted her hands on her coverall pant legs, and walked toward Randall.

Randall glanced at her with hurt in his eyes. "It's still not what you think, Jo."

"Then tell me what it is." Jo had no intention of making this easy for him. If he had even a remote belief that he could use their friendship to bully her into his affections, he was in for a surprise. "Because I have things to do, Patrolman Braddock."

"Can we take a little walk?" asked Randall. There was another flash of hurt, which he quickly masked. They walked to the back of the barn and paused. The grass was higher here. Jo made a mental note to add yard work to her list of things to do around the house. She'd neglected a lot of things in place of time spent in town with Tessa. She leaned against the building and shoved her hands into her pockets.

"Let's get the obvious issue out of the way." Randall mimicked her posture and leaned against the structure beside her, but not close enough to touch her. "I saw it, Jo, before your walls went up. And I've been thinking."

She suspected what he meant but didn't acknowledge it. "Saw what?"

He shook his head and grinned. "Okay, right to it faster." Randall looked out across their property. "Your heart beaming across your face as you held Tessa. The look I've hoped you'd someday have for me."

"Randall—"

"Wait, Jo, let me get this out. Your affection was never meant to be mine. Yeah, I thought I could overlook the fact you didn't share my love the same way. Considered sharing you, even. If you were my wife, I'd keep you safe from the verbal and physical reactions of people, and you could—very discreetly— have your liaisons. But the more I obsessed about it, the more I realize I wouldn't want you to provide me the same attention. Sounds silly, but I believed, over time, you'd realized you're meant for me. Realize your attraction to women was a phase. Now I see I'm a fool." Jo glanced at him from the corner of her eye. His expression reflected open honesty. "No way your emotions when you held Tessa would ever be mine. I don't think it makes you a bad person, Jo, but I can't say I understand how this happens."

"Are you dissolving our friendship?" She pushed away from the barn. "You will if you harm Tessa in any way."

Randall's expression was, at first, confused. "What?" Then he seemed to understand. "No, Jo. You've been my friend for four years, looking after me, the weird kid, the kid you befriended when others teased me mercilessly. Even throughout all the torturous attacks. I never wanna lose our bond. Heck, you gave me the guts to be a cop." Randall pulled his hands from his pockets, crossed his arms over his chest. "I get it. And, as your friend, I'll look out for you, both of you."

"I'm confused, Randall. Why couldn't you say this in the barn?"

He stared at her so hard, as if to gauge, anticipate her reaction. "I don't want anyone to see me warn you and your family. You need to be more cautious." Randall inhaled and exhaled deeply. When he spoke again, he lowered his voice. "I was at the station when your sister's friend came in, trying to explain his hobo theory."

Theory. So, Randall didn't believe them either. She shouldn't be surprised. "You don't believe them?"

"Actually, we do. A couple of us new guys checked out the areas of the murders."

"Did you find anything?"

Randall nodded. "We went over the reports, too. The first murders all appear to be committed by the same person." He paused. "Jo, the hobo signs are near every attack, and Mr. Tirrell saw someone at Mrs. Walters's place, but we don't think the killer is the same one for the Walters murder."

"You think there is more than one killer?" Jo knew Fiona believed the same.

Closing the gap between them, Randall leaned close. "We rookies," he gave a self-deprecating chuckle, "think Ethel was killed by someone she knew well. She had marks around her neck indicative of strangulation. Beneath the rope marks from her hanging. No other defensive wounds. You'd think there would be if a stranger came after you. Also, the other victims weren't hung. Only Ethel. The other women were all killed inside the home from strangulation, yes, but left inside their homes. And they had skin and blood under their nails, and other bruising."

Jo digested this information. Had Ethel been killed by someone she knew? Is this someone closer to home? That could only mean— "You can't possibly believe Nicholas or one of us killed Ethel?"

She must've raised her voice considerably because Randall glanced around anxiously and said, "Shush, Jo, let me finish."

Reigning in her anger, but only a tad, Jo said, "Make it quick, Randall. You're straining any remaining semblance of our friendship."

"I'm out of line here—"

"Really?"

"Listen. I meant with checking this. Me and the guys are using our time. But we got a problem. Sergeant Langford got wind of it, and he's not happy. Ordered us to back off, and toot-sweet."

Jo wasn't surprised. She didn't understand why, but Warren

didn't appear to appreciate anyone with the Cavanaugh name, and subsequently, anyone associated with them. "You did what you could. I don't want you or your friends getting into trouble. I appreciate you letting me know."

"No, that's still not it. It made us more curious. We'll be careful not to work on this at the station, but no way we're giving up." He grabbed her hand, which startled her, but she didn't pull away any further than the startled flinch. "I came so that you can choose how you tell your family." Randall squeezed her hand just short of painful, and said vehemently, "Just be careful. Fiona and Nicholas may not be safe. Maybe they're just in danger of Sarge's anger, but," he shook his head, "I think it's worse than just pissing him off."

"You think Warren would hurt them?" Jo felt the knot of tension clenched in her stomach. Would Warren be that petty? That spiteful? That dangerous?

"One more thing, Jo." Crap, there's more? "It's obvious you care very much for Tessa. Heck, the signs were all over both of you yesterday. If it turns out Warren is just an asshole, then we all live with that. If Warren isn't as clean as he should be, this household isn't the only thing in harm's way. The damage could hurt Tessa. You need to prepare for that."

Jo nodded. This information was unexpected. They needed a family meeting. Talk all of this out. On top of the list of things to do, Jo would need to prepare for any backlash on Tessa.

Chapter Fifteen

FIONA WAS RIGHT where Margaret expected she'd find her. What she hadn't planned was finding Brigid, Richard, and Nicholas in the workshop with her. She watched them from the large open doorway. Nicholas had presented Richard with an older camera, a Kodak 2A Folding Autographic Brownie, as he'd explained to them earlier in the week. Nicholas provided suggestions and pointers as Richard aimed the lens at Fiona, who went through a myriad of crazy expressions as she posed for the giggling child. Richard laughed so hard he could barely hold the camera.

"Okay, that's enough," Brigid said, lifting Richard into her arms. "Time for lunch and a nap."

"'Togaffers don't take naps," Richard whined. He looked at Nicholas.

"Rules are rules," Nicholas said. "Even for photographers."

"We can always finish later," Fiona said, kissing Richard's forehead. Margaret smiled, warmth from love flooded her. Fiona was good with him, with a lot of children, and she didn't even realize she drew them like flies to sugar. Of course, if awareness were about positive attributes, Fiona never recognized them in herself. If she didn't already love Fiona deeply and dearly, watching her with Richard would have been a clincher.

"Afternoon, Margaret," Nicholas said, slinging his satchel strap over his head, his Seneca Competitor camera in hand, and following behind Brigid and Richard. "We're off for a nap."

"Enjoy."

He grinned, then winked. "All of us will enjoy the time, except the one going down for the nap." Nicholas glanced back at Fiona. "Thanks for letting us interrupt your work."

Once they left, Margaret went to Fiona and pulled her in for a kiss. She increased the pressure, hands exploring every muscular contour of her wife's body. Gosh, she'd missed this. Fiona gently caressed Margaret's breast, thumb brushing across the nipple until it peaked. Maybe Fiona had missed the intimacy too. Margaret deepened their kiss until the need for air forced them apart. They maintained contact, Margaret's hands rested on Fiona's shoulders, Fiona's hands around her waist.

Fiona's honey-gold eyes grew hooded. "What was that for?"

She frowned. "I didn't miss a birthday, did I? An anniversary?"

Margaret slapped her shoulder, lightheartedly. "I wouldn't be kissing you if you had, silly."

Fiona's expression fell. "Then I guess you want to talk." She attempted to pull away, but Margaret held her tighter.

"I know you're having nightmares and migraines," Margaret said. "I suspect there's something more. Why won't you tell me?" She squeezed her eyes shut. Heart pounding in anticipated distress, she asked, "Are you leaving me?"

"What? No. Margaret, no." This time she was the one who pulled away, and Fiona let her. Was Fiona distancing herself with her actions, if not her words? "How can you ever think that let alone ask?"

Margaret barked an unexpected laugh. "How can I not, Fiona? We've had over four great years of sharing, loving, and growing. Of trusting. We used to trust one another."

"We still do. I still trust you," Fiona said, yet her voice faltered. Margaret couldn't say which emotion caused it.

"You can't trust me, or you'd tell me what's been going on with you. Instead, you're spending more and more time here in the workshop."

Margaret focused on the cluttered workbench of tools, multi-sized pieces of wood cuttings, and three new music boxes. Two appeared completed, one still waiting for the installment of the inner workings. The carvings were exquisite. The final product was a remarkable work of art. These were a new side to Fiona's work, one Margaret hadn't seen before now.

"I don't know what's going on, so I can't fix it. You're distancing yourself, which makes me believe you don't want to fix the problem." Margaret bit her lower lip, hoping to control an emotional breakdown, one she'd bottled up for months, from overtaking her. "Have I lost you, Fiona?"

How would Margaret survive if she had, when her life, her heart, wasn't complete without Fiona? But what right did she have to keep her hold on Fiona if Fiona didn't want her? Margaret turned away unwilling to be so vulnerable, not wanting tears to be the catalyst for Fiona staying when she didn't want to do so. "I love you too much to bind you to a relationship you don't want. I won't keep you in my life like that, honey. But please," Margaret said, ignoring the pleading tone in her voice. "Can I know what I've done wrong?"

Only a moment passed before the warmth of Fiona's body encased her back. The arms wrapped around her waist trembled.

Fiona's face pressed against the side of hers, wet with tears. "You have done nothing wrong, my love. It's me being so afraid. Afraid of losing control of things I never had control over in the first place. Afraid of losing you to my helplessness."

What? Confused, Margaret turned in Fiona's embrace until standing front to front, her arms wrapped around Fiona. Gazing into Fiona's eyes, Margaret saw the raw fear glaring back at her. "Helplessness? I don't understand."

Fiona squeezed her eyes shut for a moment. Too long a moment as far as Margaret's pulse was concerned. "You're aware of the nightmares, the migraines, and recognize they've been getting worse." Margaret nodded when Fiona paused to gather herself, indicated by the shaky inhalation of breath. "What you don't know is the blindness during and after the bouts of migraines." Fiona's anguish insinuated every syllable. "I don't know what's happening or how to fix it. How am I to protect you, support you without my sight? I'll be a burden."

Blindness? No wonder Fiona acted so distantly. Fiona was processing things as only she could—in private. "Oh baby, you shouldn't have tried dealing with this on your own."

Fiona's torment was evident, and she drew away from Margaret, swiping roughly at her eyes with the back of her hand, and then wrapped her arms around herself. "Dammit. This stupid problem has me acting like a baby."

Margaret moved behind her, placing hands and arms over Fiona's arms already held tight against her stomach. "For one thing, honey, you could never be a burden. The things you have done for this family in the last five years is more than most men do in a lifetime, in the guise of support." She placed a light kiss on the back of Fiona's neck, another behind her ear. "It is way beyond the time you let us—me especially—support you. You should never have to face your fears alone." She squeezed Fiona, released her, and shifted to stand in front of her.

When Fiona didn't look up, Margaret stepped closer and framed Fiona's face in her hands. At first, Fiona's gaze darted to fall on anything but her. Margaret was patient, acknowledged how hard showing vulnerability was for Fiona. After a moment, Fiona directed her gaze on Margaret's nose. Close enough, she thought. "I love you, Fiona. Nothing will ever change that, no matter how you fear it might. We'll find a doctor and fix whatever is wrong."

"And if we can't fix it?" Fiona's voice low and filled with dread. "Am I to be an invalid? Are you going to set my clothes out, as Brigid does for Richard?"

"If need be, yes." Margaret placed a kiss to the underside of Fiona's jaw. Geez, touching this woman, did incredible things to her insides. Just looking at Fiona's handsome features made her heart pick up the tempo, even after five years. Margaret would never—could never—stop loving her. Fiona made every cell in her body throb with heat, want, and need. Fiona was her blood, her breath. Losing Fiona would be like losing her will to breathe, to live. "I'd even go so far as to dress and undress you." She placed a kiss to the hollow at the base of Fiona's throat. She slowly skimmed a palm up Fiona's waist to graze the underside of Fiona's breast. Fiona gave a soft whimper in response. "Although, you've never had a problem with me undressing you before now. Didn't seem to mind the first time I dressed you." Margaret pictured how dashing Fiona had looked, five years ago. When Margaret believed she'd been dressing a boy named Finn. The memory caused heat in Margaret's body to burn hot. All for Fiona.

"Margaret, someone could walk—" Fiona's breathing grew ragged.

"Walk in here? I know, you're right. We will continue this later." Margaret took a deep breath to settle her pulse. Physical contact with Fiona always had her burning volcanic hot. "Patience, on my part, won't be easy." Margaret knew it had to be done, couldn't afford the distraction and single-minded focus, to the exclusion of awareness to all else, lovemaking with Fiona wrought.

She took a step back again, taking one of Fiona's hands in hers, and bumped into the workbench. Margaret turned toward the items on top, making sure she hadn't damaged anything. When her gaze fell on the music boxes, she picked up a finished one, the intricate carvings of Celtic design. "When did you start making these?" she asked. "They're gorgeous, but I don't remember you creating anything this small in previous woodworking ventures."

Fiona blushed, focused on the box Margaret held. When her eyes clouded, she cleared her throat, while balling her fingers into fists, Margaret realized the inquiry brought on a painful memory. Fiona suffered so much already. Margaret felt guilty for bringing her wife more discomfort. "Sorry, honey. You don't have to answer."

Sucking in a shuddering breath, Fiona said, "My mother's necklace used to rest every evening in a music box her mother gave her. She cherished that music box. It was the only personal possession, other than the pearl necklace, my mother owned."

"Was it lost in the fire that took your mother and brother?"

Fiona nodded. "Yes. I'd have lost the necklace too, but Quinn had that in his pocket at the time of the fire. He intended to pawn it." Margaret nearly growled at the name.

Quinn was Fiona's father, even if he also used to be the scum of the earth. Luckily for everyone, he no longer breathed. He'd been killed in Boston by a small group of women devoted to Fiona. Quinn had watched while Jimmy Bennett shot, beat, and savagely raped his daughter, claiming it the only way to show her how to be a normal woman and man-loving. His murder was a secret Margaret would harbor with her dying breath. Not because he hadn't deserved it, but for her part—her lack of intervention—in his demise. She had remained hidden away from sight while Fiona's friends beat him, while one of the women had delivered the blow that subsequently killed him.

"The music boxes are the only work I feel safe doing when blind."

"But how? These are much too incredible." Fiona chuckled. "That came out as an unintended insult. I would never insult you."

"I believe you, sweetheart, no offense taken." Fiona leaned forward and pressed a soft kiss to her forehead. Margaret wrapped her in a tight hug. "They surprised me too," Fiona said, her breath warm against Margaret's ear. "Had a carving tool in my hand when one of the episodes hit. At first, as usual," she said, giving a self-deprecating laugh, "I panicked. Then, I carefully used my tool and the wood, feeling the carvings with my fingers and thumb. It soothed me some, to be doing something productive, especially should anyone find me while blind. They'd believe me lost in thought, rather than darkness. When I remembered my mother's box, I concentrated my focus on picturing it."

She snorted. "Jo saw the work and told me it looked great, except for the splotches of blood, which I should refrain from adding to any future projects. Later, we cut up a bunch of soft-wood pieces, and I keep them close by to calm me during the episodes. I have at least one thing I can continue to do if I'm rendered entirely blind."

As always, Fiona's resiliency and determination impressed Margaret. One point nagged at her. "Honey, how often are you having these blinding episodes?"

Fiona pulled away. "Margaret—"

"Please, Fiona, honesty. Don't I have a right to know?"

A fresh flow of tears fell from Fiona's eyes. "Yes, of course, you do. And I intended to tell you. I just needed to wait to make certain."

Margaret got a flash of understanding. Fiona had wanted to come to her with not only the problem but with a credible solution. "You needed to find something you could do in the events of your blindness, to relieve us of your perceived burden on us." Fiona couldn't lose the one thing identifying her as a woman of means, a livelihood which had become her banner of a supportive member of the family, of society. "Well, honey," she said, clasping Fiona's hands in hers. "I wish it hadn't taken so long, or that you hadn't felt you couldn't come to me without the solution, but I understand."

Her steady, strong wife crinkled her nose. "Do you understand enough not to be too angry with me?"

It had been a while since the playful side of Fiona made itself known in Margaret's presence. She'd missed it, unaware how much until this moment. Fiona had always been her support, the indefatigable foundation in the storm. How many other troubles had Fiona weathered on her own? Had Margaret been so wrapped in her job and comfort with their life together, she'd missed moments Fiona needed her? Had their marriage, their partnership, really turned into give-and-take—her taking while Fiona gave? "I couldn't be angry with you, Fiona. At least not for long. But maybe you should be angry with me?"

"Whatever for?" Fiona asked, brow knitted in confusion.

"For not holding up my end of this marriage. I should've seen the signs broadcasting that all was not right with you. I should've pressed for answers sooner. Have I failed you too badly, irreparably?"

Fiona shook her head vehemently. "You could never fail me. You are my everything, Margaret. Without you, I would have given up long ago. You keep my nightmares at bay. Keep my heart full." Fresh tears flowed from her caramel-colored eyes, and she took a ragged breath. Margaret worried how long Fiona had kept these emotions bottled up. "I'm nothing without you and everything when with you. I love you."

The honest conviction in Fiona's words had Margaret crying, and she pressed her face against Fiona's. "Oh, my dearest Fiona. I love you, too—more with each beat of my heart. You needn't keep things from me. I'm here for you in good or bad. Nothing will ever change these feelings for me. It is you who inspires every breath I take."

Fiona gave her a crooked grin and a watery chuckle. "We better stop this."

"Stop what?"

"Let's just say, if we get any sappier, Jo will have to pry us from the floorboards."

The visual made Margaret chuckle. "You might be correct." Margaret brushed tears from Fiona's cheeks with the pad of her thumb. Fiona returned the favor. "Sappy or not, every word is true. You believe me, right?" Fiona nodded. "Good, because I don't think it's appropriate to start proving it by making love to you in the woodshop."

In a teasing tone, Fiona asked, "Not a fan of wood chips stuck to your bum as I take you here on the bench?"

Matching her tone, Margaret said, "If you remove them with your teeth, it could have some merit." Margaret had to laugh at the look of surprise on Fiona's tear-stained and flushed face. "And that, my beloved Fiona, is why I'll always and only love you."

Chapter Sixteen

IT WAS AN average mid-May early evening, not too warm, and even boasted a slight breeze. Not as windy as most. Excited about tonight's dinner with Tessa, Jo's nerves had her stomach in knots. Please don't be sick, please don't be sick, she silently chanted. Her heart hammered in her chest as she knocked on the downstairs door of the outer stairwell. Jo hoped the knock was loud enough to hear, not so loud as to startle Tessa.

In her hand, Jo held the gift for Tessa, a thank-you-for-dinner, and welcome-to-the-neighborhood gift. Though customary to bring sweets or flowers, she wanted this to be special and hoped it would be. She had agonized over what to bring until finally enlisting Margaret's help.

Jo found Margaret in the workshop with Fiona, both an emotional mess. Fiona must've finally told her about the illness. Jo hadn't expected this scene, or she wouldn't have announced her presence by shouting, "Hey, I'm stuck and need help," as she walked through the open door. She spun around to return them to their privacy.

"Don't go, Jo," Margaret said. Reluctantly, she twisted around. Poised to apologize, Jo swallowed the redress when Margaret shook her head. There would be no apology or questions. "What are you stuck with?"

"When you go to your girl's place, cause she's making you dinner, you bring a gift, right?" Jo shoved her hands in her pockets. "I don't know what to bring, but I wanted something special, not just what anyone else would bring."

"Aw, sweetie." Fiona shook her head and chortled. "You have it bad."

Margaret smiled and bumped a shoulder into Fiona's. Silent rebuke to stop teasing. "Quite the quandary."

Jo rolled her eyes. "That's what I said, and why I'm asking you for help. I want Tessa to know I'm serious—short of proposing—and still show her she's special."

Fiona picked up one of the finished music boxes from the bench beside her. The box had carvings of Celtic design, Fiona's mother's favorite. Jo had placed the inner workings inside the box just this morning. "It's nothing fancy, but it might be a nice housewarming gift, and thank you. Different enough gift, I think, while still making your intentions clear."

Jo's eyes widened. "But, Fiona, you worked so hard on it."

"Not that hard." Fiona shrugged. Margaret took the music box from Fiona and placed it in Jo's hands. "Tessa will appreciate you see her as an individual worthy of something unique." Margaret tapped a finger under Jo's chin. "Unique and special, just like you are."

She wanted to cry, her heart filled with the love of and from these two women. Jo had never felt less-than with Margaret and Fiona. Hoping to interject a bit of levity to break the earlier emotional tension, and the emotions she felt now, Jo said, "Thank you both. But if she accepts this and believes we're engaged, it's all on you two." Jo wouldn't mind at all if Tessa reached that conclusion.

The door opened, and Tessa stood before her in a pink shirtwaist with puffy sleeves at the shoulders and long gray skirt with pink pinstripes. Her hair was pulled back into a neat bun, a ringlet of hair on either side of the temples. She was breathtaking. "Jo, come on up," Tessa said, turned and then rushed upstairs, saying over her shoulder, "I don't want to leave the food unattended too long."

"Hasn't Warren arrived yet?" Jo asked.

Tessa laughed. "Warren is never on time, always between five and ten minutes late. Probably afraid he'd get wrangled into helping set the table or something." In the apartment, soft, instrumental music played on the radio, a delicious aroma wafted in the air, and tapered candles burned on a table neatly set for three. "I hope his bad habit doesn't interfere with your timetable for the evening."

"No, no timetable here," Jo said. Tessa moved into the small kitchen area, and Jo closed the upstairs door and followed her. A quick peek in the oven, and Tessa turned toward her. Hands shaking, Jo extended the butcher paper wrapped present. "Um... Thank you for inviting me to dinner." Tessa took her offering with wide eyes.

"Jo, you didn't have to bring anything. I'm excited you're here. That was enough for me." Tessa blushed. "I'm just sorry we had to include my brother."

Jo stepped closer and brushed a kiss across Tessa's lips. "Me too, but there will be other nights—solitary ones—for the two of us, I hope."

"As do I," Tessa said. "May I open it now?" Jo nodded. Tessa removed the ribbon (Brigid's donation) and carefully removed the paper. When her eyes glistened with the prelude to tears, Jo panicked. Had this not been the right thing to bring? Tessa ran a finger across the carvings and slowly raised the lid. The soft, tinkling tones of *Beautiful Dreamer* broke the silence. Jo was about to apologize and offer to bring whatever Tessa wanted as a replacement. Tessa, music box clutched in her hand, and launched a hug at Jo. Whispering in her ear, "This is the most precious gift I've ever received in my entire life."

Jo sent a silent prayer to the heavens. She'd give a verbal one to Fiona and Margaret later. "Your life is young, yet, which gives me plenty of chances to do better."

Tessa pulled away, blushing. "You're younger than I am, Jo. A prettier girl will catch your eye before long."

Yes, she may be young, but sometimes it felt like she'd already lived a thousand lifetimes. Moreover, how could Tessa doubt her attractiveness? "Don't know what you have and haven't been told before now, but believe me when I tell you that you are beautiful to me." Jo leaned in and gently kissed her lips, placed another on the spot just behind her jaw, and below her ear. "And irresistible." Jo felt Tessa shiver. She could have gone in for another deeper kiss but heard the turning of the doorknob.

"I'm putting bells on all the doors," Tessa grumbled softly, pulling out of their embrace and placed the music box on the counter.

"I could change the locks for you," Jo offered quietly.

Warren walked in, scowling as if this was the last place he wanted to be. He could've canceled, Jo thought bitterly.

"When do we eat?" he asked, stomping to the table and blowing out the candles. "That's a foolish waste." He plopped into a chair.

If she didn't believe it would upset Tessa, Jo would berate him for his rudeness and lack of manners. He didn't acknowledge the effort Tessa put into this evening, he criticized her attempts for atmosphere, and no brotherly hug or kiss. She couldn't remember a time she came or went from the house that someone present within didn't verbally or physically acknowledge her. It must be standard for the Langford's because Tessa turned her attention back to the meal preparation. Warren sat impatiently at the table, drumming his fingers.

"Anything I can do to help?" she asked, moving closer to Tessa.

Tessa blinked rapidly. Was she surprised by the offer? "No, thank you. Have a seat at the table, and I'll be right there." Jo sat across from Warren warily. "Here we go," Tessa said. She placed a serving platter in the middle of the table. On it was a beautiful steaming roast Tessa had thinly cut, surrounded by potatoes, pearl onions, and carrots. The divine smell, when she entered the apartment, was proving better this close. Then, Tessa retrieved the gravy bowl.

"If it tastes half as good as it smells, I'll be in heaven," she said to Tessa. Again, rapid blinking from Tessa. "I appreciate the invitation and the effort you made for this meal tonight."

Warren snickered. "Laying it on thick, aren't you?" Jo stared at him. "She needs to eat, so how hard is it to make more? You haven't tasted it, so complimenting her now is pointless. She wouldn't have invited you if she didn't like you. Not that I haven't tried to discourage the ridiculous behavior of what you both call a 'friendship.'"

"Warren," Tessa said sharply.

"It's okay, Tessa," Jo said. She glared at Warren. "I'm curious, is it only me, my entire family, or anyone who breaths that you dislike so much? What reason could you possibly have since you barely know me, or the rest of us?"

"Don't need a reason."

"No, I don't suppose you do. Although gauging from the loutish way you treat your sister, I'm not at all surprised." Tessa sat at the table, slow and silent, and picked up plates and filled them. Maybe it was best to have a silent meal anyway.

Silent and strained is what transpired. The only sound came from the clicking of utensils on plates and against teeth, the sounds of chewing and swallowing. Jo fought the urge to toss Warren out on his ass but didn't wish more strain on Tessa. The meal tonight meant a lot to Tessa, and he purposely made it uncomfortable for her, his flesh-and-blood. Despite the tension making swallowing difficult, Jo ate her fill, not in solidarity to the cook, but because the food truly tasted as wonderful as her baking. Jo made sure to tell her so, with an accompanying squeeze to Tessa's hand.

"Shit. Give it a rest," Warren snapped, pushing his chair from the table. "It's bad enough she has these...these...tendencies toward disgusting liaisons, doesn't mean I have to suffer through it."

Jo grit her teeth to control an outburst. "We haven't done anything for you to suffer through, Warren. This wonder meal doesn't fall near the realm of disgusting liaisons."

"What the hell? 'Course you have, all the dumb compliments, handholding." He paused, a glint in his eyes. "How 'bout the candles?"

"You're angry, Warren," Tessa said softly, "because you saw us kissing yesterday. There is no other reason for your extra hostility."

"This isn't supposed to happen to my sister. Why can't you just like men? It's unnatural."

"It's not like we're flaunting ourselves in public. But it's the way I am and natural to me. I can't change me, even for you."

Warren snarled and faced Tessa. "Fine, but why her? Did you know the Cavanaugh's left Boston to run away from trouble with gangsters?"

The statement startled Jo. She stood from the table, picked up the platter to take to the kitchen counter. Jo hoped to control her temper, knowing she would explode soon. With her back to them, Jo said, "We left for a new life, not because of gangsters." She spun around, extending arms behind her to grasp the counters' edge to ground herself.

"Really? I heard that's how your sister got her disfiguring scars. What went on in Boston? Why the need to change your name, Sunny?"

Tessa inhaled sharply.

The comment rattled Jo, but she didn't want him to know. She shook her head and plastered on a tight, strained grin instead. "Fiona isn't disfigured. Only an ass would look at her and see just scars. Whoever gave you your information is gravely mistaken."

Tessa rose from her chair and glowered down at him. "Enough, Warren. You're hurtful on purpose."

"Ethel told me. But only after Brigid told her," Warren said, a smug expression on his face.

Confused about why Brigid would do such a thing, panicked about how much Brigid may have shared—about all of them—Jo's attention locked on one minor and inconsequential point. What purpose or opportunity provoked Ethel to tell Warren these things?

Warren crossed his arms over his chest. "If you plan to continue this debauchery of my sister, I believe I have a right to know about the people in her life."

"Stop it, Warren. Whatever has gotten into you, I'll not have it. You're no longer welcome here. Go."

Warren appeared stunned. "You want me to leave, not her? I'm trying to protect you from a bad element." He walked over to Tessa as if proximity could help her change her mind. "You need to ask questions, Tess. Did you know Jo isn't her name? Do you know anything about her past? Even if she isn't a danger, she could bring danger to you through her family's past."

Tessa stared him down, filling Jo with a lot of pride and a hint of trepidation. Tessa was a force unto herself when ticked off. "If you cared for me as you professed, rather than see me as your cook and scrubwoman, you'd have remained silent about what you heard, accepted it as the gossip I'm sure it is. Even if it were true, you'd allow me to make my own mistakes." Tessa's finger shot forward and stabbed him in the chest repeatedly. "You had your dinner and your pathetic entertainment. You can go now."

"What about dessert?"

"Seriously? You lost the pleasure the first time you disrespected my friends."

"She's a potential heartbreak. Why doesn't she have to go?" Warren asked. "I'm blood, family."

"Right now, I'm ashamed. Leave Warren."

Jo felt queasy, the spectacular dinner a heavy lump in her stomach. She knew this day would come but hoped it would happen much later. It was best to get her past in the open. She wanted Tessa to see her for who she was, overall. Even if the information could push Tessa away. The worst part, Jo was heartbeats away from being deeply in love with Tessa, despite the short length of time they knew each other. She truly believed in love-at-first-sight the moment her gaze landed on Tessa. The feeling of home, her own home, was strongest when with Tessa. Tessa made Jo believe in permanence and futures with happy endings. But Jo's past was sordid, and the very thing to give Warren what he wanted—Jo out of Tessa's life.

Reluctantly, and with one final glare in her direction, Warren left.

"I'm sorry," she told Tessa.

"For what?"

"We ruined your special night."

Tessa raised an eyebrow. "The night isn't over yet."

Chapter Seventeen

TESSA CLEANED THE kitchen and table after she ordered Jo to the couch. She'd gone obediently, but Tessa suspected Jo anticipated they'd make a farewell tonight. The main thing about tonight was Tessa could think of only one instance Jo's past would send her running—to learn Jo was a murderess. That scenario seemed too far-fetched. And, even that prospect had circumstances to make murder doable. Whatever had happened in the past, Tessa planned on offering her total support to Jo and her family.

She'd had a good family life of her own, even if her parents felt distancing themselves the only way to deal with her and her preferences in the heart department. Warren treated her as most men did, keeping her domesticated, sweeping the other issues under the carpet. Her family seldom offered praise, believed it made a person vain. They weren't demonstrative either. Tessa longed for the touch of another.

She had a taste with Catherine but only when it suited the other woman. All too soon, she realized Catherine used her to see how far Tessa would go to please someone. Catherine grew bored before they ever reached a point of intimacy.

But Jo? Their acquaintance was still new, Jo complimented her often—honestly?—and innocently touched Tessa in casual and comforting ways. Kissing Jo made Tessa feel beautiful, wanted, desired. When Jo lightly caressed her breast—

Even now, Tessa burned with arousal at the memory. Jo might even be too good for her, despite what Warren might think otherwise. Jo was strong and caring, charismatic and outgoing, and dedicated to her family. No, nothing Jo shared could ever make Tessa turn away from her.

Tessa dried her hands on the dishtowel and then hung it on the metal rod above the sink. "That does it," she said. She left the kitchen area, sat beside Jo, and picked up one of Jo's hands in both of hers. "I apologize for Warren, even if I don't control him."

Jo gave a wry smile. "You have some authority over him. He did leave without demanding dessert."

"Too bad, it's not where it counts." Tessa squeezed the hand she held. "Sweetie, I know he brought up some painful things. If you don't ever feel you can share your past with me, I'll understand. It may seem too fast, but I have feelings for you, Jo. Feelings I think could turn into something wonderful for a long time. I'd like to know everything about you. No matter how dark. You've already told me Fiona isn't your biological sister, and you can't tell me her story. When you feel ready, maybe you can at least tell me yours."

"Tessa, I don't want you to look at me differently. Presently, you look at me like I mean something important to you. If I tell you about my past, I foresee the expression will change quickly, and not in a positive way. I would most probably lose you, Tessa."

"That won't happen," Tessa said. "But I understand you can't know that about me. Eventually, you will. We can start with small things."

Jo looked away from her. The hand she held became sweaty and trembled. Jo tried to pull it out of her grasp. Tessa held tighter. In a barely heard whisper, she asked, "What would you ask of me by way of a small question?"

Tessa playfully pursed her lips. "I like the name of Jo. It suits you. Is Warren correct, were you born with another name?"

A flicker of emotions crossed Jo's expression. It meant the memories had multiple feelings—mostly bad—associated with them. A long period of silence ensued before Jo said, "I was born Thelma Josephine Winton. When Fiona came into my life, she called me Sunny." Jo rolled her eyes. "I was far from sunny in disposition, but there wasn't talking Fiona out of it. She claimed I brightened a room. Silly, huh? Anyway, after a time, Margaret helped with the papers to make me officially Sunny Josephine Cavanaugh. Now I'm older and use Jo. Sunny seemed to indicate a child, and I don't want my name to give that impression."

Tessa could see how hard the small admission was to tell. She wanted to prod for more personal information but couldn't push and isolate Jo with her painful memories. "Thank you for sharing." She scrunched up her nose. "Mostly, thank you for changing from Thelma. Jo does suit you better." From the tension radiating from Jo's body, it was obvious to Tessa the past not an easy topic for her. They needed to get back to their relaxed conversation, the effortless physicality between them, in their budding relationship. "Most of the shops are closed now, so there shouldn't be too much foot traffic in town if you'd like to go for a walk."

Jo hesitated for a couple of minutes, finally nodding. "A walk would be nice."

Before long, they walked down the sidewalk arm in arm and chatted about the work on the shop, Jo's carpentry work with Fiona, and Tessa's reason for becoming a seamstress. "Do you plan something like this?" Jo asked. "Growing up, I never thought 'gosh, I want to be a carpenter,' but Fiona did." Jo's expression shadowed. Was it fate they continually returned to the topic of childhood? The observation hadn't been lost on Jo, either. She'd been present in their conversation but not entirely. They had walked from her end of Union Avenue to the other, crossed over, and returned. Her shop was at the bottom of Union Avenue, which led to the train depot.

Crossing back over, Jo paused at the door to her covered stairwell. "Are you coming in?" Tessa asked, unlocking the outer door and stepping inside.

Jo shook her head. "I should get home. Supper was wonderful, Tessa. Honestly. Thank you."

"I'm glad you liked it."

Ever so slowly, as if memorizing every pore, Jo stared at her, then finally raised a hand and caressed her cheek. Jo kicked the door closed with her heel, sealing them alone in the stairwell illuminated with a single bare light bulb with a long thin chain. The tenderness and warmth of Jo's touch had Tessa moan softly. When Jo spoke, her voice was low and cracked with restrained emotion. "Fiona didn't work with gangsters. She worked on the inside against them.

"Up until I met Fiona, my family seldom had a place of our own and often were kicked out for not paying rent. Eating was often a novelty and usually meant we beat most of the other homeless to fresh food, relatively speaking, from the spot where restaurants emptied the trash. Clothes were what we could scavenge." She drew in a deep, quivering breath. "My parents had just sold me to Eldon Graham for drugs. They didn't ask questions, Tessa, about what would happen to me. Wouldn't have cared. I was purchased to work in a brothel. I was fourteen years old." Jo swallowed hard, blinked back tears. Holding them at bay was a battle Jo was losing.

"When Fiona found me, Eldon had just 'tested' his newly acquired merchandise. His second-in-command prepared for his turn." Her eyes squeezed shut, as if afraid to witness Tessa's reaction to the revelation. Tessa wanted to be sick. Who could do such a thing to a child? "Fiona got me out of there and has protected me ever since. Margaret made certain I caught up in my education so I could go to a real school like normal children." Jo took a step away from her and bumped into the door. "That is why we left Boston. Fiona wanted me to have a new life and take away from me the chance of anyone recognizing me as tainted, dirty trash."

Tessa felt the damp trail of tears down her face. If she had to guess about Jo's past, using the bits Warren had spouted, she could never have envisioned the truth Jo shared with her. Jo thought her history would push Tessa away from her. Quite the opposite. Their meeting and friendship proved they shared a bonding of pure kismet, an intended destiny from God. Could it be an illusion? Certainly. Were feelings and personal revelations between them shared too fast? Possibly. Tessa, however, believed Josephine Cavanaugh her intended forever-mate.

She moved toward Jo, whose only avenue of escape was the staircase since Jo had pressed herself against the closed door. Tessa reached for her hands. Jo didn't fight her, although her body stiffened. Slow, so Jo observed her every move, Tessa wrapped her arms around Jo's waist, pressed herself fully against the front of Jo until their breasts pressed tight against each other. She leaned forward until her lips brushed the bottom of an earlobe and whispered, "You were handsome and strong to me before. Now that you shared such private pain, I can see you're even stronger than anyone I know." Tessa shifted, her lips pressed against Jo's, persisted until Jo returned the kiss. Before she realized she would say the words, Tessa blurted, "No wonder I've fallen in love with you."

Both stared at one another in wide-eyed silence, before Jo nudged herself to the side, swung the door open and ran out.

Chapter Eighteen

MARGARET STARED OUT of the bedroom window but focused on nothing. Jo hadn't returned from her dinner date, and Fiona would be upstairs soon to retire to bed.

What an awful burden for her to process. Worse, what must this situation be like for Fiona, who was living it daily? Margaret squeezed her eyes shut, pushing away the tears. Fiona worried this illness would make her a burden. Ha. If anyone had been a burden, it was her, Margaret thought bitterly. Yes, Fiona wanted to leave Boston years ago, hoping to make a new life for them all. But she took Jo from a path of prostitution, saved her body, spirit, and mind. Saved Brigid. Okay, Brigid hadn't exactly been running from anything, but she had a place of love and support, an adventure she wouldn't have had in Boston.

For Margaret, Fiona offered a safe-haven of love and appreciation. Margaret always felt the emotions, in her heart, in her world, in the depths of caramel-colored eyes when Fiona looked at her. Fiona gave her the chance to follow her dream of teaching, which her brother never allowed. Recognized her good days, comforted—sometimes with nothing more than silence and a shoulder to rest her head on—during bad days and recognized, often anticipated, what Margaret needed. And you never recognized when Fiona needed you, did you?

Reaching into her memory, Margaret realized it had always been this way. She recalled the moment precipitating Fiona's current physical troubles—the moment she'd ignored Fiona's plea and set them on this current path. A memory which would now haunt Margaret.

Margaret closed the door behind her once they entered Fiona's room. She was tired, stressed, and heartbroken at how withdrawn Fiona had become since leaving the hospital. The reason became apparent as soon as Fiona spoke. "Leave with me, Margaret. Tonight. Please."

Fiona turned to face her. "It will only take a few minutes for Sunny and me to pack, but we'll wait for you. I'm still jake with Old Man Chambers, and I know he'll give me one of his old trucks."

Tonight? "Honey, I can't leave now."

Fiona's expression was crestfallen. "Why not?"

"I have obligations, Fiona. I can't just run off willy-nilly."

"Obligations?" She took a step forward, but Fiona moved to put the bed between them. Fiona snorted loudly. "So, I'm not important enough as either your lover — one time granted — or even important enough to be an obligation."

"That's not true, Fiona. I'm just asking for a little time."

Fiona crumpled onto the chair by the bed. From the quivering in her shoulders, Margaret realized she was silently crying. On impulse driven by her heart, Margaret rushed to Fiona and dropped to her knees, clasping Fiona's hands in hers.

With an anguished whisper, Fiona said, "I don't know how I can. I don't want to be part of this charade anymore. I want to be me, be Fiona." Her head rose, watery brown eyes met Margaret's. "I can't be part of these horrible — "

Squeezing the hands in hers, Margaret said, "I understand. I'll do my best to keep you away from Eldon and Jimmy." Margaret suspected Jimmy would do his best to maintain distance for a while, rather than explain what happened with Lorraine. "I'm not saying 'never,' Fiona, only I can't leave this soon. Please, stay with me, here, for a while longer?"

"What are your feelings for me?" Fiona asked, her voice sounded small and hurt.

Looking at the torment in Fiona's eyes had her questioning what was going on with her insecurity. "Honey, what are you afraid of?"

Fiona looked away. "I'm afraid I can't protect you, can't protect Sunny. After Lorraine's death — "

Margaret cupped Fiona's cheek, the pad of her thumb brushing across her chin. "If I didn't care for you, Fiona, I wouldn't be asking for time. If you need to leave, I'll be sorry to see you go, but will understand. I wish you would stay."

"What if I can't protect you?"

"Nothing's going to happen. I love you, Fiona. Please trust me."

Trust her. What a fool Margaret had been to say those words, not to see how deeply Lorraine's murder had affected and frightened Fiona. Fiona had trusted her, and now the toll proved exorbitant for her wife. Cost her sleep because of nightmares of Jimmy's horrendous assault on her, which nearly caused Fiona's death.

Margaret sucked in a deep breath. She may have let Fiona

down then, but she wouldn't do so now or in the future. Margaret had to wait for Edward's return call, while he made inquiries for a nearby specialist to examine and consult with Fiona. She planned to use her time wisely, concentrate on Fiona and her needs. More so when the school year concluded in the next few weeks.

"Hey, what's wrong?" Jo asked from the doorway. Margaret shook her head as Jo entered the room and came to her, draped an arm across her shoulder. "Fiona finally told you, didn't she?"

She nodded. "Yes, and then I called Doc Edward."

"Did he say anything helpful? She can be healed, right?" Jo's voice rose, hope in her tone.

Margaret sniffed. Fixed, like a broken chair leg? "Fiona's not an inanimate project, Jo."

"Yeah, I get that," Jo said, face flushed. "You knew what I meant. You're upset and scared."

"I did, and I apologize." Margaret shifted from under Jo's arm and sat in the rocking chair close to the window. Jo sat on the bed, and faced her. "Honestly, Jo, after I explained the symptoms, it was the silence of what Edward didn't say that hit me with a sense of dread. Maybe I'm overreacting, but I don't think so."

"Maybe it has nothing to do with exaggerating and everything to do with being overly sensitized to what is happening to the love of your life. It's not like we can do anything but give Fiona our emotional support until we get some definitive information to work with here."

Despite her anxiety, Margaret raised an eyebrow, and teasingly said, "Ooh, listen to you all adult speaking."

"I'm in conversation with a teacher. Can't have you stuffing me in some remedial education situation. I have better uses for my summer."

"Aw, honey, I'm sorry I didn't ask sooner. How was your dinner with Tessa?"

"No need to apologize. You're a bit off-balance and understandably." Margaret remained silent while Jo squirmed at the end of the bed. Fear is the worst, Margaret prepared a conciliatory response rather than wait for Jo to gather her thoughts, but Jo finally responded. "The first part with Warren was uncomfortable, but we got through it." Jo inhaled a deep breath. "I told her about my past, Margaret. Warren brought up some with his insults about Fiona, and I couldn't let Tessa believe them."

"Oh, Jo, that couldn't have been easy." Margaret jumped

from the rocker and plopped on the bed beside Jo, her arm draped over Jo's shoulder in an expression of support. Jo must care for Tessa a lot if she shared happenings in Boston. "Are you okay?"

"I don't know, honestly." Jo shook her head. "Not in the way you'd expect. Certainly not the way I expected."

"What did she say, Jo?"

"She kissed me." Jo slowly met Margaret's gaze, and Margaret's anxiety grew at the dread-filled expression on Jo's young face. "Tessa said she was falling in love with me."

Surprised, Margaret leaned back. "Uh..."

"Yeah."

"What did you say?"

"I didn't say anything. I ran away." Jo groaned. "Ugh, like a kid, I ran away, and came straight home to the closest people I've had resembling a mom and... well, mom."

Margaret took Jo's hand. "Well, that was quite a declaration Tessa released. I probably would have run too." Margaret had done her version of running when Fiona confessed her feelings. She squeezed Jo's hand. "How do you feel about her revelation?"

Jo snorted, then said, "Scared, happy, confused. But—"

"But?"

"All I can think about is how I feel when she kisses me. I've been a little in love with her since I first laid eyes on her. Tessa makes me feel happy, comfortable with myself just as I am. I want to care for her, do care for her. When I'm not with her, I'm always thinking of her." Jo met her gaze with a furrowed brow. "Even with all that, I'm afraid it will all fall apart if I say the words aloud. What if it jinxes the relationship?"

"If you're using the word relationship instead of friendship, you're probably in deeper than you're willing to admit." Margaret grinned. "If Tessa is truly in love with you, you won't have to parrot the words back when she speaks them. She'll give you time to feel them and to adjust."

"I ran away. What if Tessa takes my reaction badly?"

"From what I've gleaned from the few times in her company, she'll recognize you were overwhelmed by the evening. You did bare your horrible past to her, after all. The disclosure is quite ponderous to the average person. Sleep on it, Jo. By morning, you'll be able to focus better."

Jo pulled her hand free from Margaret's and rose to her feet. "I feel like such a kid right now."

Margaret watched the flicker of self-annoyance skitter across

Jo's features. "How so?"

"This is what I wanted from the moment I saw Tessa. None of the crushes I had before her made me feel the way she makes me feel inside." Jo shrugged. "Now I don't know what to do with it other than feel skittish."

Margaret smiled. "Love will do that to you. Trust me, kiddo. After a good night's sleep, you may not have all the answers, but you'll feel much better."

"Thanks, Margaret." Jo bent and kissed Margaret's cheek. "Don't think I'll get much sleep, though."

"Why not? Don't plan on dreaming about the reveal and her kiss?" Margaret waggled her eyebrows.

"Nah, gonna beat myself up for feeling selfish with my problems."

"You aren't selfish. Why would you think that?"

"Fiona's issues are more important. After all, she's—" Jo rushed to the door, paused. "Do you think Fiona will be okay?"

Margaret went to her and enveloped her in a hug. "She'll be fine, honey. Fiona is strong. More than that, she has us." She flashed a wry grin at Jo. "We're her best medicine, right?"

Jo nodded. "You'll keep me updated? Tell me what Edward shares with you on the matter?"

"Of course." When Jo went to her room, Margaret returned to the rocking chair. No matter the prognosis, Margaret would be by Fiona's side, do whatever was needed. Fiona meant everything to her. But, after her phone conversation with Edward, the ball of dread, currently lodged in her heart, grew heavier.

Chapter Nineteen

THE LONG DRIVE from Pueblo to Aurora, outside of Denver, was mostly silent. Not that Margaret could fault Fiona. Her nerves were strained tighter than an over-tuned banjo string, prepared for the worse case, yet hoping for the best-case scenario. They were driving to the former Army Hospital 21, renamed in July 1920 to the Fitzsimons Army Hospital. The name honored Lt. William T. Fitzsimons, the first American medical officer to be killed in World War I.

She'd managed to get the appointment with one of the premier neurologists with the assistance from her family doctor and friend, Edward Matthews, a couple days after her call to him. Margaret didn't wish to frighten Fiona any more than she already was, but a feeling deep in her gut—especially after her latest conversation with Edward—warned this appointment might not go well in as far as prognosis.

Margaret parked the truck in the nearest hospital parking lot and turned off the engine. She glanced at her watch, noting they'd arrived nearly forty-five minutes early. Neither made a move to exit the truck. "I'm sorry, honey. Knowing the diagnosis isn't worth the strain on you." She feared the outcome, and hesitated to go inside. The distance required for the drive and the unknown possibilities resulting from this appointment had placed stressful silence between them. "We should go home, forget about this, and take each day one at a time. We'll call this a field trip or adventure for a day out."

"We're here now," Fiona said, the quiver in her voice indicated the depth of her terror. Margaret slid across the bench seat and clasped Fiona's left hand in both of hers. Sighing, Fiona squeezed Margaret's hand. "No, we need to know so that we can prepare ourselves and the family."

Margaret nodded. "Okay. We can relax over dinner when we get to the hotel." She raised their combined hands and placed a kiss on Fiona's exposed knuckles. "Or get room service and stay in." Margaret waggled her eyebrows and received a partial smile from Fiona. "We haven't been alone like this since we were first married. Of course, you were in a coma, so we weren't alone then, either." Fiona nodded as if further spoken words would put her over the edge. Margaret's teasing didn't have the desired effect.

They took their time to walk from the parking lot to the hospital. It was a beautiful day for May, warm and sunny with a slight breeze. Margaret hooked her arm around Fiona's, steered them toward the back of the building as per where she'd been told to check-in, and slowed their steps to prolong their entry time. Fiona didn't object, and the added steps in the outside air calmed them both.

Calmed until they entered the hospital.

Margaret expected to see sick and recovering patients, but what she found nearly had her yanking Fiona out of the building. Nearly. They'd entered a large open room painted completely white. The room's multiple windows opened to allow the light breeze to circulate the inside air. There were numerous couches and armchairs placed around the room. Seven people, five men, and two women, sat staggered about the furniture, some in hospital gowns, others in street clothes. Each had some form of head trauma, leaving all or most sections of their heads shaved, ugly jagged scars present, some displayed sunken flesh where bone was removed or probably crushed due to an injury. Fiona stiffened, a small whimper escaped her tightly pursed lips.

At the far end of the room was a closed doorway, and beside the door, a section of the wall cut out to provide a reception window. Margaret tugged Fiona toward reception, trying to block the sight and, in some cases, the tormented gazes following their progress. Most had a vacant expression. Two had drool puddling on the front of their chests.

Her hand was poised to ring the bell sitting on the ledge when a large-boned, blonde woman appeared from behind a row of shelving with manila folders that Margaret assumed were medical files. "How may I help you?" Her nametag read: Schneider, G., and her uniform was nurse attire.

"Um, yes, we have an appointment with Dr. Wedleby," Margaret told her. "It's for Fiona Cavanaugh."

Nurse Schneider glanced at them. "Which of you is the patient?"

Fiona's body trembled against her, where their arms joined, but she remained silent. "She is," Margaret said.

The nurse glanced at Fiona, reached a conclusion, and nodded. "Okay. Well, you're early, but I can take you back and get you ready for your examination." She glanced at Margaret. "You're welcome to have a seat or come back in about two hours."

This time Fiona's response was louder and Margaret

loosened the arm holding Fiona's, moved it to her waist, giving a supportive squeeze. "I'm not leaving her. If that's a problem, tell me now, and we'll both go."

"We only let immediate family members—"

"I'm her sister-in-law," Margaret said. She doubted the woman would appreciate it if she announced being the wife or significant other. It wasn't like their bond was recognized since she'd married Fiona in her guise of Fionn 'Finn' Cavanaugh, her deceased brother. "Her brother Fionn, my husband, is unavailable. He died. If this isn't sufficient to constitute immediate family…"

Nurse Schneider raised a bushy blonde eyebrow and looked to Fiona for confirmation. "You have no problem with this?"

"No. I want Margaret to assist with the explanations of my situation, and to hear what the doctor learns from the tests." Fiona gave a one-shoulder shrug. "I don't think I can do this on my own. I need her." Margaret's heart was ready to shatter, recognizing how much it took for Fiona to acknowledge weakness, let alone to a stranger.

"Very well, then." She moved away, then the door beside them opened, and she said, "Right this way."

TESSA QUIETLY MADE her way into the shop, so she didn't inadvertently startle Jo. Not that it would have mattered. Jo's concentration appeared to be anywhere but on the task of sanding the display case in front of her. It took a moment before Jo's vision shifted in recognition of her presence with a softly spoken, "Sorry."

"You okay?" Tessa asked.

Jo shrugged and then scrubbed both hands across her face. "Yeah, preoccupied, I guess."

"Care to share?" she asked. "I can be a good listener, promise."

Jo managed a small smile. "I don't doubt it. At least you haven't been so far. A bad listener, that is." She dropped the barely used sandpaper strip on the display's top and clasped Tessa's hand in one of her own, tugging Tessa with her onto the floor. They leaned back against the display case, Jo gently draped an arm over Tessa's shoulder. Tessa allowed Jo to pull her into an embrace. She relished these moments in Jo's arms, her cheek pressed against Jo's chest.

"This is between us?" Tessa nodded. "Fiona and Margaret

left early this morning to see a brain specialist at Fitzsimons Army Hospital in Aurora."

"About her headaches and the bouts of blindness?"

Tessa felt rather than saw Jo's nod. "Much as I'm praying for a positive diagnosis, I find I can't be too hopeful." Jo pinched roughly at her nasal bridge with thumb and forefinger. Tessa wondered if Jo attempted to staunch the onslaught of tears. "It will kill Fiona to go blind permanently. She'll think she can't protect and care for us. Sometimes I want to yell at her to knock it off, but Fiona will see herself as a burden."

"Is that why you're worried, because of Fiona's feelings of self-worth? Well, lack of them, anyway."

"What if it's worse than we imagine?" Jo asked. "It has me scared."

"When do they return?" Tessa asked. She placed a hand on Jo's thigh and rubbed the pad of her thumb in small circles. Jo and Fiona weren't blood sisters, but there was no denying the familial strength of their bond. A bond she found herself a bit jealous and a lot envious of, especially when thinking of Jo during the long hours that Tessa lay alone in bed at night. If she could keep Warren from interfering, Tessa hoped to be included in the Cavanaugh family unit. She loved, even if she didn't respect, her brother. Tessa loved Jo even more. She'd found she had a stronger bond with these women than she ever did with her flesh and blood relations.

"Tomorrow, sometime, barring anything we haven't planned for in our discussions about this visit." The statement caused Tessa to chuckle. Jo had explained some of the dynamics in their house. She wished for the same in her own, knew it would never happen.

"The family night discussion?" she asked.

Jo chuckled. "You probably think they're corny, huh?"

Tessa shook her head. "Quite the opposite, Jo. Knowing you all talk about stuff, then come to agreeable conclusions is wonderful. In my family, first with my parents and now Warren, I'm told how I should act and feel, what I will do for the sake of the family, like it or not." She gave a weak smile. "I'd give anything to be part of a family like yours."

She felt the warmth of comfort and care as Jo's hand covered hers. "You are part of our family, at least from the Cavanaugh side of the matter. You mean a lot to us, to me."

Twisting her hand, palm up, Tessa weaved her fingers between Jo's. "Thank you, Jo, that makes me feel nice inside." Jo gave a quick squeeze of their joined hands. She hoped Jo didn't just say the words to make her feel better. There was such comfort in her mind, her body, and her heart when she was in the presence of Jo. When Tessa wasn't with her, thoughts of their time together, even the silent moments, brought peace to Tessa. However, as mature as she tried to be, Tessa's head couldn't get away from one nagging question: Why?

"Why what?" Jo asked.

Tessa hadn't realized she posed the question aloud. "Nothing," she said, shaking her head and pasting on a smile. She could feel the smile was awkward, fake, by the stiffness.

Jo must have realized it, too. She shifted, stared directly at her, Jo's expression serious. "Please don't do that to us, Tessa. Don't let us keep secrets, even if we think we're protecting each other. Fiona tried to protect Margaret from worry by not telling her the truth. It hurt Margaret more, even if Fiona hadn't intended her silence in that way." Jo frowned, then looked startled. "Um, you know how I feel about you, right? You know I treasure our relationship as more than simply a girlfriend?" Tessa felt Jo's body go rigid, right before she tried to pull her hand free. "Oh, golly, what have I—"

Tessa squeezed their joined hand, used her other to latch on to Jo's elbow, and pull her body back against her. "Stop, Jo, please." Tessa breathed in deeply, slowly expelling the breath. "You've been in my heart and my head since your first hello and introduction. I know most people believe we're wrong to feel the way I feel for you, another woman, especially after such a short time, but I can't stop my heart. I want us to be together for all time."

"Then, I don't understand your question. Tessa, I want what Fiona and Margaret have with one another, even if they can't announce it like most people in love. And I don't care for the secrecy that involves, but we can live in a cave if it means I spend the rest of my life with you. Yes, we barely know anything about each other, but I want to learn everything. We haven't known one another for very long, know I'm still considered a kid, but I believe my heart and my heart wants you."

Tessa felt the tears building. "I want you, too. It's just that..." After Jo's announcement, Tessa's fears felt so stupid but unavoidable. Mentioning it now would belittle her in Jo's eyes, wouldn't it?

"No secrets and no fears, Tessa."

Focusing on their clasped hand, Tessa said, "I don't

understand what you see in me." She didn't want to see whatever expression the comment generated.

Jo was silent for such a long time, Tessa couldn't help herself. The tension of waiting for a response was tight in her chest like a fist squeezing her heart. Against her better judgment, she lifted her gaze to Jo's face. Jo's expression was honest confusion, a puzzle she was giving her best to solve.

After what seemed forever, but probably less than a minute, Jo asked, "What don't I see in you? You have a quiet, patient soul. You're tender, talented, beautiful," Jo quirked a corner of her lip. "You have pretty good taste in women. How you're single, I don't understand, but no complaining if it means I get to spend time with you."

The words, spoken with passion, even a touch of teasing, warmed Tessa's cheeks. How could she be any less honest? "You're the beautiful one, Jo. Anyone, man or woman, would love to have you interested in them. I'm homely and destined to be a spinster."

"That's where I'm confused, honey." Jo pulled Tessa against her chest. "My eyes, my heart, see only beauty when regarding you. Maybe others, even you, don't understand what I see, but isn't my opinion and, believe it or not, judgment, important to you too?"

"Thank you for liking what you see, Jo. Guess I'm a dope, forcing a compliment to make me feel better." Tessa could tell Jo meant them from her tone, even if Tessa didn't believe them toward herself.

Tessa felt the vibrating rumble of contained laughter in Jo's chest before she released it in a hearty laugh. "Is that what was happening? Fishing for a compliment? I thought this was about distracting me from worry over Fiona. No matter, it worked."

Chapter Twenty

THREE DAYS HAD passed since the dinner with Warren when Tessa heard the noise from the outside stairwell. She might otherwise have missed the sound if she weren't still awake with worry for Jo, Margaret, and Fiona, replaying in her head. There the sound was again. The rattle as if someone were trying to get the door open. Her heart thudded in her chest with panic.

Someone was trying to break into her home. Was it the same person murdering women in Pueblo? Her first thought should have been to call her brother or to call the police. She hadn't realized who she dialed until the sleep-heavy voice of Jo answered, "Hello?"

"Jo, someone is trying to break in," she whispered into the receiver.

"Tessa? Okay, honey, I'm coming. The new lock should hold until I get there but find somewhere to hide until I arrive." When nothing else was said, Tessa realized Jo had hung up.

Quiet as she could, and careful not to move too quickly and announce her location, Tessa made her way to the bedroom, grabbed a hat pin off the dresser, and crammed herself as far back into the armoire as she could squeeze, and then closed the door.

Tessa had no idea how long she waited or what she waited for, other than to hear Jo's reassuring voice. But she couldn't hear anything. Hidden away, time, and sound shut off from her. She wondered if she should open the armoire door to check if the intruder had left, but fear had her worried that she'd walk right into the arms of a killer.

Then Tessa realized she could make out slight sound, muffled shouts, and then— Was that a gunshot? Followed by more shouts. Oh, dear Lord, was Jo out there? Had she come to help Tessa, only to get in the way of the killer? Body trembling, imagining all manner of horrific scenarios that ended badly for Jo, Tessa began to cry. Pounding footsteps echoed through the outer stairwell, and then the rattle of the apartment door. Tessa clamped a hand over her mouth to stifle the startled exclamation. No sooner had she done so, then the blessed sound of Jo's panicked voice reached her.

"Tessa? Tessa, where are you?"

Tears streamed down her face as she pushed open the armoire door, struggled to her feet, and launched herself into Jo's waiting arms. "Oh, Jo, I am so sorry."

Jo's embrace grew tighter, but Tessa caught the sound of her quiet laughter. "Honey, why are you sorry?"

"I put you in danger when I called you. You could've been killed. For being a bother. I woke you. I heard gunshots. Oh God, I was—"

Jo pushed Tessa an arm's length away and stared at her with incredulity. "The shots fired were a warning. I'm fine. Have you any idea how I would have felt if I couldn't have been here for you?" Tessa stared at her and saw Jo's confusion and frustration. "I can't let anyone down again. Especially not now, not with you."

Tessa recognized her own confusion. Jo hadn't let her down. Why did she believe she had? "Jo?" Tessa never got any further in her inquiry, interrupted by a soft knock at the apartment door.

"Excuse me, Miss Langford?" Tessa recognized Randall Braddock's voice.

She moved away from Jo and turned toward the door. "Just a minute," she said, grabbing her robe from the foot of the bed and pulled it on. Jo flashed a smile, probably meant to offer reassurance. As Tessa made her way to the young officer, she felt the warm addition of Jo's hand to her lower back. The small gesture filled Tessa with feelings of safety, more so than the presence of the male police officer.

"How are you doing, ma'am? Do I need to take you to the hospital?" Randall asked.

She shook her head. "No, no, I'm fine." Tessa pointed to the couch. "May I sit down?"

Randall nodded. "Of course, my apologies." He remained standing until both she and Jo sat down, Jo grasped her hand as if feeding Tessa strength through their combined grip. "Thanks to Jo's phone call, and me working late, I arrived in time to see the perpetrator attempt to enter the premises." He smiled at her. Tessa saw in his eyes and his expressions, a resolve that would make him a great police officer. And an empathy her brother would never possess. Tessa hoped men like her brother wouldn't dissolution him from his chosen career. "I won't bore you but, suffice it to say, we caught the guy. He is in our custody." He flashed a grimace. "Also, as a matter of protocol, your brother has been notified."

Tessa nodded her understanding even if she wished he

hadn't needed to make that call. "What happens now?" she asked.

"I'll survey the scene, make notes, and go back to the station to write up my report." Randall shot a quick glance and wink to Jo, then said, "You probably saved your own life, not just hearing and alerting us, but having new locks put in. I hope an incident like this doesn't happen again but, if a next time, call the police first."

Tessa felt embarrassment heat her face. "I was scared and not thinking clearly."

"Since it worked out, I won't scold you further." Randall again glanced at Jo. "You'll stay for a while? The sergeant should be here soon." Jo nodded, and Randall moved to the door, prepared to close it behind him when angry footfall stomped up the stairs.

Tessa heard her brother's arrival and was confused by his tone. "Was the body position like the others?" Why would Warren assume her dead? And why from the killer of the other women? Had the killer changed his method?

Randall pushed the door back open and preceded Warren. "Your sister is alive and well," Randall said. Tessa was certain she caught a look of surprise, followed by a flush of anger before he schooled his features into one of concern.

"You okay?" Warren asked. Tessa nodded. Her non-verbal reassurance appeared to settle the matter enough to allow him to move on. With a toss of his head in Jo's direction, he demanded, "Why is she here at this time of the night?"

Before she or Jo had a chance to respond, Randall stepped beside Warren. "I called Jo over, considering the circumstances, I thought it best for Miss Langford to have a familiar face and a female present, until you were found." Rather than answer, Warren growled his displeasure. Randall must have sensed the growing tension because he directed his attention to Warren. "Sergeant, I'll walk you through the events. Then take you to the man we caught attempting to break into your sister's home." He stretched an arm toward the door. "After you, Sergeant." Reluctantly, Warren left. To Jo, Randall said, "I'll let you know when you can secure the premises again." Randall followed Warren, soundly closing the door behind them.

When alone, Tessa stood. "I need tea. Will you join me?" Jo followed but, in the kitchen, steered her into a chair at the kitchen table. After Tessa sat, sure to pronounce her huff of indignation, Jo moved to the stove and set the kettle to boil. Both were silent until Jo placed a cup of hot tea before her and sat in the chair next to Tessa. Jo clasped Tessa's hand, and Tessa squeezed back. "Thank you for coming."

"I will always come when you need me." She gave a lopsided grin before adding, "It's a Cavanaugh thing." Jo's thumb moved in small circles on the top of Tessa's hand. Tessa wondered if Jo were even aware it. "Can I do anything for you? Get you anything?" Jo asked.

"No, I'm fine." She sighed. "I don't want to talk about what happened tonight if that's okay?"

"Okay." Jo didn't stop the movement of her thumb as they sat in silence. Less than a quarter-hour later, a soft knock sounded at the door. Jo stood up. "That should be Randall. I'll lock up downstairs and be right back."

AT THE BOTTOM of the outer stairwell door, Jo thanked Randall for all he'd done. "I think that's the guy who broke into our house, attacked, and shot Fiona."

"Yeah, one better," Randall said. "He's probably the killer. I recognized him from the picture your sister and Mr. Tirrell brought in."

"Then I'm especially glad you were still at the station. You can show up Warren for getting the killer plaguing Pueblo, while he was dragging his feet."

Randall grimaced. "He did more than drag his feet. Be careful, will you? And take care of Tessa. She may still be in danger."

"What do you mean?" she asked. Randall glanced over his shoulder, bumping into her. The action seemed intentional. Randall shook his head and offered her a good night before he turned and walked away.

Once he left, Jo relocked the door, twisted and tugged the handle to assure it was secured. Before she made her way upstairs, Jo pulled the item Randall had covertly placed in her coverall pocket. It was a key. Not just any key. This key was the one the man attempted to use to enter the premises, Jo wondered how surprised he was to learn it no longer worked. Jo should probably be surprised by the implication, but she wasn't at all. She had no delusions of the perfidy of blood relations.

Jo swore there'd be no secrets between them. But how could she share this evidence with Tessa? This was different, right? She would let Tessa maintain her illusions of Warren. Wasn't that the loving thing to do? Jo didn't owe Warren any favors, but hurting Tessa wasn't her intent. No one other than her and Randall would know of this key being in the man's possession. She strongly doubted Warren would question why it wasn't included in evidence. Asking would only implicate him in his attempt to have his sister murdered. Jo would have to stay on her toes to assure Warren didn't complete another attempt. If she hadn't changed the locks the day before, Warren—or whoever—would have succeeded in killing Tessa. If she didn't share this development with Tessa, how could Tessa prepare herself for more of Warren's attempts? Jo swallowed back a wail of outrage.

She needed to talk to her sister, maybe bring it up in the family meeting on Fiona's return from Denver. Rubbing tiredly at her face, Jo made her way upstairs.

Jo closed the door and threw the bolts. In her absence, Tessa had returned to the couch, her legs tucked close under a crocheted blanket she'd draped from her waist down.

Quietly, Jo asked, "Can I get you more tea?"

Tessa blinked rapidly for a few seconds before she turned her attention to Jo. "No, thank you." Tessa pat the space near her feet. "Sit with me, please?"

Jo nodded, dropped on the couch, slowly expelling a breath. "You lead an exciting life, Miss Langford."

Snorting, Tessa said, "Someone else can have this kind of excitement. I prefer dull and boring if tonight was the alternative." Tessa sat up and snuggled into Jo, arranged the blanket so it covered both of their legs. "This is nice." A pause. "Jo?"

"Mm-hmm." Jo shifted, so Tessa's head rested just over her breast and dropped her arm to rest against Tessa's side and hip.

"Will you tell me how you think you let me down?" Tessa's hand brushed across Jo's stomach. "Was it in Boston?"

Jo didn't know what to say. She wanted to be upfront and honest with Tessa, but this pain went deep. Tessa's positive opinion of her could drastically change. Especially the more she learned of Boston. Tessa wouldn't gossip about the information Jo shared, she recognized that about Tessa. What if she was wrong? Her silence must've gone for too long.

Tessa said, "It's okay. I understand if you can't tell me."

The dejection in Tessa's tone broke Jo's heart. She trusted Tessa, cared for her deeply. Would this be the wedge to separate them? Jo couldn't let that happen. She told Tessa about her parents selling her to a brothel for drugs. Would this be worse?

After all, she hadn't any control over the events that had transpired five years ago. If she had only been a little faster, results could have been different. Jo drew in a deep breath. "Promise me, Tessa, if at any point this is too disturbing, you'll have me stop." Jo felt the rub of Tessa's head as she nodded.

Squeezing her eyes closed and taking a bracing breath, Jo said, "It's the reason Fiona and Margaret are in Denver. We believe the cause of Fiona's headaches and blindness have to do with what happened in Boston before we left. My parents sold me for drugs, unaware or uncaring what was in store for me. But for Fiona," Jo paused, her hand rubbed at Tessa's hip. "Maybe I should preface this first. In Boston, Fiona was known as Finn, a sixteen-year-old boy who drove and ran errands for Margaret's brother, Eldon. Fiona was so handsome as Finn, more so when Margaret dressed her in a suit and fedora."

Jo felt the vibrations of Tessa's laughter. "Oh, I can imagine she was a sight to behold. Bet you would have given her a run for the title of most handsome." Jo hoped Tessa meant it and wasn't just tossing idle compliments.

Continuing, Jo said, "Eldon was in his usual selfish-ass mode. Finn worked for him and had to do as he asked. They went to one of his speakeasies. It was a night we all shared a place in Fiona's hell."

Sobering, Jo said, "Jimmy Bennett, Eldon's next in command, had beaten and shot her, and he... he —"

"It's okay, Jo. You don't have to give all the details." Jo felt reassured with Tessa's gentle squeeze of her shoulder.

"Her Browning was near her. I picked it up and held it tight. I wanted it in case I needed to protect her. I couldn't let anyone else hurt Fiona. Margaret got there, and she'd brought Fiona's cop friend, Ian, and her friend Janice. We covered Fiona with a tablecloth. She took the gun from me." Jo gave a watery bark of laughter, realized she'd started to cry with the memory. "Made it easier to pull Fiona into my arms. Margaret begged me to let go so Ian could pick her up, take her to the hospital. Margaret had to physically pry me away."

"Would expect nothing less, honey. She is your sister in your heart, if not blood." Tessa began rubbing Jo's arm. It was a gesture that provided the comfort she needed during the telling of that horrible night.

"Fiona will always be more than a blood sister." Jo inhaled deeply. "I had to apologize to Margaret for not being there on time. If I'd been quicker, tried harder — I tried, but I was too late.

Fiona had already been hurt. Margaret told me I couldn't have done more." Jo gave a little shrug, careful not to lose Tessa's supportive arm. "Eldon refused to go to the hospital, so Margaret had to deal with him. I know she was trying to make me feel better when she had me ride to the hospital with Fiona. I was too worried to argue."

Tessa said, "That may have been part of it, Jo. Maybe Margaret felt a sense of relief that you'd be there for Fiona, the woman you both love so much."

"I can accept that reason. Anyway, Eldon Graham died that night. Fiona was in a coma for nearly two weeks, and we weren't sure if she would live or come out of the coma. We thought her survival was a miracle. At the time, it was one, a miracle, I mean." Jo felt the renewed tears as they trickled down her cheeks. "Now it appears it was merely a temporary reprieve." Jo roughly swiped at her tears. "One of the men arrested that night was Fiona's father. He had egged Jimmy on in his attack, saying it was the only way to teach Fiona a lesson. Teach her what women should expect as their place in a man's life."

Tessa sat up, cupped Jo's face in her hands. "Maybe it was a reprieve. God's will she put you all on the right paths. I see how protective you all are of one another. Sometimes, it does take a lifetime for our footprints to be placed on God's path." Tessa tapped a finger to Jo's chest. "Fiona's are protected here, making you the caring, loving, and compassionate person anyone would want to emulate. A person any other decent person would proudly call a friend."

Jo didn't know how to respond or even if she should. Could she love this woman anymore? She swallowed hard against the stark reality of her admission, even if only to herself. She shifted, Tessa lay against her side, pulled the blanket higher to cover them both. Jo kissed the top of Tessa's head. "Thank you. Now close your eyes, and let's try to get a little sleep. The morning will be here before you know it."

Chapter Twenty-one

THE TESTING WAS exhausting. Fiona returned from the last one only moments ago. She and Margaret were left to wait for Dr. Wedleby's diagnosis. Fiona wanted nothing more than for Margaret to drive her to the hotel they'd reserved for the night, and to rest cradled in the comfort of Margaret's arms. She suspected the findings would not be positive but came to a conclusion during the most strenuous of the tests she'd undergone. Fiona couldn't become like those patients seen in the waiting room. She couldn't be a burden to her loved ones, especially Margaret, but she couldn't take the chance surgery wouldn't leave her as a shell of who she currently was either.

"Are you okay? Damn, a stupid question. Of course, you aren't," Margaret said. She placed a warm hand on Fiona's lower back bared in the examination gown. Margaret placed a soft kiss on her temple and said, "I'm sorry, sweetheart."

"This is difficult for us both. I can't hold you responsible for my jittery nerves."

Margaret laid her forehead on Fiona's shoulder, and Fiona leaned back into her, needing the contact to stabilize her. "Whatever happens, we'll get through it together and as a family." Fiona caught the catch in Margaret's voice, though she tried to cover the emotion with a cough. Growling her frustration, Margaret straightened. "Where the hell—"

Fiona nearly chuckled when the door slowly opened to allow Dr. Wedleby to enter, his gaze focused on the clipboard in hand. The eyeglass lenses were so thick as to be telescopic, making his eyes appear about four times their size. Margaret, nearly caught in her outburst of exasperation, was almost as amusing. With her emotions jumbled, Fiona feared laughing at either of them now would result in her bursting into uncontrollable tears. "What's the verdict, Doctor?" she asked instead.

He pushed his glasses up the bridge of his nose with a finger, glanced at Margaret, and then settled his attention on Fiona. "Having Dr. Matthews send your medical file ahead of this visit, not to mention our telephone conversation, spared a lot of time and testing, which you may be surprised to learn would be more extensive. Unfortunately, the conclusion isn't an easy one to hear."

"Which is?" Margaret's hand, still resting on her back, stilled.

"The damage to Fiona over four years ago caused a small amount of blood to pool in her brain. The pressure, as it shifts, is straining the optical nerves."

"Why didn't Edwin fix or have it fixed then?" Margaret's sharp tone belied her fear. The scope of this issue would have been beyond Edwin's capability, she knew.

Wedleby shook his head. "It wouldn't have been noticeable, especially with all the damage done, which he did correctly monitor and repair. By all accounts, Mrs. Cavanaugh, your sister-in-law is lucky to have lived at all."

Fiona felt Margaret bristle. Before she could launch into a verbal attack, Fiona asked, "What now?"

"Well, we would cut out a small section of the skull so we could find and drain the obstruction. Once that is completed, we would stitch you up. It would take a while, but the hair will grow back, possibly enough to cover most of the scar. A scar, mind you, is a small price to pay." He glanced at the chart again. "From your medical records, you aren't a stranger to them."

Fiona wanted to shout at him, "Thanks for the reminder." Instead, she asked, "How long, without the procedure, before the damage is permanent?"

"Miss Cavanaugh, I don't believe you grasp the immediacy or the complexity of the situation."

"How much time?"

Glancing around the room, the doctor spotted the rollaway stool, pulled it closer to the exam table, and sat down heavily. "It is hard to pinpoint with any accuracy. You could become fully blind anywhere from six months to a year, barring any additional injury or head trauma." He tossed the clipboard on the table and crossed his arms. "What you may not understand is that the headaches will not only increase in pain, debilitating in and of themselves, but the clot will continue to shift. If not eradicated, the damage will eventually kill you."

Margaret gave a strangled cry. Fiona reached behind her with a trembling hand and clasped onto Margaret's hand. "I can prescribe something for the headaches, but it is not going to fix the problem, only dull it for short periods. You need surgery, and the sooner, the better."

Fiona nodded. "I understand, truly, I do. Margaret and I need to discuss this. There's a lot to consider. Margaret teaches school, and I have a business I can't ignore." Oh yeah, and she'll be my designated nursemaid if you turn me into a drooling flesh-bag, Fiona refrained from responding. "This isn't a decision I can make lightly on my own or without input from the family."

Wedleby's head bobbed in acknowledgment. He slapped his palms on his thighs, startling Margaret enough to flinch, and stood. "Please, Miss Cavanaugh, do not postpone too long. I'll hold your file until you contact me, but I hope to see you within the month." He looked directly at Fiona. "I'll have a prescription ready for you at the hospital pharmacy." He extended his hand. "It is a pleasure meeting you, though the circumstances are not the best."

"Same here, Doctor," Fiona said, returning the handshake. "Thank you." With a nod at her, then shaking Margaret's hand, Dr. Wedleby left the room. She stepped down from the exam table and began getting dressed.

Neither she nor Margaret spoke until they'd returned to the truck. Resolutely, Fiona twisted toward Margaret, who, from the tremble in her hands on the steering wheel, barely contained her emotions. Pushing her panic aside, Fiona infused her tone with as much playfulness as she could and said, "I need a hot bath, and sure could use some company."

Margaret gave a laugh that sounded like a choked sob. "Hope the intended company is me."

"Who else—" Fiona saw the twitch to the corner of Margaret's mouth. "You're such a comedian." Fiona squeezed Margaret's thigh. "It will always only be you for me. You know that, right?" Margaret nodded solemnly. "Then, get me to that bathtub."

THE HOTEL ROOM was far grander than Margaret expected, grateful for the surprise after the depressing news from the doctor. She'd been in hotels with more grandeur and opulence years ago, but this was different. Fiona's presence made it special.

Fiona made everything special to Margaret.

The bellboy placed their bags on the bed and bowed out of the room after Margaret pressed the tip into his palm. When the door closed, Fiona engaged the lock. Before she could turn around, Margaret was behind her, wrapping her arms around Fiona's waist. She nuzzled her lips to the soft flesh behind Fiona's ear and lightly placed a kiss before she whispered, "Did you want to eat in the dining room before we settle in?"

"Would you mind if we just stayed in the room?" Fiona's

head lowered, chin to chest. "You can order something brought up, but I'm not really hungry."

"No," Margaret said, "you've had a rough day, and I understand." She truly did, knew the stress would have ruined Fiona's appetite rather than increased it. If she thought about it, Margaret wasn't all that hungry either. They could use coffee, and the bath they spoke of earlier. "Let me order something light and hot to drink. We need a little something in our stomachs like it or not." She gave Fiona's waist a squeeze. "Then, we'll sit in the tub until our skin prunes."

Fiona gave a low chuckle. "Sounds like heaven. I'll prepare the tub." Fiona spun around to face her, placing a kiss on the tip of Margaret's nose.

It only took a few minutes to place an order and set out their evening clothes. Once the food was delivered, Margaret threw the bolt and removed her clothing before she joined Fiona in the bathroom.

She paused for a moment, taking in the sight of a naked Fiona in the bubble-filled bath. Margaret smiled. The bubbles would be for her, Fiona hating the feminine frivolity. All the things going on in her life and Fiona never once put herself and her wants or needs first. No matter what happened, Margaret would never — could never — find another woman whose warmth, tenderness and love could come even halfway close to Fiona's heart. As depressing as the future loomed after today's diagnosis, Margaret knew she would do anything in her power — including resigning from her teaching job — to spend every moment of every day with Fiona, for as long as Fiona needed.

With a deep breath of resolve, Margaret entered the room.

She slid behind Fiona, the water level rising to their chests. They were silent, knowing that vocalizing would be the fatal blow that destroyed the shaking walls containing Fiona's emotion. So, they sat, the hot water caressing their skin, her fingers encouraging small ripples to spin around them. Fiona shifted and pressed herself tightly against Margaret's body, and Margaret felt Fiona's palm settle against her knees.

Fiona would be working through the pros and cons, the causes and effects of every move or option available to her. This was how Fiona cared for the people she loved. This was Fiona making certain the people in her life were not adversely affected by any decision she made.

When Fiona's palm slid up Margaret's inner thighs, elbows poking up from the water, Margaret realized Fiona had reached a decision and was ready to share. Margaret understood, whether she approved or disapproved of the result, Fiona would also provide a reason — whether sound or not to anyone but Fiona — for her conclusion.

Fiona breathed deeply, the action again pressed her into Margaret, and Margaret further against the smooth contours of the iron tub. Margaret lowered her head, pressed her lips to the damp flesh where the neck meets the shoulder, and placed three consecutive kisses.

"I can't have the surgery, Margaret," Fiona said, her voice husky with emotion. She remained silent while she waited for Fiona to get through her thought process. "I won't deny seeing those people today hasn't influenced my decision, because the sight had a great deal to do with it."

Margaret squeezed her eyes shut, rewarded with the image of those in the waiting room. The doctor had explained those patients were the more serious cases, some without the benefit of quicker medical attention. He was adamant the case wouldn't be the same for Fiona. He couldn't guarantee it wasn't a possibility either. She opened her eyes when Fiona continued. "I'll let Jo take on more responsibility, especially with the driving and deliveries. For the most part, I will continue, as usual, being available when you come home from work and putting you above all else."

"But Fiona —"

"No honey, for the sake of everyone, we need to maintain the guise of normality. I won't have the family overly worried. Please, Margaret, I can't have anyone seeing me with pity in their eyes." Fiona shrugged. Margaret wrapped her arms around Fiona's waist, leaned her head on Fiona's shoulder. "The timing isn't too bad, either. School break has started. Jo is getting orders for work on her own, and we have a new addition to the family who needs to be properly indoctrinated to a house of women."

Margaret chuckled. "Increasing the number from one to four can't be as difficult a transition as dealing with just one of Ethel."

"You may be correct in that matter." Fiona snickered, then just as quickly grew serious again. "I know I'm a glass-half-empty gal, but I think we may have another big problem."

"Whatever it is, we can handle it." Margaret raised her head and reached for the washing cloth, submerged it, and raised it above Fiona's shoulders. She squeezed so water dripped across Fiona's skin, running down across her small, firm breasts.

"I don't know about that, Margaret. There are things Richard has said in his little boy innocence." Fiona twisted, facing

Margaret, her expression of serious concern. "And I'm not the only one who reached this conclusion. Nicholas agrees too."

"Agrees with what, love?" A knot formed in her stomach. What could possibly be going on that involved— "Is Richard in danger? Are we?" Margaret's pulse quickened, heart beating so hard it was sure to burst from her chest. "Dear God, Fiona, are you in danger?"

Fiona shifted again, laying half alongside and a half on top of Margaret, her fingers glided from Margaret's hip to the underside of her breast, up and down, up and down in slow, gentle repetition. "It won't be like last time. But yes, I'm a little worried. For all of us."

"Oh, Fiona, I can't—" Margaret stopped herself. No, she wouldn't doubt they could get through this together. This time, she would be there, for and with Fiona, every step of the way. Margaret sat up in the water. Placing her palms on Fiona's cheeks, she said, "Promise me, Fiona, this time we handle whatever comes together. This time you don't go anywhere without me or someone with you. Promise me."

Fiona stared directly at her. "I promise to try. But there are a lot of variables that can't be weighed in."

The sincerity in her tone had Margaret give a pained grin. Fiona would try to keep her promise. They both knew fate sometimes interfered, no matter how much preparation was made or promises spoken. She bent and kissed Fiona. "I think we need to get out of the bath. We are both shriveled, which was our goal." Margaret got out first. She grabbed a towel for herself and handed another to Fiona. Fiona bent, pulled the rubber plug, and dropped the chain over the faucet. Once Fiona had towel-dried, wrapped the towel around herself, Margaret did the same and then pulled Fiona into her arms. "I had plans to ravish you thoroughly tonight."

"Margaret—" Margaret halted the words with a finger over Fiona's lips. Fiona obediently remained silent.

"If you won't be too disappointed, I'd rather just hold you." Fiona smiled. "I'll take that as a yes." She took Fiona's hand in hers and tugged her toward the door. Margaret suddenly stopped in the doorframe to the sleeping area, and Fiona bumped into her back. She spun to face Fiona. "I probably don't want to know, but I need to know. Who killed Ethel?"

Fiona's eyes darkened with anger. She was silent for so long, Margaret wondered if she should repeat the question. Then, soft yet steady, Fiona said, "Warren Langford."

Margaret groaned. "Why aren't matters ever easy?"

Eyes returning to their lighter caramel color, Fiona said, "The worthwhile things in life never are easy. That's why we have each other."

FROM THE SUBTLE tension and uneven breathing, Margaret could tell Fiona hadn't slept any more than she had. She wasn't in the least surprised. Then the tender explorations began. Margaret recognized Fiona's need for a physical connection. She could never deny Fiona. She wouldn't do so now either.

Margaret was always amazed by Fiona's tentative touches, so tender and yet conveyed a fear of doing harm. Not once in five years had Fiona harmed her or been too rough. It was as if Fiona believed she could snap and turn into the brutal monster her father had been, like so many of the men in Fiona's life. Margaret shifted, opened herself physically, and emotionally to Fiona's exploring hands and lips. She could feel Fiona's trembling and knew Fiona was afraid, seeking comfort in their physical contact. Words were not necessary. When Fiona stretched out on top of her, Margaret willingly and gladly accepted this moment. Her response tonight would be the catalyst for Fiona's acceptance of their future together — for however long.

Fiona, mound pressed against Margaret's clit, slowly rotated her hips. Margaret dug her blunted nails into Fiona's back, felt pleasure radiate down to her feet, and shoot back up to tingle across her scalp. She moaned in response. Fiona trailed her lips and tongue down and across Margaret's chest and, leaning forward, cupped Margaret's breast in her strong, calloused hand. She tugged on Margaret's erect nipples, brushed the pad of her thumb across and around the areola, causing it to pebble.

Her body's responses to Fiona's touch never failed to surprise her. Even after five years, each time felt new and astounding, amazed her at the strength and gentleness united in Fiona's hands. Fiona lowered her head and sucked a nipple into her mouth, then lashed it with her tongue. Fiona shifted slightly, performing the same rite to Margaret's other breast. "Oh, Fiona."

"I love you, my wife. You are so beautiful," Fiona whispered, her voice held the frantic tones of near desperation. Margaret slowly opened her legs to accommodate Fiona as she glided downward. Fiona placed kisses on Margaret's chest, stomach, and hips and, finally, between Margaret's thighs, kissed the softer flesh. Fiona paused. "Margaret." Margaret heard the anguish in

Fiona's tone. "You are my heart," she said and hoped to infuse her support into the words. If Fiona couldn't finish, Margaret would again hold her in her arms. She needed Fiona as much as Fiona needed her. Instead of ending this moment, Fiona nuzzled her cheek against Margaret's sex.

"Please, Fiona, I need you," she said, not acknowledging Fiona's emotional lapse. Margaret couldn't control the twitching of her hips. It was enough. She arched to bring herself closer to Fiona's hot breath whispering across her swollen and heated folds. Margaret whimpered, then gasped as Fiona's fingers traced a languid design through her wetness.

Fiona raised her head. "You have me. Always."

Margaret groaned in frustration. "Fiona—"

"Yes, love?"

Margaret gasped again when Fiona pushed two fingers deep inside her. Her back bowed. She felt Fiona push deeper and fill her. "Oh, Fiona, yes."

Fiona withdrew, paused, and pushed in again in a quick and deliberate stroke.

Margaret's mind and body were so focused on Fiona's fingers inside her, filling her, that she let loose a jagged cry when Fiona brushed her tongue against Margaret's clit.

Shifting licks on her clit and the pounding of fingers in and out made Margaret squirm then writhe as her inner muscles clenched. Margaret's orgasm hit hard and fast, arching her back from the mattress. Waves of pleasure followed until, boneless, Margaret fell back down. The aftershocks turned to a delicate shiver. Fiona gentled her motions, slowed until finally pulling out. Fiona's lips and tongue licked and kissed her tender flesh until Margaret's sated body stilled. Fiona lay her head on Margaret's thigh.

Then Margaret felt dampness that had nothing to do with their lovemaking. Fiona was crying. Tears filled Margaret's eyes, and she didn't brush them away. Instead, she quickly shifted, sliding down to meet Fiona's position, and gently maneuvered Fiona's head on her shoulder. She felt Fiona's pain and fear in the contact of their flesh. Fiona was losing control of herself, the very thing Fiona honed to bring strength to herself and her family. She didn't need to, Margaret knew, and suspected Fiona did, too. Margaret could tell her it was all right, but voicing the sentiment would only sever the tentative hold Fiona had on her emotions. Vocalizing anything at this moment would be Margaret's undoing as well. Together they silently cried. Margaret stroked

Fiona's head with as much tenderness as she could convey in her touch. Neither broke the silence. There was no need. Moments like this were how they conveyed their love.

Moments like this that Margaret suspected would need to happen frequently before they were no longer possible.

Chapter Twenty-two

THE POUNDING INSIDE Fiona's head increased. She slowed the truck and pulled over to the side of the road and turned the ignition off. She leaned forward, resting her forehead on the steering wheel and waited out the worst of the pain. Since learning the diagnosis from the doctor, Fiona had limited certain activities, the most important being driving. She hadn't had much choice to avoid doing so this time, needing to get the chest-of-drawers to the Hager's in time for their daughter's delivery day. Luckily, two of the teenage Hager boys were on hand to unload and bring the chest inside.

Now Fiona hoped to complete the drive home without incident, but the blurring of her vision and the throbbing in her skull alerted otherwise. Now, for safeties sake, she had no other choice but to wait for this episode to end.

Fiona didn't know how much time had passed, and it had been nearly dusk when she'd started home, but total darkness consumed her when Fiona opened her eyes. The helpless feeling, which accompanied the night and the darkness, was disconcerting but not unexpected.

When she heard the rumble of an approaching vehicle, then the quick burst of a siren, Fiona felt a stab of panic. She silently prayed the officer would be Randall, the one police officer she trusted in Pueblo. Nothing against law enforcement, but Boston cops were easier to appreciate. Especially when one is your best friends' brother, like Ian Donnelly, and who treated you like a respected sibling. Luck, it seemed, wasn't to be on her side tonight.

"Get out of the truck," she heard Warren order from her opened truck window.

"Is there a problem, Sergeant?"

"I repeat, get out of the truck. Now."

Fiona took a deep breath, grudgingly accepted Warren could do anything to her, and she was helpless to stop him. She swallowed hard. In no hurry for trouble to start, Fiona slowly exited the truck and leaned against the door. "Is it a crime to stop here?"

"Why did you?" Warren asked, his tone belligerent. So, it would be business as usual.

"I wasn't feeling well. I decided to pull over for safety reasons, for my wellbeing, and for others on the road." Fiona could feel his agitation.

"Why are you out here, a woman all alone." Warren hadn't needed to note the point or make *woman* sound like something vile in his mouth. Which for him, probably was a word hard to say since he wouldn't know one if she slammed into him.

Fiona felt the stirrings of panic. She'd heard that tone of voice before, suffered the wrath of a male in need of exerting power and control. That instance had brought on this damage after a coma and weeks in a hospital. She had to stall for time, think of a way out of this situation. "I dropped a cabinet order off at the Hager's. You can check."

"How do I know you aren't up to no good now?" Fiona felt when he shifted closer. "Maybe you have buddies out here. You're from Boston, gangsters, right? Doing something illegal, Miss Cavanaugh?"

"Don't be ridiculous." Fiona clipped the title, "Sergeant."

"You've interfered with my job. Made some wet-behind-the-ears-kid take over my murder case," Warren said. He grabbed her by the shirt and shoved her into the truck. He backhanded her hard. "You made a fool out of me."

Fiona raised an eyebrow as blood pooled in her cheek. "You do that well enough by yourself. Being a brute only confirms it. Let me remind you that you blew us off when we broached the hobo possibility to you." Guess he's not worried about accusations of police brutality, she thought.

Her head felt like a sledgehammer pounded a dozen spikes through her skull. Her vision hadn't returned. She might as well give him a reason, she thought. Better he kills her outright, rather than shoot, rape, and beat her as Jimmy had done. On the positive side, there would be no audience to Warren's personal entertainment. "Is this really because of Randall handling Ethel's case?" Fiona smirked. "Or because you can't control Tessa's heart, and who she gives it too?"

"It's not right. People will talk." Fiona couldn't see but suspected his features contorted in distaste at the admission.

"Which reason pisses you off, Warren? I suspect people talking. Do you believe folks will blame you? If not this matter, there will always be something else to gossip about in town. Tessa loves Jo, and Jo her. You don't have to like it. But, if you love Tessa, you'll accept and continue to love her." Self-destructive as it was, Fiona couldn't help but add the jibe, "Is it that we'll be in-laws?" Fiona felt Warren shift before her jaw exploded with pain.

Without the closeness of his body and the hold on her shirt, Fiona would probably have dropped to the ground. She thought she vaguely heard another vehicle approach, but her stomach was roiling, her skull throbbed in excruciating pain, and Fiona fought desperately to maintain consciousness. Weak as she was, it wouldn't benefit her to taunt an angry man, but Fiona never prided herself on intelligence, that being Margaret's forte. "This is about perceptions of your manhood, isn't it?"

Warren released his hold, and Fiona dropped to her hands and knees. Then, three things happened in quick succession. Warren kicked her in the stomach, Fiona vomited on his boots, and Fiona heard tires braking on gravel just as Brigid yelled. Warren jerked her to her feet and slammed her into the truck again.

Despite her best intentions, Fiona passed out.

"WHAT THE HELL?" Brigid said. The car's headlights landed on the scene beside the road, by Fiona's truck, and she knew true fear. Warren had the front of Fiona's shirt bunched in his fists, and her body pinned against the side of her truck. The pain etched on Fiona's features, even before Warren backhanded her across the cheek, caused bile to rise in Brigid's throat. Fiona dropped, Warren kicked her, then pulled her up and slammed her into the truck.

"That son-of-a-bitch," Nicholas snarled and brought the car to a sliding stop mere inches from the truck's bumper.

Brigid's feet ate up the distance in large swallows. "What the hell are you doing, Warren?" She could see Fiona wasn't conscious.

Warren didn't glance away from Fiona, but Brigid could see the smirk on his face. "I'm doing my duty as a man of the law, with evidence of possible criminal activity transpiring. Trying to get answers, and the perpetrator is uncooperative."

She wedged herself between them, her back against Fiona. She pushed with all her strength against Warren's' chest. Brigid didn't even budge him, but Warren released Fiona and took a couple of steps back. Nicholas joined them, whispered into Fiona's ear, and wrapped an arm around her waist. Fiona was not responsive. Crap. Brigid felt when Nicholas took Fiona's weight onto himself. "She's not a criminal, and hasn't done anything wrong," she said.

"How am I to know that?" Warren shot a glower toward Fiona. "Came upon a truck, engine off, on an empty road, and I'm not supposed to get suspicious?" He looked at Brigid then. "It's bad enough," he jutted a chin toward Fiona, "her sister, is panting around my sister like a lovesick puppy. Now I'm to turn a blind eye to criminal behavior?" There, Brigid realized, was the real reason Warren abused Fiona. He blamed Fiona, at least punished her, because Tessa loved someone he didn't approve of—another woman. "She resisted my attempts to question her." So that would be his defense. His word against Fiona's, should the matter get to that point, which it wouldn't.

"Are you arresting her?" Nicholas asked, his tone casual despite the circumstances. "If not, we'd like to get her home."

Warren glanced at each of them, shrugged, and said, "Yeah, she doesn't look too good. Don't want her getting sick in my car." He curled a lip in disgust. "Already puked on my boots."

Nicholas carried Fiona and placed her in the backseat of Nicholas's car. Brigid followed. Richard jumped from the front seat into the rear, tears building in his blue eyes. He plopped down by the far door and tapped his palms on his thighs. "Aunt Fiona can rest here," he said. Careful shuffling, a quick moan from Fiona, and she lay in a fetal position with her head on Richard's lap. Nicholas held the passenger door open for her.

Just before Brigid got in, Warren walked to the front of the car. Blocking the beam of one headlamp, he created a monstrous shadow on the road. "Hey, what about the damn truck?"

"We'll come back for it after we take care of Fiona," Brigid said, not hiding her anger and frustration with him.

"Nope, can't do that," Warren said, crossing his arms over his chest, then twisted to glance at the truck and then back at Brigid. "Looks like an abandoned vehicle to me. Anything could happen to it here, all by itself." He shrugged. "Guess I could get it towed."

Nicholas tensed as if prepared to attack him. Brigid placed a hand on his forearm. "You follow me in as I drive Fiona's truck."

Teeth gritted, Nicholas said, "I'll drive the truck, Brigid. Richard and Fiona need to know you're okay. This way, you're all together." He glanced at Warren. "We need to do this together. I don't trust him if we're separated. You drive in front, and I'll follow closely."

Brigid gave a reassuring smile, but she felt anything but heartened. She rushed to the driver's side of Nicholas's car and got in. Nicholas hadn't budged from the open passenger-side until her door closed. He made a pushing down gesture with his thumb. She nodded. "Richard, lock your door." As he reached up and pushed down, Nicholas reached inside and locked the other back door then the passenger door before closing it tight. She worried Nicholas would confront Warren, but he stayed out of reach and hurried to the truck.

Once started, Nicholas stuck an arm out the open window and waved her forward. Warren stared at her through the windshield, a wicked smirk on his lips. Brigid didn't hesitate. She placed the car in gear and, ignoring the fact Warren stood in front of the car, gave enough gas to confirm her intent to move forward whether Warren stayed in his current position or not. He shifted enough to avoid the car slamming into him. She glanced at him in the rearview mirror, noted when Nicholas pulled directly behind, and said, "Hang on everyone, we're going home."

If only I truly were, Brigid thought wistfully. She would've laughed at the thought but bit her bottom lip to contain the chance it would turn into a sob. She loved Colorado, loved Fiona and Margaret, enjoyed, and loved teasing Jo. Right now, though, Brigid wished with all her heart to be with her mother, arms wrapped around, as her mother whispered in her ear that everything would be okay.

Focused on driving as quickly as possible, but without giving Warren another reason to stop them, Brigid drove the car home, silently chanting, "Please let this be okay."

MARGARET WAS IN a panic. Fiona should have been home by now. Hell, she never should've taken the vehicle out alone. Fiona was usually much more responsible and agreed to be more so after the diagnosis. Margaret understood Fiona never held her personal care the same importance as she did of others she cared about. But why would she go out alone? What couldn't wait? And so many things were changing with Fiona. Margaret feared being left behind, no longer of use to her.

Had Fiona done something stupid because of her illness? Fiona was now emotionally distant from everyone, especially after the prognosis and her decision not to have the surgery. Margaret didn't fault her, not really. She couldn't imagine how she'd react when faced with a possibility that surgery could leave Fiona with brain damage, a drooling hunk of flesh sitting— A sob burst from her lips, and she slapped her fingers over her mouth to stanch anymore from escaping.

"What's wrong? Have you more news?" Jo asked.

Margaret, lost in thought, hadn't heard Jo enter the parlor. She shook her head. "Not since I called the Hager's. They said she left hours ago." Jo had noticed the missing piece of furniture. If she hadn't, they wouldn't have had a place to start looking for Fiona.

"Nicholas and Brigid should be returning soon," Jo said. She shoved her hands in her pockets. Margaret noted how much like Fiona Jo was. You'd never guess they weren't blood related. "He and I can go out looking for her."

"You mean we can go," Margaret corrected.

"Someone should stay if she returns when we're out," Jo said.

"Brigid will be home then." Margaret shook her head to staunch the tears that threatened to fall. "I can't wait around doing nothing. She may need me."

"I'm sorry, Margaret, you're right," Jo said. When Jo pulled her into a hug, Margaret couldn't keep from crying any longer. "Jeez, I'm sorry." Jo started to pull away, but Margaret held her tighter, buried her face on Jo's shoulder.

Margaret didn't know how long she latched on to Jo, but the sound of tires braking too hard, and then the crunch of metal had them releasing each other and darting for the front door.

She considered herself an even-tempered, rational woman, but when Margaret stood on the porch and took in the scene before her, all her resolve flew out the window.

Brigid was getting out of Nicholas's car and unlocking all the doors, apparently having fully stopped by clipping the front gate. Nicholas pulled up behind his car in Fiona's truck. Where in the hell was Fiona?

On the point of panic, all sound replaced by a mind-numbing vacuum of silence, Margaret stood helpless when it turned into dread. Nicholas reached into the backseat, cradled a body awkwardly into his arms before extricating himself and his burden from the car. Dear God, Fiona. The sound came roaring back. Jo jumped into the now-empty truck and raced away. Brigid lifted a distraught, crying Richard from the car and cradled him against her chest, calming him with words whispered in his ear. Nicholas's long strides had him up the walk and on the porch. Automatically, Margaret shifted aside to allow his passage into the house, afraid to ask the question screaming in her mind. Is Fiona dead?

Nicholas paused at the bottom of the staircase. He looked at her expectantly before Margaret realized he silently begged a direction. "Up. Last on the left." He was halfway up the stairs, his hip clipping the banister under the weight of Fiona in his arms and then righted himself before she finished speaking. Margaret quickly followed, hearing Brigid enter the house, close the front door, and head for the kitchen. She felt a bit of relief that Richard's crying had turned into sniffling hiccups.

In their room, Nicholas placed Fiona on the bed and removed her work boots. Margaret stopped in the doorway. He wouldn't be removing her boots if she was dead, right? Nicholas must have recognized her hesitancy and apprehension. He glanced at her with a weak smile. "Unconscious, but alive."

Margaret nodded and moved forward. She stopped at the foot of the bed, hands clasping and unclasping. She wanted to stretch out beside Fiona and touch her, hold her. Margaret knew she wouldn't, couldn't allow anyone to witness just how much she loved Fiona. Margaret suspected Nicholas recognized the way things were between them, but they never openly talked about it. His next words confirmed Nicholas understood and wasn't appalled.

"I sent Jo to get the doctor. Brigid is making tea and coffee. Busywork from Brigid will keep Richard calmer, too." When Nicholas stepped beside her, it took a concerted effort on her part to look away from Fiona's prone body toward him. "The best thing for Fiona right now is the comfort of loved ones. I understand how guarded you need to be for others, and don't know how demonstrative you might be with her, but she'll be shocked and frightened when she wakes up." He tilted his head in the direction of the bed. "If it were me hurting, I'd want to wake up with the woman I love beside me, holding me." He gave a mischievous grin. "At least until the doctor arrives."

"Thank you, Nicholas," she said. His usual intense gray eyes held only warmth and understanding.

"I'll wait downstairs," he said. He headed for the door, where he paused. "I'd like to stay for the doctor's report."

Margaret noted his concerned expression, but there was something else beneath. Did he believe Margaret would reject his concern, push him away? "Of course, Nicholas. You're her friend and always welcomed in this home."

Oddly to her, his face brightened considerably in his relief. "Thank you, Margaret." Nicholas grasped the doorknob. "I'll bring the doctor up as soon as he gets here." He pulled the door closed behind him. There was something odd, but curious, about Nicholas. Margaret decided she liked him. Besides, he accepted Fiona and Jo for their eccentricities and befriended them anyway.

Deciding she hadn't much time, especially given the speed which Jo drove off, Margaret wasted no more time crawling onto the bed and stretching out beside Fiona. She slung an arm across Fiona's waist for a quick squeeze to assure herself her wife truly was there and breathing. She started to undo the top couple of buttons on Fiona's work shirt but was distracted by the sight of dried blood in Fiona's nose. The slight smearing of blood beneath her nostrils indicated someone had swiped blood away. Had Fiona? Had Nicholas done it hoping to lessen Margaret's shock with Fiona's injuries? Was the bloody nose part of her illness or had—

She scanned Fiona from head to foot. On her cheek, the bruising from a strike. Her clothes were in good condition if not entirely free of sawdust. Did someone hit her? Who? Margaret should have thought to ask Nicholas what had happened, how they'd found her. It would have to wait. This time was for them. Questions would only stir the emotional turmoil.

Margaret raised herself on her elbow and leaned over Fiona. She placed a gentle kiss on Fiona's usually expressive lips, now pale as the rest of her. When her lips trembled, Margaret pulled back to find Fiona's eyes opened, but her gaze unfocused.

Tears spilled down the sides of Fiona's face, pooling in her ears. "I'm so sorry, Margaret."

"Shush, honey. You've nothing to be sorry for."

Fiona gave a watery croak of disbelief. "I tried. I tried to be careful. I didn't know he'd find me."

"Rest now. We can talk about this later. Jo went to bring the doctor. Is there anything I should know about before he gets here?"

"Remember I love you," Fiona said with a sob, her body tensing.

"I never doubt that love," Margaret said. Well, she didn't doubt too much. She shifted and rested her head on Fiona's shoulders. She reached up to cup Fiona's cheek and jaw, brushed the pad of her thumb across Fiona's lips. "I'm just relieved you're safe and here with me."

"Margaret—"

"Honey, let me touch you. Before the night is over, everyone will be clamoring to check on you, so I don't know how long we'll be alone. Especially like this." The silence was Fiona's compliance. Margaret felt some of Fiona's tension recede. All too soon, footsteps sounded on the stairs. "I believe the prodding and the parade of well-wishers are ready to commence," Margaret said. She kissed the side of Fiona's cheek. Margaret climbed from the bed and pulled a chair to the bedside next to Fiona. "Are you ready?" she asked, right before the knock.

"Will it matter?" Fiona mumbled.

"Unfortunately, no." She opened the bedroom door.

The doctor insisted on examining Fiona alone, assuring Margaret it would only be a few minutes. Minutes or hours, Margaret had no intention of moving farther than the hallway outside the bedroom, which she now paced. Nicholas followed with his gaze as he leaned against the wall beside the door. Jo paced too, only her tread was more forceful and erratic. Margaret tried to offer comfort, but Jo's mood was too mercurial and volatile. Brigid opted to take Richard into her room so he wouldn't have to sleep alone. Margaret imagined Brigid needed the comfort of Richard, too.

After nearly an hour, Dr. Colby left the room, softly closing the door behind him. "Doctor?" Margaret's voice cracked. Nicholas stood erect, and Jo quit her pacing.

The doctor, voice barely above a whisper, said, "I'm pleased you were able to provide such a comprehensive medical history for me, Mrs. Cavanaugh. Regrettably, I can't conclude anything different than what the specialist stated. Miss Cavanaugh's blindness is probably permanent after this accident. Otherwise, she appears in exceptional health. I've given her a sedative to help sleep off the tension and disgruntlement. Not much I can do for her. Matter of time now."

Matter of time? Disgruntlement? Margaret's knees gave out, and she would have fallen to the floor in a heap if Nicholas hadn't caught her. Was the doctor truly that insensitive? Or was Margaret herself being overly sensitive?

"You should probably have a lie down too. Nothing you can do for your sister-in-law tonight." As if he just prescribed two aspirins, Dr. Colby said his goodnight and walked down the stairs. A few minutes later, the front door closed shut.

Jo stared at the door of the bedroom, her body trembling, her hands balled at her sides. "I'll make sure Warren stays away from her," Jo whispered, voice quivering. She spun on her heel and raced out of the house. Unlike the doctor, Jo slammed the front door.

Margaret stared helplessly at her departure, unable to move, loath to see Jo hurt—or do something stupid—and refused to leave Fiona's side, sedated or not. Nicholas made her choice for her. "Go to Fiona. Jo will be fine after she blows off some steam. I'll make sure to watch the house, and to watch for Jo's return."

Despite her worry for Jo, concern for Fiona won out. Margaret nodded to Nicholas before she opened the bedroom door. She paused, and said to Nicholas, "Thank you. You've been invaluable and a good friend to my family." She didn't wait for a response. With a deep inhale of breath and putting on a neutral expression, one Fiona wouldn't see, Margaret went inside.

Chapter Twenty-three

TESSA STARTLED AT the heavy pounding to her door as it reverberated up to the stairwell. The thud would pause for two heartbeats then resume. She couldn't imagine who would be so insistent, but it was clear they wouldn't stop until Tessa answered. She doubted someone intent on harm would pound so. Tessa stumbled down a step or two in her haste, nearly lost her footing entirely before she was able to reach the bottom and unlatch the bolt on the door.

Her heart stopped in her chest when a red-faced and puffy-eyed Jo glared back at her from the alley's doorstep. Had she been crying? "Jo? Why didn't you use your key? What's wrong?" Something drastic must have happened to send Jo's world into such a tizzy, and if her expression was any indication. Jo looked angry, frightened, and defeated all at once. Her usually unruly hair stood at angles as if she'd roughly run her fingers through the curly locks and yanked up hard. Her light-blue eyes, clouded by unshed tears, scrutinized her with a haunted gaze. Tessa's first instinct was to draw Jo into her arms to offer comfort. Angry tension radiated from Jo's trembling body curtailed the instinct, as did Jo's tightly clenched fists.

"Give Warren a message," Jo said in a voice heavy with anger and...pain? What in the hell happened?

"Is someone hurt? Should I call the police? Warren isn't here."

"No, this is personal, Tessa. Let me finish."

"Um... Okay."

"Tell him I won't come near you again, except to complete the agreed-upon work, what's unfinished."

Tessa was confused. And extremely hurt. Why didn't Jo want to see her anymore? "But—"

As if she hadn't heard Tessa's attempt to interrupt, Jo shifted her weight to stand tall and stiff. "Fiona's done nothing wrong, didn't deserve his attack. Her blindness is permanent after—" She swallowed. If audible, the sound lost beneath the rapid pounding of Tessa's heart. "I'll stay away from you if he stays away from my family."

Attack? On Fiona? What did Warren—

Okay, think, think. "Jo, please, I don't understand. Is Fiona all right?"

"The doctor just left her. She'll never see anything again." Tessa couldn't feel even a modicum of relief to receive the requested information. "Goodbye, Tessa." Jo took a step back.

Tessa panicked and grabbed Jo's arm. If Jo left now, Tessa truly would never see her again. Promises and commitments were too important for Jo to break. No, no, no. She couldn't lose Jo, not now, not when she finally found the true love she'd looked for all her twenty-four years of life. She had to stop Jo from going through with this. Somehow, Tessa had to make this right. "Please, Jo, come inside. I'll make some tea, and you can tell me what happened." The idea of never seeing Jo again hurt her heart so bad. Tessa couldn't control the tears of loneliness and frustration. "Please, Jo."

Shaking her head vigorously, voice barely audible, Jo said, "I can't, Tessa."

"You can and you will," Tessa said. "You don't dump a girl without giving her a valid reason and full explanation."

Jo winced. "Tessa." Tessa knew Jo was internally fighting the necessity to put Tessa second to family, after whatever Warren had done to precipitate this visit. She realized Jo wanted to explain, needed Tessa to understand.

She tried one last time. "Please, Jo, give me that much."

Jo's shoulders slumped. The sight of the strong, carefree woman, now broken, tore Tessa's heart to shreds. Jo moved closer to the door, but just out of reach. Head bent, gaze directed at the ground, Jo said, "I don't have the strength to do this. Please, just let me go."

"Let me support you." One simple step brought Tessa to Jo's side. She clasped Jo's balled hand in hers and tugged her into the doorway. They stood at the bottom of the stairs, the outside door closed and bolted. Ever so slowly, Tessa turned Jo to face her and pulled Jo into her arms. The moment Tessa's embrace tightened on her, Jo broke into wracking sobs. Face pressed against Jo's damp face, Tessa crooned in her ear, "I have you, honey. You're safe. Let it go."

JO SHOULDN'T HAVE come into the apartment with Tessa. Neither was in any shape to have a productive conversation. Doing so made Jo feel she was betraying her family. Rationally, she knew Tessa had no control over Warren. Rationally, Jo didn't want to lose Tessa. Tessa wasn't the enemy. She was Jo's heart.

Now, she sat on the couch, as Tessa had demanded with vehemence before she made them tea. Jo was angry at this night's events. Events so out of her control she felt helpless. Jo needed to leave, be with her family. "I have to go," she said. Tessa came into the room with a cup and saucer in each hand.

Tessa scowled. "You're in no shape to drive. It wouldn't be helpful if something happened to you, too."

"I shouldn't have even left the house. I was so angry." Jo scrubbed her hands over her face. "You're not safe either, Tessa, if Warren finds me here."

"He can't get in. We changed the locks, and I haven't given him a copy of the new key."

Tessa's calmness settled Jo and her emotions somewhat but still conflicted with what was expected as the right thing to do. Jo picked up the cup of her tea, but her hand shook, and the contents splashed onto her lap. "Dammit," Jo said. She put the cup down before popping off the couch. She paced the open length of the floor. "I must be a jinx. The trouble for Fiona got worse when she saved me. The trouble here is because Warren hates me."

"Warren hates everyone," Tessa said.

"He doesn't beat them all blind, does he?" Jo snapped. A flash of pain crossed Tessa's face and caused Jo's heart to hurt. It wasn't her intention to upset Tessa, even if she spoke the truth. What the hell was she supposed to do? Warren would continue to torment them if she didn't release Tessa. But how could she do that? Tessa meant so much to her already. Their attraction was instantaneous, at least for Jo. She was nearly certain the same held true for Tessa.

If what she believed was true, then leaving Tessa would hurt the other woman seriously. Jo didn't want to do that, especially after Tessa's ex, Catherine Dubois. Tessa would be devastated. But what other options did Jo have available?

There was only one. The family came first. Tessa would heal—eventually. Even if she didn't understand Jo's reasoning, Tessa could move on.

Jo knew she'd never move on.

"Whatever you just decided in your head, you can forget," Tessa said. Her tone brooked no argument. Tessa stood, hands placed on her hips. If Jo's heart weren't breaking, she'd tell Tessa how sexy she looked at that moment.

"Tessa, you have to understand—"

"I'll tell you what I understand. Yes, family is important. Unless it is like mine, then we're in a grey area. You want to protect Fiona and Margaret and the others. What you want and feel is important too." Tessa stomped closer to Jo, and she noticed the tears streaming down Tessa's face, eyes wide in her distress. Tessa stopped in front of Jo, taking a deep breath. "Please, Jo, don't do it." Tessa traced a finger down Jo's cheek, over her lips, and then along her neck. The finger settled between Jo's breasts. Jo sucked in a breath as goosebumps exploded across her flesh. "Please."

Jo didn't want to do anything right now but bring the light back into Tessa's eyes. Before she could curb the impulse, Jo pulled Tessa against her and pressed her lips hard against Tessa's, marveling at the passion in Tessa's returned kiss. Jo's heart stopped in a moment of panic. What if she left Tessa now, and Tessa never forgave her? If things got better, would she ever be able to win Tessa's heart back?

Tessa pulled away with a frown. "Stay with me, Jo." Tessa clasped Jo's hands. "Let me show you how much we mean to each other. How together we are stronger." Jo knew she shouldn't but didn't stop Tessa as she pulled Jo into the bedroom. Rooted to the spot in indecision, Jo watched Tessa undress and climb on the bed and extend her arms in invitation. "Get undressed and join me, Jo."

"You don't have to do this." Jo sat on the side of the bed and faced her. Tessa smiled at her. Jo made a minor shift in the distance, eased closer until they were both under the quilt. Her body absorbed Tessa's warmth. Guilt nearly consumed Jo. She should stop. Jo pulled away.

"If you intend to leave me, Jo, then let me have this. Please."

Jo leaned toward Tessa, and she came eagerly into Jo's arms. This night will probably have to last her a lifetime. Tessa didn't have to ask again. Through the material of her shirt, Jo could feel Tessa's body heat as they embraced. Jo ran her hands over Tessa's shoulders. "Off. Clothes off."

Jo did as commanded, then returned to Tessa's side. "So beautiful," Jo said.

"Not even a little," Tessa said, her lips against Jo's throat. "But I'm glad you think so."

Jo used her lips to trace the line of her jaw, then brushed Tessa's hair aside and began to kiss her ear. Tessa gasped, and Jo felt her shiver.

Slipping both hands under the quilt, Jo caressed the warm length of her back, then the smooth skin over her ribs. When Jo felt the swell of her breast against her hand, she paused. Tessa made an inarticulate sound and fitted her body closer, she put both hands in Jo's hair, drew her head closer, and kissed Jo hard.

Jo felt as if a jolt of electricity traveled directly from her lips to somewhere far lower. Jo was aware of the exquisite softness of Tessa's closed lips, then, as she pressed her mouth to Jo's, the warm satin wetness of her tongue. It entered between Jo's lips slowly, gently, as if asking permission. Then, more urgently, with an insistence that left no doubt as to what she wanted. When Tessa withdrew, Jo clutched her tighter. Their heady kisses of the other day were merely a prelude of possibilities between them.

Breathing hard, Jo finally broke off the kiss, leaned back, weakened as her hands caressed, and then rested atop Tessa's hips, glad they were already lying down. Otherwise, Jo would probably have oozed to the floor. "You're a remarkable kisser."

With a groan, Tessa said, "Shush. Need more practice." Tessa's kisses grew fiercer, more urgent. So much passion surprised Jo, but she wouldn't question. Jo held back the fear of the emotions required for intimacy, of the worry that Tessa would realize Jo not worthy of her and her body. Jo pushed the thought away. They were making love, a sweet distraction from guilt and fear. Tessa deserved her full attention. There would be time for regrets later.

Jo ran her hands over the incredible softness of her skin, and Tessa shuddered, taking Jo's hands and put them on her breasts. Tessa's nipples hardened under Jo's palms, and Jo bent to brush them with her lips. She took each hard bud in turn in her teeth, and Tessa moaned. She put her hands in Jo's hair, not gently, and raised Jo's head from her breasts. Jo watched Tessa stare for a moment, then Tessa kissed her with a demanding tongue. Jo slipped her hands around Tessa, clasped her firm buttocks and held her tighter, a knee between Tessa's legs, and she began to move against Jo in a rhythm of her own.

"Jo, please," she breathed, taking her mouth away as she gasped for breath.

Jo brushed her hand from Tessa's behind to her inner thigh and found her hot, wet center. Tessa gasped as her arms tightened around Jo while she stroked Tessa's lovely velvet wetness. Tessa trembled.

"Now, Jo," she gasped, "now."

Jo slipped two fingers inside her, stroked as Tessa's contracted walls closed around her fingers in a series of fluttering spasms. Tessa clung to Jo and gasped her name, some of the sharp, sweet pleasure that claimed Tessa, claimed Jo, too, and pierced her heart to her soul by the wonder of Tessa's throbbing center held in her hand.

As the spasms subsided, Jo put both her arms around Tessa and held her, stroked her hair and kissed her.

Jo pulled the quilted blanket over them and ran her hands along the long, warm, lovely length of her back. Relieved when Tessa sighed.

"I never expected that," Tessa said.

"You had expectations of our making love?" Jo asked, then smiled.

"I had hoped. I want you in every part of my life, Jo." Tessa sighed, this time with heavy weariness. "I don't want to lose you, not even for Warren."

"Hush. Let's not bring anyone else to bed with us, okay." Jo feigned a grimace. "Are you sure you're okay with my past? With my loving you?"

Tessa tapped Jo's nose with one finger. "Hmm," she said thoughtfully, then bent to kiss Jo, more gently this time. "Best to show you."

Through barely parted lips, their tongues met, turning Jo's blood to molten lava. Tessa's tongue invited Jo to speak her need without words. For Jo's part, her desire was now as urgent as Tessa's had been, and Jo hoped Tessa wouldn't delay much longer. As Tessa ran her hands over Jo's breasts, took her nipples between her finger and thumb, a fire flared in the pit of Jo's stomach. Jo groaned. Tessa apparently needed no further invitation.

Kissing Jo quickly, Tessa slipped a hand between Jo's thighs. Tessa found the place that Jo needed to be touched. Tessa's long fingers opened her, entered her once, and then withdrew. Jo gave an involuntary whimper. Finally, gently, with rhythmic strokes, Tessa fanned the ache of desire to a hot flame. Jo gasped, almost there. Then, when Jo thought she might faint from desire, a hot wave of liquid boiled down along nerve endings and swept Jo away to a place devoid of light and sound, as the orgasm seized her.

Neither breathed nor spoke, and Jo slowly realized Tessa looked down at her. She brushed Jo's lips with hers, smiled beautifully, and smoothed back Jo's hair.

"I love your curls," Tessa said.

"I love you." Jo had to get the words out. She had no expectations that the sentiment would be returned. Part of her hoped Tessa wouldn't say them, didn't want to wonder if it was spoken because of the moment and what they shared.

Tessa settled down alongside her and laid her head on Jo's shoulder. Jo put one arm around her. Jo was about to say something, nothing important, just words to extend the moment together. When she looked down, Tessa was fast asleep.

Chapter Twenty-four

TESSA WAS LIVID.

Jo awoke in the early hours, cleaned up her work tools and removed debris, then stacked the boxed inventory beside the shelves. She'd left a note, of course. Apologized for not staying, said it had to be this way. Jo professed her love, explained she had to look after her family, and then signed her name below goodbye.

Warren would get an ear full of her temper, then she was done with him, brother or not. Sometimes, blood wasn't enough. Warren had crossed the line. She was tired of hiding.

Now she stormed into the police station. Well, as much as she could without being too disruptive. She had manners, after all. Tessa caught sight of Warren at a sturdy metal desk cluttered with papers, his feet crossed at the ankles, and crudely resting on the left corner.

She ignored the multiple young patrolmen who rose to their feet at her entrance but gave a nod of acknowledgment to Randall on her way to her brother. Tessa gave a slight shove to his shoulder to get Warren's attention.

Warren snarled as he rose to his feet and turned in her direction. "What the hell, Tessa?" He balled his hands into fists. The action hadn't gone unnoticed by her. If the sound of shuffling steps behind her were any indication, the aggression was noted by the others in the room. Warren glared over her shoulder. "Get your asses back to work."

Tessa pivoted slightly to see Randall and three others had moved closer, their attention focused on Warren. "Miss Tessa?" Randall met her gaze. She realized he offered his support and that of the others to her. Did they believe she needed it? She remembered what Jo told her Warren did to Fiona which was the reason for this visit. These young men probably knew, too. "I apologize for the disruption, but I need to ask my brother about something." She hoped her tone alerted Randall not to go too far. Randall gave her a barely perceptible nod.

"Oh, for fuck's sake," Warren said. He grabbed Tessa's arm, just above the elbow, in a vise-like grip. She bit back her exclamation of pain. She didn't wish to incite action from her would-be heroes. Warren dragged her into an office with a windowed door, which her brother closed behind them. Tessa felt a modicum of relief. Warren would get his privacy, but anything he did wouldn't go unnoticed by the other men. "What the hell is this?"

She gulped back the shudder elicited in Warren's tone. Tessa had a purpose in confronting her brother. She had to know how far he would go to assure he had control of her life. Tessa didn't want to believe he'd started with beating Fiona, but she believed Jo over Warren, which meant she didn't need to ask him. But she did need to hear confirmation from his own mouth. "You know why I'm here, Warren. Why'd you do it?"

Warren smirked. The expression was both evil and scary. The look would have been sufficient for her, but he seemed determined to answer. He leaned close into her personal space. "Bitch deserved it. Those kinds of people corrupt good people like you. Now maybe those perverts will stay away from you."

Tessa bit her lower lip to staunch her tears. "Except I happen to love those women, Jo especially. Now, none of them will have anything to do with me."

"You're welcome."

Did he think she was thankful for his brutal behavior? "I'm not thanking you, Warren. I'm appalled." Tessa took as step back from him and crossed her arms over her chest. "Do your superiors know about this?"

Face red with rage, Warren moved so close his body was flush with hers. "No way those people will file a complaint. No one cares about them. They know it. Let it go, Tessa."

His spittle sprayed onto her cheek. Tessa nodded and wiped it away with the back of her hand. She moved to the door and put her hand on the doorknob. "Being blood doesn't excuse you or your bad conduct. I've lost the one person I loved, because of you. You got what you wanted. I hope you're happy with what it will now cost you. Don't come to my home, don't expect me to feed you, because I don't want anything to do with you." Tessa opened the door and stepped over the threshold. Randall was at her side instantly. She turned toward Warren. "You're no longer welcomed in my life."

"Damn you, Tessa." He stepped toward her, face full of fury.

Randall gently took her elbow. "I'll walk you home."

"Thank you." As they made their way to the exit, Tessa heard the hurried shuffle of feet behind her. She twisted to look over her shoulder. The patrolmen stood shoulder-to-shoulder and barred Warren from chasing after her.

"This isn't over, Tessa. Mark my word," Warren yelled as she left the precinct.

Outside, Randall asked, "Are you okay?"

Tessa sighed heavily. "No, but someday I will be." She felt the tears warm against her cheek. "Probably only when I die—like I did this morning." The moment she read Jo's goodbye.

IT NEVER FAILED to shock Nicholas how the act of confining a body to bed rest turned strength into frailty. He shook his head and grinned wryly. He stared at the muscles in her arms and realized Fiona might be weakened and paler than normal, but frail didn't apply to her. The changes—rather a growth—of the friendly relationship between he and Fiona had shifted so subtly he hadn't recognized it happening yet was strong enough to allow him to sit in this chair while Fiona lay in bed and rested. Not that that part was the surprise factor. Fiona, dressed in men's pajama bottoms and a white V-neck T-shirt, lay alone in her bed, in a house full of females, and he was trusted to keep watch. Of course, there was some irony if he delved deeper, which he wouldn't traverse now. Granted, too, the door was ajar since propriety overruled all else, even in this house.

Trust.

These Cavanaugh women trusted him, and, for the first time in a long time—if ever—Nicholas felt like an honest part of a true family. He gave a silent chuckle. The only one of them he'd originally wanted was Brigid, and she looked at him like a sibling, both ignoring their night together ever happened. After Ethel's murder, consoled and on the verge of falling in love with Brigid and summarily disabused of the notion by that woman in question, Nicholas was prepared to move on, and away from Pueblo.

He seriously reconsidered.

It's been said there's strength in numbers. Nicholas wanted desperately to be numbered among the Cavanaugh's, even as nothing more than a family friend. He rejoiced in the act of investigating with Fiona.

"Gosh, you think much harder, and you'll damage something in that male brain of yours."

Nicholas looked up and caught the mischievous grin Fiona couldn't try or wouldn't try to hide. Giving a smile of his own, aware it went unnoticed, he said, "You're supposed to be sleeping."

"Easier said than done." Fiona sat up a little, leaned tiredly against the headboard.

"Probably a dumb question, but how are you feeling?"

"Like my head's been run over by a locomotive." She gave a weak smile. "Kinda was, I guess. Run over by Loco Warren." They both chuckled, but Fiona's soon turned into a grimace. "Guess we should save jokes for later."

"Yeah, even your attempts at them." He liked that she snickered at his teasing, but it morphed into guilt when her hand clutched at her forehead. "Sorry about that." She hadn't opened her eyes since he'd been in the room. Could she tell whether she had sight or not? He didn't get a chance to ask.

"Want to tell me what you were thinking so hard about? I felt your tension way over here."

"Not sure this is the time." He glanced around the room. "Or the place."

"Serious stuff then." Fiona's eyes opened, but from her pained expression, Nicholas realized her sight hadn't returned. "Let's start with my thanks to you for getting me home." She sighed. "Can I be honest with you, Nicholas? Be personal?"

"Yes, Fiona." He leaned forward in his chair, rested elbows on knees. "I consider us good friends and, as such, learned to recognize how difficult private matters are for you to share. Anything discussed between us is and will be in confidence." It wasn't like he didn't have secrets of his own.

"I'm afraid. Afraid I won't be able to get over permanent blindness. Afraid I can't take care of my family." She pinched the bridge of her nose. He assumed it helped her staunch the flow of tears. "I don't want to be a burden."

"A burden?" He snorted. "Like they'll let you get away with it. Jo will drag you to the workshop and force you to work. Brigid will withhold sustenance. Margaret, well..." He'd witnessed often enough the love in Margaret's eyes when she looked at Fiona. "Margaret will be there every step of the way. She'll be your support, be your eyes until you learn to adjust to their loss and continue despite it."

She shook her head slowly as if the movement helped her come to terms with his words. Fiona began to gnaw her lower lip. After a moment, she spoke. "I couldn't stop Warren. There will be other situations. Situations I won't see coming. I wasn't blind when I was shot, twice, waylaid and beaten, and...and attacked by Jimmy —" Her voice held the pain of memory. Nicholas knew there was a lot more in the word attacked. He wouldn't press her on the matter. "Before, it was a figurative worry. The worst had happened to me, affected all of us. Now." She gulped hard. "Now, I literally won't see trouble coming." Fiona looked away, and Nicholas saw the gesture for what it was, her wish not to read his expression even if she couldn't see it, and apparently not wanting him to read hers. "How do I protect them?"

Nicholas stood and reached for her chin, turned her face in his direction. "Look at me." She gave a sniff. "You know what I mean. Look, I've watched you tonight. You may be scared about the blindness, but you aren't helpless. You've been adjusting and fine-tuning your other senses to compensate. Believe me, Fiona, when I tell you that the women of the house love you dearly, will never see you as a burden." He released his hold on her chin and returned to the chair. "Matter-of-fact, Fiona, I envy you. You all accept each other just as you are, unquestioningly. Have you any idea how long I've searched for just what you have accomplished under this roof?"

"What about you, Nicholas? Are you ever going to stop running?" Fiona's straightforward tone caught him by surprise.

"What makes you think I'm running from anything?"

Fiona smirked. "I'm blind, not stupid. As someone who spent her childhood and part of adulthood hiding who I was—am—I recognize the signs." She leaned back into the pillows. "Did you know I even passed myself off as a sixteen-year-old boy in Boston during my infamous gangster days? My mother and brother had died years earlier in a fire. Left me with my drunkard father. I used my brother's name. Well, his nickname, Finn, when I started working for Margaret's brother, Eldon."

Nicholas laughed gently, hoped she recognized the humor. "Sorry that I missed that...Finn. So, tell me honestly, how'd you feel about the pretense?"

"It was a mixed bag, I guess. I enjoyed the more comfortable clothes, that's for sure. Became crystal clear to me the distinction between male and female. Even as a supposed male child, my word meant more than a woman of any age. Wouldn't want to be male full time, though." Fiona snorted. "Maybe I didn't get the full experience because I was constantly looking over my shoulder, fearing exposure and stray bullets. But I wouldn't give any of the experience up. The gamble led me to Margaret. I was able to reacquaint with Fionn's girlfriend, Brigid. And gave me a sister in Jo."

Nicholas had wondered about Fiona's relationship with Margaret as sister-in-law and been confused by the timelines. He doubted anyone else was close enough to the Cavanaugh's to recognize or be told of their history. "So, am I correct that Fionn's marriage to Margaret occurred during your adventure as Finn?"

Fiona shifted uncomfortably. He wouldn't have believed it possible, but she paled more. "You could ruin my family if you speculate aloud to anyone outside this room, Nicholas."

"Which would be the last thing on my mind or in my intentions, Fiona." From the thin line of her lips, Nicholas realized his words alone wouldn't convince her of his honesty. This would be a case of tit-for-tat. "You're not the only one in the room with a tainted past, you know."

"Truly? Do tell?" Fiona turned toward him. "Does this have anything to do with what you're running from?"

"In a manner of speaking, yes." Nicholas dragged the chair closer to the bedside. He didn't want to raise his voice too loud, didn't wish to be heard by unintended ears. He trusted those who lived in the house—even if Brigid seemed to have had loose lips with Ethel—but couldn't anticipate who may come to visit. Well, he'd rather only Fiona knew what he intended to share of his history, even if Fiona chose to share with Margaret at some point. "Two years ago, I met and fell in love with a woman. I truly believed she felt the same for me. My truth was bared to her because I believed we shared love. Her response was to hire a few thugs to beat me, in her presence for whatever gratification it provided her, which was a lot, I'm certain." Nicholas paused. "As I lay bleeding on her parlor rug, Blanche proceeded to lambaste me and explain I was no more than a tool used against her father."

"Emotional cruelty can be more brutal than the physical."

"In this case, yes. But you're probably familiar with both aspects of this yourself. It's one of the reasons I feel comfortable sharing this with you. I need to warn you, Fiona, I did not respond well, or gentlemanly."

Fiona shook her head. "No one can say how they'd react in a given situation. We believe we will respond well, but when mixing emotions, all bets are off, usually at the cost of personal civility. You might shock me, Nicholas, but you won't change my positive opinion of you."

"I hope not. I'd be devastated to lose your friendship and good estimation of my character."

"Devastated is laying it a bit thick, don't you think?" Fiona said, humor in her tone.

"Only just." Nicholas agreed.

"Tell me."

Nicholas sat straighter in his seat, not that it would make the telling any easier. He inhaled deeply and forged on. "I succeeded in getting to my feet, horrified by her words, not seeing her perfidy after all our time together. Despite the pain, I managed to wrap my hand around her throat and squeeze. Fiona, I thought I'd killed her. I didn't know if I had because I snuck out the back door when she collapsed and haven't returned to her or the city. There had been ways to find out for sure, but there's no pride or release in learning unequivocally you're a murderer."

Softly, Fiona asked, "Do you, in your heart, presume you killed Blanche?"

"No, no, I didn't," he said, shaking his head. Again, she wouldn't see the action, but he believed Fiona could sense his response. "But, my word, Fiona, I was so, so angry with her, it consumed all reason."

"And you were hurt?"

He nodded. "Yeah, probably a lot of that too. I did eventually learn Blanche is alive and well. Her father married her off to the son of a business partner. I hope she's happy, but I wonder if Blanche will ever be happy. If I'm honest, I often hope Blanche is miserable. Hope she misses the independence she would have had with me."

"I hope she's miserable, too, on behalf of you, my friend." Fiona shifted the pillows behind her to sit higher. She furrowed her brow. "Let me ask you this, Nicholas. Was this secret you shared with her something to cause you great difficulty should it come to light? Something you can't reconcile?"

"Do you trust me?" he asked.

"Yes, even with the silly cookie duster above your lip." She smiled, swiping a finger across the right side of her upper lip as if taming a mustache.

"Hey, it makes me debonair."

"Makes you something, all right."

"Okay, let's leave my manly grooming for another discussion." He stood and moved to the slightly ajar door and closed it completely. When he returned to his chair, Nicholas said, "This could be the final straw in our friendship, Fiona. Losing your friendship will probably be the greatest hurt I'd suffered in my thirty years, but I'm willing to share if you truly wish to hear it."

"I do, Nicholas. I can't imagine that would cause me to shun you."

"Oh, there is a chance, believe me."

Nicholas cleared his throat. "I'll get straight to the point." He quirked the left corner of his mouth "Haven't always been this handsome, charismatic man before you. I...ah...was born Nicole Alena Terrell on October 13 of 1894, to a rich textile family in Philadelphia. Father was Horace and my mother, Bertha. I had two brothers, both older, George and Robert. Even from a young age I knew my parents, the doctors, and everyone else was blind not to see they were wrong about me. I was supposed to be a boy. I borrowed my brother's discarded clothes and only responded to Nicky. My first mistake, in a long list of them, was at the age of ten, in 1904, when I confronted my father on this matter."

He raised a brow at the memory, glad any telltale expressions wouldn't be witnessed by Fiona. "I compounded the error by announcing the mistake rest at the feet of him and mother for not siring or birthing me correctly."

Fiona flinched. "He didn't take that well, I gather?"

"Not at all. Horace, more than two hundred pounds on me, tried to slam his point home with his fists. I was unconscious for two days. Lesson one. Daddy is stronger."

"Where was your mother?"

"Buried in a bottle, I'm sure. Mother didn't contradict or defend against Father." Nicholas shrugged. "So, when I woke, I found only my frilly, girl clothes were available to dress in, which I did. And stormed into my second mistake in as many days. I confronted my parents during pre-dinner drinks. Neither appreciated my attitude or my timing. Daddy dragged me upstairs to my room." Nicholas squeezed his eyes shut as memories flooded back in vivid images, again relieved Fiona couldn't see his anguish. His silence must have lasted longer than he'd realized.

"Nicholas?" Fiona said in concerned tones. Her sightless eyes turned in his direction. "You don't have to continue."

Nicholas inhaled and exhaled loudly. "No, I want to share this, my life story, with you." He hoped the strain he heard in his tone wasn't obvious to her, suspected she heard every nuance. Nicholas believed speed was the best means over this hurdle. "Lesson two. The difference between boys and girls: boys are superior and will always take what they want."

Fiona gasped. "Oh, Nicholas, I'm sorry." Tears poured down her face, mirrored torment consumed her expression. She swiped roughly at her face. "Guess a lot of men enjoy teaching that specific lesson." Fiona swallowed hard as if the action could dispel her own memories. "You can stop if you wish."

He shifted position in the chair to collect himself and buy time. Nicholas decided to dampen the emotions with levity. "And deny you a story worthy of a radio serial drama? Never." She smirked wanly. "Two years later, a ray of light shone on my life." Nicholas smiled. "I met Gaines and Ruth Farwell. Gaines was a noted photographer in town. He was hired to take the Terrell family portrait. I was immediately enamored by Ruth. We made an agreement to meet at the small pond on the estate." Nicholas snorted. "I smuggled sandwiches out of the kitchen and brought them with me. I was hoping Ruth would show. I figured if she didn't, I'd have a snack and a longer swim."

"Did Ruth go to the pond?"

"Yeah, though she admitted she almost hadn't because she couldn't understand why I had invited her. You see, Ruth was crippled. Wore braces on her legs so she could walk. We sat for a while and ate, and then I mentioned how I missed my trousers. Well, that led to a misunderstanding. She thought I was teasing. I told her she wouldn't understand. Ruth thought I was discounting her because she was a poor, stupid, crippled girl. Which, of course, confused me more. Ruth was smart, I never saw her as common, and I thought she was the prettiest girl I'd seen."

Fiona chuckled. "Did it take more than that to convince her?"

"Oh, she didn't believe me, at first. She was so surprised that she changed the subject back to me. Then, I explained about the trousers, how I felt inside that no one could apparently see."

"Did the revelation scare her away?" Fiona's question was just a whisper as if she feared the answer. She leaned a little in his direction.

"Thought so at first. Ruth blanched and got so quiet. I backpedaled and told her I wouldn't bother her again, but she and her father would be safer if she didn't tell anyone what she knew. My father was a powerful man and would think nothing of destroying the Farwell's."

"And?"

Nicholas snorted. "She threw her arms around my neck and promised to keep my secret and always be my friend. And she followed through on her promise. Ruth Farwell gave me a reason to live. For six more years of hell, I did everything my father demanded and expected. It wasn't easy on either of us. There was something different about me. As I got older, I looked more boy than a girl, no matter how frilly the dress. I grew taller than most girls, even taller than my middle brother, Robert, and my father."

"You cared for her. I hear it in your voice."

"Yes," he admitted. "Deeply."

Fiona pushed the covering away, swung her legs to the floor, and reached toward the robe at the bottom of the bed. She frowned when she didn't grasp it in the first try, so Nicolas picked it up. "Please, allow me. Turn around." He could see her war with herself on whether to accept his help or not. Fiona turned and allowed him to help her into the robe. He stopped his assistance at that. Fiona used the bed to guide herself to the rocking chair by the window. She sat. "Need out of bed. Bring your chair over here and continue." As Nicholas brought the chair over, she asked, "Did you keep Ruth in your life?"

"Yes, for quite some time, actually. When I was old enough to leave home, I rented a room at the back of the studio and learned all I could from the Farwell's. That was the beginning of my career as N. Allen, doing freelance work for the local newspapers. I had direct access to murders that were under investigation."

"Goodness. You have experience with murders and murderers. No wonder we got as far as we did."

"I was closer than most ever knew."

"Nicholas?" Fiona said, "Tell me nothing happened to Ruth."

"Oh, no, not that," he said.

Fiona harrumphed. "Good. You know, Nicholas, we all have darkness in us. I care about you and, honestly, I like the man in this room, who has been there for me and is my friend. The man you are right now tells me all I need to know about you. Our pasts are just that, Nicholas. Past."

Nicholas leaned back again. Ruth would adore Fiona, take to her right from the first meeting; he was sure of it. He looked forward to introducing them. If he could ever make amends for the time he'd allowed to get in the way.

"GOODNESS," FIONA SAID. She hoped he believed her, that his past and whatever darkness he believed he carried wasn't important. After all, he had suffered in his childhood. She was surprised Nicholas was as well-adjusted as he presented. Nicholas was a friend. She knew all she needed to know. "My only question is why you never returned to Ruth? You care for her. Did you not part well?"

"I proposed and wanted to spend my life with Ruth. She told me she couldn't. Told me to see how far I could go with my photography." He grinned and gave a sniff. "Told me to spread my wings and, if I still wanted her, come back. She'd be waiting." Nicholas sighed heavily, apparently plopping back into the chair from the sound of it. "How could I, after my heart's infidelity? For a time, I thought I loved Blanche. Wasn't thinking about Ruth then, was I? Over the years, I did think of her often but continued engaging my heart elsewhere. It's been ten years. I'm sure Ruth has moved on."

"Maybe, Nicholas, maybe. Don't you at least want closure? Whether she has or not, doesn't she deserved to know what happened to her best friend, her first love?"

"How could she when I've been unfaithful to her? She's better off without me," Nicholas said, finality in his tone.

"Don't do this to her, or to yourself." Fiona couldn't believe Nicholas would give up so easily. When Nicholas spoke of Ruth, spoke her name, Fiona could hear the depth of feeling and warmth in his voice. From what she could gather from Nicholas's tale, the main reason for his delay could be attributed to his own insecurity. Ruth knew every secret Nicholas held. No matter his fame, the years that separated them, Nicholas didn't believe, after Blanche and Ethel, especially, he deserved Ruth's love. "Maybe she has moved on, Nicholas. But after all the two of you shared, Ruth deserves to know what happened to you. An incredible woman is waiting for news from you. You aren't giving Ruth a chance she deserves. And, she deserves to see for herself the incredible man you've become."

"What if she doesn't like who I have become? Especially after a decade."

Fiona snorted. "Seriously?" She extended a finger in his direction. "You are the famous and infamous Nicholas Alan Tirrell, aka N. Allen. What's not to love?"

Nicholas laughed heartily. "Well, there is that, of course. You're right. I'm quite remarkable."

"There we go. There's the Nicholas I know. Ego back in place."

Chapter Twenty-five

TESSA FORCED A smile and politely entertained her customers, Mrs. Russo and her daughter, Bianca. What she wanted to do is close the store and wait for a possible appearance by Jo. She missed her presence in the shop, the easy camaraderie they shared. The touches and the stolen kisses. They'd been trying to keep their meetings discreet, but neither wanted Warren's undue attention on them. He hadn't attempted to engage her with calls or visits, but Tessa had no doubts he watched her or had others doing it for him. Two could play that game. Randall was their go-between. He often let them know when Warren would be away from the area. The problem was they'd only seen each other twice since that night.

Currently, Mrs. Russo focused her attention on the music box Jo had gifted her. Although Tessa admitted to herself, of the numerous possible women who could have been in her shop, Mrs. Agatha Russo was the more welcomed.

"This is the most beautiful box I've ever seen," Mrs. Russo said. "And I've seen some remarkable work in my travels."

As the older woman went on, Tessa listened with half an ear as she focused on the three individuals quietly, save for the ringing of the bell above the door, entered her shop. The man was tall and handsome, the woman beautiful in an understated way. Between them was a small boy about Richard's age. Nice looking family new to town if the luggage were any indication. Tessa nodded toward them.

"Fiona Cavanaugh created this, you say?" The attention of both adults flashed in their direction.

"Yes," Tessa said. "I've always been amazed at her woodworking, but this," she indicated the box, "is a work of art." A broad grin lit the man's face, and Tessa's curiosity piqued. His proud beaming didn't last long.

Unaware, or uncaring of the strangers behind her, Agatha rolled on. "If the rumors are true, I wouldn't expect this. Doesn't look like the work of a gangster."

"Because she isn't," the man barked. He stormed closer to the counter, the woman and child remained by the front window. "Fiona worked with the police to bring down the gangsters, at great cost to her both physically and emotionally. Fiona saved many children, some no more than twelve-years-old, from enslaved prostitution. Young women, like your daughter, who came from good homes." As he spoke, his voice rose in temper-filled defense, but Tessa heard his pain.

The woman with him spoke his name as she protectively clutched the child closer. "One woman, her friend, was found by Fiona, chained to a bed, tortured, starved. The women used by the whim of multiple men who had a few moments to play. During the rescue, Fiona dodged most of the bullets fired at her to save her friend. Her friend died in her arms anyway."

"Ian, enough," the woman said sternly, louder. "You're scaring Adam." He appeared to have heard her this time. Tessa couldn't say if it were because of her tone his tirade had ended, or because of the little boy. Nostrils flaring, he glared at the Russo's and her in turn. "If this is the small-mindedness she deals with, it's probably best I take her home."

Tessa felt her heart stop at the words. No. No matter what happened because of Warren, Tessa couldn't lose Jo completely. She believed she had time to make everything right between them, fix them right, and strengthen their bond. If the Cavanaugh's left Pueblo that could never happen. When the comforting laughter she recognized as Jo's sounded behind her, Tessa felt her shoulders sag in relief as the tension left her. Jo came.

"Ian Donnelly, stop scaring the locals." Jo entered the room from behind her, moved around Tessa to launch herself in the man's arms. "Missed you, Detective." Jo waved to the woman who held the hand of the child, who subsequently smiled as if women threw themselves at Ian regularly. "Hello, Janice." Janice sat on the window seat, pulled the boy onto her lap, apparently satisfied Ian was in good hands. Jo released the man, stepped back and slapped him on the arm. "Apologies, please," Jo ordered.

"I'm sorry," Agatha said, as concurrently, Ian said, "my apologies, ma'am."

Tessa drank in the sight of Jo. She gave Jo her space. Tessa wasn't her brother and didn't share his views and needed Jo to understand. Tessa wanted nothing to do with Warren. But their fear of other bad behavior directed at the Cavanaugh's had them outwardly estranged. Do all the Cavanaugh's hate her because of Warren's actions? Jo said no, but Tessa didn't know for certain. Jo wouldn't want to hurt her, Tessa knew.

"Ian Donnelly, this is Mrs. Agatha Russo and her daughter

Bianca," Jo introduced. Agatha blushed when Ian took her hand and pressed a kiss to her gloved knuckles.

Bianca shook his hand rather than allow the hand-kissing but disinclined to permit her mother to take the blame for her words. With the pointed sniff, Bianca said, "I understand the impulse to protect family and friends, Mr. Donnelly. That said, had you paid better attention to mother's words, you would have realized she intended to discount the rumors in her complement of Fiona's work. Intending no gangster could create such beauty."

Tessa nodded. "Didn't look like, hence couldn't be, gangsters work." She extended her hand. "Welcome to Seamlessly Stylish. I'm Tessa Langford."

Ian stared at her intently but shook her extended hand. "Tessa Langford? As related to—" The rage returned to his eyes.

"Yes, well," Bianca said overly loud. "I believe it's time I take mother home." She hooked an arm through her mother's, tugging as they moved to the door. Agatha stopped, turned toward Ian, and said, "I never meant harm, Detective Donnelly. Rest assured, I shall staunch any further gossip as I can. Miss Cavanaugh has a new verbal protector." At Ian's nod, they left.

However, it appeared Ian wasn't finished with Tessa. "You're related to the man responsible for Fiona's current condition?" It wasn't a question, his gaze hard. When he crossed his arms over his chest, Tessa suspected he challenged her. What did he expect of her? He knew, obviously, who had hurt Fiona. Did he believe the siblings were cut from the same cloth?

Raising her chin defiantly, Tessa said, "Yes, his younger and only sister."

What Tessa didn't expect was Jo coming to her defense. She stepped in front of Tessa. Jo said, "Let her alone, Ian. She's not like Warren. Tessa is—" Jo stopped to rub at the pained expression on her face. They couldn't be together because of Warren. Had they officially dissolved the relationship? Were they no longer girlfriends? Would this be the official dissolution? Was hiding their relationship too difficult for Jo? "She's mine. Tessa is my girlfriend, no matter who doesn't approve. Including you."

Tessa didn't know who was more surprised by the statement, her or Ian. She wanted to pull Jo into her arms to express her appreciation but didn't know how Jo would react to open displays of affection. More so, Tessa didn't want to break down in her own emotion-filled responses.

Ian hesitantly uncrossed his arms. His features softened a little as he stared at her over Jo's shoulder. Then, his gaze switched to Jo. "You sure? She seems a bit surprised."

"Long story. I'm sure you're tired from the train ride. I'll take you to the house." Jo and Ian went to Janice, the child, and picked up the luggage. Summarily dismissed, Tessa started for the back room. "Tessa?" Jo said her name softly, but her hesitancy recognizable. "I know I'm interfering with your business, but," Jo paused, her expression pleading. "Would you join us?" Tessa blinked rapidly to stem the flow of tears. She didn't trust her voice, not willing to betray her confused emotions. Tessa nodded. "We'll give you a moment to lock up. It'll be a tight squeeze just so you're prepared." Jo gave her a smile. "Meet you at the truck?"

Tessa rushed to secure her apartment, the back stairwell, and then the front door. She wiped at tears of joy. She had wanted time with Jo, wanted to explain to the Cavanaugh's how sorry she was, and Jo was extending the hand to allow her to do so. Unsure of the reception she would receive at the house, Tessa nervously slid next to Janice so she was in the middle of the seat, but silently vowed to withstand anything if it meant even a few moments more with Jo.

The ride was silent, with only the sounds of the truck's engine as Jo drove them to her home. Tessa was certain she would be able to hear the heartbeats of the occupants if her own wasn't drumming in her ears. Her pulse quickened, along with warmth that flooded her system at the tight contact with Jo's thigh in the confined space. When they pulled up in front of the house, Ian exited the truck first and assisted Janice and the little boy—who had yet to utter a sound. Jo's strong hand on her thigh stopped Tessa from following them. "We will be right there," Jo said at Ian's curious glance.

Margaret and Brigid were ushering them inside, but Tessa hesitated from looking at Jo, afraid and uncertain of what she'd find in her lover's eyes. Jo really wants her to participate in the family gathering. Or was this a way to ambush Tessa as the next best target for Warren? Tessa quickly disabused herself of that, though. Jo wasn't the type to backstab her, or anyone, like that. Her heart was too tender.

"You're afraid," Jo said. She pulled the key from the ignition and pocketed it.

"Yes. But I understand if—"

Jo scooted closer, her voice a caressing brush against Tessa's ear. "I've missed you." Tessa tried to swallow the sob ineffectually. "I've tried to stay away as I promised. It is so hard. The harder I try to push you from my thoughts, the more you consume them."

Tessa was afraid to look at Jo. No matter what she saw, any expression from Jo would release the torrent of tears, she was barely able to contain. Instead, she said, "Miss you too. I'll accept whatever your family wants, even to punish me. I never wanted this to happen."

"Oh, honey," Jo said. "My family has no plans to punish you. Look at me, please." Tessa turned to face Jo, who clasped Tessa's hands in hers. "I don't want to anger Warren, Tessa, but it has been so hard to pretend I don't care for you, don't want to spend time with you." She inhaled deeply. "I'll do my best to continue with the pretense, but this is my family, and you're my heart. I want you to be part of my life."

"Oh, Jo, I want that too." Tessa squeezed the hands, holding hers. "I understand your reasoning for wanting to leave me, but I've never wanted, never loved anyone as much as you. If you need me to stay away, I will. Please, Jo, don't make it forever." Tessa remembered a comment Ian made at the store. Lowering her gaze, Tessa asked, "If they take you back to Boston, will you go?"

"We are not going anywhere, sweetheart."

Tessa shook her head. "You don't know that, Jo. Ian was pretty angry."

"Let's not worry about that right now." Jo brushed the pad of her thumb across Tessa's chin and up her jaw. "No matter what's decided, I won't leave you behind, understand? We will get through this. Trust me."

"I do, Jo, trust you. I don't intend to stop."

Jo smiled at her. "Margaret is staring at us from the porch. We better get inside before she gives us the teacher look."

"Heaven forbid," Tessa said. Her heart felt much lighter as she and Jo joined the others inside.

MARGARET WATCHED JO and Tessa from the porch. Anyone had to just look at the two, and it was obvious how much they cared for one another. She wished times were different. That love alone could be enough. Janice joined her as Jo and Tessa walked up the sidewalk. "They're cute."

"But it's not going to be easy for them."

"It never is." Janice placed an arm around Margaret's waist. "Jo's grown into quite the young woman."

"Yes, she has." Margaret said. Jo and Tessa entered the house and Margaret said to Jo, "I'm glad you two decided not to spend the evening in the truck," she teased. She reached for Tessa's hand and gave a squeeze, then released it. "Tessa, I'm glad you could join us. Welcome. Fiona's resting, but I'll wake her in a little while. Could you both help Brigid get everyone settled?" They acquiesced and went into the house.

Margaret dropped her head to Janice's shoulder. "Glad you came. Your letter arrived only an hour ago."

Janice squeezed her waist and waggled her eyebrows. "Surprise."

Margaret laughed. "Yes." She paused. "What's going on, Janice? You wrote about a visit, and that Ian would be with you. You didn't mention a child. Something you need to tell me? Are you and Ian—"

"God, no." Janice snorted. "He learned I was coming this way, and lovelorn Ian decided to play escort. He came for Brigid, not for any real assistance. Although," she shrugged, "he's been pretty good with Adam." Janice lowered her voice to barely a whisper. "Ian's been beside himself with all the news. Doc Matthews mentioned Fiona's health. Just before we left, he updated us about her blindness."

Margaret frowned. "How did he know?"

"Ha." Janice rolled her eyes. "You know the rich love to gossip. She told her parents and news got around from there. Ian has maintained contact with Brigid's parents. I guess it's been beneficial. Ta-da, here we are."

"And Adam?"

Janice dropped the arm from Margaret's waist and stepped away. She heaved a heavy sigh. "As you know, I've turned your house into an orphanage."

"Your house for a fair price," she corrected.

"True." Margaret watched Janice fidget. She was about to prod her to continue, when Janice said, "Adam's been through a lot and wants friends like any other kid. He doesn't realize when the older kids tease him, they're mean. I worry what will happen to him when he's old enough to figure it out. Compound that matter with the fact that most families looking to adopt a child don't want to deal with any issues, like nightmares, a boy like Adam comes with. He's already been taken in and returned by three families, which doesn't include his biological parents." Tears fell down Janice's face. She sniffed, and Margaret pulled her into a hug. "Fifth home would be me. And what do I do? I put him on a train and a sixth home."

"Why did you bring him here? Can't be because you missed my sparkling personality. Wait." She furrowed her brow. "Do not consider hitting on my wife again."

Janice stepped back and swiped at the tears and gave a watery chuckle. "In my defense, she was posing as a handsome male. How was I to know?"

"Posing as a sixteen-year-old boy."

"Po-ta-to, Po-tah-to."

Margaret shook her head. "Are you still a consummate flirt?"

"Well." Janice drew the word out.

"Okay," Margaret said. "Back to Adam."

Janice exhaled loudly. "He needs a home. One that will love him and teach him, in a manner that a great kid deserves. Show him what a real family is."

"Janice. This isn't a good time."

"Hear me out, Meggie. Please." Janice took her hands in both her own. "This is a perfect time. It's the only way you can have a child of your own. Fiona needs this. I haven't known her for as long as you, but I have a pretty good idea she needs to focus on being useful. She won't be able to concentrate on being blind if she has Adam around."

"Or, it could achieve the opposite."

"Meggie, honey. There's another matter to think about." Janice turned away as if she didn't want to face Margaret for her next disclosure. Margaret balled her hands in anticipation. "I had a long talk with Edward. I know what Fiona has to look forward to." She winced. "I didn't mean—"

Margaret couldn't speak, afraid she'd completely break down. After a moment, she asked, "What has Adam got to do with Fiona's diagnosis?"

This time Janice pulled Margaret into a hug. "Together, you raise Adam, and he learns from you both. Maybe he takes on characteristics of Fiona. In years to come, you have a common link, a reminder to bring even a modicum of peace in her absence."

"I don't know if I can." Margaret pulled away and turned her back on Janice. "It's bad enough to know what will happen. What if his reminding me doesn't bring peace, but horrible pain? Don't you think this is hard enough?"

"Okay, I understand. I just thought—" Janice moved to the screen door. "I guess I hadn't thought hard enough. But know this. When I got Adam, all I could visualize was you and Fiona beside him. I'll take him back with me. Destroy the paperwork."

Janice opened the screen door.

"I won't be rash. Let me talk to Fiona." Margaret was divided on the matter. Janice had reasonable points. "Guess I should disturb her, quit giving her too much brooding time. Better fill Jo in on the new development, too, since she'd be an aunt."

FIONA HEARD THE mumbled voices outside her bedroom but didn't acknowledge them. She used the toe of one foot to keep the movement of the rocker going. If they wanted to speak to her, they made no move to knock on the door or to enter. Just as well. In her current mood, any human interaction would not go well. Not after the day she had, and it was only a little before supper time. Fiona thought she recognized the voices from a long time ago. She focused for a moment. The voices were from five years ago.

Her attention was caught by the sound of the knob turning and the soft rustle of clothing, followed by the softer sound of tiny footsteps as they approached her. Fiona focused on the quiet noise. The tread was young and light, the footpads too close together to be an adult. A child and a small one. Her first thought was that Richard came for a visit. She dismissed that quickly since there wasn't any familiarity with the movement. She felt a frisson of panic. Had a neighbor's child wandered up to her room to see the freak? Poised to call out to Margaret, a small, hesitant hand on her knee kept her momentarily silent.

"Can I sit with you?" the child asked. Fiona hesitated, unsure how to respond. She didn't get the opportunity. The child climbed up onto her lap, wiggled into a comfortable position, and leaned his head on Fiona's shoulder. Her action unconscious, she pulled him closer into an embrace, her arm around his small body, even as panic filled her. Was this child here to torment her? How did he get past the family? "What's your name?"

"Adam."

"Adam, what?"

"Dunno," he said. "Gonna be different."

Perplexed, Fiona asked, "Why?"

"Because." Small fingers gently traced the scar on her forehead. "You hiding?"

"Why would you think I'm hiding?" she asked, surprised at his directness.

He shifted on her lap, then she felt tiny hands framing her face. "You alone. You sad." From the size and weight of the little boy, an assumption until told otherwise, Fiona suspected he couldn't be more than three, maybe four years old. What did a child at this age know about sadness? "You punished?"

"What makes you ask that?"

Again, he touched her scar. "I got a bad boo-boo too. No one wants me. Miss Janice says I go to special mommies." Janice? Janice Hartwell? Was that one of the voices which sounded familiar just a moment ago? What was either of them doing here? And boo-boo? A birth defect or scar of his own? "Is your boo-boo because you were punished?"

Fiona felt his barely perceptible nod before he clasped her hand while lifting a leg onto her knee. "I was bad, punished," he repeated, raising the pant leg.

He pressed Fiona's hand against his bared leg, making her immediately aware of the scars from severely burnt flesh. She gasped. His leg, at least the part available to her touch, was covered in scarring. The pain this little boy must've suffered, and as a punishment. The very thought made her want to cry. Would her open emotional reaction frighten him?

Fiona bit her bottom lip to suppress herself from a response. Instead, she asked, "Why did you ask if I was punished?"

"You sad. And your eyes funny."

She gave a chuckle at that. No longer able to see, Fiona couldn't look at the reflection, adjust to how the world saw her. How Margaret saw her. How did this child become so perceptive? "My eyes are different because I'm blind. I can't see."

"Oh." He leaned back against her, nearly draped across her chest. "I'll help you if you want." He sighed wearily, and Fiona smiled. "I'm tired, though."

"So am I," she admitted.

"I hope you get to be my new mommy," he whispered.

Fiona wrapped her arms around him, secured him safely in place. Whoever the intended woman was to be his mother would be lucky to have him. That would never be her, especially now. How wonderful would it be, to teach, to love, to leave a reminder of her behind? Margaret would need someone to love, to focus her empty hours. Life could be cruel in so many different ways, like burning a child as punishment. What kind of monster did that to anyone, let alone to a toddler? Fiona nudged the chair into a slow rocking rhythm, leaned her head back, and closed her eyes. His breathing steadied in sleep. Fiona kissed the top of his head, her lips tickled by soft, thick curls. She wondered at the color of his hair. Did it resemble Jo's from when they first met, all curly and blonde? At least she was lucky to have an opportunity to raise Jo.

"Sweet dreams," she whispered.

Moments later, the chair stilled, Fiona's head lulled to the side as she too slept.

Chapter Twenty-six

MARGARET DISLIKED DISTURBING the loving scene before her. Fiona held the small child so tenderly, even as they both slept soundly in the rocker. With all that had happened in the last couple of weeks, Margaret wondered— and worried— how Fiona would react when she learned more about the child in her arms. Surprised that Fiona hadn't called for his removal. Margaret was curious about how this scene transpired. Not that she expected Fiona to be cruel to anyone, least a child, but a strange little boy had invaded her personal space. And Fiona's lap. Margaret smiled and locked this vision in her mind forever.

Much as she wanted to spend longer watching, it was dinner time, and six people downstairs waited on their arrival. Margaret went to the rocker and placed a kiss to the top of Fiona's head. "Fiona, honey, you need to wake up." Margaret watched as Fiona's brow furrowed before she blinked rapidly to clear the sleep from her eyes.

"Guess I didn't dream up him."

Margaret settled a hand on Fiona's shoulder. "No, honey, you didn't dream him. We need to discuss him quickly since the family is waiting for dinner."

"We have company, other than him, I mean?"

"Yes, Janice and Ian are here."

"This little guy theirs?" Was that a hint of disappointment?

Margaret chuckled. "Most definitely not." She cleared her throat, nervous about sharing the news without any preparation for the blunt reality. If this conversation had come before Fiona's blindness, Margaret would have expected a positive response. She didn't know what reaction to predict with Fiona's depression. "His name is Adam." She hesitated. "Adam Graham."

"Graham?" Margaret noticed Fiona's arm tightened around the little boy. "How—"

Rubbing Fiona's arm, Margaret explained. "Janice turned the house into a home for abandoned and orphaned children. She works to find these kids permanent homes." She paused. "But no one adopts a flawed child."

Defensively, yet quietly, Fiona snapped, "Adam is not flawed." Fiona snapped her mouth closed, seeming startled by her own reaction, her teeth gnashed.

Margaret drew a footstool close to the rocker and took Fiona's free hand in both of hers. "No, not to us, but he is to the rest of the world. That is why he is now ours. If we want him."

"I don't want to be daft, Margaret, but I'm confused. Maybe my blindness has made me stupid."

Margaret cupped Fiona's cheek. "Not possible, Fiona. You're the brightest woman I know. Never doubt that fact. According to the paperwork, my brother—" Fiona tensed, but Margaret pressed on. "My brother and his wife died in an automobile accident. His last wish was for family, me, and my husband Fionn to be his guardian. Adam is the closest we could possibly expect for a child of our own."

Fiona stayed stiff and silent, tears streamed down her face, Margaret wasn't sure what the reaction meant. So focused on Fiona, Margaret wasn't aware Adam was awake until he spoke. "Don't you want me either?" The hurt coating the question nearly broke Margaret's heart.

Maybe Fiona's too. Suddenly Adam was crushed in Fiona's embrace. "Oh Adam," Fiona said, her voice breaking. "You're not going anywhere." Fiona stood and clutched Adam against her chest and pulled Margaret into a hug. "Adam's right where he belongs. He's with his aunties."

"Is aunties like mommies?"

"As close as we can be for you, Adam," Fiona said.

Margaret didn't know how long they stood in the embrace, sensing a renewed energy, maybe hope, in Fiona. The moment was broken, and Margaret suspected there would be many more, when Adam asked, "Can we eat now?"

Adam grinned mischievously.

Margaret laughed. "You little scamp."

Fiona settled Adam on the floor. He promptly took one of their hands in each of his tiny ones. "Lead the way, Aunties." Margaret laughed as they left the bedroom, hand-in-hand.

This new change in her life was the second-best day of her twenty-seven years of life. Meeting Fiona was her first-best day.

DINNER WENT WELL. Everyone had a wonderful time catching up. The best topic for the night being Adam and welcoming him to the Cavanaugh clan. During the meal, Fiona felt the tension that radiated from Tessa, seated on her left. As everyone rose from the table, Ian offered to help Brigid clean everything after a little more social time in the parlor. Fiona reached toward Tessa. "Could you give me a moment, Tessa?" Fiona understood Tessa's discomfort. For the young woman's sake, and for Jo, she figured to nip the distress while manageable.

"Certainly," Tessa said. Fiona sensed she was made more nervous by the request, but Tessa sat back in her chair.

"Is everything all right?" Jo asked. "Fiona?"

"It's okay, honey," Tessa said. "We'll be right there."

Fiona detected Jo's hesitancy but, after a breath or two, Jo left the room. Fiona shifted her body to face Tessa, hoping to convey openness. She'd didn't know if it worked as she couldn't visually see to gauge Tessa's expressions. Now she had to rely on her other senses. Inwardly, she shrugged. This was the hardest to get used to with her blindness. "What are your intentions toward my sister?"

"I...I care for Jo." Tessa swallowed hard enough for Fiona to hear. "Actually, Fiona, I'm in love with your sister. I've had feelings for her since the first time I set eyes on Jo. I'll do whatever is necessary, or required, to spend my life making her happy."

"Do you and Warren share the same personality traits?"

"No, never," Tessa said defensively. "I couldn't hurt people the way he does. Fiona, I would never—"

"My point, Tessa. You need to be cognizant of the fact that you're not Warren. Yet you're afraid I, and others in this house, will believe you are. Maybe hate you for it?" she asked.

"I would understand if you did despise me." Fiona heard the despair in Tessa's voice. "I'd also understand if you take Jo away from me and move back to Boston."

"To Boston?" Fiona wondered where that notion came. "Why would you think that?" She heard a knuckle crack and wondered how hard Tessa was wringing her hands.

"Ian mentioned it in my shop this morning."

Fiona snorted. Poor Tessa. "Was he upset when he brought it up?"

"Yes."

"Ian gets a little overprotective. We just ignore him." No, the statement wasn't true. She smiled, remembering how many times Ian had been there for her. Fiona never ignored Ian. He had always looked after her like an older brother. "I can't speak or stop Jo from making her own decisions, Tessa. But understand, I have no intention of leaving Pueblo. This is our home, for better or worse. Also, no matter what you assume, no one in this family paints you with the same brush as Warren." She stood. "Only one way for this family to turn against you, Tessa. Hurt Jo. Then the Cavanaugh's will turn on you like a tornado."

"I would never intentionally hurt Jo," Tessa said.

"Glad to hear it." Fiona offered her arm in Tessa's direction. "How about we join the others before Jo comes hunting for us?" She felt Tessa curl a hand around her elbow. "I'll try not to bump us into any walls. Still getting the hang of this."

JO PUSHED HERSELF off the wall she'd been leaning against. She worried about Tessa. She watched Tessa walk toward the parlor, hanging on Fiona's arm as they entered. Tessa led Fiona to the empty space next to Margaret on the settee. After Fiona was settled, Tessa made her way to Jo. "You okay?" Jo asked. She trusted Fiona to be civil, but Fiona had come to harm because of Tessa's brother, a matter they were all coming to terms with handling.

Tessa wrapped an arm around her waist. Jo's heart leaped at their contact. Tessa's smile was beautiful. She squeezed Jo's waist. "She asked about my intentions for you."

Jo waggled her eyebrows. "And they are?"

"Not that," Tessa said, her cheeks reddened, and she slapped Jo's hip. Tessa's voice deepened into a throaty whisper. "At least I didn't mention those intentions to your sister." Jo felt surprised at Tessa for making the remark. Did she recognize Jo's nervousness? When Tessa dropped her head on her shoulder, Jo slid an arm around Tessa's waist. "Fiona reminded me I'm not Warren. Said I'm here on my own merits."

"Are you okay with that? If you're uncomfortable with us, I can take you home."

"No, Jo. I want to be here with your family. They are great, if not a bit scary." Tessa raised her head. "I want to be here with and for you."

Jo pressed a kiss to her brow. "Thank you. I'm glad you came, too."

She looked around the room at the other occupants. Janice sat in the lone overstuffed chair and watched the boys. Richard and Adam were on the rug playing with an assortment of toys. Brigid and Ian were on the couch, with Brigid watching the boys, and Ian watching Brigid. Nicholas, a new constant for Fiona and the family, also sat on the couch. Margaret and Fiona were on the settee, holding hands, Margaret quietly speaking in Fiona's ear. Jo grinned. If the expression on Fiona's face were any indication,

Fiona was the happiest she'd been for a long time.

Much as the idyllic scene warmed her, Jo brought up the topic not addressed yet. "How long are you and Janice staying, Ian?"

Ian pulled his gaze from Brigid. Jo wondered if he realized everyone recognized the obvious effort. "Two days. Janice needs to get back to the other children. Me? Well, I can't expect crime to stop while I've been away, either. I just need to ask if any of you will be joining us?" Tessa's hold on her tightened almost painfully, nails dug into Jo's flesh. She gave Tessa a reassuring smile.

Janice spoke up. "We'd love to have you back home, but we aren't demanding it, of course."

Adam's head popped up, a worried look on his face. With unexpected speed, he surged up from the floor and squeezed himself between Margaret and Fiona. "I stay with my aunties, right?"

Fiona clasped his small hand in hers. "You aren't going anywhere, tiger." Margaret had tears in her eyes as she placed a palm on his thin little thigh.

Ian stood and offered a hand to Brigid. Jo noticed Brigid didn't release it once she stood. "This isn't a decision to make lightly." He glanced at her, then where Margaret and Fiona sat. "Think about it. For now, Brigid and I are going to put the boys to bed, and then clean up the kitchen. We will see you in the morning." Ian, Brigid, and Richard left the room and headed for the stairs. Adam hesitantly placed a light kiss on Margaret and then Fiona's cheek, getting a snug hug and peck in response. Damn, Jo thought, the addition of the little guy is just what this family needs. Adam rushed up the stairs as fast as his small legs could manage, catching up with Ian, who picked him up for the remainder of the trek.

"After all Adam's been through," Janice said, also getting to her feet, "I never expected he'd transition so quickly. I hope you aren't disappointed with the name I chose."

"He's perfect. His name, Janice, is perfect," Margaret said, taking Fiona's hand in hers.

"Janice, I can't—" Fiona stopped and took a deep breath, the intensity of her joyous emotions on her face and in her tone. "We owe you so much for this. If there's any way I can repay you, you ask."

Janice walked over and knelt in front of Fiona. Her palms rested on Fiona's knees. "Oh, my sweet Finn and beloved Fiona.

Seeing the delight on your face," Janice started to weep, too. "Watching Adam interact with us and not sit silently in the corner, alone? This is my payment. Look, I know what the—" she stopped, glanced at Nicholas, then Tessa questioningly.

Jo understood her hesitation. "Tessa and Nicholas are part of the family. They know about the prognosis from Denver." Jo hadn't fully explained the diagnosis to Tessa but didn't bring that up. She hadn't wanted Tessa to feel more guilty than she already did.

This made Janice sob harder. "Oh, Fiona, I'm sorry. But I know you will make a significant, as you already have, impact on Adam. If you ever need anything from me, ask. There are so many people who love you and owe you much. We're here for you and Margaret." Janice gave a watery smile even though Fiona couldn't see it. Janice tossed her head in Jo's direction. "Hell, we'll even help squirt over there if you ask. Even if she quit being a cute kid for a cuter adult."

"I'm honored," Jo said with teasing sarcasm.

"You should be," Janice said, standing again. "Well, I'm off to bed now. We'll catch up more tomorrow."

After Janice left, Jo tugged on Tessa. They moved to the couch and sat beside Nicholas. Jo hoped to brighten the mood, which grew quiet after Janice's comments. Enthusiastically, Jo said, "So, Margaret, you finally made me an aunt."

"We're all aunts, Jo," Margaret said. "Adam is allegedly Eldon's son, at least for the paperwork's sake."

"Maybe outside of this house," Tessa said. "Adam already knows you as his parents." Tessa gave a shocked expression, and an abrupt inhale of breath. "I'm sorry. Not my place."

"It is, Tessa," Fiona said. "You're part of the family now. Which means you get to speak freely and take part in decisions and discussions."

"Certainly," Margaret agreed.

Tessa relaxed beside Jo. Jo playfully punched Nicholas in the shoulder. "You're awful quiet tonight."

Nicholas swiped a finger across his thin mustache. "I was internally conducting serious consideration to a crucial matter."

"That sounds ominous. On the murders? Have you something new?" Fiona asked.

Nicholas shook his head. "No, I think we're on target with what conclusions we've arrived at so far. We've done all we can in that matter." Jo knew Fiona and Nicholas suspected Warren of killing Ethel. They didn't believe her death part of the other mur-

ders in town. Out of deference to Jo and her feelings for Tessa —
and because they also liked Tessa — Nicholas spoke vaguely on
the subject. He rose above Jo's already high estimation of him.
Nicholas rose from the couch and tugged down his vest, straightened his tie, then clasped his hands behind his back in a contem-
plative gesture. "Horribly forward of me, but I would appreciate
your deliberation on an offer. My services as Adams' godfather."

Fiona grinned, stood, and extended her hand in his general
direction. "I would consider it a fantastic honor and blessing for
all involved. If Margaret has no objections."

As Nicholas shook Fiona's hand, Margaret wrapped him in a
tight hug. "No objections, Nicholas. You are now the unofficial,
in the eyes of the church, godfather of our wonderful little boy."

Nicholas beamed with pleasure, bowed to Margaret, and
addressed the room in general. "Perfect. Then if you'll excuse me,
I have a private celebration over a glass of scotch waiting in my
hotel room."

When only the four of them remained in the parlor, Jo pulled
Tessa closer and draped her arm across her shoulders. "Eventful
as the evening's been," Jo said, "I wonder when the other shoe
will drop."

Margaret shook her head. "Let's hope it isn't tonight."

"I agree," Fiona said. "So, Tessa, are you sure you can handle
this patchwork family?"

"This was the best night I've had, Fiona. I gladly welcome
many more in the future."

The statement filled Jo with delight. She'd didn't ever want
to lose Tessa. They still needed to walk a fine path, hide their
interactions from Warren. Jo certainly looked forward to a time
she didn't have to avoid Tessa when outside this home.

At this point, unfortunately, it appeared only divine
intervention could clear that path completely.

BRIGID AND IAN, who presently wiped dry the last pan,
finished with clearing the dining room and washing the dishes.
She was a little surprised he'd offered his services and not just his
presence. Moments before, he'd been wonderful at putting both
the boys to bed. He read to them from one of Richard's picture
books. Her heart felt full, but her head grew confused. Spending
time with Nicholas encouraged Brigid to think a lot of Ian. Older
now, and a detective rather than a beat cop, Ian had grown into a
remarkable and more handsome man. For a moment, Brigid

wondered what Fionn would have achieved had he lived. Would they have become man and wife? Would he have become a cruel drunk, like his father?

"I enjoyed the diversion," Ian said. He folded the dishtowel over the drying bar.

She smirked at him. "You enjoy watching ladies work in the kitchen?"

Ian pulled out a chair from the table and indicated she should sit. When she did, Ian perched himself on the seat to her left. "Enjoy spending time with you, no matter the task."

Brigid felt the heat of a blush immediately and lowered her head, not able to meet his gaze. "You don't have to say things like that, Ian."

"It's the truth." He cleared his throat. "Are you seeing the fancy fella in the parlor?"

"We've spent time together." Brigid wondered if Ian knew what intimacies that statement entailed. How would he take the information? Would he think less of her? Judge her? She wasn't ashamed. Heck, most considered her an old maid. Brigid would not let anyone make her feel tawdry on the matter. "No, we do not see one another, not the way it may suggest. Nicholas and I aren't compatible other than in friendship. With Richard to consider, I have a lot more to contemplate."

Ian cleared his throat. "Brigid, can I be totally candid with you?" Brigid nodded. She tensed at what might come next. "I know you loved Fionn and devastated with his death. By giving you space to grieve, I nearly lost you. Until Fiona became Finn." The disguise had been a surprise for her, too. She'd worked for the Graham's, Margaret's family, and been shocked the first time Fiona entered the house. Fiona had been impersonating a teenage boy, using Fionn's nickname of Finn. She'd looked so much like her older brother that Brigid thought his specter had come to haunt her. "I had always wanted you to be mine, Brigid, but Fionn had your affections first. I couldn't go against my best friend." Her hands became engulfed in his larger ones. "Seeing you today reminded me that my heart never pushed you out, nor forgotten you."

He slid from the chair on to a knee. Brigid was shocked, her eyes wide. "You don't have to love me, Brigid. I've enough love to compensate both of us. Marry me and let me provide a home for you and for Richard."

Emotions waged war in her head and her heart. Ian would be a great husband and father. She knew it meant leaving Fiona in her worst hour as she adjusted to her blindness. But, oh, how she wanted to go back east. Back with her parents. "Fiona and Margaret need me, especially now."

"Fiona will understand, believe me," he said.

Yes, Fiona was selfless enough, even if she did need her, or anyone. The merits of the proposal were great. But she wanted more than just an offer based on the past. "Would you court me first?"

Ian grinned. "Gladly." He tilted his head. "It will give me a chance to win Richard's favor, too." All the old feelings of how wonderful Ian was came rushing back to Brigid. She wanted to be a wife and mother. Needed the stability Ian was offering. Brigid realized long ago she wasn't inherently strong like Fiona, or like Margaret and Josephine. Brigid needed someone to support her. Was the revelation even fair to Ian?

"I see you're conflicted. Sleep on it, Brigid. Know that you don't have to return my affections. Maybe, someday, you'll grow to feel as I do, and love me back. No matter your feelings, since I know there's some affection toward me, let me be a beau, then a husband to you, and a father to Richard."

Brigid felt the tears stream down her face. Some were tears of relief at the offer. Some were tears of joy Ian had professed his devotion. The thing she wanted most was being offered— stability. She had, in fact, had stability here, but not in the manner she needed. She wanted her own family home and life. Brigid would be a fool to turn Ian's offer down.

"If you aren't having sport of me, Ian, I'll agree."

Ian beamed a smile at her.

If it didn't work out, Brigid thought, at least I'll be back with my mother.

JO HAD ADAM perched on her hip, as she and Tessa gave their goodbye hugs to Brigid, Richard, and Ian. Margaret stayed close to Fiona's side. She knew this farewell was hard on Fiona. Added to the burden, few, outside of the family, were privy to Fiona's blindness. They had agreed to keep it quiet for as long as possible. "How are you holding up, honey?" she asked, head bent close to Fiona's ear.

"Fine, I guess." Fiona's hand found hers, and Margaret ignored how it would appear to outside observers, given they'd be correct whether they knew it or not. Eventually, any observer would realize Fiona was incapable of maneuvering the people and obstacles of the busy train station if they cared to examine them close enough. She wished Fiona could have seen the signage about the ladies of the evening, and the police direction on their appropriate and expected behavior and their curfews. Margaret hadn't remembered seeing the signs when they'd arrived five years ago. Granted, it was a trying time for the whole family. Telling her about them had made Fiona smile, but it lost some of the humor they could have shared if they'd been able to read them together.

The day already held such sadness, even a little humor was better than none. She, too, would miss Brigid and Richard. It had been great to see Ian again. Fantastic to visit with Janice and learn of the wonderful things she'd accomplished since their separation. Margaret was pleased to learn Janice had put her party girl days behind her. Margaret's family and friends were growing up and moving on.

"Do you think our Brigid and Ian are really happy?" Fiona asked.

"Yes, honey, they are. Truly. Brigid and Richard couldn't do better. Ian will be a great husband and father. He has Nana and Claire to help." Nana Donnelly, Ian's mother, had helped Margaret's own mother during her illness. His sister, Claire, had been a close friend to Fiona.

Fiona nodded. "I'm glad Brigid was able to move beyond Fionn."

"And Nicholas?" Margaret couldn't help but notice their interaction. After Ethel's death, the stirrings of closeness and then the distance they perpetrated had been strange to watch.

"Nah, that rapport was more a friend comforting a friend." Fiona leaned even closer to Margaret's ear. "I worried a bit, though, that Brigid might try to garner a relationship with Langford."

Margaret chuckled. "Thankfully, the spark was quickly diminished. No one should be that desperate."

"I'm glad Tessa doesn't share his qualities — or his lack of any good traits."

"Touché," Margaret agreed. "Here come Brigid and Ian."

Brigid pulled Fiona into a hug. "Please don't be angry with me for leaving."

"Never. I've always only wanted you happy. Ian will take care of you and Richard. He's like a brother to me, so I can finally have you as my sister-in-law," Fiona said, grinning.

"I'll do my best to make them both happy," Ian said. He

nudged Brigid toward Margaret's side so he could better focus on Fiona. "It's been wonderful seeing you again. Mother and Claire will be relieved to know you are all right." He took Margaret's hand in his, then Fiona's. "Should you ever decide to come back home, let me know. I'll be here, immediately, to get all of you."

"Thank you for the offer, Ian," Margaret said, "but we're happy here. This is our home." She knew Fiona shared her position on the subject.

Ian shrugged. "Gotta tell Mother I tried, as she wouldn't forgive me if I hadn't done so."

He and Brigid moved away, and Janice took their place. "It's been a pleasure, my old friend."

"Watch who you're calling old."

"Figuratively, Meggie." Janice heaved a weary sigh. "Last chance, my dear's—"

Margaret scowled and took a menacing step forward and lowered her voice. "If you offer yourself to my wife, so help me, Janice."

Janice gave a full-throated laugh. "I know better." She turned toward Fiona and gave her a full-body perusal that Margaret was glad Fiona would never see. "You're still a handsome woman, Fiona. Even without the suits. Miss the newsboy cap, too." Janice shook her head. "No, I want to make certain I didn't overstep myself with Adam."

Fiona gave a throaty growl. "My nephew-son stays here with his auntie-mother's."

"Just wanted to make certain," Janice said. "Couldn't ask for a more perfect family. All right, dears, I'm off. Don't be strangers. Come visit."

Margaret knew she meant well, honestly offered the invitation. Deep down, Janice knew as surely as Margaret, they would never be able to accept.

The call for boarding was given, and they waived their final goodbyes, as their Boston-family boarded. Margaret wrapped an arm around Fiona's waist. "As good as friends visiting us is, I'm looking forward to time alone with you and Adam."

"Are you sure you're okay with raising Adam?"

Margaret frowned. "Why wouldn't I be? He is perfect. Cavanaugh through and through, even as a Graham."

Fiona gave a weighty shrug. "Not like I'm capable of giving you a child. Now, I may not be around to see him to adolescence, let alone manhood."

Tears filled Margaret's eyes. "Oh, honey. Adam couldn't be

more your son if he'd been of your blood. Every minute the three of us share is, and will be, precious."

"Everything okay?" Jo asked, Adam still on her hip. Tessa smiled warmly from Jo's side.

Margaret squeezed Fiona's waist and caressed Adam's cheek. "Wonderful. Just telling Fiona how lucky I am to have the perfect family. Let's all go home."

Adam leaned forward and wrapped an arm each around her and Fiona. "Auntie's go home."

Beaming a smile, Margaret ignored the tears that fell. Happy tears were always welcomed.

Chapter Twenty-seven

"WHAT IS THAT smell?" Margaret asked. She stepped into the kitchen just as dark smoke rose from the cast iron skillet Jo was tending at the stove. Adam giggled from his seat at the table next to Fiona, who currently made exaggerated facial expressions for his benefit. They'd placed Adam in the chair Brigid used, but he wanted to sit next to Fiona. Margaret couldn't take offense because Adam would often offer Fiona his assistance.

Best of all, he'd opened up a little bit at a time and bonded with all three of them in the last two weeks. The one concern they seemed to have was his reluctance to leave the house. It didn't pose a problem yet as the family was still adjusting to the loss of Brigid and Richard in the home, Jo's sulking because she had to avoid Tessa, and Fiona's learning to maneuver the house and journey to the barn for her work.

"Ugh, why can't I ever get this right." Jo removed the pan from the stove, placed it on the potholder on the counter by the sink, and opened a window. "Brigid made this look so easy." Margaret stood behind Jo and looked down. Their collective stomachs would pay for this debacle later. "It's fine, honey. Still edible," she lied. "After school is out, I'll be able to assume this responsibility for the summer."

"Glad I don't have to see it," Fiona whispered.

"What did you say?" Jo demanded as she spun and nearly bumped into Margaret.

Adam giggled again, not able to squash it behind his hand.

Fiona appeared to struggle with holding the laughter back and asked, "Any more toast need buttering?"

"Maybe Jo do the jam," Adam said.

"Does," Margaret said automatically.

"Good idea, Adam. She can't ruin that," Fiona said. She pursed her lips. "I don't think."

Jo stomped her foot. "All right, you two. You're welcomed to take over."

Margaret turned away from Jo as she struggled to maintain her own chuckle from escaping. She sat at the table, her attention fell on Fiona, glad to see her interact with the family instead of moping in her room. Despite another burned breakfast they'd still force themselves to eat. Margaret loved the playful atmosphere.

"Wouldn't be a problem if Tessa were here," Jo mumbled, dishing out the blackened remains of eggs and ham. A single tear slid down her right cheek. "She can cook."

Adam's head bobbed up from the inspection of his breakfast. "Tessa make cookies?"

"The very best," Jo answered with a strained smile.

Jo sat at the table, and Margaret gave a pat to her shoulder meant to offer reassurance. "Hold out a little longer, honey. We'll figure out some way. Maybe Warren will come around." Fiona and Jo snorted simultaneously. "Well, it would be nice."

There was a knock at the back door, and Nicholas opened it enough to stick his head in. "Everyone decent?" Even Adam joined in the chorus of no's. "Goody," Nicholas said. He stepped inside and closed the door behind him. "Uh-oh. Jo's turn to cook?"

"Ha, ha, funny. Keep it up, and I'll sit on your chest and scrape off the fuzz you call a mustache."

Nicholas guffawed. "Bad morning?" He sat in the empty chair across from Jo.

"Something like that," Margaret answered for Jo. "I believe the fault is with the skillet." She grinned at him when he responded with a quirked eyebrow. "You're more than welcome to join us."

Adam wrinkled his nose and nudged his plate forward. "You can have mine."

"Adam, finish your breakfast," Margaret said.

"Okay," he said, voice sullen.

"You'll need your energy," Margaret said. "You'll be coming to school with me today. It's the last day, and I thought you'd like to be with the other children."

Adam paled. He didn't say anything for a long time, then asked, "Do I have ta? I wanna stay here."

Fiona's brow furrowed. "It'll be good for you to get out, be around other kids."

"Wanna stay here." His voice was so quiet. Margaret wondered if he'd been punished for speaking his mind.

"Are you afraid the other kids will be mean?" Jo asked. Adam shook his head. "'Cause, if they are, Auntie Jo will give them her mean look." She crossed her arms and presented her fiercest scowl.

Nicholas gave a feigned shudder. "Goodness. Remind me to stay on your good side."

"Are there any reasons you don't want to go?" Fiona asked.

Adam shrugged. Not able to see, Fiona reached out, settling a hand on the top of his head. "Sweetie, if we know what's bothering you, we can fix it."

Margaret leaned forward and placed her elbows on the table. "I'll be with you the whole time and never leave your side. None of the children will say or do anything to hurt you." Adam squirmed in his chair. Margaret sighed. She didn't want him afraid but didn't want to incite emotional trauma by forcing him to do what he wasn't comfortable with doing. "I'd hoped you would want to spend time with me today. Maybe I can find someone to come by and look after you."

Adam's expression revealed guilt. He was too young to be remorseful for emotions he probably couldn't identify. "I'll go with you."

"You don't have to if you're not comfortable, Adam," Margaret explained.

Nicholas raised his hand, schoolroom style. "Ooh, can I have his cookie."

"I get a cookie?" Adam asked as if that might be the only catalyst for his compliance.

"Aunt Margaret always has snacks and games for the last day. Bet you could talk her into more than one," Fiona said in a stage-whisper.

"I won't force you to come, Adam. I can bring a couple back for you." She stood. "I'll go see if I can find someone to watch you while I'm away. Nicholas and your aunts have a lot to do in the workshop today, or I'd let you stay with them."

Adam got down from his chair, with only a little assistance from Fiona, and rushed toward her. "I'll go. It's okay." But his tone suggested otherwise.

"Are you sure?" she asked. Adam nodded. "Thank you, Adam." Margaret returned to her chair, and Adam crawled into her lap.

FIONA WALKED OUTSIDE with Nicholas and Jo, ready to get some work completed. She fully intended to concentrate a lot of time with Margaret and Adam over the summer. Today, they had to fine-tune a piece or two, which they would load on the truck so Jo could make the deliveries. After today, any work done would be completely Jo's commissions and responsibility. She could tell Jo looked forward to creating her own reputation, one beyond just being the youngest Cavanaugh sister. Jo needed this opportunity for self-growth and self-awareness, especially since the business would be solely hers when Fiona died.

Fiona was better at maneuvering the workshop without serious harm to herself or the tools, products, and tables. Fiona sat at her most comfortable workstation and sanded the few blemishes from her latest work before it would be labeled complete. Off to the left she could hear Jo and Nicholas loading the truck. Fiona grinned, picturing the perfectly groomed Nicholas working beside her tomboy sister, both probably perspiring with their efforts, as they chatted away with each other.

The gentle rasp of sandpaper across wood settled her. Fiona took this opportunity to rehash the odd reluctance to leave the house that Adam displayed at breakfast. What could be troubling the child to cause such distress? She was happy he agreed to go with Margaret, though hesitantly. Fiona decided she'd talk with Margaret tonight, discuss ways to broach the topic with Adam. They needed to find a resolution as a family.

"That's the last one," Jo announced. "I'll get these dropped off, and then Cavanaugh Sisters can, for the most part, go on hiatus."

"Are you sure you don't want me to come along?" Nicholas asked. "I'm just as capable of unloading as loading."

"I'll manage. Besides, I'll have help at each of the three stops." Jo snickered. "Some men aren't bothered by the way I dress when the wives are home. They're expected to treat me nice, or their women tend to devise some nasty forms of penance." A pause. "Fiona?" Jo strode closer to her. "It's looking rather grey out today, will probably rain." Fiona suspected where the weather update would lead. "Would it be all right if I drive downtown? Just in case I see anyone I know?"

Fiona bit her lower lip. She hated that Jo needed to suffer through subterfuge. But Fiona would have done and did, anything to find clandestine moments to be with Margaret. She at least had the guise of being male to assist in her efforts at the time. "Be careful, sweetie. Warren's not the sharpest tool in the workshop, but he's certainly sneaky enough to consider the same weather patterns as cover for furtive behavior."

Jo kissed the top of Fiona's head. "Not to worry. I'll be cautious." She squeezed Fiona in a tight hug. "Rest up. After today, Margaret and Adam are going to run you ragged."

"Love you, Jo." Fiona tapped the arms around her. "I hope you can find a few moments with Tessa. She's pretty swell."

"Yes, she is. Thanks, Fiona. Be back." Then Jo was racing to the truck and driving away.

"Wish life could be more accommodating. For everyone, especially young people in love." Fiona placed the sandpaper and box on the worktable. "I appreciate you helping."

"Nothing you wouldn't have done for me. Can I make a suggestion?" Fiona nodded. "Let's take Jo's advice. We'll go back to the kitchen, I'll make us coffee, and we can talk." A silent interval, then, "If you're amenable, I'd like your commentary on a matter, personal to you, but concerning a topic that we covered a couple weeks ago."

Fiona could sense his tension. "That was long-winded. Are you saying you have questions relating to your feelings for Ruth? And they can only be answered from an invasion of my personal life?"

"Wow, I'm glad you speak the language of awkward — and avoidance." Nicholas chortled. "Coffee first?"

"Of course." Always the gentleman, Nicholas escorted Fiona across the yard to the back door, seated her at the table, and fussed around the kitchen as he made coffee. All made Fiona grateful. "So, what's on your mind, Nicholas?"

Fiona heard the solid clink of saucer and cup placed before her, in a not-so-subtle announcement of its location. Then, the slow scrape of chair legs on the floor before he sat. "Done a lot of soul-searching since my confession two weeks ago, which dredged up a lot of my feelings for Ruth."

"Is that not a good thing?" she asked.

"Not if you consult the horrors of my sleepless nights. I've done Ruth a disservice, haven't I?"

"And to yourself, Nicholas. Were you able to reach a decision?"

Nicholas inhaled deeply. "Just that she's a chapter I really need to finish. When she refused to marry me, I thought Ruth didn't love me with the same fervor I did for her. But, maybe, she strode closer alongside the truth than I recognized. Did I love her because of what she knew or despite it? When Ruth pushed me away, told me to find to my guiding star, I hurt with one more rejection. And, unlike with my biological family, loved her enough that her dismissal was soul-wrenching. I think part of me believed I hated Ruth for what I perceived as her perfidy."

"She simply wanted you to be certain, Nicholas." Fiona could follow this path of his. Nicholas would leave soon. She didn't fault him wanting to do so. He truly did need closure. "Ruth needed you to do this for her, too. From what you told me Ruth battled her own demons. Did you love her because she stood by your side, and you owed her—"

"It wasn't like that," he said defensively.

"We know that, but did Ruth? She was shunned and stared at for her deformity all her life. Then, along comes someone who wants to be with her anyway. Could she have talked herself into believing you pitied her?" Fiona leaned closer to him, sliding the coffee cup toward the middle of the table, rested her elbows on the top. "One thing I know about, Nicholas, is being haunted by the monsters of our past. The hardest struggle in life is to see them for what they are and move beyond them. The struggles won't always go away. But we can compartmentalize them, stuff them in the back corner of a mental cupboard. Silly as it may be if others knew about our family meetings, it's what keeps us together and strong. Because we communicate."

"How'd you get so smart?" Nicholas asked. "Fancy thinking going on there as well."

She rolled her eyes and leaned back in her chair. "Helps to be in love with a teacher. Margaret is above me in so many ways. But she doesn't see life in that way. She is her best when I accept the exuberance when sharing a point of view, explaining in magnificent detail a topic that has caught her attention. Yes, sometimes she gets to a place where, true to my own upbringing and station, Margaret needs to dumb-down for me. The stupid street kid who never finished school."

"Neither Margaret or I consider you stupid. That's a hateful word. You have an intelligence that comes from the heart. Because of being a street kid."

"Thanks." She grudgingly accepted his compliment. "I do pick up things and, it benefits me, and Margaret sees I'm a better person for it. She knows my reactions are from wanting to be the best person I can be for her. And our love of each other, my love of her passion, humor, and understanding are why I love her so deeply." Fiona suspected the future was as scary for Margaret as for her. She wanted eternity with Margaret but would have to settle for a handful of days, months, maybe a few more years. If she were lucky. Fiona needed to eke out every ounce of time they had remaining. Margaret should never doubt that Fiona loved her with everything she had to give. Fiona felt his hand on her arm. She apologized, swiped at tears she now felt fall.

"No need. The purging of this type of fluid is good for the body." Nicholas gave a comforting squeeze. "You alright?"

Fiona sniffed and giggled. "Was that a fancy way to say crying is okay?"

"I do what I can." His tone was teasing. She liked that best about him, his efforts to bring humor to temper an emotionally charged situation. "As you were saying, communication is important. Something Ruth and I should have done before emotions took over."

"And why Margaret and I may take a step forward with Adam and find it prudent to often take two steps back. It'll take time, but we'll figure out Adam's fear."

Nicholas expelled a heavy breath. "Which brings me to a personal question. Before that, I'd like to say I pass no judgments but seek clarity."

"That sounds...scary. Never good if you have to preface with a disclaimer."

"You can't judge my sincerity in my expressions, so I hope you believe—"

"Just ask your question, Nicholas." Why was he so awkward?

"Why did you accept Adam? Not that he's not a great kid. I mean, you have so much going on with your health."

"My slowly dying—or quick, under certain circumstances. Leaving behind the one brightness in my heart, Margaret. Those same reasons are why I can do it."

"It was awful presumptuous of Janice. What if you and Margaret declined?"

"Janice knew that wouldn't happen." Fiona wondered how best to explain. "Will Adam work as a painful reminder in the future? Probably. He'll also be a reminder of happier times. Will it be hard for Margaret to be forced to raise a child on her own? Yes. But I hope Adam will be the catalyst for her to get up every morning. Jo will help as she can but has her own life to think about."

"But Fiona, why a child with obvious issues? He's afraid to leave the house. Won't that make raising him a lot harder?"

"For a time. Yes. We need to isolate the reason for Adam's fear." Fiona reached for her coffee and finished the now cold liquid. She repressed a shiver from the repulsive taste.

Nicholas noticed and moved away from the table. "Let me refresh your cup," he said. "Weak coffee is bad enough. Cold coffee is criminal."

"Thank you." Fiona waited until he returned to the table. "The easiest way for me to explain this is by using us as examples." She cleared her throat. "Despite your horrible upbringing, Ruth showed you a more positive outlook because she believed and cared for you. My childhood started out okay but was quick to turn negative. If I hadn't met and been loved by Margaret, I could have met a brutal end. I don't want to believe I'd have given into the criminal element, but I can't say for certain."

"I assume Jo would have met an unfortunate end too."

Fiona winced at the reminder of what Jo's future had held. "None of us are unscathed. Which is why we will do everything we can to put Adam on a proper path to achieve his fullest potential. As a family we will help him overcome the worst of his fears as best we can. There aren't any guarantees, but we'll never know the possibilities if we don't try."

"You're a better person than I am, Fiona."

"How so?"

"Don't know if I could take on the responsibility of another person's emotions, and like Adam, physically damaged child and expect a positive outcome."

"Ah, but you can't discount the possibility either. There are so many children in need of loving care and support to keep them from surrendering to the dark recesses' life offers. Maybe you need to ask yourself—if your reunion works out—how beneficial Ruth could be, or how she would react to the chance to do so for another life. Because given the prospects in our lives in this day and age, this is the only way for us to have a chance to influence another's existence."

Chapter Twenty-eight

MARGARET RELEASED THE children for the summer break. Adam silently sat at a desk in the front row of the classroom, a picture book opened, but he wasn't reading. Instead, Margaret noted his surreptitious glances at her, and sometimes at the door. She finalized grades into the individual report cards before the beginning of a summer off from teaching. An older woman, with greying hair pulled into a tight bun at the back of her head, walked in as if cued. "Hello, Mrs. Goodman. Ready for summer?"

"Oh my, yes. I get to catch up on my knitting and quantity time with my grandchildren." Mrs. Goodman wrinkled her pert little nose. She was the epitome of the expectation of a sweet grandmother. When she passed Adam, she smiled down at him, gave a hello, and brushed her hand down his back. It was a tender exchange, but Margaret thought she caught a sadness and — was that a tear?

"Quantity time?" Margaret raised an eyebrow. "Shouldn't you mean quality?"

Mrs. Goodman giggled. "And I would mean it if my old bones could keep up with them. Can't say whether the children find the quality intended. So, before they exhaust me into a somnolent state, I aim for quantity."

"I understand," Margaret said. And she certainly did. Some days the students were so exuberant, she felt she needed to drag herself home. "What can I do for you?"

"Wanted to privately take this opportunity to collect all the report cards, and wish you a wonderful summer," the older woman said, moving around the desk. Margaret stood respectfully and was wrapped in a warm hug. In Margaret's ear, she whispered, "Congratulations and best wishes with little Adam. He'll be a blessing to your already blessed house."

Adam wasn't ready for school, but she had explained to the principal and his secretary, Mrs. Goodman, the change to her circumstances. There would be times she would need to bring him to work. Would he even be school age by the time she lost Fiona? Her chest responded as if a vice squeezed her heart at the thought. Stop it, she reprimanded herself, focus on having her now. "Thank you, Mrs. Goodman. May you have both quality and quantity time for the summer and beyond." Mrs. Goodman left after a final goodbye. She was certain Adam looked relieved at her departure but still wary. Margaret remembered the information Janice shared about Adam's past. From his reactions, she believed she understood Adam's concern.

Okay. Time to focus on Fiona and Adam.

Margaret assured all was cleared from her desk, pulled her handbag from the bottom desk drawer, and slung it on a shoulder. She crouched beside Adam. "Wanna talk?" He shook his head. "Worried Mrs. Goodman had come to take you away?" Adam shrugged. "Well, let me tell you, young man, you aren't going anywhere. You belong to and with us, Adam Graham, always a part of the Cavanaugh clan. Okay?"

Adam reached over and embraced her neck with small arms in a fierce grip. "Promise?" he asked.

"Promise," she said. "I'll pop anyone in the nose if they try to take you from us. Not even Jack Dempsey could take you from me." Adam released her and stood beside her and looked up, an expression of amazement lit his face. "If you think I'm tough, Auntie Fiona is even stronger."

"But she can't see," Adam said, his tone confused.

"Don't let that fool you. Auntie Fiona is ferocious when protecting her family. You know some of our secrets aren't to be shared outside the house, right?" Adam nodded. "When you're a little older, we'll tell you the reason Fiona has her scars. How protective she can be for us. But it's so secret, people might hurt her if they knew, so we have to keep the secrets in our heads and hearts. Okay?"

"Okay."

Margaret extended her hand, which he took with a watery smile. "You ready to go home?" Adam placed his tiny hand in hers. Together they left the schoolhouse.

The day was grey, and the wind was picking up speed. Margaret considered calling to see if Nicholas was around to pick them up, but figured they could make the few blocks to and over the Arkansas River to the opposite side before any storm arrived. It was nice to exercise her legs and spend time with Adam before she started supper to celebrate the end of the school year. Then a relaxing evening with the family. Inwardly, she gave a naughty grin. And a not so relaxing evening with Fiona.

They walked about two blocks when a dirty, white, diaper-delivery van pulled up beside them. Two men got out. Margaret pulled Adam close to her when she recognized them as two of the bullies from the visit to Tessa's shop over a month ago. The fat one pointed a gun at them. "Get inside," he demanded. Before the scene registered, the other grabbed Adam and yanked him from her, thrust him into the man with the gun. She made a fist and slammed it into his face. He quirked a grin and returned the favor.

"Love it when broad's play rough," he said. Margaret was woozy. When the man grabbed her at the waist and propelled her to the open doors of the van, Margaret used her nails to rake gashes down the left side of his face. His response was to toss her inside, where she landed on piles of laundry bags, filled with what smelled like soiled diapers. "Maybe we can have some fun together when this is over." He climbed in beside her. "Hurry up, Donald," he growled.

"Damn, Walter. The kid won't hold still," Donald said. Adam fought to get free but never uttered a word.

"Then sock him one," Walter said.

"No, please don't," Margaret said. At her words, Adam glanced at her. She held her arms out. Donald tossed him toward her. As Donald closed the back doors, Adam climbed over the bags and into her embrace. Walter got into the passenger seat, and Margaret glanced to the front, which opened to the driver's seat. A laughing Thomas Gendry stared back at her. "Someone will call the police," she said.

"Let 'em. Langford is ready if they do," Thomas said, his grin spreading.

"What do you want with us?" Margaret held Adam tight to her chest. He nestled into her body. So this was really about Warren Langford and his further punishment of the Cavanaugh's. "Warren not man enough to do this himself?"

Thomas raised a shoulder. "He's gonna come to Daddy's telephone company. You and the kid can go after he's done."

"And I've had some fun." Walter leered at her, and she felt dirtier than the soiled cloth surrounding them.

Thomas turned back to the steering wheel and drove. Over his shoulder, he said, "Better check with Langford. Don't know how much he's willing to ignore."

"I'll take my chances," Walter said, his eyes grazing over her insultingly.

Margaret focused on the bloody furrows she'd given Walter, wondering if she and Adam would get out of this alive. Resolving to fight if she could, but accepted she may have to suffer Walter's assault if it meant protecting Adam.

She closed her eyes and kissed the top of Adam's head in

silent reassurance. Another attack planned for the woman Margaret loved with every fiber of her being. How much more could Fiona take? Would this be the day she lost her forever?

THE PHONE CALL made Fiona's entire body tremble. Luckily, Nicholas was still at the house. His presence and help were a balm that kept her from cracking up or breaking down entirely. The caller had been Thomas, and he demanded Fiona come to the telephone company, alone, downtown. If not, he'd settle his dispute with Fiona by harming Margaret and Adam. What perceived feud did they share? Why take her family as hostages? Hell, she was blind — not that many knew — so it wouldn't take much to ambush her. Holding back the panic after the call was nearly impossible. Fiona wondered how the spoiled little weasel got possession of her wife and son. He'd told her it wouldn't do any good to call the police. That information let her know Warren, to whatever extent, was involved.

Fiona and Nicholas drove to town. Often, Margaret stayed late to grade papers and prepare lessons plans, so Fiona hadn't been overly concerned when she hadn't arrived home on time. She hoped Adam enjoyed the day but worried how this turn of events could emotionally damage him.

"That sonofabitch hurts Margaret or Adam, and I'll kill him."

"You need to calm down, Fiona. Won't be much use to them if you're caught off guard," Nicholas said. She appreciated his being the voice of reason. Didn't change her stomach aching with the heavy ball of worry. "We have to think. You know this is a trap, right?"

Fiona did know, which only added to her distress. This situation was so much like the one five years ago. That reminder had her seesawing between panic and rage. With Jimmy, Fiona was aware of the possible circumstances she walked into then. This time she didn't just face a hateful opponent on her own. Margaret and Adam's safety needed consideration. "Don't have a lot of options. What are you suggesting?"

"Well, Thomas made the call, which means Walter and Donald will probably be involved. His ego will want to play in front of his puppets. They're known bullies, so will be relying on strength rather than smarts." Nicholas must be getting closer to town as Fiona heard the increase in activity from the open car window. She wondered how much longer until they reached their destination. "I don't think this is Thomas's idea. If anything, his gripe is against Jo, not you. It leaves me to believe we're dealing with Warren. Warren's the one who thinks he has a legitimate grudge. But Warren isn't going to show himself without cause. He has too much to lose. Which means he'll be hiding until all his little ducks have positioned things in a neat little row."

"So, Warren could or couldn't be there?" A headache was building from the stress. This had a worst-case scenario written all over it. Being a cop, Warren had a lot to lose if the situation and whatever he'd planned went badly. He couldn't have loose ends. Couldn't have his part in this get out to his superiors. If Warren was personally involved, he couldn't leave witnesses, which meant them all. Fiona couldn't see how she and her family would possibly get out of this alive if Warren and flunkies had their way. Fiona would make certain, if anyone suffered, it would be Warren.

"Warren has an ego of his own," Nicholas said. "I think he'll want to take a risk—for the adrenaline rush if not his ego—and witness your downfall personally. Which gives us our advantage."

"Which is?"

Nicholas chuckled. "His focus on the outcome and not the process."

"You've lost me. How does Warren's ego work in our favor?" Fiona's emotions fluctuated all over the place. She couldn't grasp what track Nicholas's thoughts were taking.

"Thomas called and told you to come, right?" he asked.

"Yes." Fiona grew frustrated. "Please, Nicholas, get to the point."

Nicholas's tone grew conciliatory when he continued. "He gave no direction to leave whoever brought you outside, which means he doesn't know you're blind or didn't consider a second person. Warren may also be unaware of your blindness in thinking he'd just taught you a lesson, not irreparable damage."

Fiona nodded, understanding. "I go in alone."

"Exactly. If you think you can pull off being sighted," Nicholas said. "Either way, we're outnumbered. We've as much an element of surprise as Thomas or Warren. There's also the obvious fact you and I alone are brighter than the four of them put together."

"I can agree with your assessment, but remind you we don't have their combined strength. Don't forget the added disadvantage that one of us is blind."

"Hey, only when it comes to my heart," Nicholas quipped.

She chuckled, appreciated his use of levity to keep her from going over the hysterical edge. "We can assume my family is held on the third floor of the building too."

"How so?" Nicholas asked.

"The telephone company is where she had the field trip earlier this month for her students. She told me the layout when she made the arrangements. Margaret explained the switchboard operators were located on the second floor. The first floor holds the offices and reception area, which will be closed this time of day. That leaves the third floor as the most likely place for anything close to nefarious. That floor is for maintaining the supplies and storage. Thomas, or Warren, will want to limit witnesses."

Fiona felt the car come to a stop, heard when Nicholas shut the engine off.

"Why bring them back here? Why not stay at the school?" Nicholas asked. "Better chance of privacy, I would think."

She snorted. "Please tell me you don't really expect to understand a disturbed mind. If I were to hazard a guess, it would be because Thomas's father owns the building, so Thomas's presence wouldn't be unexpected. As for Warren, his appearance would be unremarkable, I guess, as a policeman. Also, the police station is located right across the street. Easier for him to step in and out with minimum detection."

Nicholas barked a laugh. "Take this as a compliment, Fiona, please. But it seems to me you understand the warped mind just fine."

"Thanks," she said with sarcasm. "Are we here?"

"Yes. So how about I get you close to the door, you go in and try to play nice with the idiots? Oh, and not get killed by Warren or Thomas. After a few moments, I'll follow you inside." He snickered. "Probably save the day and my godson. Hero of the hour."

Fiona shook her head. "You know, Nicholas, sometimes, like now, I want to throttle you."

"Aw, you do love me."

True to his word, Nicholas brought her close to the intended destination, explained the entrance was four strides ahead with the door on the right. "Okay, here goes nothing."

RANDALL COULDN'T SHAKE the feeling Sergeant Langford was up to no good. It went beyond believing Warren exuded *icky* from his pores. This feeling telegraphed the sergeant was up to something more insidious. Randall knew it in his bones. He glanced up toward the darkening skies. A storm was rolling in.

He hadn't expected to see Fiona and Nicholas standing outside the front entrance of the Telephone Company building. The same building Warren entered not too long ago. What the hell was going on? Hell, why was Nicholas walking away? He'd just left Fiona defenseless against someone as dangerous as Warren. She was only one woman, after all. And, hadn't Jo—albeit with reluctance—stated Fiona lost her sight after an encounter with Warren?

Before he could think better on the matter, logical thought to alert someone or bring help along, Randall crossed the street and entered the building.

Then stopped immobile. The door closed, and the soles of Randall's shoes squeaked on the linoleum from his abrupt halt. Donald and Walter stood in front of him with...were those finger gashes on his cheek? Both held Spalding bats, Donald, on his shoulder, and Walter repetitively slapped his against a palm. The sounds of slow footfalls—Fiona's—echoed from the enclosed stairwell. If they let her through unhampered, then she waited for a different fate.

"Looky here, Walter," Donald said. "It's Jo's girlfriend, the cop."

Walter sniffed insultingly. "Nah. Randall here ain't a girlfriend, just a sissy." They inched their way to either side of him. Randall automatically reached for his service weapon. "Tsk, tsk," Walter said. "Play nice."

A blow to the side of his head dropped Randall to a knee, one hand to the back of his head. He'd turned to watch Walter, while Donald took advantage. Luckily, for Randall, physical activity wasn't the fatter man's forte. The hit hurt like the dickens but didn't incapacitate him.

The distinctive click of a gun's hammer pulled back caused Randall to stiffen in anticipation, and Donald and Walter to bite back the teasing laughter, gulping audibly. Okay, maybe not a bad sound to hear at all, he thought. Randall tried to turn and see who stood behind him, but the blow made him queasy and dizzy.

"Would like to offer you the time to get hold of yourself but would prefer you to do so with all due haste, if you please."

Take my time but hurry, Randall thought with frustration. Only Mr. Tirrell would speak at odds like that and expect to be understood. With a deep breath through his nose, Randall got to his feet and pulled his weapon free from the holster. "Good job," Nicholas said. He stood, his legs a bit wobblier than he'd like. "If you'll keep an eye on the riff-raff."

"What the hell's going on?" he demanded through gritted teeth.

Nicholas shifted until he stood at the bottom of the staircase. He jutted his chin to where Donald and Walter now stood together. "Gendry has Margaret and Adam upstairs somewhere."

"Son of a —"

"Exactly." Nicholas placed a foot on the bottom step. "You okay here?"

"Yeah, but I should go up there," Randall said. "Sergeant Langford's up there, too."

"Suspected as much." Nicholas grinned. "I'd let you take this if you hadn't just been clobbered with a bat. More than that, Braddock. If this doesn't end well, you'll need to make certain the true and correct version is given." Without a sound, Nicholas was gone.

"Hey, Randall," Donald said. "We haven't done anything."

"Except assault a police officer in the line of duty."

"Donald will make it up to you, won't ya?" Walter suggested, then elbowed Donald in the rib with an elbow. "He's got money. Oh, and Langford said it would be okay. So, we're sorta helping the police. All you need is a little forgetfulness."

Randall smirked. "Gonna run through town in dresses?" Both stared in total incomprehension. "What it would take for this sissy to forget and let you go." A too-long pause before understanding reached them. Hesitantly, they nodded. Randall shook his head sadly. "Aw, you took too long. Can't believe either of you would find redemption." During the conversation, Randall noted a door off to the side of the room that appeared to be the main office of the phone company. He needed to get upstairs, keep the situation from escalating. Keep the Cavanaugh's safe.

"We can take him," Walter sneered.

"Nervous hand. Gun could go off." Randall grinned. "You're my first target, Walter. Donald's only got his flab to help him." Donald whimpered. Short, firm waves of his weapon toward the right, Randall said, "Carefully boys, and walk backward." They did. "Okay, stop," he said. They were even with the door, a small square of wood reading: supply room, and a key seated in the lock. "Open it, Walter." Walter's hand trembled as he turned the knob. How quickly bullies transformed into babies with the turning of the table. The door opened. Randall felt a modicum of relief to find the closet, barely two square feet, held form papers on the only shelf, one bucket, and a stack of neatly folded rags. Nothing else. Nothing to aid in their immediate escape. "Inside, boys."

"What the hell, Braddock?" Donald sputtered, his expression registered panic. "I'm not going in there. I hate tight places. You know that from school."

"Should have thought of that before you assaulted a police officer and became accessories in a kidnapping." Randall pulled back the hammer with his thumb. "Here are your two choices. One, I shoot you fleeing the scene. Two, you get in the closet." Randall shrugged. "Closet gets you Walter's company. If I shoot you, you're the coroners' problem. Oh yeah, and dead." Donald pushed Walter into the closet and followed him inside. "Not my preferred choice, but I'll honor it."

There was a pounding on the door from inside as soon as Randall closed the door, locked it, and pulled the key free. He shoved the key in his pocket. Donald's strained voice sounded, muffled by the door. "Don't forget about us here, Braddock."

Randall snickered. "I'll try not to but, with this head wound, no guarantees." The pounding became more insistent. He stuffed a chair, the top rail wedged beneath the doorknob. Then, he pushed and dragged a desk to wedge against the chair to hold it from slipping free.

He felt better, Donald and Walter were out of commission. Randall headed for the stairs, his progress a lot slower than Nicholas's, and quieter than Fiona's. Every instinct told him to be cautious and prepared. The resolution to this situation was important to him. But more so for the Cavanaugh's upstairs, and to Jo—whom he owed so much.

Chapter Twenty-nine

FIONA'S HEART POUNDED so forcefully in her chest, she felt sure it would burst through her ribs at any moment. Her senses heightened, she prayed her heartbeat didn't announce her arrival before she was prepared to face Thomas—possibly Warren, too.

On the landing to the second floor, Fiona stopped and listened. She expected to be accosted or shot at any moment. Nothing. What the hell were they waiting for? She presented an easy target.

On her left, Fiona heard multiple voices of the telephone operators as they went about their business dispensing callers, making transfers, and talking amongst themselves between duties. Ahead, the same sense of someone's presence. Were her fear and tension making her hear what may not be there? Fiona didn't have to question herself any longer. The rapid movement shifted the air in front of her. A hand clamped over her mouth as she felt cold metal pressed to her temple, tension and excitement vibrated through the body of the man behind her. Recognition struck her, but Fiona couldn't place him immediately. Until the whisper in her ear.

"Payback time and no Jo." Thomas Gendry. If he was here, Warren must have Margaret and Adam. "Let's go," Thomas said, his voice harsh in her ear. He all but dragged her up another flight of stairs, the hand clamped across her mouth painfully, the barrel of the gun bruised as it bit into her flesh. Thomas, apparently reaching his goal, relinquished his hold as he shoved Fiona to the floor. A few feet ahead, Fiona heard Margaret whisper her name, fear, and a hint of relief in the tone. "Here she is," Thomas said, "let's get on with it."

"Not so fast," Warren's voice sounded off to her right.

"You promised—"

"Shut up," Warren ordered. Fiona knew when Warren moved from his position, not just from his heavy footfalls, but from his hate as it rippled in the air between them. With the none too gentle prompt from his foot into her hip, Warren said, "About six-feet at ten o'clock." Fiona wasted no time making her way in that direction, crawled on hands and knees, and uncaring of the picture she presented. "And nothing stupid, or you'll all get it."

"What the hell's that about?" Thomas asked.

"Shut the hell up." Warren must know about her permanent blindness.

Adam and Margaret's hands each touched and tugged her closer. "Are you okay?" Margaret asked. She cupped a cheek in her gentle appraisal. Adam remained silent, but he mirrored a touch to her cheek, his fear and concern telegraphed in small fingers.

Fiona found Adam's face with one hand, drew him closer, and placed a kiss to his forehead. Then Fiona did the same to Margaret. Behind her, Fiona heard Thomas mumble, "I'm gonna be sick." Had the situation been less life-threatening, Fiona would have given them a reason to be sickened by kissing Margaret fully and passionately, if this were a goodbye. These men were already on the brink of violence, and she wouldn't add to the volatility. "Did they hurt you?" she asked.

Adam shuffled close to her ear and whispered, "A mean man hit Auntie Margaret."

The heat of her rage filled Fiona. Before this was done, Warren would pay for that. Margaret must have sensed her furor. "I'm fine," Margaret said. "It's what they plan next that has me worried."

Fiona worried too. She suspected Warren had no intention of letting them live, although she was curious how he intended to deal with their bodies. He could shoot them, and probably would. He was a coward at heart, and guns expedited his cause. The telephone operators were a floor below. They would be witnesses to any sounds of gunfire. The scheduled time for business close time over, so any scuffling should be suspect. Why hadn't someone been alerted already?

"What now, Warren?"

Thomas snickered. "You get to show me how tough you are, all dressed and acting like a man."

"What of the people downstairs?" she asked.

Warren said, "Had them lock themselves in the room for their safety. I told them I had reason to believe the killer had broken in and hidden away up here. I, of course, as a duty-bound police officer, would do whatever necessary to apprehend the foul criminal." Foul criminal, she thought. It sounded like a case of pot and kettle, both being black and not recognizing the same.

So, any noise they made was already explained away. The people below believe themselves safe and part of Warren doing his civic duty. "I suppose you enlisted the help of the rich bully by agreeing to let Thomas prove—or try to prove—his manhood?"

"You bitch," Thomas said. She shouldn't provoke him, not with Margaret and Adam as hostages, but angry men made mistakes. Fiona needed every advantage she could get.

Heavy steps sounded before she was hauled backward and away from her family. "Wait," Warren bellowed. She felt Margaret reach for her, received the barest brush of her fingertips, and then heard the distinct sound of flesh against flesh before Margaret cried out. "Enough, Thomas," Warren said.

Thomas guffawed. "But it's fun. Besides, it's really pissing her off." Fiona didn't know which her he referred to, but the remark covered either. She couldn't see Margaret's face but suspected her equally livid.

Warren dragged her away from Margaret before he released her. Once again, she felt the cold steel against her temple. "Don't move." Fiona didn't. She needed to get her family out of this but had no idea how to accomplish that end. Wondered, too, if Nicholas saw what transpired and if he now gauged the proper time for his intervention.

Time to move this along. "All right, Warren. You've had your show of power. Let Margaret and Adam go and finish whatever you intend with me. Just know if that little prick hits Margaret again, I will kill him."

"Brave talk from a blind woman," Warren said.

Fiona grit her teeth. "Stating a fact."

"What the hell?" Thomas sounded surprised.

"It changes nothing," Warren said.

"Yeah, blind or not, I'll kick your sorry ass," Fiona said.

"We'll see. Okay, Thomas, you're about to get your wish. Over here. No, you stay where you are. Move again, and I'll shoot the boy." Fiona's fury continued to build. He had threatened serious harm to a child. Not any child, but hers. She had to rein in her emotions, or she'd be worthless to properly defend them. Fiona got to her feet, her hands clenched and unclenched repeatedly at her side. "You're an ass, threatening children."

"What? Don't I get points for letting Ethel's whelp live? Stupid bitch didn't even leave me the house in the will. I was supposed to get it and the brat when she changed the will, which she was supposed to do when she dumped the fancy bastard."

"Nice to know Nicholas and I had you pegged. You'll pay for her murder."

"Who will tell? No one will believe you." They hadn't found

any evidence, so he had that matter correct. He would get away with murder. Warren continued. "Better. This is what's going to happen. For helping me, Thomas gets his chance to beat you up."

"I'm supposed to just stand here and take it?" she asked. She may be blind but not entirely defenseless. If either of these men— males—believed Fiona would make this assault on her family easy for them, they were dumber than they looked.

Warren barked a laugh. "You have a free run to protect yourself as best you can."

"Let my family go."

"No, I want them to watch. After you're dead, if these two agree to keep this matter completely secret, they live. Same for you, of course."

"And if I kick Thomas's spoiled ass?"

"You won't." Warren sounded sure of himself. Fiona knew he had no intention of letting any of them live. Warren had too much hate in his blood. She would do everything in her power, until her dying breath, to protect Margaret and Adam. Fiona hoped if that were to be the outcome, she'd do whatever it took to assure both these idiots fell with her. "To give you a little assist," Warren said, continuing his soliloquy, "the room is large but filled with crates. There are broken and new telephone switchboard consoles against the walls, too. The center space, where you're standing, is cleared. Do whatever you need to damage each other, but try not to destroy too much else. An abundance of destroyed items would be hard to explain, even for me in the apprehension of a killer."

"You don't have to worry, Sergeant," Thomas said. His tone dripped with arrogance. "This will be quick."

The first blow was too. Fast. Straight to the jaw. Fiona stumbled to the right as she focused on the sounds around her. Warren hadn't moved, and she figured he probably wouldn't, not until Thomas finished his little display. Thomas, on the other hand, pranced about like the obvious victor. He believed her easy prey. For the moment, Fiona intended to let him believe the notion as he circled her, bouncing foot to foot. He alternated hard, heavy, open-palmed hits to various parts of her body. Thomas became the clever cat as he toyed with the helpless Fiona mouse.

Fiona bid her time. Listening. Eventually, Warren egged Thomas on. Thomas probably looked for an easy means to bring her down. She listened for any signal from Thomas. She realized he figured she couldn't defend herself. It didn't take long.

He was nearly finished with his second rotation around her when Fiona heard it. The short puff of air, not quite a snort, which stated his superiority in the battle he believed already won. Thomas paused, shifted body weight to the balls of his feet, and swung with his right arm.

Fiona dodged the blow, twisted her body right, and rammed an elbow into his abdomen. Bending forward, to protect his stomach, she assumed, Thomas wouldn't see the same elbow slammed down toward his back. Thomas dropped to a knee. Fiona wrapped an arm around his neck, as Thomas simultaneously wrapped one around her leg. Both fell to the floor, each losing their holds. Fiona knew she couldn't stay in that indefensible position, rolled away, and regained her feet.

A crashing roar sounded from outside and vibrated the building.

Thomas paused, and Fiona used the opportunity to sidle closer while she launched a punch to the general vicinity of Thomas's face. Her blow landed on the side of his head. She felt him turn in her direction. Fiona responded with an immediate left swing, and then a right. Both blows landed. She repeated until she realized he had moved out of reach.

Thomas launched himself at her. Fiona twisted, reached out her arm to wrap around his neck again, but the back of her head and upper right shoulder exploded in pain. Fiona vaguely heard Margaret's shouted warning as dizziness consumed her. She tried to get her bearings but could barely keep herself from dropping to the floor, waves of nausea consumed her. Fiona was losing the battle to maintain her awareness. She couldn't focus, couldn't gauge where Thomas was within the room. Where was Warren?

The weight of her failure to protect her family nearly suffocated Fiona. Then she heard running footfalls and another scream from Margaret. Finally, came another darkness, different from her blindness, as she felt herself falling. Falling.

Chapter Thirty

THE RAIN KEPT most of the shoppers from the town, which didn't bother Jo. She and Tessa talked about what Warren had done to Fiona, but they avoided physical contact with one another and kept verbal communication strictly to business. Devious as Warren was, Jo didn't want to be caught doing more. She and Tessa were cautious, but one could never tell.

The floor beneath her vibrated before a loud roar came from outside. The noise pulled Jo's thought back to the present. The windowpanes shuddered in their frames in response. Rushing out the shop door, Jo glanced around for a reason behind the noise. Tessa rushed toward her position from inside the shop. One man was walking down the sidewalk, head bowed beneath his hat, collar turned up against the sudden onslaught of rain.

Then Jo saw it. A wall of water rushed down toward them from the top of the street. Jo hollered for the man to hurry toward them, but he ignored her, lost in his panic. Jo raced into the shop, grabbed Tessa and hauled her toward the back of the shop. Tessa strained against her for a moment, yelling above the roar. "What's happening?"

"Flood," Jo hollered back. She tightened her grip. Behind her, the shop's front window shattered into pieces, raining glass into the wall of water and sludge rushing in, the sharp pieces sliced into exposed flesh. Nearly to the stairs, Jo gave another pull on Tessa, only to have her feet knocked from under her.

Tessa screamed, and Jo labored to maintain her grip. She regarded the water that rushed into the store was pulling at everything into its wake, and the water level rose too quickly. Tessa became heavier in her grip, and Jo tightened her hold, worried how much longer she could maintain it. Her clothes were heavy from saturation. Jo wrenched Tessa closer. It was apparent to Jo that Tessa's dress had become so waterlogged, the floodwaters would soon drag her under.

At the bottom of the staircase, Jo wrapped her legs around the newel post base of the staircase and, once anchored, yanked frantically at Tessa's skirt.

After a quick flash of panic, Tessa realized Jo's intentions and aided her in the garment's removal. Once the soaked material was freed and sunk into the rapid swirls of cold, muddied water,

Tessa grabbed a baluster and latched on with both hands. Even in her panicked state, she looked into Jo's eyes. "If you wanted my clothes off, you had only to ask," Tessa said, teeth chattering through her teasing.

Jo smiled, then kissed Tessa's nose. "Put your arms around my neck and wrap your legs around my waist." Tessa did as she asked, then buried her face in Jo's neck. Using the handrail, Jo pulled herself up the stairwell, feet unable to maintain footing on the tread because of the rising water. One thing Jo appreciated is the water made Tessa more buoyant.

Another burst of fast-moving water slammed into them, and Jo clasped tighter to the handrail. Tessa followed suit with her legs, locked them tighter around Jo's waist. Jo's arms were tiring, holding them through the rising and rushing waters. Her hands were numb from the cold water. Jo didn't know how much longer she could keep her grip.

Alarm filled her when her feet lost purchase on the tread. The water pulled violently. The onslaught slammed her head into the wooden rail and forced Tessa below the water. Stunned, but making her fingers continue the hand-over-hand motion, Jo managed to reach a step above the current water level.

Tessa gasped and sputtered for air as Jo brought them to lay sprawled across several stair treads, bodies shaking from cold and fear.

Jo's fingers and palms were red from strain and exertion. The floodwater wasn't going any higher, thankfully. "You okay?" she asked when Tessa got her breath back to a normal rhythm. Tessa nodded in a feeble motion. "Let's get you upstairs and into some dry clothes."

Another nod from Tessa, then Tessa's eyes widened. Jo glanced around to identify the cause of Tessa's alarm, but the motion made her dizzy. "You've cut your forehead," Tessa said. Tessa got to her feet and yanked on Jo's shirt to get her to follow. "We need to clean and dress the wound."

"I'm fine," she said, even as pain filtered through her head. With slow, deliberate steps, Jo followed Tessa the remainder of the way upstairs. Tessa appeared to have recovered from their ordeal quickly now that she had a purpose. The last few steps sapped Jo's residual strength. It felt like an eternity passed before the apartment doorway opened before her.

Tessa rushed around the kitchen, collected items and deposited them on the table. Jo only vaguely aware, her focus locked on the pale flesh freed from the garment. Tessa, Jo noted with appreciation and remembrance, had long, beautiful legs.

"Stop grinning like you've gone mad and get over here."

Jo followed the request, but with less grace than usual. She felt too lightheaded and unsteady to continue her leering. Her body came down from her adrenaline rush, and the pounding in her head became more noticeable. As did the awareness of the warmth that dripped down the side of her face. Jo brushed blood away with the palm of her hand, and absently wiped the blood on her water-soaked coveralls.

"Stop that," Tessa said as she rushed to Jo with the washcloth in her hand. Tessa wrapped an arm around Jo's waist as she pressed the cloth to Jo's forehead. "You need to sit down before you fall down." Jo complied and giggled when she realized the command left Tessa's pale legs and cotton clad hips on display before her. "What is so funny?" Tessa asked.

"Not funny," Jo said. "Happy." She reached a hand to caress the hip closest to her. "You're beautiful." Jo could get away with her behavior since there was no way Warren would interrupt for a while.

Tessa stilled. Her voice deepened as she said, "And you're concussed. You banged your head pretty good. It has you off balance and out of sorts." Tessa centered her attention on her ministrations to Jo's wound.

Jo, however, focused on her hand where it rested on Tessa's hip. Why were things in life so hard? These feelings she had for Tessa were what was significant. She simply wanted to love and be loved. Not only by her family but by this woman. Her Tessa.

She abhorred Warren's hatred, because if forced them to remain or appear to stay apart. How long before the strain of the charade worked for real? Jo wanted to do right by Fiona, keep her out of harm's way. And this time, it was in the form of Warren instead of Jimmy. She couldn't stop Jimmy Bennett from what he had done, to Fiona and Lorraine, now dead, and probably a host of other women. If it hadn't been for her attraction to Tessa, Fiona would have never been noticed by Warren. Jo was entirely at fault. She brought her family into Sergeant Langford's view.

Guilt tore at part of her soul. The other part of her soul couldn't accept blame for following her heart. She loved Tessa. Jo knew with the certainty of her heartbeat, and she couldn't walk away from her. Heck, just overtly avoiding and keeping to a minimal contact had been torturous. How could she give Tessa up completely and survive?

Lost in thought, Jo hadn't realized Tessa moved until she

asked, "What is wrong?" Jo blinked rapidly to focus on the brown eyes that stared at her with concern and love. Tessa had shifted to her knees, her hands clasping Jo's.

Jo felt the tears on her cheeks. She reached for Tessa, pulled her forward into a tight hug. She couldn't—wouldn't—let Tessa go. Hand to the back of Tessa's head, Jo said through trembling lips, "I love you, Tessa." Jo slid from the chair, pulled Tessa closer until she settled snug against Jo's body. "I can't let you go."

Tessa wrapped her arms around Jo, mimicked Jo's fierce hug. "I love you, too, Josephine Cavanaugh. Please, don't let me go."

Jo had no idea how long they stayed in their position. Moments? Hours? The lights had gone out in the interim, and the apartment was lit only by the natural light of late afternoon as it filtered through the windows. She felt a shiver ripple through Tessa's body. Jo became aware of how cold the bared skin was under her hands. She felt chilled herself. "You're freezing, honey."

"Well, you're soaked through," Tessa said, "and I am half-naked. Somehow, Pueblo has flooded, nearly taking us away with it. And we will probably waste away here on my apartment floor."

Jo laughed. "Yeah, but together." Tessa laughed as Jo squeezed the soft flesh beneath her palm. "We need to get you warmed up and dry. Then we need to see what's going on outside."

In Tessa's bedroom, Jo went to the window while Tessa removed her remaining wet clothes and replace them with dry ones. The distraction would keep Jo from wanting to watch the display of flesh begging her to hold and caress, to assure herself that Tessa was truly well and unharmed.

Her head throbbed. The discomfort was quickly forgotten with the sight below.

Floodwaters raged and sucked anything not bolted down into its wake. The sight was startling enough. What proved more horrific was seeing people swept away in a powerful flow of water. Jo sent up a silent prayer that her family was safe and away from this tragic onslaught.

Jo heard the terrified scream of a child above the roar of the flooding water. She opened the bedroom window and stuck her head outside. On the fire escape of the building next door, a little girl of about eight stood crying from three steps above the water level, focused on a half-submerged man as he tried to pull another child from the current fighting them both. The man had nearly hauled the boy safely to the fire escape before they were slammed by debris. The man howled a cry as the boy was yanked away into the rushing water, and other screams were nearly drowned out by the flood's deafening progression. Jo wasn't aware she'd added her own voice to the thunderous cacophony until arms wrapped around her waist and dragged her away from the window. "Oh, dear God, what if my family is caught in this?"

"Calm down, Jo," Tessa whispered in her ear. "There is nothing you can do. For them outside or for your family." Jo spun in Tessa's embrace, dropped her head onto Tessa's shoulder, and cried. Jo didn't know how much time had passed before Tessa spoke again. "You need to get into dry clothes, Jo."

Jo leaned back and swiped at the residual tears. "I'm not wearing one of your dresses, honey. Won't fit for one, and this isn't church." She nearly melted at the bright smile Tessa flashed her. "I'd rather catch pneumonia from wet overalls than put on a dress." Jo brushed two fingers along Tessa's jaw. "Dresses are for beautiful girls like you."

Tessa blushed. "Thank you, but you're the only beauty in this room."

Jo cupped Tessa's cheek, and said, "Not to me, Tessa. In my eyes, you're exquisite in your loveliness. Anyone who can't see this is a fool." She shrugged. "Not that I'm unwilling to fight anyone who would consider taking you from me."

"No chance of that happening." Tessa unhooked the straps from the bib of Jo's overalls. "I only have eyes and loving feelings for you. Now, take your clothes off."

"Tessa?" Jo's mouth went dry at the sensual tone that underlined her command. They'd been together intimately, touched nearly every part of one another, but Tessa seeing all of her in the light of day frightened her. Plus, there was a flood outside, which was an occurrence so unexpected in this part of southern Colorado.

And she just watched a man lose a child.

Was her own family safe? How would she survive without Fiona, Margaret, or little Adam?

"Hey Jo, look at me." Tessa clasped Jo's hands and squeezed, which brought her out of her sullen thoughts. "Your family will be fine, you'll see. Cavanaugh's are made of pretty sturdy stuff." Tessa released one hand and flicked a finger to Jo's nose.

Jo could not help but smile. "I love you, Tessa." She pulled Tessa into a tight hug.

"I love you, too, Jo. I don't want to lose you, but I cannot change who my brother is either. I don't know how to make this right." Jo felt the trembling in Tessa's body.

"We'll figure it out, I promise. Even if we have to leave." Jo leaned back and scrunched up her nose. "Even if I have to be nicer to Warren."

Tessa laughed. "Let us not be extreme, Jo. He is my blood, even if I can't make the promise of civility toward him." Tessa pulled away completely, closed the curtains across the window enough to hide them from view, but keep some light in the room. She then headed for the armoire. "I was saving this for your birthday, which I don't know the date of yet, or for Christmas." She pulled out a brown paper package tied with a lavender ribbon. "I will just have to think of something else for you."

"Tessa, you don't have to give me things. Just seeing you happy — even if I haven't helped with that lately — is all I want."

"I feel the same, Jo," Tessa said and held the package for Jo to take. "Right now, you need these." Jo moved to the bed and placed the package on top of the duvet. She carefully untied the ribbon and pulled back the paper. Inside was a beautiful shirt of baby blue hue and a pair of pleated trousers in black. "Oh, Tessa, these are wonderful." She brought her gaze to Tessa, who reddened and looked down at the floor.

"Not that I don't adore you in tight T-shirts and coveralls, but I thought you might want something different to wear. I know it's rude and presumptuous as if I'm ashamed of how you dress because I'm not. I kind of thought you'd consider this your courting outfit."

Jo smiled and removed her wet clothes. She heard Tessa's breath hitch when she was naked. She went to Tessa, lifted Tessa into her arms, and walked her to the bed. Jo carefully lay her down and settled alongside her. Tessa's breathing quickened. "Let me properly thank you for my gift."

Tessa groaned. "Jo, it's the middle of the day." Jo kissed the expanse of Tessa's neck. "And there's a crisis going on outside."

Jo slowly removed Tessa's clothing. "There's a crisis inside me, too. I want you, Tessa." She cupped one of Tessa's breasts in her hand, skated her thumb across a nipple until it pebbled to a hard bud. "I need you. Let me show you just how much."

"But—"

She replaced her thumb with her mouth. Tessa sucked in a ragged breath. Jo released the hardened bud with a soft, popping sound. Tessa moaned, and Jo grew more elated, wanted to see how many noises she could inspire Tessa to make. "No buts. If we're meant to die in this flood, I can't let it be without sharing our love. If we're to die, let it be together."

"If we are meant to live," Tessa said breathlessly, "let it be forever."

Chapter Thirty-one

NICHOLAS STAYED CLOSE behind Fiona but far enough away so everyone in the room wouldn't learn of his presence. He hoped Randall remained able to keep the two other bullies at bay.

He'd nearly jumped Thomas on the level below when he grabbed Fiona and again when Warren kicked her. Using every ounce of restraint, Nicholas waited and examined the area. One thing was apparent. He would never be able to enter the room completely without being seen. When Warren yanked Fiona from her family and dragged her to the center of the open storage room, Nicholas reached into his satchel and grasped his gun, scanning for a location better suited as an advantage point. The roar from outside unexpectedly flowed up the stairs and into the room.

Margaret and Adam were huddled together beside the room's only window, Warren stood beside them and blocked what little daylight seeped through the dirty panes of glass. Nicholas nearly snickered aloud when Thomas's teasing attitude was dampened by solid blows from Fiona. He was proud of her fighting spirit and skill, recognized her determination to protect her loved ones.

Any plans Nicholas may have had for a stealthy rescue disintegrated when Warren lay his gun on a nearby crate and picked up a broken length of two-by-four. What pathetic animals preyed upon children and women, fighting a blind woman, too? He should have expected the action. Fiona had won the encounter. Warren was apparently a sore loser.

Nicholas released the hold on his gun, pulled his hand from the depths, and launched himself at Warren just as Warren slammed the board against Fiona from behind. Momentum had Warren drop the board when Nicholas hit him. Gravity carried Nicholas, unable to stop when his legs tangled with Warren's, and they both broke through the glass and out of the window.

Nicholas expected to land on the fire escape, but the metal landing hung about a foot away. He released his hold on Warren, self-preservation demanded he reach for the metal structure and let the sergeant fend for himself. Instead, Nicholas dangled from the side of the building by his satchel strap. He glanced up and noticed he was caught on a protruding bolt that once held the metal staircase to the side of the building. The strap tugged painfully as it strained to hold his weight.

The roar was louder now, nearly drowned out Warren's scream as he fell three flights down and landed in the unexpected churning of floodwaters. Behind him, through the broken window, Margaret and Adam sat beside an unmoving Fiona. Warren's gun was clutched in Margaret's hand as she aimed it at Thomas.

In his ear, Nicholas heard the rending of leather as the strap holding him tore free. He had an instant to decide between sliced fingers with an attempt to go back through the window. Or to propel himself toward the damaged stairwell of the fire escape.

The decision was made for him by the final separation of the strap holding him in place. He grasped onto the satchel, which held all his secrets and his livelihood. Nicholas closed his eyes as his body dropped.

RANDALL HADN'T TAKEN more than two steps when the roaring sound from outside increased in volume. The stairwell's overhead light flickered. He ran to the door and peered out the small frame of glass, noted the street and sidewalk quickly disappeared beneath a flow of water. His body became immobile, uncertain of what he should do. He needed to get upstairs, protect the Cavanaugh's from Warren. Would Donald and Walter be safe where they were in the closet? Would the water get into the building? How much could he expect to result from the deluge? Even as the questions raced through his mind, the first tendrils of water seeped beneath the door and swirled around his booted feet. Randall couldn't take the chance something drastic wasn't about to happen. The increased pounding from his heart certainly beat a warning of dire portent. He pushed aside the obstacles he'd recently placed in front of the supply door, unlocked and pulled it open. Two startled faces stared back at him. Gun back in hand, Randall ordered, "Upstairs, now." All three rushed toward the stairwell.

"What the—" Walter didn't finish his question.

A bicycle broke through the front window, propelled by the torrent of water gushing in its wake.

Donald and Walter didn't even hesitate on the second-floor landing, confirming for Randall they knew exactly what was occurring upstairs and sought safety with the leader of this debacle.

A scream, followed by another, echoed down from the third floor. When the men ahead of him turned away from the sound, intent on running off, Randall pointed his gun in their direction. "I don't think so, fellas. Up you go."

The third floor was of an entirely open area. Numerous crates and other telephone-related items were piled high, creating barriers that prevented an immediate assessment of the room and its occupants. Above and strategically placed to support the roof were numerous concrete pillars. Randall heard Margaret's worried voice then. "Fiona, honey, please wake up." Randall shoved a hand hard into Walter's and then Donald's back to urge them to move forward. "Go."

In the center of the room, Thomas stood over an unconscious Fiona, Adam at her side, Margaret next to him with a revolver pointed unsteadily at Thomas. He gave another nudge to each man until they stood next to Thomas.

"Where is Langford?" Randall asked.

Thomas responded. His shoulders slumped in silent acknowledgment of the unexpected changes in the situation. A situation he could no longer sneak out of. "Pushed out the window by the fancy fellow."

Randall glanced toward Margaret for confirmation. She nodded dismally. He didn't have to worry about Warren sneaking upon them. Also, Randall was now the ranking owner of this ghastly situation. "Mrs. Cavanaugh, if I could further demand your assistance in maintaining the weapon on these boys?" When she nodded, he directed the three men to walk to the wall. "Okay, boys, on your knees and face the wall."

"You gonna shoot us?" Walter asked, his tone whiny with insecurity.

"Are you always going to be an idiot?" Randall heaved a sigh. "Stupid question. Of course, you are." He glanced around to see if there was something to bind their hands but found nothing. Once the three men complied he said, "Cross your legs at the ankle, hands behind your head, and lean your forehead against the wall." The position would be uncomfortable and awkward for them but would alert him if they tried to get up.

He made his way to Margaret, knelt beside her, and carefully removed the gun from her trembling grasp. She didn't resist him. When the gun was no longer in her hand, Margaret reached forward and pulled Fiona into her lap. "Can you tell me what happened?" She did. She began from when Thomas and friends abducted her and Adam until Nicholas and Warren fell through the window

Shards of glass littered the floor. Most apparently flung onto the ground outside with the momentum of the two men. A few jagged pieces remained in the frame. Randall cautiously avoided impalement as he stuck his head through the opening. He didn't know if the weight of Warren and Nicholas had released the fire escape from the outside wall or the force of the water flooding the street. Either way, it hung about a foot from the building. Neither man occupied the metal structure.

Randall looked down at the rapidly flowing water. They must have fallen to their deaths. Death nearly assured with the force of water hastening through the street below. Good riddance Warren, Randall thought, not the least bit guilty about the loss of his life. He regretted the loss of Nicholas, friend of the Cavanaugh's, whose life would be mourned. Only a miracle could save anyone caught in the murderous rage of the water below.

MARGARET FELT A moment of relief when Fiona regained consciousness. She'd torn a strip of material from her slip to use as a binding for Fiona's head wound. The bleeding appeared to have stopped. Her poor beloved wife. Life seemed to oppose her at every chance. No, she corrected herself. Despite opposition, Fiona managed to retaliate with life. The handsome woman cradled in her lap was the impetus for life to so many. Without Fiona, Margaret may survive, but it would be as an empty shell. Once again, her beloved Fiona rallied against the weight of negativity, trying to entomb her.

Fiona's eyelids fluttered open. Then a tremulous smile curved her lips. "Hey."

"Hey yourself," Margaret said, relief answered Fiona's smile with a grin of her own.

"Guess I'm not dead," Fiona said. "Think I'd be able to see again if I had died. Probably wouldn't have the monster headache either." Margaret gently applied pressure to Fiona's chest when she attempted to sit up. "Guess Thomas kicked my ass."

Margaret snorted. "Not hardly. He lost. Warren intervened by slamming the board to your head." She smiled down at her wife even though she could not see Margaret's response. Fiona would feel it from her. She lowered her voice and leaned closer to maintain privacy. "Watch your language in front of our son, Fiona." Margaret reprimanded gently. Tenderly, she added, "And know I love you."

Fiona pulled her closer and gave Margaret a fierce hug. Margaret felt the tremor of the myriad of emotions coursing through Fiona, and released her when the trembling stopped. She tugged Adam into their embrace. Margaret hoped to convey both their love and support through their combined physical contact.

The intensity of their moment was dampened when Randall joined them. He sat down on the floor a foot from them. Close enough to protect. "Didn't expect this," he said.

"What is happening?" Margaret asked.

"Apparently Pueblo is flooding. Better relax, because we'll be here a while."

He stretched his legs out in front of him, leaned back on his arms.

Margaret realized at that moment how much Randall had grown up. He would do all right for himself in his chosen profession. Jo had done well when she'd befriended this young man. Although she suspected the answer, fearful of Fiona's reaction, she asked, "Nicholas?"

Fiona shot upward into a sitting position with a groan. "Where is he?" She tilted her head, Fiona's way of focusing on the sounds surrounding her. Margaret looked to Randall. He shook his head. "I'm so sorry, Fiona." Margaret held Fiona tightly while Fiona silently cried.

IT WAS A hot June day, less than a week after the flood. Jo rose to answer the doorbell, left Fiona and Margaret at play with Adam on the parlor rug. Tessa watched with a broad smile while stitching in a corner chair. Her family. The Cavanaugh clan. She was a little surprised to see Randall, cap in hand. He, like most of the law enforcement in Pueblo, had been busy over the last couple of days with recovering those lost in the flooding, and everything that comes after such a catastrophe. He looked exhausted; his usual sharp appearance disheveled. Sweat stains and mud unusual for him under normal circumstances. Despite it all, Randall looked happy and in his element. She knew it would be a long time before Union Avenue, and other areas in the flood plain were returned to normal. Possibly years. The destruction had a positive outcome — two if you counted losing Warren, not that she'd say as much in front of Tessa. With the loss of the store and most of her inventory, no one questioned Tessa when she moved in with the Cavanaugh's. A lot of people had opened their homes to help families and friends who lost everything.

"Hello, Jo."

"Randall, come in." Jo motioned him inside. "We're in the parlor." While Margaret and Tessa greeted Randall, Jo noticed Fiona reflexively pulled Adam closer to her side farthest from the doorway. "What brings you our way? Not that we aren't happy to have you visit. Plus, we know you've been working a lot of hours."

"Yeah, but it seems I'm also expected to get some sleep," he said with an embarrassed grin. He shuffled his feet and ran his fingers through his ginger-colored hair. "Since you were instrumental, Fiona, in helping solve the murders, I wanted to update you that we had the man in custody. Unfortunately, he drowned in the flooding."

Fiona picked up Adam, rose from in front of the couch where they played on the floor to sit on the cushion. Adam nestled into her chest. The little boy must've realized this talk was important because he remained silent. "The man was responsible for all the murders?" Fiona asked.

Jo noted Randall shifted so he wouldn't accidentally glance in Tessa's direction. Everyone in the room, except Tessa, knew Warren killed Ethel. They also knew Warren had sent someone to hurt Tessa. None of them would reveal the secret. Tessa meant too much to Jo, to all of them. "That is what all the reports reflect," Randall said.

"No need to protect me," Tessa said. "I know Warren was responsible for Ethel's murder and helping to kidnap you." Jo's eyes widened. "I didn't want to believe him capable, of course. But when I confronted him at the station, I saw a side of him I hadn't witnessed before then. I'm sorry."

Fiona nodded. To Tessa, he added, "We aren't alerting anyone else. We," he glanced at everyone in turn, "wanted to protect you from any gossip or inquiry."

"And don't blame Jo and us. We couldn't bear to see you hurt." Margaret rose from the floor. "Thank you, Randall, for letting us know. Can we offer you anything to eat or drink? You must be famished as well as tired."

"Thank you, Mrs. Cavanaugh. But my mother has a meal waiting." He glanced down at his uniform. "Promised to attend to my laundry too. I just wanted to offer your family a bit of closure."

"We appreciate that, Randall. You're welcomed here anytime." Margaret smiled at him.

Randall nodded, obviously pleased with the open invitation.

"Good night, then."

"I'll walk you out." Jo followed him out the door and onto the porch. She lowered her voice. "Is there going to be a problem with the others involved with the incident at the Telephone Company?"

"You're worried about the police learning the truth about Warren?"

She smirked. "Of course. We've all been through enough. We just want to move on—not look over our shoulders forever."

"It won't come from me. Other than your family, Jo, I'm the only one who knows the full truth." Randall slapped his cap on his head. "We're friends, right? I won't jeopardize that. Don't expect Donald and Walter to spill the beans about Warren, as a rumor seems to have made it to their cell. Cops don't like it when you attempt to shift blame to a dead cop."

Jo leaned over and planted a quick kiss on his cheek. She smiled at the instant reddening of his cheeks. They could live with Warren being touted a hero or whatever, as long as Tessa wasn't hurt by the extent of Warren's perfidy.

"Josephine Cavanaugh, are you accosting an officer of the law?"

"Not hardly," Jo said. "I see it as a proper thank you for going above and beyond the duties of your rank." She shrugged. "Besides, yes, we are friends. You wouldn't deny your friend an offering of gratitude, would you?"

Randall shook his head, then snickered. "I'm glad you and your family moved to town."

"Glad you survived it."

"So far, anyway," Randall said. He walked to his car. "Get back to your family, Jo. May you all have a wonderful night."

"Thanks to your news, Randall, we will." He waved as he drove away. Jo spun on her heels and rushed inside, to her family.

Epilogue

Six months later

MARGARET LEANED BACK against the counter, drying her hands on the dishtowel when Jo rushed through the back door. Gusts of biting cold January wind followed in her wake before she shouldered the door closed, snowflakes scattered and crashed into nonexistence against the floor from the warmth of the room.

"Have any trouble with your drive?" Margaret asked as Jo toed off her snow-encrusted boots on the rug by the door.

"Nah, no more than usual," Jo said. She lay a small package on the table before she pulled off her gloves and unbuttoned her jacket, then draped it across the back of the chair. Jo's curly blonde hair crinkled with static when she pulled the knitted hat from her head. "Where is everybody?"

Margaret draped the towel over the dishes in the strainer before responding. "Tessa's upstairs, putting Adam to bed for me. Christmas wore him out, but now he's moved on to questions about New Year's Day." She moved closer to Jo and the table. "Fiona's in the parlor. There's a plate for you warming in the oven."

"Great, I'm starved. The meeting in town took longer than I expected. Snow doesn't look like it will amount to much, but that wind is a doozy." Jo retrieved her plate from the oven and plucked a fork from the strainer. "Is it okay if I take this upstairs? I'll remember to bring it back down."

"What you mean," she said, grinning, "is Tessa will remember."

"Yeah, yeah, it gets done." Jo kissed her cheek. "I'll say goodnight to Fiona and be upstairs if you need me for anything. How is she today?"

"Tired, quiet, but our beloved Fiona nonetheless." Jo nodded, her expression saddened. "Good night, Jo." Jo was almost into the hallway, a green bean thrust into her mouth when Margaret noticed the package Jo brought in with her. "Jo, what's this?"

Jo shrugged and said, "It's addressed to you. The return address has the name as N. Allen."

Margaret felt lightheaded. Nicholas? But— "Margaret? Everything okay?"

"Yes, everything is fine. Go to Tessa and eat." Margaret suspected the plate would be cleaned of its contents before Jo made it to the room she shared with Tessa.

Left alone, Margaret pulled the brown paper package closer and dropped into a chair. Jo had been correct about the sender. Margaret remembered Fiona telling her N. Allen was the name Nicholas used for his photography. Everyone had believed he'd perished with the flood, like Warren. Why had he waited so long to contact them? At least he could have let Fiona know, stopped her grieving his death because of Warren's hatred of them.

Margaret tore open the wrapping, ripped the return address free from the rest, and stuffed it into the pocket of her dress. Inside was a cloth-wrapped bundle and two envelopes, one thick envelope addressed to Fiona, the other thinner to Margaret.

Margaret opened hers.

```
Dear Margaret,
    I'm certain this is a surprise. All will be
explained in the letter to Fiona. As you must
read it for her, you'll both learn more about
why I didn't offer an explanation before now.
    Included, if you haven't unwrapped it
already—I know how impatient women can be with
gifts—is something I thought you would want. Two
things to be precise. The top item is for the
household. A keepsake I picked up during my
travels.
    The second is self-explanatory.
    If you ever need anything, Margaret, don't
hesitate to ask. The inclusion of all the
Cavanaugh ladies and little Adam in my life has
made me a better person. Thank you.
Your friend,
Nicholas
```

Margaret refolded the letter, stuffed it back in the envelope, and tucked it away in her pocket with the address. She removed the cloth to reveal two five-by-seven picture frames. The top picture was Ian, Brigid, and Richard, all dressed up as if going to church. Margaret smiled. Brigid and Richard had finally completed their family, and they were a handsome group.

The second frame held a picture of Fiona and Margaret in a tender embrace. The love they shared captured perfectly. The picture was taken in the workshop about nine months ago. Margaret remembered the day vividly. It was the day she confronted Fiona, believed Fiona was leaving her. Instead, she learned Fiona suffered physically and tried to keep her troubles hidden. Tears poured down her cheeks. Nicholas had provided a reminder of her love, to last well beyond Fiona's remaining days on the earth. She cried harder. It was many minutes before Margaret was able to pull herself together. She picked up the envelope Nicholas addressed to Fiona and made her way to the parlor. Margaret would bring their photo to their room later.

The flames in the fireplace where all that illuminated the room. Fiona no longer needed lights and Margaret appreciated being able to see the furniture without incurring bodily harm. Fiona sat on the settee that faced the window. Even in the coziness of the firelight, Fiona looked tired. Margaret noticed the changes of the last couple of weeks, the lethargy in her limbs, the longer periods of sleep. Margaret wanted to lash out at a God who set so many painful hurdles for Fiona to jump, one who slowly took the reason for Margaret's heart beating.

Margaret inhaled deeply. Enough of this self-pity. Fiona was still here, sharing so many moments of love and tenderness that was purely Fiona. "Kitchens cleaned up," she said to announce her presence. Margaret lit the lamp beside the settee.

"Come, sit with me," Fiona said as she patted the empty space beside her. "Everything okay? You took longer tonight." Margaret sat close to Fiona, rested her head on Fiona's shoulder, as Fiona embraced her.

"Fine. Jo brought a package home. There's a picture of Ian, Brigid, and Richard. They look very happy."

Fiona smiled. "I guessed as much from their phone calls. Having proof is nice. Why didn't they let us know the picture was coming?"

Margaret raised her head to kiss Fiona's jawline, then sat up, but didn't disconnect the physical contact between them. She lightly tapped the envelope to Fiona's thigh. "Because the picture and this envelope addressed to you, came from someone else." Fiona's brow furrowed, probably trying to suppose the possibilities. Margaret didn't pause too long, decided the quicker the announcement, the sooner Fiona could process. "They are from Nicholas."

Fiona gasped. She was silent for a long time. Margaret assumed to process the information. "Nicholas? But how?"

"I assume that's where this envelope comes into play. Would you like me to open it and read it to you now? Or would you want to do this upstairs?"

"Here, now. If I let you wait, you'll have to change, wash up, putter around, and then get to it."

"I don't putter around," Margaret said, her tone equally teasing. Margaret opened the flap and pulled out the folded papers inside. She shifted so Fiona could nestle into her side as she unfolded the sheets of paper. She didn't pause to count them, knowing she would finish every word unless Fiona stopped her. There was no way to gauge how the words would affect Fiona. She'd been devastated in her belief that Nicholas died. "Ready?" Fiona's nod was barely perceptible.

Margaret read.

My dearest friend Fiona,

Please don't be too angry with me for my extended silence. After Warren and I went out the window, my satchel caught on the remaining pieces of fire escape still attached to the outer wall. I eventually fell into the rapid water, broke my leg, a couple ribs, and my wrist. As you know, I couldn't very well let the locals, especially those who knew me, uncover my truth. I managed to get away before I collapsed and couldn't go further.

I guess the powers that be were looking out for me. I found a place hidden away, which belonged to a retired schoolteacher, who nursed me back to reasonable health, enough for me to travel.

Margaret, I appear to be blessed with the gentler and caring side of educators, not the ruler-wielding and sharp-tongued harridans of my day.

After four months I managed to make my way to Philadelphia and Ruth. It seems she continued her father's business and was doing good for herself in her father's semi-retirement. It only took a moment of gazing at her to realize I had run away from more than my father. Of course, Ruth's, "What took you so long?", helped confirm this.

Ruth and I had a small private—and totally inadmissible—wedding. We spent our honeymoon in Boston, hence the family photo of the Donnelly's. After speaking of my friendship with the Cavanaugh's, Ruth wanted to visit the places that created my remarkable friend and friendship. She adores you already.

I miss you, Fiona. All of you, actually, if I'm honest. I would never have realized my true feelings for Ruth had I not witnessed the love between you and Margaret.

My only wish and my deepest hope are that you'll hang on as long as possible. Ruth and I would love to visit. See how Adam is getting along, see Jo and Tessa. I hope they worked things out.

I know you aren't in control of this. But you are a fighter, my friend. I hope soon we can see one another, and you meet my Ruth and partake in some of that stubborn sass, which is exclusively Fiona Cavanaugh.

My thoughts, prayers, and hopes to see you in the not-too-distant future are with you. Above all, I recognize you have shown me how to be a better human.

Lovingly,

Your friend no matter what,

Nicholas

Margaret folded the letter, stuffed it back into the envelope, and placed it in Fiona's hand. She put an arm around Fiona, pulling them closer together. She realized they both had silent tears on their faces.

Fiona was the first to break the silence. "Isn't that just like a man? Bossy." Fiona snorted. "Won't be because I have so much to still teach Adam. Or that leaving you will be the hardest task possible in my whole life. No. I have to fight so the snooty Nicholas Tirrell can visit and show off his Ruth."

Margaret chuckled. "The nerve of the man."

"In truth."

If Fiona's indignation paused or slowed her illness, then Margaret planned to fan the flames. So far, willpower alone kept Fiona with them. "I think you should, too. Not because Nicholas commanded it, but so you can give him what for when he does get here." Margaret wasn't ready to lose her heart, her true love. The matter was inevitable, a battle with indefinite time. Fiona was losing the battle if her recent lethargy was any indication. Hopefully, this missive from Nicholas would be the boost she needed to fight a bit longer.

Fiona reached for her cheek, sat up, so they faced, somehow locked her sightless gaze into Margaret's. "Every day I am relieved and blessed when I wake, feeling you beside me, spending time with our nephew-son. I'm glad to have closure with Nicholas, rather than all the horrid things I imagined." Margaret welcomed Fiona's tender kiss, let Fiona set the tone and pace. "I do my best to fight because eternity wouldn't be long enough for your love, to share in the joy that is you, Margaret." Fiona sat back a little. "I most certainly won't do it just to appease some willful man."

This time Margaret pulled Fiona into a kiss, one she hoped explained all that lived in her heart. Share the passion only Fiona could incite in her. Out of breath, Margaret gathered Fiona into her arms. "That is my girl. I love you, Fiona Cavanaugh."

"And I love you, Margaret Cavanaugh, my wife, auntie-mother to our wonderful boy."

Margaret pulled away and grasped Fiona's hand in hers as she prodded her to stand. "Let's finish this properly upstairs."

"Now who's being bossy?" Fiona asked teasingly as they made their way to the staircase and their bedroom.

Margaret couldn't know how long she had left with Fiona, but she didn't plan to waste a single moment of loving her.

The End

Afterword

The events in the story were purely for fictional entertainment. The Pueblo flood, however, is entirely real. But I have taken license with the timeline.

The historic flooding took place on June 3, 1921. A cloudburst deposited over half an inch of rain in a matter of minutes. As the rains fell, the Arkansas River and Fountain Creek swelled to over fifteen feet, before receding. Two hours from the storms start, the entire wholesale district and most of the business district of Pueblo were flooded with water ten feet deep, destroying most of the downtown Pueblo. Some reports have the death toll as high as 1500 people, though the count was hindered by the fact the debris and sludge left in the flood's wake washed away or buried many who were never recovered.

Assisting with the flood damage and carnage is the fire that broke out in a lumberyard, the flood carrying the burning lumber through the city streets.

It took Pueblo three years of the community banding together to rebuild. The city was running again by 1924.

About the Author

Sharon lives in Colorado, enjoys finding new trails to hike and playing mahjong, although not simultaneously as she's awkward enough under normal circumstances. She served in the U.S. Marine Corps—Oorah! Sharon currently works as financial and program assistant for Nursing and Forensic Nursing Programs, for the UCCS, Nursing College.

More Sharon G. Clark titles:

The Magic Found in Chaos

A disgruntled Gradyln warrior, Belzan, is preparing to destroy the woman who severed his hand and banished him — and all those important to Kareina. Using the fear of the people of Kellshae as a catalyst to building his army, Belzan incites hatred of magic wielders, and the basic need of men to get their women under control.

Gionne needs to bring Kellshae's first oracle to Zheirger Keep, but must traverse the unsettled land filled with angry magicked people, and the common people killing those with magic. Time has Gionne wondering if she may have been rash in her actions to break up with Jahq. Hatred is tearing Kellshae apart. Is it too late to make amends before all hope is lost?

Jahq hasn't spoken to Gionne for nearly three years, has barely left her rooms in the Keep. Now her mothers are asking Jahq to accompany Gionne from Gradyln to Zheirger. She knows this mission is important to Kellshae, and that her absence should make her disappearance afterward easier.

Jahq accepts one former lesson above all: Gionne's rejection was worse for her than any monster Bahalkar spit up from its depths.

ISBN 978-1-61929-312-0
eISBN 978-1-61929-313-7

Chaos Beneath the Moonbeams

The age of magic has been over for nearly three centuries; finalized with the War of Harmony. Even the gods willingly melt into forgetfulness, letting mortal life grow as it would, for good or bad. Not all the gods had agreed unanimously. So, when a mortal man decides to release a banished god for his own purposes, nothing will ever be the same.

Kareina of Clan Gradyln has posed as her twin brother Karr (with the aid of minor forbidden magic) for over a decade, since Karr's disappearance and Kareina's kidnapping and torture. Even Caldier Hassid, her father, forgets her true gender. So, when Hassid agrees to a betrothal between Karr and Mayliandra, it's up to Kareina to figure a way out of it. Meanwhile, someone has brought the old god T'Dar from the depths of Bahalkar to bring back the old ways of chaos.

Mayliandra of Clan Bredwine, about to be given to the fierce Sher Karr, doesn't know if she should be happy for the opportunity to leave her home, where she's nothing but a servant; or, petrified her future husband will learn her secret. Although Mayliandra intends to do her duty to her clan, she can't help wishing Karr were his dead sister, Kareina.

ISBN 978-1-61929-252-9
eISBN 978-1-61929-253-6

A Majestic Affair

A decade ago, Tiara Summers was forced to leave her home with her alcoholic mother, and contact was lost with her father and friends. Tiara built a profitable construction business in Colorado Springs and, if not exactly happy, is comfortable with her life. Then she receives a letter from her father asking for help with a horse, which means returning to Silver Waters, Colorado with all the old memories of kisses and running away...and Jayce.

Jayce Mansfield trains horses for a living. Her focus is specializing the equines for stunts in the movies. Then Tiara returns, though her father is AWOL, and Jayce sees promise in a second chance. Hopes for the happily-ever-after she'd envisioned for them are reanimated, until Jayce realizes the sweet, caring teenager that left ten years ago has turned into a bitter woman.

When a little gangster in a purple limousine comes demanding Tiara give over her father's horse, situations and emotions only become more complicated, compelling Tiara to run again.

Can Jayce get Tiara to realize she belongs in Silver Waters, that they belong together?

ISBN 978-1-61929-178-2
eISBN 978-1-61929-177-5

Into the Mist

Lieutenant Kasey Houston has snuck off the USS Console, to join the Marines in their fight against the Japanese soldiers, in May of 1945. She is a psychiatric nurse, and when the Marines of her unit are all killed, she attempts to take out the enemy. However, a strange gray mist is in the cave, and the enemy soldier releases a grenade that buries her in rubble.

Captain Andrea Knight is locating the occupants of an exploded building. She comes upon a woman without identification and in WWII era uniform. Andrea after learning Kasey is from the past procures documentation to establish Kasey as a Military Advisor to the Militia.

Andrea and Kasey are to meet with the officials and militia, who want them to be a bodyguard for the Ambassador of the United Church. His mission: to explain the severity of the threat of the terrorist gangs and Bad Billy. The United Presidents refuse to believe the threat bad. The Ambassador tries to explain he's capable of stopping Billy by using powers they both possess.

Bad Billy requests a rendezvous and stipulates that Andrea come alone. Kasey pleads with Andrea to ignore the message, and is shocked to learn later that Andrea has gone anyway. Meanwhile, Andrea realizes how much she loves Kasey although she is afraid to admit it. Can she avoid her worst fear that Kasey could be returned to her own time before an opportunity ever presents itself to act on her feelings?

ISBN 978-1-935053-34-7
eISBN 978-1-935053-34-7e

Tears Don't Become Me

GW (Georgia Wilhelmina) Diamond, Private Investigator, dealt in missing children cases — only. It didn't alter her own traumatic childhood experience, but she could try to keep other children from the same horrors. She'd left her past and her name behind her. Or so she thought. This case was putting her in contact with people she had managed to keep a distant and barely civil relationship with for fifteen years. Now the buried past was returning to haunt her. When Sheriff Matthews of Elk Grove, Missouri, asked her to take a case involving a teenaged runaway girl, she believed it would be no different from any other. Until Matthews explained she had to take a cop as partner or no deal. A cop who just happened to be the missing girl's aunt...

Erin Dunbar, received the call concerning her niece from an old partner, Frank Matthews. It should have been from her sister, but their estrangement, compounded by her having moved to Detroit, kept that from happening. Now she would have to work with a PI. One had nearly killed her and Frank years ago; she expected this one would be no different. Matters were only made worse by discovering it was a "she" PI — a Looney-tune one who gave new and literal meaning to: "Hands Off." For the sake of her niece, Erin would put up with just about anything, until...

GW seemed to be strangely affected by this case and Erin, to her chagrin and amazement, was strangely affected by her. If Erin could solve GW's past, give her hope, could they have a hope of finding her niece?

ISBN 978-1-932300-83-3
eISBN 978-1-61929-039-6

Speakeasy, Speak Love

Fiona "Finn" Cavanaugh wants to move west, leaving the tenements and her abusive father far behind. When she saves Margaret Graham from the local street bully, Fiona doesn't realize how the ramifications will change her life, her plans, and especially her heart. Eldon Graham, Margaret's brother, offers Finn the chance to work for him, and make more money than anyone else "his" age. For Fiona, this could mean a chance to save faster to meet her goals–and spend more time with Margaret.

Margaret Graham comes from a family of some consequence and has finished a college degree to be a teacher, but is thoroughly under her brother's rule. He believes her education is nice, because it will land her a prominent husband. He has his partner in crime, Jimmy Bennet, at the top of the suitor list. Margaret, at first, is confused and frustrated by the immediate attraction to a mere boy-child when she and Finn meet. She learns the truth, but the knowledge–and the fact Fiona works for her brother–could cost Fiona her life.

The heat between Fiona and Margaret nears a boiling point; and, when rival gangsters, and Jimmy, turn up the heat on the Graham businesses, things become so dangerous that neither woman may survive long enough to leave for a better life, or explore their burgeoning love for each other.

ISBN 978-1-61929-334-2
eISBN 978-1-61929-335-9

MORE REGAL CREST PUBLICATIONS

Melissa Good	Moving Target	978-1-61929-150-8
Melissa Good	Red Sky At Morning	978-1-932300-80-2
Melissa Good	Storm Surge: Book One	978-1-935053-28-6
Melissa Good	Storm Surge: Book Two	978-1-935053-39-2
Melissa Good	Stormy Waters	978-1-61929-082-2
Melissa Good	Thicker Than Water	1-932300-24-4
Melissa Good	Terrors of the High Seas	1-932300-45-7
Melissa Good	Tropical Storm	978-1-932300-60-4
Melissa Good	Tropical Convergence	978-1-935053-18-7
Melissa Good	Winds of Change Book One	978-1-61929-194-2
Melissa Good	Winds of Change Book Two	978-1-61929-232-1
Melissa Good	Southern Stars	978-1-61929-348-9
Danielle Grainger	Wrecking Bernadette: Book One in the Bernadette Series	978-1-61929-428-8
Jeanine Hoffman	Lights & Sirens	978-1-61929-115-7
Jeanine Hoffman	Strength in Numbers	978-1-61929-109-6
Jeanine Hoffman	Back Swing	978-1-61929-137-9
K. E. Lane	And, Playing the Role of Herself	978-1-932300-72-7
Kate McLachlan	Christmas Crush	978-1-61929-195-9
Kate McLachlan	Hearts, Dead and Alive	978-1-61929-017-4
Kate McLachlan	Murder and the Hurdy Gurdy Girl	978-1-61929-125-6
Kate McLachlan	Rescue At Inspiration Point	978-1-61929-005-1
Kate McLachlan	Return Of An Impetuous Pilot	978-1-61929-152-2
Kate McLachlan	Rip Van Dyke	978-1-935053-29-3
Kate McLachlan	Ten Little Lesbians	978-1-61929-236-9
Kate McLachlan	Alias Mrs. Jones	978-1-61929-282-6
Lynne Norris	One Promise	978-1-932300-92-5
Lynne Norris	Sanctuary	978-1-61929-248-2
Lynne Norris	The Light of Day	978-1-61929-338-0
Schramm and Dunne	Love Is In the Air	978-1-61929-362-8
Rae Theodore	Leaving Normal: Adventures in Gender	978-1-61929-320-5
Rae Theodore	My Mother Says Drums Are for Boys: True Stories for Gender Rebels	978-1-61929-378-6
Barbara Valletto	Pulse Points	978-1-61929-254-3
Barbara Valletto	Everlong	978-1-61929-266-6
Barbara Valletto	Limbo	978-1-61929-358-8
Barbara Valletto	Diver Blues	978-1-61929-384-7
Lisa Young	Out and Proud	978-1-61929-392-2

Be sure to check out our other imprints,
Blue Beacon Books, Mystic Books, Quest Books,
Silver Dragon Books, Troubadour Books,
and Young Adult Books.

VISIT US ONLINE AT
www.regalcrest.biz

At the Regal Crest Website You'll Find

~ The latest news about forthcoming titles and new releases

~ Our complete backlist of titles

~ Information about your favorite authors

Regal Crest print titles are available from all progressive booksellers including numerous sources online. Our distributors are Bella Distribution and Ingram.